BECKY
MELBY

YESTERDAY'S
STARDUST

LOST SANCTUARY

Book Two

BARBOUR
PUBLISHING

Print ISBN 978-1-61626-239-6

eBook Editions:
Adobe Digital Edition (.epub) 978-1-60742-870-1
Kindle and MobiPocket Edition (.prc) 978-1-60742-871-8

Scripture taken from the HOLY BIBLE, NEW INTERNATIONAL VERSION®. NIV®. Copyright © 1973, 1978, 1984, 2011 by Biblica, Inc.™ Used by permission. All rights reserved worldwide.

This book is a work of fiction. Names, characters, places, and incidents are either products of the author's imagination or used fictitiously. Any similarity to actual people, organizations, and/or events is purely coincidental.

For more information about Becky Melby, please access the author's website at the following Internet address: www.beckymelby.com.

Cover credit: Studio Gearbox, www.studiogearbox.com

Published by Barbour Publishing, Inc., P.O. Box 719, Uhrichsville, OH 44683, www.barbourbooks.com

Our mission is to publish and distribute inspirational products offering exceptional value and biblical encouragement to the masses.

 Member of the
Evangelical Christian
Publishers Association

Printed in the United States of America.

DEDICATION/ACKNOWLEDGMENT

In loving memory of my mom,
Edith Parish Foght,
who went home to Jesus on June 16, 2011.
In her 93 years, she lived out the quote we found in her scrapbook:
Only one life twill soon be past.
Only what's done for Christ will last.

A special acknowledgement to the staff and kids—
past, present, and future—
of Common Grounds Coffee House in Burlington, Wisconsin.
I will always be grateful God allowed me a season
of being part of something that truly makes a difference.

Thank you to:

Bill, for loving me and living on hot dogs and peanut butter while I finished this.

My kids and grandkids for the fun, messy, noisy crowd we make when we're together.

Cathy—Thank you for your blessing on this project. Dani and Nicky and a host of other characters would not exist without you. Thank you for your steadfast friendship.

My father-in-law, Irvin Melby, for sharing true stories of his father's bootlegging days.

Cynthia, for always helping me see God's hand and purpose in everything.

Kathy, for on-going prayer and for weekly talks and walks.

Jan, for printing this out in tiny print so you could carry it with you to edit.

My Bible study sisters, for praying for this book and the people who will read it.

Rebecca Germany and JoAnne Simmons, for opportunities and nudges.

Jamie Chavez, for wonderful editing and being so much fun to work with.

The neighborhood where much of *Yesterday's Stardust* takes place exists only in my head. . .and now yours. The storyline is based on a problem common to most larger cities and is in no way intended to reflect negatively on the beautiful city of Kenosha, Wisconsin.

PROLOGUE

Look for the silver lining when e'er a cloud appears...." The song and the familiar rhythm of needle tugging thread freed Francie Tillman to dwell on all that might finally be going right.

Curled in the white-painted rocker in the corner of her shop, she sang along with the Radiola as she stitched, counted her blessings, and tried to ignore all that was unfixable in her life.

She had her own business, the kind of friends who stuck closer than family, and maybe—she threaded the thought into a prayer—they were finally safe.

Safe.

Bits of plaster dust clung to the wallpaper beneath the framed print she'd just hung—black clouds threatening, trees bent with the wind, a cluster of terrified people fleeing the impending storm.

"Somewhere the sun is shining. . ." Her voice echoed in the windowless room as she sang. ". . .and so the right thing to do is make it shine for you."

The picture reminded her of the day she'd discovered where to hide in the storm.

"A heart, full of joy and gladness will always banish sadness...."

The music didn't mask clanking tools and sputtering motors on the other side of the wall, nor the scrape of chairs and an angry stream of Italian above her, but they were predictable sounds, the backdrop of her new world. Never again would she complain about a predictable life.

She sewed the final stitches on the voile overlay that flowed in angled layers over snowy, calf-length satin then snipped the thread with ivory-handled scissors. Holding the wedding gown against her chest, she struck a Greta Garbo pose in front of the mirror. She tried to imagine gliding down the aisle with yards of Italian lace floating from a diamond tiara and ribbons trailing from a spray of calla lilies. The vision blurred. It wasn't her dress. There would be no white satin in Francie Tillman's future.

But that was all right. She had all she needed. And some she didn't.

She hung the gown on the dress form and covered it with a sheet then took a second glanced in the mirror.

The floral "One Hour Dress" she'd made in forty-eight minutes from leftover polished cotton had rumpled and would never do for meeting with her biggest client yet. She closed the door on quiet and order and took the stairs down to the shadowed passage that led to the part of her life that wasn't going right.

In her upstairs room, with humid, late-afternoon air ruffling the eyelet curtains, she kept the song alive as she changed into the peach-colored silk charmeuse. "So always look for the silver lining, and try to find the sunny side of li—"

"What're you gettin' all dolled up for?"

Suzette leaned on the door frame, ashes cascading from the end of her cigarette. Coffee stains streaked the housecoat she'd worn for three days.

"I have a fitting." Francie aimed her answer at a clear glass button on her shoe. She couldn't bear looking up at her sister's once-beautiful eyes, or at the way the billowing gown engulfed the figure she'd once envied.

"Who's the hoity-toity this time? Wait. *Shh*." Suze held one finger to her lips. "I heard you talking to Renata. It's the mayor's wife."

Francie nodded and sat on her vanity stool. "Please keep it to yourself." She pulled a book out of the narrow middle drawer.

"Sure. I get it. None of your beeswax, Suze. Fine." Suzette walked to the far side of the room, to the twin bed that matched

Francie's except that it hadn't been made in weeks. "I'm tired."

You're always tired. Francie jumped up, grabbed the cigarette before it hit the rug, and then took a deep, slow breath. From the front room, the radio speaker her nephew called the "giant tiger's mouth" spilled Paul Whiteman's voice, "...strolled the lane together, laughed at the rain..." Francie sat back down, picked up her pen, and spoke to Suzette over her shoulder. "I told Franky to come to the shop when he wakes up."

"Mm-hm." The slurred syllables dissolved into a raspy snore.

"...we cried together, cast love aside together—"

A distant noise froze her pen in midair. A gunshot. Francie jerked and turned toward the window, waiting, not breathing.

Nothing. A car backfiring, maybe, or just memories playing havoc with her mind.

She opened the back cover of her five-year diary. The glue had dried on the picture she'd pasted there. Hard to explain why she'd felt the urgency. Renata had told her to heed the nudge. "Listen to Jesus, *mia amica.*" Maybe the Lord had warned her. Or maybe she was just being paranoid. She couldn't yet convince herself the danger had died.

She fingered the end of the yellow satin ribbon sticking out of the book and opened to the date it marked. Her gaze traveled up the page through four Septembers to her fifteenth summer.

September 14, 1924
    Leaving Theo will be the hardest thing I've ever done
in my life. I love him more than life, but Suze needs me, and
besides, I was never cut out to be a missionary's wife. I know
I was created for something big, and it will begin in Chicago.
I'll get over Theo and he'll get over me. I just hope not too soon.

Four years had passed. She hadn't gotten over Theo, and the one time she'd seen him, he'd said he was still in love with her. She focused on the blank slot at the bottom of the page. White, empty space, a new September 14 waiting to be filled. Setting pen to paper, she left Theo and her dreams of something big in a past she'd moved beyond.

Life would be perfect if not for the problem sleeping in the same room with me. Today I'm doing a second fitting on Mrs. A. Tomorrow Renata and I are going to a Women's Society Meeting at the First Congregational Church. I called Mama yesterday. She actually talked—

A scream shattered the quiet. Francie jumped up and ran to the window. In front of the restaurant, her best friend knelt, sobbing beside her husband, who lay bleeding and motionless on the sidewalk.

CHAPTER 1

Last night's applause lingered in Dani Gallagher's mind like footprints pressed in wet sand. With the tip of a pencil, she lifted the florist's card on the bundle of Gerbera daisies festooning the corner of her desk then tunnel-visioned back to her computer.

The popcorn sound of keyboards capturing the pulse of Tuesday, July 10 slowed her adrenaline for several pithy sentences—until her phone binged an incoming text message.

A parade of exclamation marks marching behind an all-caps CONGRATULATIONS triggered a maverick smile. Just as her lips widened enough to show her teeth, a flash bounced off her screen.

Looking up through dancing spots, she met Evan Carr's smug eyes peeking above the telephoto lens of his three-thousand-dollar obsession. Unruly brown curls and too-long-to-be-fashionable sideburns framed the elfish face of her zany sidekick. Something flat and green was wedged under his arm.

Evan winked. "I'm calling it 'The Face of Victory.'"

A deep cough bounced off the oatmeal-colored walls of her cubicle. "More like 'The Face of Gloating.'" Mitch Anderson, Kenosha Times feature editor, leaned his elbows on a fabric-covered partition. "You proved me wrong, kiddo. I didn't think you were ready for the big leagues."

Dani answered with a smile tinged with just a smidge of smugness.

Evan shoved aside papers and a microwavable container of Campbell's Italian wedding soup and made a place for his posterior on the corner of her desk. He held out a package wrapped in green tissue. "A little something from all of us."

"What is it?"

"One way to find out." He picked at a piece of clear tape.

Dani slid her finger under a fold. The paper tore with a satisfying rip. Matted in sage green and framed in gold, her face stared back at her from page 1, section C, of yesterday's edition.

Her lips parted as her reflection superimposed over her picture. "Thank you."

Evan leaned over the frame and cleared his throat. " 'Kenosha Times Reporter Wins National Award. Danielle Gallagher receives Chase Award for her series 'Children of the Risk—The Age of Electronic Neglect.'" He took a sip of her hour-old coffee. "Good work, blondie."

"So what's next?" Mitch shoved his glasses back to the bridge of his nose.

"Back to the real world." She drew out a martyr's sigh. "Counsel meetings and school board elections. Lucky me." *Unless. . .* She restrained the urge to spring out of her seat like Donkey in the *Shrek* movies. *"Oh! I know! Pick me! Pick me!"*

The balding man who held her future in his pudgy hands gave a slow, torturous smile. "You've only been here, what? Four years? Still a rookie in my book." He clicked his tongue. "However, the extenuating circumstances of a national contest win just might persuade me to give you a chance. Say a three-month trial period to razzle my socks off with a few more scintillating stories?"

"Serious?" She discarded any pretense of acting mature and professional.

"As a shark attack." He shot a two-finger salute from the middle of his forehead. "Give me some weekly stories on kids. Good, bad, every kind of kid. But I want you working on another series like this one." He tapped the frame. "Something big and meaty, something—"

Her desk phone rang.

Evan laughed. "More accolades?"

One eyebrow arched at Evan, she copied Mitch's signature

salute and answered the phone. "Dani Gallagher, feature reporter, how may I help you?"

Silence.

"Hello?"

"Danielle?"

"Yes. Can I help you?"

"This is China." A quiet voice edged with steel.

Dani turned away from Mitch and Evan and covered her other ear as she matched a picture to the voice of a girl she'd interviewed in April. Sixteen, heavyset, long hair dyed black with a purplish-red cast. Dark eyes, tipped up at the corners, encased in thick strokes of liner, lashes clumped with mascara.

"You remember me?" A shaky timbre quaked the words. Fear, anger, maybe drugs.

"Of course. Are you all right?"

Silence again and then a tight "No."

"What's the matter, China?"

"You were wrong."

"Wrong about what?"

"You said I should leave Miguel." Her voice shook, grew even weaker. "You said I had to stand up to him and let him know he couldn't push me around."

"Did you?"

A laugh. Low, almost vicious. "Yeah. Yeah, I did."

Dani switched the phone to her other hand, wiped her damp palm against her thigh. "What happened?" Her pulse hammered against her eardrums as she waited for an answer. "China?"

Seconds passed. "You said he was just using threats to manipulate me."

"What happened?"

"He beat me—good this time. But then he said he was sorry, and he cried. I can't stand that. I can't ever stand that."

"Where are you? Are you hurt?"

Again the laugh. "Of course I'm hurt."

Dear God... "How bad? Have you seen a doctor?"

"He won't hurt me again."

"Where are you? I'll come and get you."

"Can't you listen? This isn't about me. This is about you—what you did. I was gonna give in; I was gonna stay, but then I remembered what you said. You said I was worth more than that. You said nobody has the right to beat on somebody else. You said I deserved somebody better. Well, there isn't anybody better." Her tone escalated. "He was the only guy that ever loved me, and you took him away."

The pulse beat intensified, pounding China's words through her denial. "Where is he now?"

The next sound could have been a laugh or a cry on the verge of hysteria. "In Hell, probably. Where you should be. You killed him."

"China, I—"

"You ever read *Romeo and Juliet*? Bet you could write a nice story about that. A real, true Romeo and Juliet."

"China, stop it. Tell me what happened." *Romeo and Juliet.* "Did he—"

"Yeah. Right in the head. He pulled the trigger, but it was your fault."

Ice lodged in Dani's veins. "I'm so, so sorry, but you have to listen to me."

"No. Not anymore I don't." Another long pause. "I called the cops." Her voice fell flat. "They'll be here soon. I should go. I don't want to see them take him."

Dani pressed her hand against her eyes. Evan gripped her shoulder. She grabbed a pen and scribbled *Check police calls. Suicide?* Evan nodded and took off at a run. Mitch crouched, put his hand where Evan's had been, leaning in toward the phone.

"Are you alone, China?"

Another laugh, high and eerie. "No. Miguel's here. You believe in spirits? Maybe he'll come back as someone else. Maybe he'll come after you for what you did."

Dani dried her palm and gripped the phone to steady the shaking. The quick change in China's voice scared her. Maybe she'd already taken something. She took a deep breath and commanded her voice to be calm. If she could just keep her talking until the police got there. "It's not my fault, and it's not yours either. Miguel was messed up; you told me that yourself. What I said was the truth.

He didn't have the right to hurt you. No one does. That's not how love works."

Muffled sobs answered her.

"I'm so sorry, China. I know you loved him, and I'm sorry he didn't get the help he needed, but you have to believe you weren't wrong to stand up to him. You're a precious girl. Your life is valuable." As she talked she opened a drawer. Scanning file tabs, she grabbed a yellow legal pad. Flipping through pages, she found the one from her interview with China.

"Remember how you told me you'd like to be an occupational therapist? Why does that interest you?"

The crying quieted. Dani visualized her sitting in a corner, hugging her knees and rocking, mascara streaming down her face.

"My friend's little brother got his hand smashed. When he got the cast off, I taught him how to draw." She took a convulsive breath. "His family said I was like one of his therapists. They gave me a necklace. A heart necklace."

"That must have made you feel good. Can you see yourself—"

"Somebody's gotta clean this place. The wall is—" A gasp, followed by a low keening wail cut through Dani, sending chills down her back.

"Tell me where you are. I'll stay with you when you talk to the police. You shouldn't be alone."

"Why did you tell me to leave him? He'd still be here. . . ."

"Let me come and get you, and we'll talk about it."

"The cops just drove up. I didn't want to be here."

"It's good that you stayed. They'll have to ask you some questions."

"I'll tell them the truth," she rasped. "I'll tell them Danielle Gallagher killed him."

⚜

Dani didn't protest when Evan pried the phone from her hand. He held his iPhone in front of her face. "Three blocks from the Marina. Squads got there about two minutes ago. Sound like your call?"

She stared down at the address on the map and nodded.

"Who is she? How do you know her?" Mitch picked up her

13

canvas bag, set it on her desk, and stood.

Evan bent over her. "Talk to me, Dan. You're not looking so good."

"Remember China?"

"The girl who only let me take silhouettes?"

She nodded and looked up at Mitch. "Vito Savona—he works here in maintenance—jumped my car one night when I was doing research for my series, and he told me about this guy in his neighborhood who's heavy into a gaming community. China is the guy's sister. I interviewed her, and she opened up about other things. Her boyfriend was threatening her. I told her to leave him. She did. And now he"—her voice cracked—"he shot himself."

"Find her." Mitch pulled her keys out of the dish on her desk. "This is it. Your story. This is your 'What's next.'"

Evan grabbed her elbow as she stood. "Look at her. She's white as a sheet. She can't—"

"I can. I have to."

"Why?" Evan's grip on her elbow tightened. "Stop and think. Is this really about a story? Or is it about rescuing that girl? That's not your job. It's—"

"Yes. It's about all that. And throw redeeming myself into the mix." As she picked up her bag, her hair spilled across her face, shielding her from the concern that threatened her self-control.

Mitch squeezed her shoulder. "Can you go with her, Carr?"

"No. I have to be at the courthouse in fifteen."

"She'll do okay. It's never easy when you've got a personal connection, but this will be good. Just remember, you gotta draw a line between reporting and social work." Mitch raised the salute again. "Stay safe, kiddo."

"I'm the kickboxing diva, remember?" Her voice quaked.

"That's right." With a laugh, Mitch strode back to his glass-walled office.

"You don't have to do this."

She lowered her chin then raised it. "If I'd kept my big mouth shut, that kid would still be alive. I should—"

"Whoa." Evan grabbed her by the shoulders. "I heard you say it wasn't your fault, and it's not. Somebody had to tell her to get out of there. Maybe you lost your objectivity. Maybe you forgot you were a reporter for a few minutes. But you acted out of compassion; you listened to your gut." He lifted her chin. "We work for God first, Dan."

Dani answered with a sarcastic laugh as she swiped at her wet cheek and threw the strap of her bag over her shoulder. "Go take some pictures, Evan."

CHAPTER 2

Nicky Fiorini kicked his sweat-soaked sheet to the floor and sucked a deep breath. Hot, stagnant air did nothing to ease the panic roused by the dream. Sitting up, he stared at the clock with one eye then glared at the spikes of afternoon sun stabbing through holes in the shade. If not for the dream, he'd still have another hour of escape.

The nightmare hadn't haunted him for months. He'd hoped he'd finally banished it, but the gunshot sound his subconscious conjured to shatter his sleep reverberated through his mind as intensely as the real one had.

A day's worth of stubble scratched his palms as he rubbed his face. He stood and pulled back the shade. Nothing stirred on the street below but a mother tugging a resistant child by the arm.

What had he hoped to see? Would the aftermath of a real fight be somehow comforting? Someone else's crisis instead of the one that stole his peace? Keys jangled. One scraped his thigh as he stepped into the flour-dusted jeans he'd discarded after tossing his apron and climbing the stairs at four-thirty this morning. He rolled his shoulders and grabbed a shirt from the drawer. When was the last time he'd fully relaxed? Four years, at least—back in his midtwenties when his biggest stresses were date nights ruined by his cheating father forgetting to show up for work.

Life was simple back then. Before the nightmares.

He picked up the sheet and shook it out, spreading it over the bed so the woman who'd filled the gap his mother left wouldn't have to.

A siren wailed in the distance. Someone else's crisis.

"Nicky!" Footsteps pounded the stairs. "Did you hear that?"

"Hear what?" He took two strides to the hallway, his pulse quickening at the tone in his sister's voice.

"A shot. I was in the kitchen. Alonzo"—she reached the top of the stairs and folded her arms across her belly—"said it came from across the street. He called the cops."

"Did he see anything?"

Dark hair streaked across pale skin as she shook her head. "He thought he heard a scream. A woman." Eyes wide, she leaned against the wall. "Shouldn't we do something?"

"No." Nicky pressed his hand against the rigid cords at the back of his neck. The sound was real, and just yards away someone lived out his nightmare. "The police will handle it."

His sister closed her eyes. "It's just like. . ." Tears brimming, she turned and ran down the stairs.

She'd disappeared into the kitchen by the time Nicky nodded. His fingers curled. His thumb wrapped over them, but the splotch of patched plaster at shoulder height on the wall stopped him from using his fist. This time.

Voice low and gravelly, he whispered, "I know."

♔

From where he stood, the red and white ambulance concealed the driveway across the street. Nicky turned away from the knot of gapers on the corner. Speculations ricocheted like errant rifle shots. Gang related. . .revenge. . .murder. . .suicide. . . Some said they'd met the young couple who'd lived there several months. Others said the upstairs apartment was a drug house.

Only one person appeared disturbed by the shooting. His sister.

If he thought she'd welcome it, he'd have wrapped his arms around her, but he wasn't going to play the fool in front of that crowd. As he walked away, his bare foot slid on a wad of soft gum. Without acknowledging it, he kept walking.

Turning into the parking lot, he let out an explosive sigh. Twenty yards ahead, fresh graffiti covered the bottom half of the vacant building next to the restaurant his family had owned for generations.

A basketball-sized red circle overlapped a four-foot-high white 7 on a green background. Not an ad for soda pop—the red dot stood for things that birthed nightmares.

He walked over to the two-story building and swiped his finger across a granite block. Rust-red grit—a combination of dirt and spray paint, coated his fingertip. Arching his neck, he gazed up at the fortress. No windows, no openings other than two garage doors in front. By today's standards, it was an ugly structure, violating every current building code.

Yet it still spun dreams in his head.

Pulling out his keys, he turned his back on the green and red wall and strode back to the building he'd lived in for twenty-eight years. A building with no room, or reason, to grow.

He opened the outside door of the storeroom. What was it with builders in the 1920s? Or was it just on this block that windows weren't fashionable? He closed the door behind him, fastened the chain lock, then wedged the door open as far as the gold links would allow. A muggy draft, cool in comparison to the stagnant air inside, seeped through the two-inch space.

Ceiling lights in rose-covered porcelain bases lit the three-hundred-plus square feet. Pink roses climbed trellises on the scuffed and yellowed wallpaper, and floor-to-ceiling cherry wood shelves lined three walls. In the center of the room, a wrought iron table, legs fashioned of trailing, winding vines, sat bolted to the hardwood floor. Decades ago, someone, most likely his great-grandmother, had gone through a lot of trouble decorating a room built for storage.

His great-grandmother's touches remained in other ways. Her crucifix hung by the back door. For much of his childhood he'd prayed to it. He knew the exact moment he'd stopped praying to the figure on the cross and started talking to the living God. He also knew the exact moment he'd stopped.

Nicky hoisted a thousand-count box of white paper bags onto the table then walked over to his computer desk in the corner and sat on a three-legged chair. One more thing in need of fixing.

In spite of an array of amputated table legs, stained tablecloths, and bent silverware demanding his attention, he'd always done his best thinking here. It was where he'd hid when he was eleven, the day his mother left, the day he promised to become a better man than his father.

It was where he came in the middle of the night for a break from reality. Here, he gave rein to hopeless fantasies where candlelight flickered on starched white tablecloths, music swirled around jeweled women and men in dark Italian suits, and whispered compliments floated on the cool air over a backdrop of clinking crystal. Here, the illustrious Mr. Fiorini bowed to his guests in his Luciano Carreli tux.

Here, visions spawned. And died just as quickly.

He was born a century too late for his dreams.

The air was thick and hot and hard to breathe as Dani ran down the concrete steps from the *Times* building. She unlocked the door of her 1990 Geo Metro. Chips of blue paint crumbled onto her open-toed sandals. The car, a gift from her grandmother and named in her memory, bragged of 58,000 miles on its odometer. It was dying of sheer age and boredom.

A blast of heat wafted up at her as she opened the door. She slid in gingerly, keeping the backs of her bare arms off the gray vinyl.

She stuck the key in the ignition, holding her breath as she turned it. "Come on, Agatha." The car responded with a familiar *click*.

"Behave yourself. We've got a job to do." She jiggled the steering wheel and wiggled the key, but none of the usual tricks succeeded.

A thundering rap on the hood jerked her head.

"Agatha *testardo* again?"

Dani wiped the dampness from her top lip and nodded at the burly little man whose hairy, ape-like fist curled on the hood of her car.

Vito Savona could have retired from maintenance five years earlier but claimed the peace and quiet would kill him. "You going home, or you on a story?" A stubby cigar dusted Agatha's nose with ashes.

Dani leaned her head out of the window. She wouldn't tell him she was headed to his neighborhood. If he knew she was going alone, he'd refuse to jump her car or he'd jump in with her. "I've got a story." *Or the fallout from one.* "Not that Agatha cares."

Vito smiled and patted the hood. "You leave her to me. I got a way with old ladies." He unhooked a ring with two keys from the chain on his belt. "You take mine. I'll get to Agatha after work."

"Oh, Vito, not again. You'll be late for supper."

"If I come home on time, Lavinia thinks I'm sick. You don't let me work on Agatha, I'll have to go to bed with a bowl of milk toast. Take my car."

"You're my angel, Vito." She got out and planted a kiss on his cheek.

♔

Out of habit, questions sifted into logical order as she drove. But how did the who-what-when-where fit into a bigger story? She had no intention of making this about Miguel—of exploiting the despair of one young man or exposing the raw grief of a single family. . .or the girl who would spend the rest of her life second-guessing her decision to walk away from abuse.

There were universal truths in every human interest story. To make her readers care, she had to cull them out. What was Miguel's deepest need? To be loved? To belong? To feel a sense of purpose and know that his life mattered?

Or was she projecting her own heart's desire onto a boy she'd never met?

The air conditioner in Vito's car didn't work. The heat intensified the suffocating smell of stale cigar smoke. By the time she reached the neighborhood everyone referred to as the Swamp, her blouse was wet and sticking to the seat. She pulled a hair band out of her bag and tied her hair up, steering with her knee as she pulled the wet strands off her neck and away from her face. Yet in spite of the heat, her fingers were still cold and clammy.

She didn't need a GPS to tell her she'd found the house. Two cruisers and an ambulance, their rotating lights muted by the blaring sun, sat in front of a house sided with gray shingles. On the porch above dilapidated steps, a child's swing angled on rusty chains. She drove slowly, taking mental notes on the area.

A small redbrick grocery store, two of its four front windows boarded and plastered with beer signs, occupied one corner of the block. Next to a Laundromat stood two mirror-image houses, one white and well kept with pink petunias spilling out of flower boxes. Its twin sported a garish green with peeling salmon-colored trim. Across the street from the ambulance, a neon sign jutted out over the sidewalk proclaiming BRACCIANO ITALIAN AND AMERICAN CUISINE.

Breathing a prayer, Dani let reason take hold. She shouldn't be here. As she lifted her foot off the brake, a shadow reached out from the north side of the house then morphed into two paramedics wheeling a draped form on a stretcher. Behind them China leaned on the arm of a police officer, her hands clenched over her mouth, her face streaked with black.

Dani pulled away. Barely conscious of where she was heading, she drove toward the lake and parked at the marina. Numb legs carried her to a park bench facing the water.

Heat shimmered on the sidewalk. Two boys flew past on skateboards. The cloudless blue dome of sky dissolved into gray-blue where Lake Michigan met the horizon. Her gaze followed the boys until they were out of sight then turned back to the water, where white triangle sails bobbed like plastic toys in a bathtub. A seagull swooped, grabbed its dinner, and took off. It soared and then hovered, gliding effortlessly on the wind.

It was all too tranquil, too incongruous with China's tears and Miguel's shrouded body.

"It's all your fault. Why did you tell me to leave him? He'd still be here. . . ."

Dani turned her back to the lake and the laughter. *Lord, what can I do?*

No answer came. She walked to the car and drove back. The ambulance was gone. A single police car remained. Investigating a possible crime scene.

She went home and sat on the outside steps, staring at manicured lawns and expensive cars. And her watch. An hour passed in a haze of trying not to think. On shaky legs she stood, walked to her car, and drove back to the house where Miguel had died.

The police car was gone. Onlookers had moved on with their day. From the street, all looked peaceful. As if life continued, uninterrupted, in the neglected gray house.

She parked on the side street and walked along the south side of the house to a white door marked 5351 ½ in orange crayon. Through smudged windows, she eyed narrow steps leading upstairs. The door opened without a sound. The temperature and the cloying smell of old grease increased with each step.

A thin curtain of faded green dotted swiss hung across the window in the upstairs door, offering no privacy. A pink refrigerator stood in one corner. A chrome-legged table covered with dirty dishes, wrappers, and overflowing ashtrays sat against the outside wall. Large blue plastic bins, all apparently empty, lined the floor in front of the cupboards.

Dani knocked. From somewhere next door or the apartment downstairs the Beatles sang "Eleanor Rigby." She knocked louder, waited, then tried the door handle.

It didn't budge. She pulled a pen and notebook out of her bag. *China. I need to talk to you. Call me as soon as you can. Danielle.* She wrote her cell phone number, tore out the paper, and slid it under the door.

Two steps down the memory of China's words stopped her. *"A real Romeo and Juliet story."*

Would the police have taken her in to fill out forms or answer questions, or would they have done that here? Was she still inside, huddled in a corner somewhere or trying to clean up the mess?

Shutting her eyes against the scene playing in her head, Dani grabbed the handle again and pushed against the door. The handle stayed rigid, but the latch gave way. She fell into the room.

"China? China, are you here?" She walked through the kitchen, stopping at a doorway. Every nerve fiber told her to leave. What if the police came back to finish their investigation? What if China— or someone else—came in behind her? She shivered, took a deep breath, and entered the room.

Her eyes locked on a stain on the wall behind a mattress on the floor. For the space of several seconds, she couldn't breathe, couldn't move. Her gaze lowered to a pillow and she gasped.

Her knees suddenly felt like rubber. Her hand shook as she swiped at the perspiration on her upper lip. She took a deep breath and forced her eyes to scan the room. Unframed pencil sketches, held in place by masking tape, decorated all four walls. Drawings of doors, parking meters, manhole covers. She walked around a stack of empty cardboard boxes, past the mattress, to the only other doorway.

A bathroom, tiled in black and white, and surprisingly clean. The bottom edge of the closed shower curtain hung inside the tub. The curtain bulged in one spot. Dani shook her head as her vision blurred, took another breath and held it, then opened the curtain.

Her breath rushed out in pent-up relief. The tub overflowed with dirty laundry—women's clothes mixed in with men's jeans and shirts. Dani lifted a white T-shirt. Beneath a tear in the ribbed collar a distorted, black-outlined 7 emblazoned the front.

She ordered her mind to think like a reporter. She'd been on police calls. They'd never affected her like this.

It's never easy when you've got a personal connection.

She closed the shower curtain and took in the details of the small room. A cardboard box sat on the floor, haphazardly filled with cosmetic bottles, brushes, shampoos, and curling irons. In the open medicine cabinet, two shelves held men's deodorant, aftershave, toothpaste, and razors. Two shelves were empty. With the tip of her finger she opened cupboards and drawers. More empty shelves. Had Miguel come home and caught China packing?

Streaks of dampness remained on the counter. Dani could picture a hysterical girl scrubbing her hands.

Had she found him dead or witnessed the horror?

An icy chill crept up her back. Did the police believe it was suicide?

The insanity of being there hit her full force. She backed out of the bathroom and retraced her steps, not looking at the mattress this time. Untucking the tail of her blouse, she wiped the door handle on both sides, ran down the steps, looked around, and did the same with the outside door.

Heart slamming her ribs, she ran toward the alley. Two garbage cans overflowed with papers, clothes, and books. A plastic milk crate sat on the ground between them, filled with spiral notebooks. The front one, every inch of its cover decorated with ink drawings, was labeled "Algebra." Dani bent, flipping through them. West Civ., Psych., Spanish. Wedged between them was a black leather book, worn and frayed at the corners. MY DIARY was lettered in muted gold across the front.

Looking both ways again, she grabbed the crate and ran to Vito's car. She tossed the basket in the backseat, slid behind the wheel, and drove around the corner.

In front of the Laundromat, a little blond girl rode a bike with training wheels, a twenty-something man close behind. At the end of the block, an elderly man shuffled out of the grocery store, newspaper under one arm.

The dash clock read 5:56. She drove around the block and parked on the one-way street next to the Italian restaurant. China would return sometime, if only to gather her things and run.

Until the sun went down, she'd have a perfect view.

September 12, 1924

Toying with the broken strap of her overalls, Francie compared the gown she'd just sketched with the one in McCall's. "Mine's better," she mouthed.

Downstairs, the screen door opened and bounced against the frame. Daddy's barn boots stomped the wood floor. "You'll be going to Mrs. Johnson's tonight?"

"Of course," Mama answered, her voice tight with the strain of Friday. "I would appreciate it if you would tell Francie to go with me."

"She's fine here."

"I'd rather she not—"

"She's fifteen, Signe. Not a baby. She understands what I need to do to keep the farm."

"But if there's trouble. . ."

Daddy laughed. "If there's trouble, Francie just may be the one to break it up."

Mama huffed the kind of sigh that ruffled the hair hanging over her forehead. Francie heard her gathering her things. She scrambled off the bed, crawled through the open window, and jumped onto the roof of the shed.

When Mama poked her head into the shed, Francie was sitting on the three-legged stool, laying the bowl ring from the milk separator out on a clean flour sack to dry. Mama smiled. "Good girl. I'll be off now. Stay in the house tonight."

"I will." Pretending to stretch, she slipped both hands behind her back.

A lie doesn't count if your fingers are crossed.

Half an hour later, she lowered onto her belly in the hayloft, careful not to dislodge a single blade of straw. The open door framed an orange ball of sun, low and huge, melting into the pines above their valley. Through the spaces between the boards, she had a perfect view of Daddy's "office." Beyond the curtain that separated the office from the rest of the barn, Applejack nickered and Tess answered with a soft snort. Francie rested her chin on her hands and waited.

Almost dark. And Friday. Something would happen tonight.

Daddy lit kindling in the stove, poured water from a dented bucket into the iron kettle, then filled a small pan with sugar. He wiped off the old, scarred table and set a tin cup in the center. "Thirty-five cents a pint, gentlemen," she'd hear him say. And then the stories would start. Stories of birthing calves and record rainfall, of life before the War. And the War.

Mama spent Friday evenings reading to Mrs. Johnson. Francie was always invited, but there were too many things a fifteen-year-old girl would rather do than sip tea and read the Bible to an old lady. Things like listening in on Daddy's "business." And hoping for another good fight.

Below her the door opened. She hadn't heard a car. Daddy looked up. His eyes widened. "Signe? Is something wrong?"

Mama never came into Daddy's office. Francie couldn't see her face, but she could hear her breathing like she'd been running. Her brown shift quivered over wide hips as she caught her breath. She held something out to Daddy. "Carina is ill. I came back to get

25

slippery elm. She got a letter for us by mistake." Mama thrust an envelope at him. "From your daughter."

Francie pressed her face into the boards. Suzette had left home going on three years ago. They hadn't heard from her since.

"*My* daughter?" His eyes lit with a rare smile. "Well, what does she say?"

"She says"—Mama hissed the words—"we have a grandchild."

Daddy's jaw slackened. Tired eyes widened. "A baby?"

"No, Henri. A child. A two-year-old boy."

"And she just tells us now? Is she—"

"Married? Of course not."

His hands knotted into fists. "What does she want? She knows she won't get money."

"She wants Francie."

Daddy gave a laugh that sent shivers down Francie's back. "I will not lose another daughter." He held his hand out for the letter. "Hide the envelope. We may want her address." He tossed the letter into the raging flames in the stove. "Francie cannot hear of this."

CHAPTER 3

The shadows disappeared. A slight breeze stirred through the open car window. Dani stretched and rubbed her eyes then pulled the front of her shirt away from her belly, letting the air dry her hot, sticky skin. Every pore in her body cried out for a shower, and her stomach growled. The smells coming from the restaurant called to her.

She'd made a call and found out the police had taken China in for questioning and then released her. The woman at the police station who always gave Dani more information than she was supposed to had no idea who China had left with or where she'd gone.

Three hours and still no sign of her. She'd come back for the rest of her things, wouldn't she? Or send someone for the half-packed boxes? Or would she just walk away, leaving every reminder of life with Miguel behind?

Doubts danced on the night breeze. "What am I doing here?"

"*This is your 'What's next.'*"

Mitch's commission warred with Evan's warning—"*You don't have to do this.*"

"*I can. I have to.*" China was out there somewhere, hating herself for what had happened, blaming Dani for starting the Domino chain that led to a gunshot.

A cold clamminess circled her mouth. Her fingertips tingled. She needed food.

Vito's car door creaked as it opened. Through the red and gold of BRACCIANO lettered behind iron bars on the front window, she spotted a small table facing the street. A perfect vantage point. After reshaping her ponytail, she looked around, hoping no one was watching. She still had the guilty feeling she was doing something wrong.

Fresh paint and the neon sign seemed to be the only updates the outside of the restaurant had experienced in decades. On the second story, each tall, narrow window had its own wrought-iron balcony.

A bell dinged overhead as she opened the door. The rich scents of oregano, sausage, and fresh-baked bread intensified her hunger.

Dani surveyed the red-walled room crammed with tables covered with checkered tablecloths and surrounded by black-lacquered chairs with red cushions.

The thin, long-legged girl walking toward her with a stack of menus under her arm looked to be in her late teens. Her nametag read "Renata Fiorini." Anger snapped in dark, red-rimmed eyes smudged with mascara. As if she'd been crying. Black hair, short in back, hung over one eye. Half moons of silver decorated each ear. She wore a short black leather skirt with a wide zipper up the front and a white button-down blouse.

"Welcome to Bracciano." She pronounced it Bra-CHA-no, and her tone was anything but welcoming. "One?"

"Yes, please."

"Over here."

"Could I sit right there by the window?"

The girl slapped the menu on the table. A button slipped open at the top of her blouse, revealing a tattoo in the hollow above her collarbone. Reddened edges indicated fresh work. Dani stopped a gasp as she stared at the stretched and warped 7.

The girl tugged at her shirt, her face pinking as she turned away. She walked to the far side of the room and returned moments later, blouse buttoned, face once again pale. She smacked down silverware rolled in a napkin and a glass of water. "You ready to order?"

Dani smiled at the menu she hadn't opened. "Do you have calzones?"

"Yeah."

"What kind?"

The girl sighed. "Spinach or sausage."

"I'd like a spinach calzone, please."

"Anything to drink?"

"Just water."

Without even a nod, the girl walked away.

Dani walked to the restroom. She splashed cold water on her face and neck, hoping for some revival. The eyes that stared back at her from the small cracked mirror above the sink looked older than the image in yesterday's paper. Victory no longer tasted sweet.

She dried her face and turned, catching her image in a full-length mirror on the back of the door. Smoothing the front of her rumpled peasant blouse with a damp hand, she tightened her abs and pulled her shoulders back. The smocking on the shirt she'd found at her favorite resale shop allowed the fabric to flow over her hips, concealing the fact that she hadn't been to the gym in three weeks. She thought about brushing her hair or refreshing her lipstick, but that all took effort, and she wasn't going to be seeing anyone tonight who cared what she looked like. Snapping off the light, she opened the door then walked back to the table.

A lamp glowed in the downstairs apartment across the street. Dani began to let herself relax. If China came home she'd have to turn on a light, and Dani could see windows from two of the upstairs rooms from where she sat. She pulled out her legal pad and pen, drew a slanted 7 then scribbled it out. The tattoo, the emblem on the shirt in the bathtub—gang signs. She'd heard of the Sevens. And they weren't the only gang in the Swamp.

What am I doing here?

A rush of angry Italian from the kitchen slammed over her question. A male voice followed by the waitress's, equally harsh. Thanks to Vito's frequent peppering of Italian, Dani could pick out a few words.

A minute later Dani's order smacked the table in front of her. "Anything else?"

"No, thank you." She smiled at the girl. "Bad day?"

The girl rolled her eyes. "Bad life. Bad family."

"Parents?"

29

"No." She blinked hard. "My brother. King of the Universe."

Dani laughed. "That makes you royalty, too, you know."

The girl swiped at tears and smiled weakly. "Yeah. Part of the Royal Pain family. I'm disowning them."

"Smart move. Who wants to be related to someone suffering from delusions of grandeur."

This time she actually laughed. "Hope you like the calzone. It was made by the king himself."

Dani cut into the stuffed pastry. Melted cheese pooled around her fork and stretched like a bungee cord when she lifted it. She took a bite and closed her eyes. Italian heaven. She studied a poster on the window advertising a new all-you-can-eat Italian buffet on Friday nights. Ravioli, chicken marsala, baked ziti. She might just have to come back sometime. With friends, for a happy occasion.

In the growing darkness, the light filtering through the first-floor windows across the street outlined the broken swing. Black windows stared at her from the upstairs apartment. Resting her fork on the plate, she picked up her pen.

She recorded the scene in Miguel's living room as objectively as she could. She outlined questions and topics to research. *Signs of suicidal behavior. Statistics. Demographics. Effects of suicide on peers. Copycat suicides. Miguel's age—check obit. Substance abuse? Prior record? Gang involvement?* She filled the page then turned to a blank one and gave vent to her feelings.

I just want to talk to China. I want to tell her it wasn't her fault— but was it mine? Why didn't I tell her to take him seriously, to call a suicide hotline? Why didn't I call for her? When will I learn to just ask questions and not meddle? If she does anything to hurt herself I'll never—

Renata returned. Her eyes sparkled. "Is everything okay? Would you like dessert?"

"No thanks. Everything was delicious. Things okay with you now?"

"Yeah." She grinned. "I just told my brother he was suffering from delusions of grandeur. He almost fell into the tortellini." She set the check down on the table. "Thanks for your help. Have a good evening." With a wave, she walked back to the kitchen.

Just before closing her notebook, Dani's eyes fell on *When will I learn to just ask questions and not meddle?*

Maybe never, she thought, ripping out a sheet of paper. She folded it in half and wrote a quick note then left it on the table, covering it with a generous tip.

Renata—The calzone was royally delicious. I don't know about your brother, but I know that God, the real King of the Universe, loves you very much.

♔

The temperature dropped with the sun and made sitting in the car bearable. Dani locked the doors, leaving the windows open a crack. She reached in the backseat and pulled out the diary. In spite of its obvious age, she hoped it was China's. It wasn't. The inscription in the front read *To Francine from Mama and Daddy. Happy 15th Birthday. December 4, 1923.*

She put the book back in the milk crate. It would be an interesting read sometime when she could focus on something other than the house across the street. Wedging her bag behind her, she leaned against the passenger door, slipped off her sandals, and rested bare feet on the dashboard in front of the steering wheel. She'd wait another hour or so, maybe until midnight.

♔

"Hey, kid! Open the door!"

Dani bolted upright. Red and blue lights splashed the dashboard, sidewalk, and side of the building. She'd fallen asleep. Was she dreaming? The hammering on the window matched the pounding of her pulse.

"I said open the door! Get out or I'll—"

"Cool it, Nicky." A calmer voice spoke over the angry one. "He's probably passed out."

Dani sat up, trying to remember where she was. She turned, only to look straight into the beam of a flashlight. The light shifted. As her vision cleared, she stared at the gold and blue of a Kenosha City Police badge.

The scene in the apartment flashed before her. Her hands turned cold and tingly. How could she have been so stupid as to walk into that apartment just minutes after the police left, and then to park

31

across the street? If they had any suspicions that Miguel's death was not suicide, wouldn't they have the place under surveillance? And if China had given them her name. . .*the note.* Had she picked it up or had she left a calling card complete with phone number? Hand trembling, she rolled down the window.

"Step out of the car, please."

As Dani obeyed, squinting in the light, an angry hiss emanated from the figure behind the officer. "Got a problem, Nicky?" the officer asked, never taking his eyes off her.

" 'Step out of the car, please,'" the man behind the officer mocked. "You sound like you're talking to your mother."

The officer shook his head and ran the flashlight from Dani's head to her toes. A look of surprise crossed his face, and the light switched off. "May I see your driver's license, *ma'am?*"

"Huh?" The shadowy figure stepped closer into the hazy, yellow light of the street lamp.

Dani reached into the car. Her hand slid toward her open bag. The officer raised one hand. "Take the bag out of the car first, please."

Pulling it out by one strap, Dani noted the officer's hand resting on the handle of his holstered revolver. She drew out her wallet, pulled out her license, and handed it to him.

"May I see your vehicle registration, please?"

How could she explain the car? "It's. . .not my car. I'm just borrowing it."

"Yeah, right." This from the dark-haired man in jeans and a white T-shirt.

"Who owns the car?"

"Vito Savona. He's a friend—I work with him. Mine broke down and he loaned me his, and"—she closed her mouth, aware that too much talk could sound like she had something to hide.

A glance passed from the officer to the other man. The look clearly said, "I hope you feel like an idiot."

The man with the dark hair shrugged, looked down then suddenly up again. "You gonna believe her? Just like that?"

The officer sighed. "No. I'm going to call it in, but you want to go call Vito? You want to deal with Lavinia at two in the morning? You go call, and I'll question your car thief some more."

The man muttered under his breath as he turned. "How'd you ever get to be a cop, anyway?"

Stifling a smile the officer yelled, "Shut up, Nicky, and bring us some coffee." Turning the full force of his smile on Dani, he held up one finger. "Stay right there. This'll only take a couple of minutes." He walked back to the squad car.

Dani watched his face in the glow of his computer. He shut off the flashing lights before he got out. "No thefts reported, and your record is clean. Sorry if we scared you."

Dani's brain processed slowly. Why wasn't he questioning her about Miguel? Suddenly, part of the conversation registered. "You know Vito?"

The man laughed. "Everybody knows Vito. Nicky and I went to school with his boys. Every kid in the neighborhood knew if he got kicked out of the house, the Savona's door was always open—or if it wasn't, we knew how to pick it with a credit card and a bobby pin. 'Course we knew we'd get a lecture and a kick in the butt, too."

He nodded toward the restaurant. "Unfortunately, some of us just remember life's kicks, not the hospitality." The look in his eyes typed a mental note. There was a story here.

The man removed his cap, revealing buzz-cut blond hair. "So, prove to me you didn't steal Vito's car."

Dani warmed to his smile. "I think you just did."

The officer raised his left brow and cocked his head.

"Why would anyone steal from a man who would give you the shirt off his back before you asked for it?"

He laughed again. "You obviously know Vito. I'm convinced." He extended his hand. "Todd Metzger. The suspicious dude is Dominick Fiorini."

"Ah." His royal high-and-mightiness in the flesh?

"So, you homeless or something, Danielle?"

Dani laughed, partially from relief the questions weren't headed in a different direction. The booming beat of a rap song thundered from a low-slung car approaching the corner. The distraction gave her a chance to formulate an answer. The car rolled to a stop.

"Hey, Sergeant Metzger, whatcha' think?"

"Sounds great, HoJo, but tamp it down. It's two a.m."

The boy's compliance surprised Dani. In the relative quiet, the sidewalk no longer vibrated. "We keep the peace just for you, okay?" He gave a wicked smile. "Maybe we go wake up the Vamps."

"Maybe you go home and quit worrying your mama."

The boy laughed and pulled away, squealing tires as he turned. Todd shook his head. "Now, what were you saying?"

"I was just waiting for a friend to get home, and I fell asleep."

Nodding in the direction of the disappearing taillights, he said, "Not the best part of town to camp out in."

She was about to respond with a lame answer when the "suspicious dude" approached with what could only be called a sheepish look on his face. His lack of eye contact with the sergeant was obvious. He looked directly at Dani. "Vito wants to talk to you."

The officer smiled but didn't comment as Dominick turned and led the way into the building. He opened a side door and walked in, leaving Todd to catch it before it could hit Dani. Todd shrugged. "Sorry. He flunked Manners 101."

"Sounds like you're used to apologizing for him."

"Always have. In his defense, he's seen too much in this neighborhood. And Vito's car was stolen twice last year."

Dani stood for a minute, adjusting to the fluorescent-lit room. A massive, flour-dusted table took up the center, one half covered with mounds of rising dough, the other crammed with loaves fresh from the oven. She stared at the dark-haired Dominick's profile as he pummeled a mass of dough.

The pounding stopped, and he began shaping with the hands of an artist, the muscles in his arms flexing. His fingers pulled exactly the right amount of dough to shape and twist breadsticks with the speed and ease of a master.

Footsteps pulled Dani's attention from the performance in front of her. Dani turned. Renata, in flip-flops and a baggy shirt and shorts she'd probably been sleeping in, held a phone, long curled cord looped over her arm. Surprise registered on the girl's face. "You?" Her brow furrowed. "I don't know what's going on, Vito," she spoke into the phone, "but here's your car thief."

As Dani took the phone, she nodded in Dominick's direction. "His eminence?"

Renata nodded, a smile lighting her dark eyes. "Wanna kiss his ring?"

"Maybe I'll request an audience when he's in a better mood."

"Won't happen."

Dani put the phone to her ear. "Hi Vito." She couldn't help the apologetic, little-girl voice. "I'm sorry."

"You okay? Did that piece of junk break down on you?"

"I'm fine. The car's fine. I was just waiting for a friend to get home, and I fell asleep. I'm sorry they had to wake you up. Tell Lavinia I'm sorry."

"Forget it. Why didn't that *stupido* kid believe you? Always making mountains out of mole hills, that kid. And a worse temper than me. Don't you let him get to you, you hear? Don't let him mess with your head. You tell him if he lays a finger on you, I'll rearrange his face, okay?"

Dani laughed. "I'll tell him, Vito. Now kiss your wife and go back to sleep."

"Now that we're awake maybe I do more than kiss—"

"Hey." Lavinia's voice cut over his. "Dream on, old man."

Dani was laughing as she turned back to face the table where Todd the policeman smothered a piece of fresh bread with butter then sprinkled it with garlic salt. He held it out to her. "So, Vito gonna press charges?"

"Nah, but he did ask for my shoe size."

Renata laughed, "Cool. Cement shoes—everybody's wearing 'em."

Todd opened his mouth then shut it as the tip of Dominick's knife slammed into the table. Dark eyes turned on Dani as he pulled it out and pointed the blade at her. "I don't know who you are or what you were doing out there, but sleeping in a car in this neighborhood is a really stupid, brainless thing to do, and laughing about it is even stupider."

Renata rolled her eyes. "Lay off, Nicky."

"No, I won't lay off. And I won't lay off you, either. You haven't got any more sense than she does, hanging around with—"

"Wait a minute." Dani glared back at him. "Don't start on her. It's me you've got a problem with, and I think you've made your point."

"I haven't gotten even remotely close to my point. I should have left you out there and let the Vamps or the Roses make the point."

Todd put his hand on Nicky's shoulder. "Cool it, Nick."

Nicky shrugged the hand off, never taking his eyes off Dani. "You know how happy you'd make some homey, lyin' there like you're wearing a sign saying, 'Here I am, dumb and stupid on a silver platter. Come and get me.'"

Dani slapped the piece of bread on the table. "I accidentally fell asleep in a locked car."

"You think a locked car with the window open three inches is protection? Tell that to the kid across the street who got shot in his own house this afternoon."

"He didn't get shot. He shot himsel—I don't have to listen to this."

Bare feet slapped as she ran out the door and onto the sidewalk, "dumb and stupid on a silver platter" echoing in her head.

CHAPTER 4

Dani eyed the clock as she stumbled in the door. *"Everyone should have at least one three a.m. friend."*

She'd heard it at a seminar last year and decided the night she'd heard it, to find out if she did. Anna Nelson had answered in a panic on the second ring. Evan had answered on the fourth with a yawn and a "What's wrong?" Both ended up laughing.

How many people have *two* three a.m. friends? And was it wrong to wake them both? One to vent about the enraged Italian who'd screamed at her—the other to describe the Roman statue of a man in a white apron who shaped dough with hands that would put Michelangelo's to shame?

She kicked off her shoes and felt her way to the bathroom without turning on a light. Anna would make her laugh, make her forget the horrible day at least for a few moments. And then she'd ask questions, and then she'd agree with the silver platter comment.

Evan would make her pray for the cranky Italian who thought he ruled the universe.

She splashed water on her face and went to bed, still dressed, determined not to dream about a stained wall and a shrouded body and flashing lights.

After two hours of pretend sleep, she got up and grabbed her gym bag. An hour of ducks and jabs, strikes and blocks, and she was drenched in sweat and finally spent enough for the sleep she no longer had time for.

⚜

Vito met her in the parking lot on Thursday afternoon, Agatha's keys in hand.

"She's purring like a spoiled baby."

Dani gave him his keys. "Thank you, Vito." She kissed his cheek. "You're my angel." She pulled her checkbook out of her purse.

"Angels don't come in packages like this one. Put that away. You want to pay me, come have supper at my house."

"How does your wife fixing supper for me make us even?"

"It makes her happy. And when Mama's happy. . ." Dark eyes sparkled.

"Everybody's happy." She laughed. "Fine. But I'm doing dishes."

"Deal. Monday night, six o'clock. She's got the menu figured out already."

Monday? Not Saturday? Or Sunday? She didn't question, just thanked him and got in her rusty oven of a car. "Glad to have you back, Aggie."

"You don't have to do this." Ignoring the little voice in her head that sounded like Evan, she drove to the neighborhood where seven was not, as described in the Bible, a perfect number.

She parked in the alley several doors down from the apartment where Miguel had put a bullet in his head. The place where her story would begin. She'd follow the ripples, the concentric circles lapping out from the house on the corner.

In a skirt and blouse, with sunglasses on and hair down, no one who'd seen her on Tuesday would recognize her. She stashed her wallet in the glove compartment and locked it. Taking only her phone and keys, she got out and walked past the back of the shabby gray house on the corner.

The mound of trash had doubled in size. Clear garbage bags full of canned and boxed food teetered on boxes of clothes, an old dresser, chair and—her stomach lurched. The stained pillow sat between a smashed television and a stuffed yellow rabbit holding a felt carrot.

38

Eyes focused on the gravel beneath her feet, she turned right and let out a breath she didn't know she'd been holding. As she walked toward the corner, pulse tripping, she pulled out her phone and punched a listing she'd called at least a dozen times in forty-eight hours. *Answer, China. Answer.*

"The number you have dialed is unavailable."

Suddenly not wanting to feel so alone, she punched Anna's number.

"Hi! This is Anna's phone. Leave a message because, whoever you are, if you have this number, you're im—" Dani pushed the red button. What good was a girlfriend if she spent all her time with her boyfriend?

Three doors down, two long-legged boys of fifteen or so sat on a front porch. *Hi guys. Name's Dani. I work for the* Times. *Either of you know Miguel Reyes? How has his death affected you? Does it make you appreciate each day? Make you want to change the way your life is going? Does it scare you to think how quickly his life was snuffed—*

One of the boys waved. "Nice skirt. Nice..."

She quickened her steps, pretending not to hear his assessment of her body parts. Not the place, nor the outfit, to start interviewing.

A woman on a ladder, paint can in hand, nodded to her.

Dani waved. "Nice color." Her face pinked. *The house trim, not you. Please don't take that wrong.*

"Thanks." The woman did a double take. Or was it her imagination? Did a pale blond seem as out of place here to anyone but her?

As if in answer, two girls in short shorts giggled past, arms and legs as white as hers. Except for the tattoos.

"Nice shoes," one whispered. The other giggled.

If she had any hopes of mingling, it wasn't going to happen in stilettos.

On the opposite side of the street, the Italian restaurant anchored the far corner of the block. Without a single explanation in her head, she crossed the street. She passed three houses in various shades of white and disrepair and then an old two-story building with two wide garage doors. A grassy area, maybe twenty feet wide, stretched between the building and Bracciano. Green space. Did neighborhood kids flock there to play kick ball? Would his highness, King of the Universe, allow it so close to his kingdom?

A bell chimed. She looked up and blinked twice as the king himself stepped onto the sidewalk with a white-haired couple. The couple kept walking. Dominick turned.

Shiny black hair drifted over one eye. He shook it away. One hand landed on narrow hips, displaying tanned muscles under a tight white T-shirt. A white apron, folded in half, wrapped his waist and hung at an angle. Dark eyes squinted. He nodded and held the door open. "Coming in?" His strained tone might almost be called civil.

"No. Just out walking. Thank you."

Eyebrows rose. His head tilted to one side. "Seriously?" He said it with as much disdain as could be squeezed into four syllables. "You really don't get it, do you?"

Fingers choking her phone, Dani folded her arms across her blouse. "It's the middle of the afternoon, and it's a free country."

He took a step toward her. "Really?" He swept his arm toward the restaurant. "Notice anything unusual? Do you see bars on the windows at Mangia or Ray Radigan's? It may be a free country, sister, but there isn't a lot of freedom in this neighborhood. I can point out two drug houses on this block alone. You think their customers feel free? You think. . ."

Dani's temperature rose with each word. Spinning away from him, she marched two yards. And slammed her heel into an iron grate. Swooping forward, nose to outstretched knee, her hands hit the sidewalk, stopping her momentum. Before she could right herself, Dominick Fiorini knelt at her feet.

"Are you all right?" Genuine, or deftly faked, concern drenched his words. Dark chocolate eyes intensified the heat on her face.

He smelled of warm bread and sandalwood.

Broad hands lifted her foot from her shoe and yanked at her stiletto. Freeing it, he slid it onto her foot. "There you go, Cinderella."

Swallowing wasn't an option. Her tongue fused to the roof of her mouth.

"Now go home and stay safe." His soft words slid over her like butter on fresh-baked rolls.

She nodded and turned away. Five steps toward the corner, her tongue loosened enough for a hoarse "Thank you."

⚜

A yellow-tinged newspaper clipping floated out of the diary as Dani set it on her kitchen table.

July 29, 1928
Two Armed Men Shot in Jewelry Store Holdup

She picked it up and read the lead.

Jewelers Row saw yet another robbery this week as three gunmen broke into Walbrecht's Jewelers on Wabash Street and absconded with more than $10,000 worth of cut diamonds, rings, and necklaces. The take would have been much higher, however, if an anonymous caller had not tipped off the police at the very moment the heist was unfolding.

Now that was good journalism. She'd love to see the look on Mitch's face if she worked the word *absconded* into a piece. She set the clipping aside, took a sip of Tazo Calm tea, and reread the inscription inside the cover. On the opposite page, perfect penmanship spelled out *Francie Tillman, Osseo, Wisconsin.*

She turned to the first entry.

January 1, 1924

A new year and all these pages waiting to be filled with plans for adventure! Nothing exciting ever happens around here, but I won't be here forever. As soon as I graduate I'm moving to New York City. I'll get there even if I have to walk. I'll show my sketches to someone at Harry Angelo if it kills me!

"Who are you, Francie Tillman?" A quick calculation told her there wasn't a chance she'd still be alive. Turning the book over, she opened it from the back. Just to look at the final date. She didn't want any more of a spoiler than that. On the inside back cover was a sepia-toned picture of a young woman with a brimless hat pulled

41

low over her forehead. A sash, darker than the hat, was tied on the right with a massive bow.

"Love your style, girl. You were lucky. Fashion got off track in the fifties and never recovered." Had Francie lived through any of that fashion nightmare era? Dani set the book down and got up to fill the tea kettle. While waiting for it to boil, she remembered a call she'd ignored earlier. She took a deep breath and listened to her voicemail.

"Glad you liked the flowers, honey. Dad and I are so proud of you. Soon you'll be writing for the *Sun Times* or the *New York Times*. This is just the beginning. Love you."

Rubbing her right temple with one hand, she dialed her best friend with the other.

"Hi! This is Anna's phone. Leave a message because, whoever you are, if you have this number, you're important to me." *Beeep.*

The second number got her a real human. "Hey, you okay?" Once again, Evan's concern brought her close to tears. "Any word from China?"

"Nothing."

"Just as well, maybe. So how are you doing with the fame and fortune side of your life, Miss Chase Award? Feet on the ground yet?"

A flash of her three-point landing, butt in the air, hands on the ground, with Dominick Fiorini kneeling at her feet, started a hard-to-squelch giggle. "No more head in the clouds. Just listened to a message from my mom."

"Always good for a reality check."

Resting bare feet on the coffee table, Dani settled back on a giant black couch pillow. "I'll be a nothing until I write for the *New York Times*."

"Keep strivin'."

She sat up and plucked an olive from what was left of her supper salad and stuck it in her cheek like a piece of hard candy. "I called to get. . .What's the opposite of a reality check?"

"A lie."

"Yeah, that's it." She chewed the olive.

"No prob. You're an average writer, a mediocre dresser; you'll never be really successful, but you'll be relatively happy; you drive like a girl, but you're supposed to. People don't mind inviting you to par—"

"Stop!" The olive lodged halfway to her esophagus. She hacked it up. "I said lie to me!"

"I did. You are a seriously brilliant chick, and if I wasn't just swamped with girls my own age wanting to date me, I'd fall head over heels for your brain."

"Just my brain? Don't answer that." She picked up the diary. "I found something. In the trash behind China's apartment."

"Perfect place to get story material. And rats."

"Thank you for that picture. Now shut up and listen to this." She told him about the book.

"Wonder how it got here from up north. What's the date of the last entry?"

"September 14, 1928. I didn't read it, but she stopped in the middle of a sentence. How mysterious is that?"

"Read me something."

"Here's January 2, 1924: 'Mrs. Johnson gave us her Marshall Field's catalogue. All the models look like Suze, at least the way I remember her. If I only drank water for a month and did calisthenics all day long, I could never look like her. It's not fair, but doesn't stop me from working on it. Maybe someday styles will change again and curvy girls will be the bee's knees.'"

"Hmm. She's a workout freak like you. That really could be story material—how 'what a girl wants' hasn't changed all that much in a hundred years."

She sat up straight, nerves tuned to the low hum of adrenaline racing to ignite with an idea spark. "You could be right."

"I am, generally. Hey, the guys are coming for study in a few minutes."

"Okay. See you Saturday? You're going to the funeral with me, right?"

"Unless some big story breaks, I'll be there. Against my better judgment."

"I don't need your better judgment. Just your camera." The teakettle whistled and she lunged to stop the noise. "I don't want to go alone."

"I'm amazed you're going at all. You're the bee's knees, girl."

September 15, 1924

Francie spit out a word forbidden by Miss Ellestad and threw her empty syrup pail at the ground. "One more month. Just one more month." Four more weeks of sitting in front of Earl Hagen and his nasty mouth and she would be gone. She had her Christmas money. Four more Saturday nights of minding the Huseby children and she'd have enough for a train ticket. There'd be no Christmas presents for anyone this year, but Suzette needed her. Hugging her books to her chest, she ran down the hill, away from the laughter.

A whistle split the autumn air. One long, one short. "Vait up." Francie grabbed a low limb and swung around. Mad as she was, she almost laughed. She still wasn't used to Theo Brekken's man voice. When he'd left school in the spring, he'd been a boy like all the rest of them. When he returned, a shadow darkened his upper lip and a voice like his father's carried across the room. A preacher voice.

Plowing gold leaves with his boots, Theo half slid to the bottom of the hill. He skidded to a stop two feet in front of her and held out her lunch pail. The crisp air turned heavy. She'd known Theo since she was five and he was six. He'd asked her to marry him when he was twelve. She'd said yes. Since then, they'd held hands every day on the way to and from school. Never, in all that time, had she felt awkward around him. But never before had his eyes simmered like Rod La Rocque's in *The Ten Commandments*. She took the pail.

"Earl is just *dumme*."

She kicked moss off a rock and shrugged. "Sticks and stones."

Theo laughed. Gentle. It rumbled in her belly. "You do not always need to be strong," he said.

"I just. . .don't care. You're right—he's dumme."

One corner of his darkened lip rose. Because she'd gotten the accent right or because she'd failed? His head tilted to one side. "Vhy—" His brow furrowed as he reshaped his mouth. A summer at home with a mother who spoke little English had deepened his accent. "Why would Earl say something like that?"

She took two steps, head down as if she were searching for

something. Like an answer that wasn't a lie. Or the truth.

"Francie?" His man voice slid over her like summer sun. "It is not true, is it?"

Bread crumbs skittered in the bottom of her pail as it banged against her hip.

She slowed and glanced at Theo. His father's eyes looked back. Grown-up eyes. She watched a squirrel dig a hole at the base of an oak tree, hiding his plunder from the world.

"Is it true?" Theo touched her arm. "Your father is bootlegging?"

In her head, Earl's jeers drowned the concern in Theo's new, strange voice. Eyes smarting, she ran up the hill toward home. Reaching the top, she scanned the valley. A truck sat in front of the barn. Gold letters painted on the shiny black side spelled out HENDERSON MAPLE SYRUP CO. EST. 1919. Theo wouldn't know not all the gallon cans held syrup, but the sight made her skin prickle.

She whipped around, almost banging into him, took him by the hand, and led him to her rock. Sitting down, she patted the flat slab and Theo joined her, his arm almost touching hers as they faced into the sun.

"What are you going to do when you spring this place, Theo?"

He ran his hand through hair streaked with blond. It fell back over his forehead. "You know vhat I am going to do. But I am not in a hurry. I do not see this as a prison. I wish you did not."

Drawing her knees to her chest, she pulled her dress down to her ankles and wrapped her arms around her legs. "After I leave here, I'm never going to shuck another ear of corn or slop another pig or muck another stall or churn butter or—"

Theo laughed. "Who is this very, very rich man you vill marry?"

"I'm going to Chicago, Theo." She spoke softly, looking away from the hurt in his eyes. She couldn't tell him she was leaving next week. Theo had the power to make her change her mind. "And after that, New York. And then I'll study art and fashion in Paris."

His chin rose suddenly. Wide eyes turned on her. "France?"

"Of course, France. I'm part French, you know."

"You are part Chippewa. Why not go live on a reservation for adventure?" He picked up a chunk of sandstone and chucked it down the hill.

"Come with me." Her voice rose just barely above a whisper.

He stood. "God has called me to India, Francine. You have known that for years." He turned his back and spoke over his shoulder. "And I believe, with all my heart, that He has called you to be a missionary's wife."

CHAPTER 5

Evan steered Agatha away from Dani's apartment on Saturday afternoon. "Are you sure about this?"

"No." She turned to the second page in the diary. "Listen to this."

"You're sidetracking."

"I'm not. You'll see. It's actually kind of a setup for what we're doing." She angled the book toward the window. " 'January 11, 1924. Massive snow last night. Drifts to the top of the chicken coop. Storms are bad for business. No suppliers, no customers. Daddy and Applejack have been plowing for hours. I shoveled in front of his office. Mama didn't like that. She thinks if she pretends Daddy's business doesn't exist, it will disappear. If it does, so will the farm.' "

Evan raised an eyebrow. "What's the business?"

"I haven't read enough to know for sure, but I have a guess."

"1924. Bet there was a still in that barn."

"Or her father just sold it. She talks about 'suppliers.' " She turned several pages. " 'January 19. Last night Mr. Nielson came to Daddy's office. He talked about the War. The French and American soldiers sometimes talked all night to the Germans who were in their own trenches ten meters away. They became friends, but as soon as their orders were given, they shot each other! I hate guns. If men have guns they will find reason to use them.' "

"You're right, it sets the tone for today. 'If men have guns, they will find reason to use them.'"

Dani closed the book and took out her phone and legal pad. "Back to work."

She scrolled through the Hansen-Lendman Funeral Home site and scribbled notes. "The founder went to the Oriental School of Embalming."

"Creepy bit of trivia. It would make a great segue into the grieving girlfriend with the oriental name."

Dani wrinkled her nose. "You can be very crass when you want to be." She turned her phone to vibrate. "I don't know if I'll use any of this, but I want details just in case." She stared out at luxurious lawns surrounding massive Victorian homes. "I love this part of town. I want a time machine."

"I can see you living on this street. Twirling your parasol and batting your eyes as you spy on your rich neighbors and record all their sordid little secrets for the *Times* gossip column." He flipped the turn signal as the gabled mansion came into view.

Ivory trim surrounded porches, porticos, garrets, and a round turret. She imagined the view from the top window—the green lawns and branching sidewalks of Library Park, a clear look at the library's cupola-topped red roof. Agatha followed a silver van into the driveway and beneath a carport.

Ten minutes before the service began, and only a dozen cars were in the parking lot. Evan pointed at a shiny black car with bowed fenders and a white roof. "Javelin. Homegrown sweetness."

Dani recognized the distinctive style of an American Motors car. "Nineteen. . .sixty-eight?"

"Close. Seventy. Seventy-one, maybe. And not a speck of rust. Somebody's put some work into that baby."

They parked at an angle next to the van and watched three kids, late teens, get out. Short skirts, tight pants, stringy hair. Dani craned her neck in search of tattoos but didn't find any. She pushed her hair away from her face and took a shaky breath.

Evan pulled the keys out and dangled them over her purse. "Not too late to back out."

"I know."

"We don't belong here.".

Her fingers grazed a white envelope as she put the keys away. "I know that, too."

⚜

The opening bars of "Angel" slid through ceiling-mounted speakers and wound around the half-empty chapel. Nicky folded his arms across his sport jacket. The haunting melody always transfixed him. Sarah McLachlan's smooth voice caressed lyrics that fit like a second skin, as if she'd written them for him as he waited for a second chance, always feeling not good enough.

Beside him, his father shifted in his chair and shielded his mouth with his hand. "Who plays junk like this at a funeral?"

Who goes to a funeral of someone they've never met? "Good PR," would be the answer. His dad hadn't seemed to notice the blocks surrounding Bracciano had changed. Like the human body replacing cells every seven years, the people were new, but the place looked older. And neighbors hadn't been neighborly in over a decade.

In the front row, a forty-ish woman, Hispanic-looking, clung to a tall, broad-shouldered African American man as she sobbed. The man wrapped both arms around her. Next to the woman a young boy stared straight ahead, his face blank.

The song dragged on. *Fly away...*

Though Nicky felt nothing at the moment, he heard the couple's thoughts. As if having once sat that close to a coffin had heightened his grief senses. *Why didn't I see it coming? Why didn't I stop it? If only I had...*

Fourteen people filled the chairs in front of them. Nicky turned as if stretching his neck and counted over his left shoulder. Seven more. He did the same over his right and froze as his gaze locked on the too-innocent face he'd kneeled in front of two days ago. She stared back, eyes filled with pain she couldn't possibly feel. Only one reason a reporter would sit in the back row of a funeral.

She was doing a story.

His jaw clenched. A box in the hall closet at home held clippings written by a woman like her. A woman who'd mastered the art of replicating empathy.

49

"That must have been terrifying for you. It's easy to second guess, isn't it? If you could change one thing, one moment, what would you have done differently?"

Questions pressed against the inside of his skull—the same unanswered pleas causing the couple to sob and cling to each other and the boy to stare vacantly.

Like the boy, he chose not to feel.

⚜

"Miguel's life was shorter than you, his family and friends, hoped it would be, but our lives are not measured by the number of years, or days, or hours. Our lives are measured by the amount of love we give and the quality of joy we experience." The man at the microphone raised the corners of his lips as if looking in the mirror and trying to copy a picture of a smile. Dani looked down at the black-and-white photo of Miguel and his parents, at the en dash between his birth and Tuesday afternoon.

"One thing I know beyond the shadow of a doubt after talking to many of you is that Miguel Reyes loved his parents and..."

The man—no title decorated his name in the program—droned on with generic words about a person he'd never met. He spoke with glittering adjectives of a man who'd displayed his joy for life with a 9 mm pistol. Dani stared at the child who must be Miguel's brother as hopelessness filled the room like invisible, scentless gas.

"Miguel was a listener. Friends could count on him to hear them out and to offer wise advice."

Dani bit back a laugh. Maybe the description was true. Maybe there were times the boy had been a model friend, but none of the speaker's words shed light on the reality China had shared with her three months ago. Nothing hinted at his jealous, paranoid nature, at the way he stalked her when she went out with her friends, texted her incessantly when he was out with his. No one in the room could guess by the eulogy that the boy they memorialized was capable of flashes of rage that left bruises that faded and emotional scars that never would. Dani wrapped her fingers around the rolled program.

Several rows from the front, Dominick sat with a man she guessed was his father. Dani tried to read the tight line of Dominick's

50

mouth, but she had no frame of reference. She'd only seen him angry. Except for one strange out-of-context moment. The distinct angles of his profile would be easy to sketch.

A frustrated sigh rippled onto her shoulder, snapping her out of contemplations that had no place at a funeral. Evan glared at the man at the podium and folded his arms across his chest, apparently sharing her frustration at empty, meaningless words.

"...are tempted to grieve for him, we must remember that our sorrow is for ourselves alone. It is good that we grieve, for it means we have loved, but we need always remind ourselves and each other that he is in a place untouched by pain. A place..."

Really? What makes you so sure? She fought the sadness with an imaginary leap over chairs and a shove to the man at the podium. *Don't listen to him! There's real true hope, people!*

A song interrupted her sermon. The Indigo Girls sang "Closer to Fine." Evan sighed again and shook his head. "What a waste," he whispered.

She nodded. A captive audience searching for direction, and the whole service came off like a talking Hallmark card. Her eyes burned as the song touted the pointlessness of seeking meaning in life. Who did it comfort? Would the family feel less guilt, less grief, if they were convinced life had no purpose?

"Miguel loved his music. His friends have shared some of his songs with me. I was touched by his poetic ability to put words to the challenges and disappointments common to the human condition. He was a contemplative person, who questioned everything...."

But got no answers. Dani silently repeated Evan's observation. *What a waste.*

"...work on relationships and not take each other for granted. Each day is a gift...."

Nicky closed his eyes as the speaker prayed; he wasn't sure to whom. *Life can't be a gift if there's no giver, mister.* The guy hadn't mentioned God once. It didn't take somebody tight with God to notice the glaring lack of anything religious. Halfway through the message, Nicky had started imagining Gianna, the woman who'd taken over his mother's job, reacting to the service. He could see her high-heeled foot swinging in time with her agitation, her mouth puckered, her long nails clicking on the open program. But Gianna wouldn't stop at body language. She'd park herself by the door and give each person a "God word."

Like she'd done four years ago.

"The Lord has a plan for you, Nicky. He'll pull you out of this and move you beyond the sadness. You'll see. You can turn your back on Him, but He won't let go of you."

He hadn't believed her promise at the time, and he wasn't buying it yet.

The speaker stopped praying, or whatever he called it. No "Amen," the words just stopped. Nicky stood with his father and turned.

The back row was empty.

CHAPTER 6

D epressing."

Evan took the keys from her and walked around to the driver's side. Agatha sputtered when he turned the key.

Not now. She didn't want to see the little band of people filing out to cars marked with orange flags. The engine coughed twice then started. Evan backed out of the parking space. "Where to?"

She leaned her head against the door. "Go to the beach where we can talk to kids who didn't know Miguel." As they neared the lake, she rolled the window halfway down and breathed in the cooling air. "I should have listened to you. We shouldn't have gone."

"Maybe. But maybe it was good that we were two more bodies in a mostly empty room."

"All those hurting people looking for answers and hearing nothing. Imagine if somebody had gotten up there and told them about God knowing the pain of losing a son and how He longs to comfort those who mourn. I wanted to grab the mic and start preaching."

What kind of message did the angry Italian need to hear? *God loves you no matter what. He forgives you. He can help you forgive.* She pictured his expression when he'd turned around and recognized her—surprise morphing into hostility. *What's your story, Dominick?* The reporter in her wondered about the source of the rage.

Maybe it wasn't just the reporter in her that wanted to know his story.

Evan stopped at a stop sign. "Do you really feel up to talking to strange kids right now?"

"Let's look for some of the kids we talked to in April. That way they'll be strange, but not strang*ers*." She rubbed the rigid muscle on the top of her shoulder. "I need a diversion and a story for next week."

"So are you looking for good, bad, or ugly kids for this story?"

"Bad. Who wants to read a story about perfect kids?"

"Their parents. The ones who buy papers."

"Oh. Them. I'll get to their kids eventually. When I'm in a better mood." She closed her eyes and fell silent until Evan pulled into the Eichelman Beach parking lot.

"What questions are you going to ask?" He reached in the back seat for his camera case.

"I don't know yet. Mostly I just want to get reacquainted, build relationships."

He shook his head. "There's that fine line again."

"What 'fine line'?"

"The one Mitch told you not to cross. Reporters ask questions. Social workers build relationships."

"Right. And I'm just going to walk up and say, 'Remember me? The reporter? I know you don't know or trust me, but I'd like you to spill your guts right here in my notebook, please.'"

"Ick. That's disgusting." He opened his door. "Fine. Let's go forge some lifelong friendships with people half our age. 'Hello, juveniles, we are here to build deep and meaningful relationships and save you from a future of substance abuse and crime and incarceration and—'"

"They're half *my* age. You're practically one of them. Now hush up and take pictures."

⚜

Three boys lounged in the shade of the concession stand. Dani recognized two of them. "Mouthwash," she said out loud.

"In your glove compartment."

"No. His name." She punched Evan's arm. "That tall kid—remember him? His parents are into that war game."

54

"World of Warcraft."

"Right. What do they call him? It's some brand of mouthwash."

"Listerine?"

"Duh. You're worthless."

"Well, maybe it'll come to you when we get out there and *scope* out the situation."

Dani turned slowly and narrowed her eyes at Evan. "Grandma Agatha had a saying—'Why be difficult when with a little more effort you can be impossible?'"

"And that pertains to me how?"

After a slow eye roll she got out and led the way to a picnic table. "Okay, Scope and. . .we met his friend with the backward cap, didn't we?"

"I'm paid to remember faces, not names. But I do remember him. He had a story that reminded me too much of me. Broken home, controlling mother, father who never says a word unless he's screaming. He's an insecure kid trying to look cool."

"Aren't they all?"

Two girls crossed the sand toward the boys. "And here come the girls who remind me too much of me. Working too hard to look good for the cool, insecure guys."

"You and them and the girl in the diary. Nothing new under the sun, is there?"

Dani stuck her hand in her purse and fingered her favorite pen. "What would you say to them if they'd listen?"

"Give it up. Stop trying to please everyone. Stop blaming yourself because your parents are too messed up to know how to love you. Pursue God because really knowing Him is the only thing that will make that emptiness go away." Evan stopped for a breath. "But they won't listen."

"Doesn't mean we can't convey truth on some level. 'Preach the Gospel at all times. If necessary, use words.'"

Evan nodded as he snapped a series of pictures from a distance that wouldn't allow the kids to be easily identified. The girls copped poses, the boys laughed. After a few minutes the girls swayed off, taking full advantage of the audience watching their backsides.

Dani picked up her bag. "Let's go."

Scope waved as they approached. "It's the reporter. Cool story. You doing another one?"

"Yes." She stuck her hand out. "Nice to see you again, Scope." She turned to the backwards cap guy. "Sorry, I don't remember your name."

"Broom." Bony shoulders shrugged.

Scope nodded at the third boy who hugged a skateboard like a little kid clinging to a teddy bear. "This is Zipper."

Dani raised both eyebrows. "Dare I ask?"

The boy aimed a slit-eyed look at Scope. "Just Zip."

"When he was like eight, he got his tongue stuck in his jacket zipper." Scope reached behind Broom and slapped Zip on the back. The boy only glared. "Zipper makes him sound like a stud."

Dani laughed. "I'd like some input from you guys for another story. Mind if I ask some questions?"

Broom looked down at the pavement between his shoes. Zip stared, unblinking. Scope was the only one who showed any sign of hearing the question. He looked at Evan. "Do I get my picture in the paper again?"

"I just do what the lady says."

Dani sat down cross-legged on the blacktop and pulled her yellow pad out of her bag. "What do you guys do all day?" She directed the question at the only kid with a voice.

"Sleep, eat, hang out here."

"Any of you have a job?"

"We do today." Scope nodded toward a pickup pulling into the parking lot.

Dani recognized the driver. "That's your dad, isn't it?"

Scope nodded. "You really messed with his head with that thing you wrote. In a good way. He's outta the game."

"Really?"

"Yeah. And today he's paying us to paint our porch." Both thumbs shot up. "It's like a reverse Tom Sawyer thing." He stood. "He's paying us 'cause we made him think we hate it."

"But you don't?"

"Nah."

Broom smiled. "We paint even when—"

"Hey, we gotta go." Scope waved. "We're here all the time if you got more questions. Or wanna take pics of my sweet face."

"We'll find you." Dani laughed and watched them slog away as if they dreaded the work ahead.

Evan scratched his head. "So they like to paint. Next time I'll bring my collection of wall art photos. Maybe they can autograph a few shots."

"How's your exposé going? Any answers to the proposals you—"

Her phone buzzed. By the time she found it in the bottom of her bag it had stopped. The voice mail chime gonged. She punched the number.

"Danielle, it's Mitchell. I want to see you in my office at eight sharp Monday morning."

❦

Hands compressed into fists, Dani paced the width of Mitch's office. "Was it a man? Angry voice, slight Italian accent?"

"I didn't take the call." Mitch looked over the top of his glasses. "You think you know who complained?"

"Yes." She unclenched her fists but couldn't keep them relaxed. *Dominick Fiorini.* How could she have entertained one second of a Cinderella fantasy about a man whose life goal seemed to be to make the world a more miserable place? "What did he say, anyway? I'd like to report a funeral crasher? It wasn't invitation-only. I had as much right to be there as anyone else. I knew the guy's girlfriend, and I thought she'd be there. I thought I could talk to her and. . ."

"Save her." Evan's words taunted. *"That's not your job."*

"And interview her for a story at her boyfriend's funeral?"

"No! I mean, I might have used something she said, but just in general. I just want to talk to her and make sure she's doing okay and—"

"*I* know that. But somebody who was there legitimately grieving over the loss of a friend or family member knew you worked for the *Times* and knew you didn't have any real connection with the kid." Mitch took off his glasses and ran a hand over his face. "It makes us look like vultures preying on misfortune."

Duh. "That's kind of the definition of news, isn't it? If no one is suffering, we have nothing to report."

Sucking his lips in, Mitch shook his head. For a split second

Dani was sure she saw amusement in his eyes. "If a teacher kicks the bucket and all two thousand of her past students attend the funeral, you can blend into the crowd. When a crack addict blows his brains out and twelve people show up for his funeral, your being there becomes an ethics problem. Add the minor detail that his girlfriend blames you for the guy's death, and we've got ourselves an issue."

"What did whoever talked to the guy—the caller—tell him?"

"That we'd slap the backs of your hands with a ruler and make you promise never to do it again." The amusement she'd glimpsed earlier spread across his face. "There. I said I'd have a talk with you, and I did."

"So you don't think I was wrong to be there?"

"I think you were gutsy. I like that about you, Danielle. You'll do what it takes to get a story. Just keep it legal, Miss Gallagher, and you'll never hear me complain." He picked up a pink phone message slip, crumpled it, and pitched it at the wastebasket. "Go get 'em, tiger."

Dani stood. "How can I find out the name of the caller?'

"It was an anonymous call."

She nodded and walked toward the door.

"Danielle?"

"Yes?"

"Let it go. You might be wrong about who called, and if you're right you'll only make things worse."

"Right." Sure. You bet. *Not.*

By midmorning, fatigue hit like the flu. She took the rest of the day off. Mitch didn't bat an eye when she said she needed a personal day.

Inside her apartment, she dropped her purse, kicked her shoes toward the kitchen, and slogged to the bathroom. In the shower, she shut out everything but the *thrum* of water on tile. Steam rose, shrouding the room.

She dressed in worn-thin cotton shorts and an oversized shirt imprinted with *Snow White*'s Sleepy. Walking into her kitchen, she said an automatic prayer. The rent she paid for her above-garage apartment was nothing short of a miracle. Less than a week's wages for tile floors, marble counter tops, and a breathtaking view. Her landlord was a deacon in her church. As her mother had taught her young, it's who you know that matters.

She took a chicken potpie out of the freezer. While it baked, she tore lettuce into a salad, added vinegar and oil and a sprinkling of oregano. Settling into a faux suede chair, she stared through rain spatters at the green lawn of the Kemper Center and the lake beyond it. In the 1860s, the original building was home to Wisconsin's first US Senator. Later it became an Episcopal school for girls. The chapel, with beams the color of dark honey and an intricately carved altar, was a popular wedding venue. *Someday, maybe.*

She took a bite of salad. The smell of oregano brought a face to mind. Dark eyes narrowing at her while the mournful notes of "Angel" bled into the room. Her fingers tightened reflexively around her fork. She'd stomped out of Mitch's office this morning and straight to her computer to look up the phone number for Bracciano. Every word she'd use to put Dominick Fiorini in his place strained at the tip of her tongue as the website popped up.

Italian restaurants close on Mondays.

With no place to go, her irritation had brewed in her head, building pressure until it sent her home early.

She flicked through song titles on her iPod. Nora Jones matched her mood. Soothing, mellow. Guitar chords led into "Come Away with Me." Her head and shoulders swayed with the notes. Dark eyes came back into focus. Strong hands cradling her foot as if they held a fragile kitten.

Stop!

The timer buzzed. She ate at her little round table to the sound of rain and piano music. After cleaning up the kitchen, she slid into bed. She set her alarm for five. That would wake her, if she fell asleep, with enough time to dress for dinner at Vito's. She propped brown and blue pillows behind her. As she folded the geometric pattern of her bed spread over her belly, the diary slid to the floor. She winced and crawled to the edge of the bed. The book lay open. Her gaze landed on an entry at the bottom of the page.

June 24, 1928
Busy but fun night at Bracciano again.

⟡

September 30, 1924

"We have no choice." Daddy folded his hands on the kitchen table and looked at Francie with sad, tired eyes. Mama sat in her rocker, head bent over her Bible. Her lips moved but made no sound.

Daddy stared into the coffee Mama had poured half an hour ago. He hadn't yet touched it. "I know you've been saving the money from the Husebys for Christmas, but this is an emergency. We owe Doc Volden too much. He won't come out again unless we can pay, and Applejack won't make it without help. I've tried everything I know to do for obstruction and it's not working."

Francie nodded. Tears stung, spilled onto her cheeks, and left darkened spots on her overalls. She had found Suzette's address and sent a letter saying she would be there by the middle of October. She couldn't tell her parents. So here she sat, looking like a selfish, spoiled child, crying about money while her favorite horse writhed in pain in the barn. "I'll go get it."

"Thank you." Daddy stood, put on his old plaid coat, and took his hat off the hook. "I'll ring the doc from the feed mill."

The door opened to the cool, late-afternoon air. When it shut, the room seemed to close in around her. Stew simmered on the mint-green and cream-colored stove. Francie remembered the day Daddy brought it home. "Things will be better from now on," he'd said back then. He bought the icebox the same year. Mama had oiled and shined its golden wood every day for months. Now black fingerprints surrounded the handle. The War had been good for farmers. But it didn't last.

She stared at the Currier and Ives print above Mama's chair. *Home to Thanksgiving.* In the picture, snow covered the ground and the barn roof. The front door of a cozy house stood wide open as a woman in a long dress greeted guests. Oxen pulling a wood-sided sled; a dark horse was harnessed to a sleigh. A peaceful scene of life on the farm. Francie turned away and walked up the stairs.

CHAPTER 7

Monday. Finally. The day most people dreaded was the day he lived for.

Nicky stared at his reflection in the flawless black finish on the car hood, threw the polishing rag onto Todd's workbench, and slid into the car.

Squinting through the garage door at the glare of midafternoon sun ricocheting off concrete, he groped for the sunglasses he'd left on the bucket seat a week ago. He slid them on then turned the key in the ignition. The Javelin purred as he drove out of the garage.

He parked facing the street, got out, and rolled down the door on the single-car garage. Sweat trickled down the back of his neck. He wiped his forehead with his arm. Only a real mental case would run half a mile to pick up his car so he could drive a mile and a half to the park in air-conditioned comfort to go Rollerblading in the middle of July.

If the shoe fits.

He climbed back in. Todd and his brother had done the bodywork, and he was slowly paying them off. Two more payments to Todd and the Javelin would be his, free and clear. Since Nicky didn't own a garage, Todd kept it in his—in exchange for using it whenever Nicky was working.

He turned up the radio on the way to Simmons Island Park.

He parked the Javelin then got out and sat on the ground to lace his skates. After using the bottom of his torn Kenosha Kings T-shirt to mop his face, he stood and pushed off. In minutes the muscles in his calves burned with the welcome strain. He wove around a middle-aged woman walking a cocker spaniel. Beyond the breakers, the lake shimmered, white sparks glinting on the waves.

Miles of pavement and a free afternoon stretched ahead of him. He breathed in the lake air and exhaled all thoughts of a struggling business and a rebellious sister.

♔

Rena Fiorini slid her notebook into her dresser drawer. Working on a new song usually lifted her spirits. It didn't work today. She wasn't looking forward to meeting Jarod.

Someday, maybe, she'd have choices.

Hoisting her bike onto her shoulder, she thudded down the stairs toward the propped-open back door. Someday she'd own a house with an attached garage in a safe neighborhood.

Right. And someday pigs would sprout wings. Her skate bag swung into the wall as she descended. The narrow stairway mirrored the rest of her life.

A door opened behind her. "Where you off to?"

Rena froze. She hadn't heard him come home. Her father's voice, heavy with sleep yet tinged with suspicion, switched on her defenses. She turned and gave him her best little-girl smile. "Morning, Daddy. Sleep good?" *Or was it strange to be in your own bed?*

His face softened as she spoke. He nodded. "How's my little Wren?"

"Great. Looking forward to a day off. I'm going to the park."

"Alone?"

Going alone. Not being alone. "Yep."

"Where's Dominick?"

"I don't know." *And don't care.*

"Family night tonight?"

Where had that come from? Dredged from the deep, dark recesses of their pathetic family history. They hadn't spent a Monday night together in over a year—since the last time he'd had a revelation from God and turned a leaf that lasted almost four weeks. "Wow, that would be fun, but Nicky and I have plans. Maybe next week."

As usual, his expression melted her. He pouted like a spoiled little boy deprived of a cookie, and once again she became the parent. "How 'bout I make breakfast just for the two of us tomorrow? Prosciutto and mozzarella frittatas, okay?" She ladled on the accent so heavy she could have been his—God rest her soul—sainted grandmother. As her father slowly retracted his pout, she wondered if the great-grandmother she'd been named for had been anything like the Fiorini legend she'd become.

She walked the bike into the street. Her foot hadn't left the ground when she heard her name from across the street.

"Hey, Gianna."

"Where are you off to on this gorgeously hot day, Renata-bata?"

Rena smiled. It was the same question her father had asked, but this silly nickname and the smile changed everything. "The park."

"Lovely." Gianna shifted her bucket of cleaning supplies to her other hand as she walked across the street. Perfectly straight teeth glimmered from her perpetual smile. Rena's aunt described Gianna as a "Sophia Loren caricature." The comment was mean, but it did kind of fit. Her nose was too large and her mouth too wide to be pretty, yet she carried her large-boned height with a transfixing grace, and her smile dazzled.

Gianna leaned in for a kiss on the cheek. "Enjoy." She wiped moisture from her upper lip. "Nicky home?"

"Nah. But Dad is."

"Ohhh." Gianna drew out the word. The smile stayed but stiffened. "Where is he?"

"In his room."

"Mmm." Gianna glanced at the restaurant and back at her car. "I have some shopping to do." Her eyes lit. "Wouldn't you rather go to Kohl's with me than exercise?"

"I'd love to, but. . ."

"But you're meeting someone."

"Well. . ."

One artfully shaped brow arched. A manicured hand rested on the waistline of Gianna's peach capri pants. "A male someone."

Rena cringed, looking up at the window over the stairway, as if her father stood there reading lips.

"Is he a good boy?"

There were a million ways a person could interpret a question like that. "He's wonderful." *Well, he used to be.*

"Would I approve?"

She *would* have to throw that one in. "He's not Italian, if that's what you mean."

"That is not what I mean, and you know it." Hash marks formed between the sculpted brows.

"His parents go to church."

Gianna shook her head. "God doesn't have grandchildren."

Rena looked at her feet. "I know."

"Be careful." Gianna patted her arm then dropped a kiss on her forehead. "Guard your heart. . .and the other parts you shouldn't share."

Cheeks warming, Rena nodded. "Love you." She lifted her foot and rode off the curb.

"Love you to the moon."

"And back." She shot the automatic response over her shoulder and got on her bike. She'd been saying it as long as she could remember. Rena had no memories of her first three years before Gianna swept into their lives. On Gianna's one and only dinner date at the restaurant with Carlo Fiorini, she'd figured him out. She'd jilted him but fallen for his motherless children, convincing him to hire her as a nanny and housekeeper.

Rena had given the woman reason to quit more than once, and today could well be one of those days. *If* she got caught.

But she wouldn't.

She rode past old two-story houses with porches and imagined, as she always did, what it would be like to grow up in a real house instead of above a restaurant. A couple walked along the sidewalk holding hands, and she let herself wonder about that, too. What would it be like to have someone who spoke words of love rather than want? But it worked both ways. She used Jarod, too. She gave him what he wanted, and he kept her safe. Right now, until she found a way to break free, that's all she needed.

She squeezed all her doubts into a manageable lump as she rode into the parking lot. Like an ice cube, painful until it finally melts. And it would.

Her pulse skipped at the sight of him. She chained her bike to the rack. It never hurt to keep a guy waiting a little while. She walked across the parking lot, conscious of every move she made in her tight shorts and how her tank top edged toward her shoulder, showing off her tattoo.

He leaned against his car, long legs stretched out and crossed at the ankles. His muscles bulged when he folded his arms across his chest. He lowered his sunglasses. Just like a movie star. She might not love him, but she loved the look of him.

But she didn't like the look of his eyes today. Seeing him like this in the middle of the day was way different than at a party at night when everybody else was smoking. It made her feel somehow not good enough. Why did he want to get high before meeting her?

With a deep breath and a forced smile, she snuggled into the arms he opened for her. "Better get our skates on."

Jarod laughed. "I thought the skating thing was just what you made up to tell your brother."

Rena couldn't tell if his laugh was aimed at her or the situation. "You didn't bring skates?"

His laugh erupted into a sound she knew was directed at her. "I don't *own* skates." His fingertip traced the tender area around her tattoo. "We got better ways to—"

The sound of tires crunching gravel swallowed his words. Jarod swore and shoved her away. Rena turned to see a foreign-looking car with chrome wheels pull into the parking lot. Sliding his fingers into his front pockets, Jarod motioned with his chin, a gesture telling her to walk away. Private business. She was used to that. But she wasn't used to a car like that, or a man in a jacket and tie. He rolled the passenger window down. Jarod walked over, all cocky like some kind of thug on a cop show. He leaned into the open window.

They talked in hushed and hurried voices, and the man drove away.

Rena knew better than to ask.

Jarod pulled his hands out of his pockets. "Now, where were we?"

As his hand touched her skin, she closed her eyes and pretended she was somewhere else.

♲

Nicky ripped off his shirt and tucked it in the back of his shorts. He slowed his pace. A subtle breeze blew off the lake, cooling his skin as the sweat evaporated. He felt good. The workout was purifying, purging his body of toxins and his mind of a build-up of negative thoughts.

It freed him to dream.

The old dream had to go, but Bracciano had to change with the times. If they didn't, they could go under. He wouldn't let that happen. Their specialties had been handmade only by a Fiorini for over eight decades.

It was time to move.

For months, the thought had been pestering like a persistent mosquito. He'd tried killing it, but it kept returning. Twice he'd opened his mouth to broach the subject with his father, but each time he imagined the vein in his father's forehead pulsating, the dark eyes smoldering. His father hated change.

Except when it came to women.

A dark blue Jaguar pulled out of the parking lot as he skated toward the Javelin. Gleaming alloy wheels caught the sunlight and spun it.

Welcome to the new Bracciano, sir. Nicky imagined the voice of the young valet he would personally train. *Enjoy your evening, sir.*

I intend to. I've heard marvelous things about your chef.

Chef Dominick is the best, sir.

He smiled to himself as he rolled to a stop. Feeling like a new man, he lifted his face to the sun. As he turned toward the car, his thoughts froze. Two kids leaned against a beat-up car, lip-locked in an almost obscene embrace. A cloth bag hung over the girl's shoulder. A bag exactly like—

His breath caught. Fingers spasmed into fists. "Renata!"

CHAPTER 8

I ced tea's done." Dani set the pitcher on the counter and looked over at Vito's wife.

"Thank you. Why did God not give me a daughter?" Lavinia glanced toward the front door. "Check on the garlic bread, okay?"

Lavinia was up to something. *Please, Lord, not another blind date.* Ever since the first time Agatha broke down at work and Vito invited Dani to dinner, Lavinia had been trying to find a "nice Christian man" for her. They'd introduced her to two of Vito's nephews, their mailman, and the guy who installed their water softener.

The garlic bread was still on the pale side. "Just a couple more minutes." Dani closed the oven door. "I'll set the table. Just the three of us?" *Please.*

"Why don't you toss the salad?"

The salad looked sufficiently tossed, but she picked up the tongs and repositioned the cherry tomatoes.

The clang of the front door opening made her jump.

"The police force has arrived," Vito shouted from his recliner in the living room.

Lavinia picked a tomato from the salad bowl. Her eyes glittered. "Come on in the kitchen, Todd."

"*Lavinia!*" Dani stomach seized. *This can't be happening.*

Running fingers through gray-streaked curls, Lavinia shrugged.

67

"Why didn't I think of him before? A cop and a reporter—a match made in heaven. Don't tell me he didn't turn your head."

"He didn't turn my head. *Yenta*."

"Ha. I don't believe you. He's cute; he's single. You're pretty; you're single. Chemistry, I tell you."

Dani pointed a fork at the little round woman who stood eye to eye, challenging her to admit her attraction to the policeman. The stare down lasted only seconds. Dani laughed. "What a conniver. I seriously didn't think about the guy once after I met him."

"We'll see. I listen to God when He gives me a nudge, and He tells me something's going to happen here tonight. Something for your future."

Something like getting arrested for accessory to murder?

Lavinia pinched her cheek. "Be a good girl and put the salad on the table."

There was nothing to do but smile and act polite and pretend her abs weren't going into convulsions as Todd Metzger walked in, wearing jeans and a polo shirt. Okay, so maybe her head turned just now. Just a little.

"How's my Italian mama?"

"*Stupendo*." She pinched his cheek. "How's my pale Norwegian boy?"

"German."

"Whatever. You're all pasty-faced."

Todd laughed and turned to Dani. "Nice to see you again, Danielle."

"Dani."

"Whatever." He mimicked Lavinia's tone. "Nice to see you again, Dani."

Lavinia pulled a pan of mostaccioli from the oven. She looked at Todd and nodded toward the basement door. "Call the troops."

"Troops?" Dani stared at the door handle turning beneath Todd's hand. The knot in her gut wrenched tighter.

"Soup's on!"

Footsteps. The door opened wide. Renata, the waitress—Dominick's sister—stepped into the room. Behind her strode the King of the Universe himself.

Lavinia! The scream stayed in her head as she greeted Renata.

The girl shrugged. "Call me Rena." Lavinia pulled a pan from the oven. "Nicky, you remember Dani."

Dani nodded at the man who'd tattled on her for crashing a funeral. *Stupido.* She knew other words, thanks to Vito, but she wasn't that kind of girl.

Dark eyes narrowed as he returned her nod.

Headed toward the table with the steaming pan, Lavinia walked between them.

Nicky plucked a piece of pasta, dropped it into his mouth, and closed his eyes. "*Dolce signora*, I am in love." The sharp angles of his jaw softened. "When will I learn to cook like you? When will you come to work for me? I steal your recipes and still nothing I make is like this. *Delizioso.*"

Lavinia set the pan on the table. The reluctant smile teasing the corners of her mouth as she raised her hands and shook her head spoke of a history of forgiving against her will.

There were stories in this house.

Vito's recliner squeaked. "Let's eat," he said as he walked into the room. He took his chair at the head of the table. Lavinia sat at the opposite end. Dani ended up next to Todd and across the table from Rena and Nicky. Vito folded his gorilla hands and lowered his head. "Bless us, O Lord, and these gifts which we are about to receive from Thy bounty, through Christ our Lord. Amen."

Todd picked up a basket of garlic bread and passed it to Dani. "So you're a reporter."

Wherever this was going, she already didn't like it. "Yes."

"That explains what you were doing the night we met."

"*The night we met.*" It sounded like a line from a chick flick.

He rubbed the sandy beard stubble on his chin. "I just have to wonder—"

"Todd." Vito pointed at a cut glass dish. "Have a pickle."

Todd smiled and picked up the dish. Lavinia pointed a fork at him. "Tell Dani about the concert at your church."

One shoulder shrugged. "We're doing sort of a coffeehouse thing." He cleared his throat. "I'll write down the website before we leave."

"He's so modest. Todd's a drummer. An excellent drummer. You like rock music, don't you, Dani?" Lavinia nodded and her chin jutted slightly forward and to the side.

"Sure, but I lean toward the quieter stuff." Dani aimed her answer at Todd. "Chris Tomlin and Matt Redman's worship songs, and Colbie Caillat, Jamie Cullum, Nora—"

"Jones?" Rena leaned forward. "That's Nicky's kind of music. Bet you like Katie Melua's stuff."

"I"—she swallowed hard—"Yes. I love 'The Flood.'"

"Nicky just bought—"

"Rena." Lavinia picked up a glass dish. "Have a pickle."

She took the dish and passed it. "Have a pickle, Danielle."

What's going on? It seemed like everybody was working off a different script. Lavinia was trying to set her up with Todd, and Rena acted like she was trying. . . No. Just her imagination. *Change the subject.* "What do you do for fun, Rena?"

The girl darted a glance at her brother. "I hang out with friends."

Nicky's seemingly permanent scowl deepened. *Stories.*

"Mostly I just work."

"Well, you're good at that. Some waitresses I've met never smile." She gave a half wink that could pass for a nervous tic. "I think it must be the working conditions."

"Yeah, I love my job." Rena gave a carbon copy of the half wink.

"The food was delicious. And the atmosphere so"—she raised one eyebrow—"friendly."

Rena coughed on a bite of mostaccioli. "That's us. The happy Fiorinis. Our happy family has been giving that place a happy atmosphere since 1923."

A chill shimmied up Dani's back. Should she tell Rena about the diary? It wasn't the kind of secret she wanted to keep to herself.

She'd read a dozen or more entries before falling asleep. Not enough to figure out how the girl who started in Osseo ended up in Kenosha. She could have skipped to the final year of the diary, but she hated reading endings first. "I love old buildings and the stories behind them. Do you know much about your family history?"

"I don't, but Nicky does. He listens to my grandfather's old stories."

70

Lavinia poised a spoon over the pan. "If you like historic buildings, you should see the house on Third Street Todd grew up in. Not far from you, Dani." She turned to Todd. "Dani lives in the cutest little apartment across from the Kemper Center. You two are practically neighbors."

Could you be any more obvious, Lavinia? Dani arched her brows at Todd. "But I wasn't *born* into the Mansion District. So you come from *ooold* money."

"No, I come from ingenious parents who bought a run-down mansion and turned it into three apartments. My peeps are land*lords*, not land *barons*, and they bought it when I was in high school. I actually grew up in an upstairs apartment two blocks from here. He pointed a butter knife at Nicky. "At least I'm not descended from the mafia."

Nicky closed his eyes for a millisecond and shook his head. "Have a pickle, Metzger."

Dani pushed aside her plate. A streak of whipped cream was all that remained of the chocolate chip cannoli. "Delicious." It was at least the third time she'd said it.

Nicky stood. "Anyone want more coffee?"

So he does have a thoughtful cell in his body. Dani watched the bulging-over-biceps gray shirt disappear behind the cupboards hanging over the counter that separated the kitchen and dining room. This was her chance to corner him. And blast him.

Before she worked up the courage to follow him, he was back with the coffee pot. He refilled every cup, including hers. When he got to Lavinia, he bent and planted a kiss on her cheek.

"What's that for?"

"For dinner. And for putting up with me."

Lavinia blushed.

Maybe she wouldn't blast him. Maybe she'd just ask. Dani picked up her plate and stood. "Guess I'm on KP duty." She followed Nicky into the kitchen.

"You called the paper." She waited for him to turn around.

He slipped the pot back into the coffee maker. Seconds passed

BECKY MELBY

before he looked up at her. For a long time. Without a word. Then finally he nodded. "I'll help you with dishes."

What?

"You will not." Lavinia materialized from out of nowhere. "This is your day off. Get out of here. Go enjoy that car for the rest of the night."

Todd walked in carrying a stack of plates. "She's right, Nick. I'll help with dishes."

Not a chance. Dani had no intention of being left alone with the cop and his questions. "I think the girls should do dishes and let the men shoot pool or something. Rena, come help me."

Lavinia shook her head. "I have something to show Rena in my sewing room."

Nicky grabbed a pad of paper from the refrigerator and scribbled something on it. Todd peered over his shoulder. "What're you doing?"

Something vaguely resembling a smile lit his dark eyes. "I'm giving the woman my phone number." Without making eye contact, he thrust it into her hand and walked out.

Todd picked up a dish cloth. "What was that all about?"

She slid the paper deep into her back pocket. Her hand shook as she reached for the towel. "I have no idea."

⬥

Todd washed and she dried. Through glasses and silverware, they chatted about their jobs. While seemingly engrossed in scraping the burnt edges from the mostaccioli pan, Todd tipped his head and stared at her over his shoulder. "You're covering the story, aren't you?"

"Story?" The wide-eyed stare might buy her the moment she needed to figure out her own story.

"Don't pull the dumb blond routine on me. Do you know how many times I see that look every day? 'The speed limit's twenty-five? Really?' He batted his eyes. " 'Why, officer, I thought the sign said *fifty*-five.' "

Dani laughed. "Makes you all weak in the knees, I bet."

Rena padded into the kitchen in bare feet. "Makes him all weak in the head more like."

72

"Watch it, girl."

Rena yawned. Wiping her hands on the dishtowel, Dani smiled at the girl with the black 7 healing above her collarbone. "I'll take you home. It's not safe to be out at night in this neighborhood."

⟡

"...and he went all ballistic on me right in front of Jarod. He can't accept that I'm not a little kid anymore, and I'm not a moron...."

Dani rolled down a window. In defiance, maybe. They were parked in the same spot where she'd fallen asleep in Vito's car. Finally the venting trickled to a stop. She looked up at dark kitchen windows that had blazed last week at two a.m. "Nicky works strange hours. Why doesn't he bake during the day?"

"*Tradizione.* It goes back to wood-burning ovens or something. You bake at night when it's cool, and that way if something burns or flops you have time to do it over. Nicky's weird. He says he wants to change things, but he's stuck on old school stuff."

"Old school like wanting to know where you are and who you're with?"

"I'm three months away from eighteen. My great-grandmother had two kids by my age. He needs to chill."

"What do you do when you're not working? Are you with Jarod all the time?"

A tiny crease formed above Rena's nose. "Most of the time, but we hang out with...other people, too." She shifted in her seat. "Do you have a boyfriend?"

"No. Not since college."

"How come?"

She loved the directness of teens, but it could be disconcerting when they tried to turn the tables. "I guess the honest answer is I'm way too picky. I've been disappointed too many times by guys who aren't who they pretend to be."

Rena folded her arms and leaned her head against the car door. "Yeah..."

"Sounds like you know what I mean."

"I grew up with people who let you know what they were thinking. Nicky gets upset with me, he blasts me. Jarod's all closed

73

up." She made a fist and held it out. "Like that."

"What attracted you to him in the first place?"

"I felt safe with him." She blinked, as if sweeping away a mirage. "Todd asked if you were covering the story. Did he mean about Miguel?"

"You knew him?"

"Yes." She ran a finger under the lashes of her right eye.

"And you know China?"

Rena's head tilted to one side. "How do *you* know her?"

"I did a story awhile back about families affected by online gaming. I interviewed her. Do you know how I can get ahold of her?"

"You're the one who told her to get rid of Miguel, aren't you?"

A sharp breath rasped in Dani's throat.

"She told me she talked to a reporter. You told her she was too good for him, didn't you?"

Dani rubbed her hands against her knees. "Did she tell you what she thought about that?"

"She figured you were right, but she couldn't walk away from him until she had somebody to protect—" Rena bit her bottom lip. Her foot tapped against the door.

"Was she afraid of what Miguel would do?"

Rena fingered the door handle.

"Rena." Dani quieted her voice. "Was Miguel involved in a gang?" *Are you?*

The foot tapped faster, giving the impression she might bolt at any minute. Tears spilled onto pale makeup. "Yes."

"Was that why China was afraid to break up with him?"

Choppy hair batted her face. "She was going to run, go out of state, but he caught her and. . ." In the glow of a streetlight, pooled tears glimmered. "The guys in. . . A lot of guys are like Jarod. China and I talked about that a lot. It's hard when people keep secrets from you, when you don't feel you really know them or that they don't really want to know you for who you are."

"Is Jarod part of the gang?"

Rena picked at dark nail polish. "Are you doing a story on what happened to Miguel?"

"Yes. And no. I don't know if I'll use his name, but can't you see where his story could touch a lot of people? Maybe stop somebody else from taking the same path?" Rena didn't comment. "I want to do a story on kids in your neighborhood, about"—the focus of her story suddenly crystallized—"gangs and why there's so much crime here, and what can be done about it. I want to talk to kids and see what's going on in their lives. Miguel's death is just kind of a starting point."

Silence. Rena chewed one fingernail then another. "You said you wanted to talk to China. What did you want to tell her?"

"That Miguel's death isn't her fault. Or mine. I'm worried about her. Do you think she's capable of hurting herself?"

"Maybe. Her family's getting her out of here. I don't know where she's going, but they're leaving Friday. We're doing our own memorial thing at the beach Friday night, and they won't let her stay for it. That's seems wrong, but I get why they're doing it." She turned to the window and folded her hands. "If you did a story on kids in gangs, not hard-core bangers, but people on the fringe who were in danger of getting deeper, the ones who aren't beyond hope. . .what could happen? To you. Or us."

Dani didn't react to the last word, the girl's admission. "I don't know. There would be a risk, I suppose, that someone would retaliate. I wouldn't use names of minors, maybe not even the name of the gang."

"But you wouldn't want to keep it all generic, right? 'Cause the goal would be to show adults, parents, and teachers and people like that, what's really going on so they could do something—make a safe place for kids to hang out or"—knuckles pressed into her lips; tears brimmed—"a way to get out."

Do you want out? For once, she held the question in. "It could work that way. I always hope my stories will stir someone to act."

"Then I'll help."

"So I can start with you? Are you willing to answer some personal questions?"

A faint smile brightened the tear-streaked face. "How 'bout I just take you somewhere where you can start getting answers yourself?" She reached out and touched the ends of Dani's hair.

"Have to do something about this first." She fingered the sleeve of Dani's retro gauze shirt. "And this."

♔

September 30, 1924

Francie's legs felt weighted as she climbed to her room. One end of Daddy's old leather satchel pushed out the curtain nailed to the crate beside her bed. She'd already filled it with stockings and undergarments. She closed her diary on the lines she'd written an hour ago. Tonight she'd write about giving up her money to save Applejack. And not going to Chicago.

As she picked up the coin-filled jar, the putter of a car motor wafted through the open window. The syrup truck braked to a stop in front of the barn.

Daddy was gone, and Mama wouldn't know what to do. If they didn't get this delivery, there'd be nothing to sell. She climbed down the steps, skipping the last two altogether. "I'll go sit with Applejack." She set the jar on the table, took her coat, and ran to the barn.

Two men stood in Daddy's office. Francie smoothed her hair back. "My father was called away on an emergency. I can help you."

She'd seen the older, stouter man often from the hayloft. He doffed his hat, showing a mostly bald head, and shot a questioning look, part amusement with maybe a hint of fear, at the other man. Francie followed his gaze and for a moment forgot to breathe. Eyes greener and more intense than any she had ever seen gazed back at her. Slicked, jet-black hair parted in the middle, high cheekbones, and a smile that showed an amazing dimple on his left cheek. He wore a tweed hat and a dark gray coat belted at the waist. Francie's knees weakened.

His right eye twitched. Almost a wink but not quite. "Glad to meet you. Do you know when your father will return?"

"He went to fe—call the vet." She couldn't use a word like "fetch" around a man like this. She walked across the room, opened the flat middle drawer in Daddy's desk, and pulled out the ledger. Two years of eavesdropping and snooping around the office came to her aid. "I believe we'll be needing three gallons this time." She closed the book and turned around.

76

Baldy shifted from one foot to the other. Clearly he was not the decision maker.

"I assure you I am fully acquainted with my father's business dealings." The words sprouted without thought. Daddy wouldn't be so quick to call her incessant reading "foolishness" after this.

It occurred to her that neither of the men had introduced themselves. Clutching the ledger to her chest, she stared at Green Eyes. The man nodded and looked at his partner. "Everything copacetic?"

"Whatever you say. I don't know about this, but whatever you say."

Green Eyes grinned. "There ain't nothin' I can do. . ." he sang, " 'Tain't nobody's business if I do, do, do, do."

Francie blinked hard. Leaning back, she misjudged the space between her back and the desk and banged into it. The man could sing! "That was swell," she gushed, sounding as lame as a three-legged horse. "Sara Martin." Mama would die if she knew she'd ever heard that kind of music.

"Sara Martin indeed." He took a small bow.

Baldy shook his head. "We'll tell her hi from you."

"You know her? Personally?"

"We'll be seeing her in Chicago next—"

Green Eyes silenced him with a hard look. "So, shall we get down to business?"

"Yes." Her voice sounded like the youngest Huseby boy.

"Fine. That'll be fifty-one dollars, Miss Tillman. Three gallons at seventeen clams per."

Strength rushed back into her legs. The man was trying to gyp her! Daddy would be none too pleased if she let them walk away with fifty cents more a gallon than the stuff was worth. She smiled, wide eyed, playing the dumme girl he thought her to be. "I'm sorry, sir, but I believe that will be forty-nine dollars and fifty cents."

His Adam's apple lowered then bobbed to the top of his neck. "Sharp cookie. Okay, forty-nine fifty it is."

She tried not to feel his stare as she opened Daddy's safe. Who was this man? Dressed like he just stepped out of a magazine, with a voice better than some she'd heard on the radio at the mercantile.

What would it be like to dance with him under a mirrored ball across a polished floor in— "*Chicago?*"

"Excuse me?"

She whirled around, money box in hand. "You're going to Chicago?"

"Maybe. Who wants to know?"

"I do." She lowered her voice. "My sister lives there. She needs me to watch her little boy, and I told her I'd be there by next week to help, but all the money I've saved has to go to pay the vet to treat our horse. If I could get a ride with you, I wouldn't be any trouble at all."

Green Eyes stroked his chin. "What would your daddy say about you riding with us?"

She glanced toward the door and straightened her shoulders. "He wouldn't need to know."

Both men hooted, louder than some of Daddy's customers after a few pints. Baldy shook his head. "Sorry, sister."

Green Eyes squinted and looked her over from her hair to her boots. For the longest time, he just stood there. Francie counted out the money and set it on the table. Finally his left eyebrow lifted. "How old are you?"

Her hands slid behind her back. Her fingers crossed. "Seventeen."

Green eyes closed for a moment. She was sure he wasn't falling for it.

"Can you drive?"

Her heart flip-flopped. She'd driven the Huseby's brand-new Model T pickup from their house to the barn with Mrs. Huseby sitting beside her, telling her what to do, but just to be sure the not-quite-lie wouldn't count, she tightened her crossed fingers. "Yes, sir."

"You'd have to be ready to go in five minutes."

"Not a problem." Sara Martin's words giving wing to her feet, she ran out the door. " 'Tain't nobody's business if I do, do, d—" She slid to a stop. The safe. She'd forgotten to lock it again. Spinning on her heel, she ran back.

The two men sat at the table, smoking. The safe was closed.

Under the gaze of cool green eyes, she opened it.

The box was empty.

CHAPTER 9

What had she done?

Rena sat in bed, knees pulled to her chest. Tree branches, quivering in the night breeze, cast flickering shadows on the sheet. She chewed a second fingernail. The first was bleeding.

Her idea could get both of them in way more trouble than the reporter knew. Maybe she should take it back.

But maybe it was her only hope.

She pushed a button on her phone to check the time. 1:38. Giving up on sleep, she turned on her lamp and got out of bed. Rummaging through the bins in her closet, she found a box of too-small clothes she'd set aside to donate. She pulled out two pairs of jeans and three shirts. The pants would have to be shortened, but they should fit. She fished a handful of earrings out of the pile on her dresser. Another piercing or two would help. What kind of reaction would that suggestion get?

If she did back out, would Dani go to the cops or to Nicky? She hadn't shared all that much, but the girl with all the questions could figure things out.

What if she went ahead with the plan and Jarod figured it out? Or a story came out in the paper that brought cops crawling all over the neighborhood? Would things get better? Or way, way worse?

Like the wolves in a nightmare she'd had after that horrible night a year ago, fear circled.

Closing in on a wounded animal.

⚜

Dani opened one eye and stared at the clock. After three hours of fighting with her sheet, she'd apparently won the battle. It lay on the floor in a twisted mound.

She pressed the heels of both hands to her temples, wishing the pressure could stop the thoughts. *You gotta draw a line between reporting and social work.*

Yes, she wanted to help Rena get out, but the bottom line was still the story. Lots of reporters went incognito to get the scoop. In college she'd spent a day at the mall in a wheelchair, recording people's responses to her. This was no different. It wasn't a lie, it was research. She was an actress on the stage of life. An actress for a cause. The more awareness she brought to the lure and danger of gangs, the more chance there was that someone would do something about the problem.

And she wasn't doing anything illegal.

She exhausted every possible rationalization and still didn't have an ounce of peace, but turning back didn't seem the right option either.

Maybe Rena would change her mind and call. Maybe Evan wouldn't answer the message she'd left him. Or maybe he'd say no to what she was going to ask and then that would be her answer, too. No. *Sorry, Rena. Thanks but no thanks. Not going to risk my life for a story.*

Sometime after three she fell asleep. In one of many disjointed dreams, Nicky Fiorini took Agatha's keys from her and baked them inside a spinach calzone.

⚜

Dani's phone rang at five-thirty in the morning. Sitting bolt upright, she fumbled for the phone. Evan. Flopping back on the pillows, she answered in a barely audible croak.

"Rough night?"

"Mostaccioli. Cannoli."

80

"Ah...the oregano morning after. Thought your message sounded a little weird. Sorry I didn't return your call. Had my phone on vibrate, and it was after midnight when I saw it. So what's up? What are you getting me into now?"

"Do you know what time it is?" She flipped a pillow onto her face. "I'll tell you at work."

"No. You'll tell me in twenty minutes when I pick you up."

"Evan. No. I had a horrible night and—"

"Okay, fine, if you won't do a favor for me I guess I can't do whatever it is you want me to do on Fri—"

"I'll do it." She sat up again. "What am I doing?"

"It'll only take about an hour. I'll get us to work on time."

"Sure." Whatever it was, she wasn't in a position to refuse.

"I'm making coffee for you. Hazelnut. Smell it?"

"Hurry."

"I'll be there in twenty."

Ten minutes into a hot shower, Dani regained full consciousness. Hazy snips from another dream surfaced in the steam, sending chills skittering down her back. She was sitting at a picnic table by the lake, watching the sailboats. She could even remember the colors—a striped red and yellow sail dipping and rising on surreal vibrant blue waves. And then someone tapped her shoulder. She turned. China stood next to her, her face lined with hideous black streaks. Intense relief washed over her, but as she reached out to hug her, China placed a gun in the palm of her hand. The barrel was still hot.

She turned the water temperature down, rinsing in the slowly cooling water until her skin tingled. As she dressed, the sick feeling of the gun in her hand remained.

When she walked out of the bedroom in a sleeveless poor boy shirt from the seventies and plaid peddle pushers, Evan sat at the counter with his back to her. "Morning," he said, "you decent?"

"Ugly, but dressed."

He turned and held out a travel mug of coffee. "You are particularly retro this morning. Let's go. I want to use this light." He put his keys in her hand. "In fact, I want you to drive the H1 so I can get some shots on the way."

"That's a first."

81

"I'm so crunched for time I'll chance it."

"Crunched for time? As in an official deadline? As in *Urbanart* likes your idea?"

Evan beamed. Dani hugged him then ran ahead of him down the steps and opened the driver's side door of the Hummer. She drove in silence, turning, slowing, and stopping at Evan's commands. The click of the shutter formed a backdrop to a replay of her talk with Rena.

She had to get on the inside to be trusted. That's just how it worked in this business. Sure, there was a risk. The Swamp wasn't a safe place, though she wouldn't admit that to Nicky.

Nicky. Did he really expect her to call him? Why? So he could apologize? Or shoot her down again?

It took effort to channel her thoughts back to Rena and this coming Friday night—and what kind of chances a reporter should take for a story. There was a risk, but it was Kenosha after all, the town she'd grown up in. It wasn't Afghanistan. Or even Chicago.

If Evan said yes, so would she. Evan had acted in a few dramas at his church. They could pull this off.

"Park up there." Evan pointed toward what appeared to be a vacant building. Finding a place along the curb where she didn't have to parallel park the monster, Dani put the H1 in PARK.

Evan jumped out. She watched him crouching, backing up, then jumping up on the concrete base of a light pole, taking several shots of the side of a redbrick building. Colored swirls outlined in black covered the bottom four feet of the wall.

She hadn't painted much since college, but she could easily summon the exhilaration of a fresh, blank canvas. If conscience and ethics were not an integral part of her, a forty-foot-tall span just begging to be painted would present an incredible rush.

Evan finished more photo-gymnastics and jumped back in. "All done. Thank you. Now, what's this favor you want from me? I put my Friday night in your hands."

Dani sucked in a breath and locked her eyes on his. "How would you feel about putting your *life* in my hands?"

CHAPTER 10

A cobalt sky outlined the red roof of the Kemper Center as Dani backed Agatha onto Third Avenue. She straightened the wheel and took another swig of strong morning coffee. "It's Thursday, right Agatha?"

Tired didn't begin to describe the increase in the pull of gravity on every muscle in her body. She'd tried reading the diary again last night, but she'd only made it through a few entries before falling asleep with the old leather book in her hands. At this rate, it would take her five years to read the five-year diary.

Her phone rang. She answered on a tired sigh without looking at the display. Only Evan would call at this time of day.

"Hi Dani. It's Rena."

"Rena. Aren't teenagers supposed to sleep till noon?"

"I wish. I haven't slept all that great since Monday."

Me neither. Are you backing out? Disappointment entwined with relief. "What's up?"

"I was wondering when you're coming to get the clothes."

Dani glanced at the clock. Nicky would be sleeping, wouldn't he? "I could stop by right now if you have them ready."

"Sure. I'm going to the store with my dad in a couple minutes. I'll put the bag on the bottom step. You can just walk in."

"Great. Thanks."

"There's something else. I need you to promise you won't tell Nicky anything, okay?"

Dani rubbed the nagging ache in her left temple. "I can't give you a blanket promise, Rena, but I can promise I won't say a word unless I see you're in real danger."

"Well then I can't—"

"Immediate danger, I mean. If someone's pointing a gun at you I'm not going to keep quiet."

"Oh." Rena's laugh was shaky. "I guess I'd want you to do something then. It's just that I saw him give you his phone number, and the more I thought about it. . ."

"I don't know why he gave me his number. I don't have any intention of calling him."

"I think you should." Rena's voice sounded suddenly older than seventeen.

"Why?"

"Because I heard him talking to somebody last night." She paused, a bit of melodrama Dani was coming to see as a Rena trademark. "I think he knows where China is."

"How would he—"

"I have to go. See you tomorrow night."

⚜

Dani glanced at the time in the bottom corner of her monitor. 1:03. Four minutes since the last time she'd checked. She picked up her phone, wiped her palms on her knees, and scrolled through her contacts until she reached the Ns and the number she'd added just yesterday. Why, she couldn't have said at the time. Pushing the little green phone icon, she held her breath.

"Hey, it's Nick. I'm either sleeping or up to my armpits in marinara. Yeah, disgusting, I know. Anyway, leave a message, and I'll get back to you as soon—"

Her desk jarred. She jammed her finger onto the END button and jerked around.

A stack of books sat on her desk.

"I'm really getting into this." Evan parked his derriere next to her monitor.

Dani wiped the dampness from her top lip and slid her phone into her purse. She picked up the top book. "*Gang Slang.*" Arching an eyebrow, she looked at the second one. "*Gang Intelligence Manual—Identifying and Understanding Modern-Day Violent Gangs in the United States.*" On the third title she gave up trying not to laugh. "*My Bloody Life: The Making of a Latin King.*" She put one hand over her face, fingers splayed. "Evan. They're just kids."

He grabbed another book and held it up, his expression dead serious. "So were some of these."

"*Home of the Body Bags?*" Maybe it was a week and a half of lousy sleep. Maybe it was the constant second-guessing. Whatever the cause, the result was laughter on the brink of hysterics. Tears streamed down her face, and she doubled over. "I'm s—sorry." She tried twice to quell the spasms but only succeeded in making things worse.

"Come on. Let's go get fresh bad coffee, and I'll tell you all I've learned."

She followed him to the elevator. The door opened and two men in perfectly pressed shirts got out. One held a camera case. Evan exchanged several lines of chitchat then tugged on his rumpled shirt as the door closed. "You think I should dress more professional?"

"Nah. You wouldn't be you." She nodded toward the door. "I can't imagine asking one of them to come with me tomorrow night. You're adaptable. They're way too GQ."

"Wait till you see me tomorrow night. I be wearin' creased khakis-and-a-cuff wit' ice in ma grills." Grinning, he pointed to his teeth. "Urbandictionary.com. Very handy."

"Don't you *dare* talk like that. You'll get yourself killed, pseudo-gangsta." They walked into the cafeteria and made a beeline to the coffee. "That would be a good name. Hey, cool ta meet ya, name's Pseudo-G, homey." She picked up two paper cups and filled them.

Evan rolled his eyes. "Name's Razzi, chick."

"Rotsy? How'd you come up wi—oh! Razzi! As in paparazzi."

"You got it."

"Clever." She set the cups at an empty table. "Very clever."

"So what's yours?"

"I hadn't thought about it. Clearly, I'm not as street savvy as you."

"What're you wearing?"

"Some of Rena's clothes. And I'm dyeing my hair bright red."

"Yuck. But we can work with it." Evan pulled out his phone, punched a few keys, and swiped the screen. "Bittersweet, blush, brick, burgundy, cardinal, copper, coral, crimson, dahlia. Oh, that's a good one. Dahlia, dahling."

"Very gangish."

"Flaming, florid, flushed, fuchsia, garnet, geranium, pink, puce—"

"Yeah." Dani rolled fists toward her wrists and stuck her elbows out. "Don't mess wi' me. Name's Puce."

"I can see it tattooed on your bicep. Okay, moving on. Scarlet, vermilion, carroty, cerise—that has promise—flame, magenta, poppy." His eyes lit. "That's it! You're Poppy. I'm Razzi." He slapped his knee. "Baby, baby, we belong together," he crooned.

"Poppy, huh? Short, catchy, with some drug overtones." She rolled her eyes. "Go back to the other one you said had promise."

"Cerise."

"That's it. Cerise." She let it play on her tongue. "I like it."

Evan sat down across from her and grabbed a stack of sugar packets. "One for Cerise, one for Razzi." He doled them out like a card dealer.

"Any second thoughts?"

"Are you kidding? I'm always up for an adventure. And I feel safe with a five-foot-two kickboxer to hide behind."

"I got your back, Razzi. But seriously, it's not too late to"—her phone vibrated—"back out." She scrolled to the text message. "It's from Rena." Her spine straightened as she read the message. CHINA JUST WENT INTO THE APARTMENT. I THINK ALONE.

She showed it to Evan, pushed her chair back, and stood.

"What are you thinking?"

She shoved her cup toward Evan. "What do you think I'm thinking?"

"I'll go with you."

"No, you won't." She pointed a finger at him and winked. "Can't blow your cover, Razzi."

She turned and sprinted out of the cafeteria, ignoring Evan's pleas for her to stop and think.

Across the street and a block from the restaurant, Nicky slowed his steps and looked at his watch. Three miles in just over twenty-six minutes—a PR. Bending over, he put one hand on his knee and mopped his forehead with the bottom of his shirt. Anger had fueled his run. It wasn't a huge thing, wasn't even his responsibility, but when he'd awakened to new additions to the graffiti on the old garage next to the restaurant, it felt like a slap in the face.

Too close to home. Too close to Rena. His anger shifted to his parents. Dad was in a buddy-buddy phase again. He cycled, like Wisconsin seasons, through alternating bouts of failure and trying too hard. Though undependable and unpredictable, he did manage to make his kids feel loved.

Unlike the woman who gave birth to them.

Nicky ran a hand through dripping hair, lifting it off his forehead. As he reached the corner, a woman caught his eye to his right. Black pants came to mid-calf. Her shirt was the color of a ripe peach. Blond hair floated around her shoulders.

Dumb and stupid on a silver platter. The girl who hadn't called.

Can you blame her? If he'd had time to think, he would have asked for her number instead. So he could call her and. . .what? Seeing her here completely obliterated the momentary desire to apologize. What had he been thinking?

He knew the answer to that. He'd been thinking he didn't want to let Todd win. Again.

She walked with her chin up, a bounce in her step, a sway to her hips. She walked like an open invitation.

The girls around here, the ones who wanted to stay safe, walked with a swagger. A touch-me-and-you-die swagger. Not a sway.

He slowed, almost to a stop, watching the hypnotic swing of her hips and wishing for a garden hose, knowing it might take more than a rush of cold water to shock him back to a normal pulse.

In the middle of the block, she jaywalked across the street. Heading for the house where the kid had killed himself.

He wasn't about to get mixed up in whatever she was up to. But he might just watch. He backed toward a scraggly maple tree.

"Nicky! Hi!" She waved like they'd spotted each other across the grocery store.

"What are you doing here?" He didn't much care that he sounded like he was demanding an answer from a two-year-old. In spite of the voice in his head reminding him he didn't want to get involved, he slipped his shirt on and strode toward her.

Her face colored, giving it a much healthier glow than she'd had under the sickly yellow of a streetlight the first time he'd seen her. "I was just. . .wanting another one of those spinach calzones."

At two in the afternoon? *Right.* "You must have very flexible work hours."

"Yeah, well, that's one of the perks of my job." She wiped her top lip where tiny beads of perspiration formed. The girl squirmed like a bee on a bug zapper. Nicky found it fascinating.

"Yeah. So now that you haven't admitted you're here to gather juicy facts about something, what's the story about? Urban renewal?" He waved his hand, taking in the entire intersection. "Not a whole lot going on in this neighborhood." A screen door opened and closed somewhere not far away, but he couldn't see it. With her hand at the back of her neck, she turned her head, a gesture he guessed he was supposed to view as just a stretch. "Looking for someone?"

"I'm. . .no. . ." She stared at her feet.

Very pretty feet. Toenails matched her pinky-peach blouse. Nicky waited.

Her chin lifted. A pent-up breath whooshed through puffed cheeks.

"Kind of old news here, isn't it? Shouldn't you be on to something new and equally gruesome?"

Her gaze hardened. Something in his gut tightened. He needed to loosen up. What was it about the girl that brought out the worst in him? He tried on a smile. "I've had some dealings with reporters in the past. My attitude's a bit skewed."

"That would explain you calling the paper to tell them I was at the funeral."

Apologize. He'd made the call in the funeral home parking lot while waiting for his dad to stop gabbing. He'd felt stupid the second he'd hung up. "You had no right to be there." Old, hibernating feelings roused. "Have you ever been on the other end of what you do? Ever had a reporter in your face, asking questions, playing on your emotions? Waiting for you to crack and say some—"

A car door slammed in the distance. She turned away from him as a dirty red car pulled out of the alley. Her shoulders dropped. She faced him again, eyes closing for a moment, lips pressed so tight they blanched.

The rusty voice of what must be his conscience whispered in his head. "Look, I'm sorry. Like I said, I've had some bad experiences. I shouldn't have"—he swallowed, took a deep breath, and looked over her shoulder—"made that call. I'm sorry."

A faint smile tipped perfectly shaped lips. "That cost you, didn't it?"

"Wow." Her comment hit like the cold water he'd needed a few minutes ago, but for some odd reason made him smile. And not much did that. "A guy humbles himself and admits he made a mistake, and you just rub his face in it."

"I'm sorry." Her expression didn't reflect her words. "It's just that. . .never mind."

It's just that I came off like a total jerk the first three—make that four—times we met. He nodded toward the house behind her. "What are you doing here?" Same question. Different tone.

"You're right. I'm working on a story. About kids in this neighborhood. Gangs, to be specific."

"So you thought you'd wander around the Swamp looking for some nice gang kids to interview."

A muscle tightened visibly on her jaw. The nagging rusty voice screamed in his head. What was he doing? And why? "Want pictures?" He pointed toward the newly defaced garage. "I've painted the back wall of that building three times this summer. The paint doesn't even have a chance to dry before they're back marking it up like a psychedelic 7UP ad."

The girl's pupils seemed to dilate. "Can I see it?" Energy practically buzzed off her like the hum surrounding high-voltage wires. Strange girl.

"I guess."

"I have a friend who's doing a photography exposé on urban art."

Nicky sputtered. "Makes it sound so. . .artsy."

She shrugged. "Maybe it is."

Really strange girl.

⚜

She should have just let him back away, but she was sure he'd seen her. If she'd had a plan in her head before yelling to him, maybe she could have come off with some degree of common sense. As it was, she now appeared exponentially more ignorant than the other two times he'd caught her here.

She scampered to keep up with Nicky's powerful strides. Squinting into the sun as they crossed the street, she read the inscription on a stone in the arched garage door. "1924. So it was built the year after the restaurant."

Nicky nodded.

"Can't you just see this street back then? Model Ts, guys in celluloid collars and wing-tip shoes. Women in cloche hats with pearls down to their knees."

Nicky turned and stared at her then led the way through the green space.

Dani backed away from the depiction of a white-gloved hand wrapped around a warped, Salvador Dali-style painting of a green bottle. Rivers of red ran from a red dot on the label. Clearly intentional. "Who did this?"

"Local artists." He kicked gravel with the toe of his shoe. "If it were my property, I'd set up a security camera." His voice was tight, restrained.

"The Sevens?"

"You've done your research."

You have no idea. "It's my job." She stepped closer to the wall. "It takes talent to do something like this with spray paint."

"If that's what you want to call it."

"You have to admit it ads color to the alley." She swept her arm to include the parking lot behind the restaurant and the backsides of houses and businesses backed up to the gravel alley. "It livens things up."

"It's illegal."

90

She'd never used *curmudgeon* in a sentence before. This seemed an appropriate time. "Has anyone ever vandalized Bracciano?"

"No." A dimple teased his right cheek. "They wouldn't dare."

She smiled back, the dimple having sucked all words, including *curmudgeon*, from her lips.

"You said you needed to talk to me. You want to ask what I know about the guy who killed himself?" His eyes seemed to darken. His expression made her want to back away. "Or are you back in my neighborhood because you have a death wish?"

Even when the guy was being rude, there was something weirdly charming about him. "It's mine. I was hoping to talk to China, Miguel's girlfriend."

"What for?" He looked up and to the right. She'd taken a class on body language once. Which direction did eyes shift when people had something to hide?

She turned back to the dripping, blood-red ball. "I interviewed her a few months ago for a series I wrote."

She looked into Nicky's eyes, needing, for some undefined reason, absolution from him. "I gave her some advice. I told her to break it off with Miguel. And she did."

"That's why he killed himself."

"Yes."

"And she blames you."

She nodded.

"You did the right thing. He's the one who made the wrong choice."

"That's what I keep telling myself. But it wasn't my place. As a journalist I'm supposed to report the facts, not get involved in the story."

"You might have saved her life by what you did."

"Maybe." She blinked away the sting in her eyes.

"You acted on what you thought you should do. That's way better than being left with regret." He crossed his arms over his chest.

Dani wasn't so sure Rena was right about her brother always saying what he felt. She had no doubt there were things Nicky Fiorini kept hidden in a tightly clenched fist.

91

"Do you know where she's staying?"

He held her gaze with an unblinking stare. "I might."

She waited, looking back with an unwavering stare.

"The guy who owns the house across the street said she's living with her aunt. Turns out she used to work here. Carmen James." Again, the shift of the eyes to the right. "She lives in Wilson Heights."

Her pulse quickened. Another neighborhood she'd be dumb and stupid to walk through. "Thank you."

"Promise me something, okay?" His voice took on the Prince Charming gentleness she'd heard once before.

"What?"

"Don't go looking for her by yourself."

"Okay."

"I'll go with you."

Who was this man? "Thank you."

"Now, do you really want a calzone?"

"No. I mean, yes, but some other time."

"Let me know when you're coming. I'll make one just for you."

Just for you.

His chin dipped, making his gaze slice deeper. "Might even sit down and join you."

Did she want that?

She looked over at the restaurant, imagining freshly painted trim against new brick, neighbors chatting on front porches, and the alley where they stood a safe place for a game of stickball. The way it might have been in June of 1928 when Francie Tillman had a 'fun night at Bracciano.'

Breathing shallow, fingers tingling the way they had the first time she dove off the diving board at Washington Park, she answered her own question. *Yes. I want that.* She looked into eyes that masked stories she wanted to hear. "I found something across the street. If you're interested, I'd like to show it to you."

Nicky tipped his head to one side, hair tumbling across his forehead. "I'm interested."

September 30, 1924

Arms spread out like one of the thieves on the cross, Francie gripped two hooks on the inside of the cargo box. Her muscles ached from shivering, but every time she let go of the hooks to hug her coat closer to her body, the truck hit a rut or turned a corner and she lost her balance on the upturned pail. She had no idea how long they'd driven, but her bottom hurt from too many jarrings and hard landings on the bucket, and her stomach growled fiercely. Tears surfaced whenever she thought of the stew on the stove at home and Mama's face when she would read the letter Francie'd left.

She'd saved Daddy's money. When she'd threatened to scream, Baldy turned it over. She just hoped he'd given her all of it.

Hooga-hooga. The horn blared, the truck swerved. The chugging of the motor slowed. More ruts. She imagined a long dirt road like the one linking their farm to the main road. For a moment she wished they'd changed their minds and were taking her home.

Gritting her teeth, she fought tears. Suzette needed her. Her nephew needed her. How were people treating him? Were they calling him the names she'd heard for Halla Gudmundson's baby? The little girl was in school now, but Mama's friends still whispered about Halla not knowing who her daughter's father was. People could be so mean while sounding like they were doing God's work.

That was why Daddy never went to church and why he hadn't made Francie go after she got confirmed. The fight he'd had with Mama still rang in her head.

"Francie would learn more about genuine compassion sitting out in my office than in a church pew," he'd said.

"Can you really fool yourself into thinking you're doing God's work when you sell liquor to weak-willed men and then listen to them ramble in their drunkenness?"

"I may not do it in the name of God, but I do more for the 'least of these' out there at that table. . . ." They'd thought she was sleeping, but she'd heard every word. She remembered his loud, heavy sigh. "If you people just once acted like the man you claim to follow, maybe he wouldn't have died in vain."

Mama had gasped. "That's blasphemy."

"Is it? When's the last time you even gave the time of day to somebody outside the walls of your church who's down on his luck?"

"The Missionary Society collects money and packs boxes for—"

Daddy had laughed, cutting off her words. "You take money from people who can barely put food on their tables and then you sit in your righteous circles and pick them apart while you pack your boxes for the poor children in China."

The fight had ended with Mama crying, Daddy marching to the barn, and Francie not returning to church.

The truck lurched. Brakes squealed. Her shoulder slammed into a crate of syrup cans. She heard the doors open, and Baldy and Green Eyes talking in hushed tones. "All clear. Get her."

With a soft whine, the rear doors opened.

"Get out." Baldy motioned with his arm. She could just barely make out his silhouette in the moonlight. "Get behind the wheel."

In the dark? They expected her to drive in the dark? "Where are we?"

"Nowhere. Just sit here and follow that truck when it pulls—"

A dog barked not far away. A door opened. "Rusty!" A woman's voice.

"Shh!" Green Eyes grabbed her arm and yanked her to the other side of the truck. His arm went across her chest, and he pressed her back against him. A hand clamped over her mouth. His breath touched her ear. "Not a word."

"Rusty, come here now!"

Francie's heart hammered in her throat. Her knees quivered. The door closed, and Green Eyes' arms relaxed, but he didn't move for several long moments. "Sorry, doll," he whispered. "Didn't mean to scare you. We're borrowing this truck from a friend, see, and he said his Ma wouldn't like it, so we have to make sure she doesn't know. He said she'd be sleeping by now, but looks like she's a night owl. We'll have to push the truck out onto the road. Think you can see well enough to follow?"

Moonlight cast ghostly tree shadows along the roadside. Francie nodded. She could see. Could she remember how to drive?

"Good girl." Green Eyes took his hand off her mouth and stroked her cheek with his knuckles. His spicy scent spun images of far-away countries where women dressed in rich-colored saris and men wore turbans and rode camels. "We're going to make a good team, you and me."

Her heart slowed. The trembles of fear transformed to jitters of anticipation. It was only for a night and a day. Tomorrow night she would be in Chicago, safe and sound with her sister. Until then, she could cram in enough excitement to last a long, long time.

✥

"Get rid of her."

Francie huddled in the corner of a metal cage just large enough to lie down in. She had no idea how she'd gotten there. A few yards away, Green Eyes and Baldy sat at a table with a gray-haired man with glasses. The high-ceilinged building was bigger than the barn back home. The truck she'd driven and the one they claimed they'd borrowed were parked inside along with at least two others.

Perspiration trickled down her sides in spite of the damp cold.

"She's just a kid." Green Eyes blew smoke directly at the man.

"Too bad. She's seen too much."

Green Eyes crushed his cigarette in an ashtray. "She came in handy."

"I bet she did." The gray-haired man's laugh echoed off concrete walls.

"When that cop stopped us, she played him big time, convinced him I was her big brother teaching her how to drive. Even got him to laugh. The guy forgot all about looking in the back of the truck."

"So you made a smart decision to take her along, but we don't need her now."

Green Eyes glanced her way. "What if we just keep her?"

Spine straightening, Francie leaned forward, arms wrapped around her churning stomach.

Green Eyes nodded. "A little hush money could go a long way. She's got nothing. Dirt poor folks. We take her to her sister's, keep her supplied with everything a gal could want, and use her when we need a dame for cover."

95

The gray-haired man shoved his chair back, stood, and walked over to the cage. "You listening to all this, sweetheart?"

Francie nodded, sure she'd vomit if she opened her mouth.

"What d'ya think? You good at keeping secrets?"

Her eyes felt stuck wide open. She nodded with more force than before. Whatever they asked, she'd agree to, as long as it got her to Suzette's.

The man tapped a finger on the end of his nose. "Do you understand there'd be consequences if you told anyone about our little business venture? Consequences to your sister maybe, or your parents? Seems there are things about your Daddy's farm the authorities might be interested in."

"There's a kid," Baldy added. "Her nephew."

"Convenient."

Bile burned her throat. She swallowed hard. She would not give this man the satisfaction of seeing how scared she was. "I understand." Her words rasped in her tight throat.

"So we have a deal then. Tag here seems to be sweet on you, so I'll put him in charge. He'll take you to your sister. I'm thinking maybe you'll have to play it like you two got a thing for each other so's your sister doesn't wonder where all the pretty things are coming from. You got yourself a rich boyfriend, girly, without even tryin'. When we need you, Tag'll just come 'round and pick you up for a little romantic getaway."

Grasping the bars of the cage, Francie pulled to a stand. Her gaze locked on Green Eyes. So his name was Tag. Strange name. Probably not his real one. He stared back at her, a slow smile spreading across his face. His lips pursed. He kissed the air and winked.

Francie felt suddenly warm.

How bad could working with him possibly be?

CHAPTER 11

Rena stood out of sight in Bracciano's empty dining room, gaze riveted to the front window. Pulling her phone from her apron pocket, she tried to control the jerking of her fingers as she punched Jarod's number. "Answer. Answer," she whispered, praying his phone was on silent.

Outside Nicky pointed toward the far end of the garage building, and Dani followed him. Just as they disappeared around the corner, Jarod answered.

"My brother's coming around the back of the garage."

Jarod responded with a whispered curse and broke the connection.

Why was she protecting him? If he got caught, he'd go to jail and she'd be free.

Unless he brought her down with him.

Flying through the swinging doors, Rena dashed through the kitchen. "Hi, Dad, be right back. Front's empty." She flashed a fake smile and pounded up the stairs, down the hall, and into her father's bedroom. Bending down, she pressed the top of her head against the screen, straining to see the garage next door.

From this angle, she couldn't see a thing. But if she held her breath, she could just barely make out words.

". . .in there?" Dani asked.

"I've wanted to know. . ." Her brother's voice faded.

Her phone buzzed in her hand. "Jarod?"

"I'm inside." His voice was low, breathless, the way he used to talk when he called her in the middle of the night to say he missed her. He hadn't done that in months, and now the voice gave her the wrong kind of chills. "Let me know when they leave."

"You didn't leave anything outside, did you? Anything they'd—"

"What kind of"—she held the phone away from her ear while he spewed his favorite words—"do you think I am?" The clock on Dad's dresser clicked four times. "You really don't trust me, do you?"

Trust? You won't even tell me what it is you're hiding in there. "I'm just worried about you. I want you safe." The lie left a bitter aftertaste.

"I got everything. It's clean."

Clean. Like a person finally off drugs. "They're leaving. Walking toward the street."

"Okay. I'm going home." He didn't bother saying "I love you." Again.

She turned away from the window and headed for the stairs, ready to act like nothing was wrong.

Even though everything was.

⚜

"It's midnight in the Midwest. Hope you're with the one you love in this first minute of Friday, and if you're not, I hope you're enjoying a 'simple little kind of free' like John Mayer. This is 'Perfectly Lonely.'"

Nicky sang along as he fed pasta dough into the cutter. The lyrics spoke of belonging to no one. The song usually left him feeling free. Tonight it just made the night seem heavy. He turned off the machine and shut off the radio.

The music didn't stop. Muffled guitar chords filtered through the vents. Rena's voice rose above the sweet, clear notes. He walked to the foot of the stairs.

Two steps up, he recognized the song. The words lodged beneath his ribs like a fist.

"Shed a tear at your grave today/a single crystal drop/then I stood and watched it hit the stone/catch light and fade away. . ."

He waited for her to finish then walked upstairs. Rena sat on the floor, eyes closed as she tuned the strings. Nicky leaned on the doorframe. "Sounded good."

"Thanks." She swiped at damp cheeks. "They're having a memorial for Miguel down at the beach tomor—" She glanced at the time on her radio. "Tonight. I traded shifts so I can go. I thought maybe I'd sing it."

She hadn't answered any of his questions all week. Would she close up now if he tried again? He walked over to the bed and sat on the floor facing her. "How well did you know him?"

"Not very well. I'm kind of friends with China, his girlfriend."

"Can I ask why you didn't want to go to the funeral?"

Rena stared at her fingernails. "Miguel's parents were really nasty to China. We stayed away because of her."

" 'We' as in you and Jarod?" Acid rose in his throat along with the name. "Or you and Trish?"

"All of us." She reached behind her for a tissue and blew her nose. "A bunch of us kind of stick together. Take care of each other, you know?"

He knew. His chest burned with what he knew. "People are saying Miguel was one of the Sevens. Is that true?"

She shrugged and tossed the crumpled tissue at a black wastebasket. "I heard that, too."

Nicky wrapped his arms around bent knees and waited until her eyes finally wandered back to him. "Are *you?*" *Dear God, let her say no.*

"No." She gave a soft laugh that neutralized the pain beneath his sternum. "You're slipping. You used to know everything going on around here. The Sevens are only guys. No girls allowed."

"Thank the Lord for that."

"Yeah." She ran the edge of her thumb across the strings. "Can't really see myself carjacking."

"Me neither." He picked a beaded bracelet from the floor. Red, white, and green. A nagging feeling, like the warning of distant thunder, fluttered in his belly. "Funny. We're talking about the Sevens and I find a bracelet with their colors." The cords on the sides of his neck stiffened until they hurt.

Rena laughed again. "Those are *Christmas* colors. Man, are you paranoid." She swiveled toward her dresser, opened her bottom drawer, and pulled out a pair of socks. Red, white, and green. White snowmen, holly leaves, on a red background. "It matches these."

Totally unconvinced, he nodded. "Danielle Gallagher was across the street today."

Rena picked up a yellow plastic guitar pick. "I saw you talking to her."

"Did you know she interviewed Miguel's girlfriend?"

"Yeah. She's doing another story on crazy teenagers or something, huh? What were you and reporter lady doing out back?"

"A friend of hers is a photographer. He's going around taking pictures of graffiti. 'Wall art' he calls it."

"Some of it's kind of pretty."

"Those kids need to get a life. There's nothing pretty about vandalizing somebody's property." He stared at her, watching for any sign of guilt.

She stared right back. "It's nice we have Todd around so much. Nobody would dare do anything to our place."

"Is that what it is? Is that why they leave us alone? Or is it because you live here?"

Her eyes shot wide. Her fingers whitened on the neck of the guitar. "Get. A. Grip." She metered it out as if he didn't speak the language. "You gotta quit thinkin' stuff like that. You're gonna drive yourself crazy."

Nicky ran his hands over his eyes. "You know why I go nuts on you sometimes."

"I know."

"Raising you hasn't been a piece of cake." He threw the socks back.

"But you've done a good job. Now it's time to retire."

"You wish." He shook his finger at her. "When you're married. Maybe."

"That's exceptionally demeaning and sexist, even for you."

"It's the truth. At least around here. I won't feel like you're safe until you have some six-foot-twelve, four-hundred-pound guy looking after you."

As she laughed, he weighed the next question. "Which brings

us back to the conversation that didn't go so well last week. Can we talk about Jarod?"

"Not now. Maybe after tonight. I've got too many emotions going on right now."

"Fine." He slapped his knees and stood.

"You do that just like Dad."

"What?"

"The knee slap thing."

"That's exceptionally demeaning, even for you." Ruffling her hair, he said good night. He walked into the hallway then turned back. "It was nice to hear you play again."

She strummed a chord. "I should have closed my door. I didn't think you could hear me over the radio. That song has to get to you."

"It does." He ran his hand along a spot of patched plaster in the hall. "But it's a good one. You should write more. Maybe a happier one."

"Yeah. Maybe I will."

Halfway down the stairs he heard her say "Someday."

⬮

Rena curled in a ball on the bare mattress. The cold from the stone walls seeped into her. In the hesitant light from her lantern, she stared at the four streaks above the door. They'd once scared her. She'd been sure the dark brown stains were blood. Now they were simply a part of her hiding place. She turned off the lantern to save the battery and welcomed the darkness. Jarod had left the little room a mess. Beer cans littered the floor. She felt violated all over again. It was her place, hers alone. She never should have let him in.

Tears ran across the bridge of her nose. She didn't even know who she was crying for anymore. It had started with Miguel and moved on to every loss she'd ever experienced, including her mother. She'd once told Jarod she sometimes cried for her mother. He'd laughed. "Don't waste your tears on somebody who ditched you." It was the last little part of her heart she'd tried to share.

God, can you hear me? Did thick stone walls, or doubt, block her words?

She had to do something. She'd go somewhere. Maybe China would take her with her.

101

Is that why they leave us alone? Or is it because you live here?

If she left home, or even just left Jarod, the restaurant wouldn't be protected and neither would she. She picked up her phone and called her best friend. Trish answered with a sleepy voice and stayed silent as she spoke her fears out loud and searched for a way out.

When she finally ran out of words, Trish sighed, loud and harsh. "Don't be stupid, Ren." Her voice raked exposed nerves. "Jarod's your force field. He's what's standing between you and what happened before. You're not going anywhere, and you know it."

Rena curled her hand, pressing her phone to her chest, and sobbed again for a future that could not be.

CHAPTER 12

It was just beginning to get dark on Friday night when Evan turned Agatha onto the gravel road leading to the private beach. They'd agreed the H1 didn't fit the image. The air was cool, tinged with the smell of rain. Dani opened the window. Thoughts bounced like the strands of hair whipping her face and neck.

Doubts about the night ahead competed with anticipation of tomorrow. Nicky had suggested lunch at Petrifying Springs Park. She'd bring the diary and a notebook. He'd bring lunch. She couldn't shake the sense that it felt like a date. A wave of dizziness disoriented her every time she thought of the quicksilver shifts in his attitude—and her response. She didn't want to be one of those women who caved at a smile. Or a chiseled profile. Or shadowed brown eyes with stories to tell. Or a "just for you."

As she smoothed the frayed edge on one of many holes in the skinny jeans she'd hemmed during her lunch break, she planned what she'd wear tomorrow. And hoped the wash-off tattoos would really wash off and the Rock'n Red temporary hair color was really temporary.

No one seemed to notice as they found places on the outside of a circle of maybe thirty kids surrounding a bonfire. Dani drew her knees to her chest and dug her bare feet into the sand. A hush, almost a reverence, hovered over them. Whatever she'd been expecting, it wasn't this.

Evan snapped pictures and made it look like he was just texting or scrolling for music on his phone.

Rena left a group of girls and sat next to her. She pointed at the magnetic stud in Dani's nose. "Hey, *Cerise*. You look good."

Dani introduced her to "Razzi" then nodded toward the cluster of kids Rena had just left. "What did you tell them?"

"I said you guys knew China so I invited you."

"China's gone? You're sure?"

"Yeah. I heard they were leaving really early this morning. It has to be killing her not to be here."

"Which one is Jarod?"

"He's not here. I knew he wouldn't come." She jabbed stiffened fingers into the sand.

A dark-skinned girl in a red shirt stood up and walked toward the fire. The others quieted.

"I wrote a poem for Miguel. It's called 'Dark Angel.' Um—I guess I'll just—uh—read it now." The paper in her hands shook as she began.

> *Always standing in the shadow,*
> *always centered in the storm,*
> *you reached for light, but never felt it,*
> *you begged for peace, it never came.*
> *Like a fading star's glowing path,*
> *your death points us to light*
> *and makes us cry for peace—*
> *the peace you never knew.*
> *Your quest goes on*
> *in those you leave behind,*
> *in us you will live on, dark angel.*

When she finished reading, she slowly ripped the paper and let the pieces fall into the fire. As the last piece sparked and hovered above the flames on the waves of heat, she wiped her tears. "Good-bye, Miguel."

Another girl stood. Rena leaned close to Dani. "She's Miguel's stepsister."

The girl ran the back of her hand across her face. "This maybe sounds like I'm dissin' Miguel, but I'm going to read it 'cause maybe somebody else is dealing with feelings, and I think it's okay to let it out and not keep all the junk inside."

Clearing her throat, she read from a pink paper. "This is so unfair. It hurts so bad, and I can't do anything to make it go away. It didn't have to be this way. If only you would have told someone. No one knew how bad you were hurting. You didn't give us a chance, and now it's too late, and we're left with tears and memories and guilt. Sometimes the sadness is so thick and black I can't even breathe. Getting mad helps 'cause then I can blame you and not myself, but I always come back to the whys about me. Why didn't I see? Why didn't I listen? Why didn't I know? Why couldn't I stop you?" She let the paper fall into the fire along with her tears.

Dani wiped at her own tears, and Evan squeezed her hand.

Rena stood and walked over to a guitar leaning on a boulder near the fire. " 'Cause I've kind of been through this once before, I just want to say that the really intense pain doesn't last forever. And one day you wake up and you remember the good times, and you can laugh without feeling guilty, and then you know it's okay to go on." She strummed several chords. "I wrote this for someone else, but I hope it can maybe give somebody here some hope." She began to sing in a voice that was startlingly sweet and clear.

Put a flower on your grave today,
A single, perfect rose.
Then I stood and watched the petals curl,
Turn brown and blow away.
Shed a tear at your grave today,
A single crystal drop,
then I stood and watched it hit the stone,
Catch light and fade away.
Left my sadness at your grave today,
And walked out on my own,
Knowing who I am is part of you,
And you're not far away.
Stopped to listen at your grave today

For laughter on the wind.
Then I stood and smiled as memories
Took wings and flew away.
Came to whisper at your grave today
Of going on alone,
Then I stood and said good-bye to you,
And turned and walked away.
Left my sadness at your grave today,
And walked out on my own,
Knowing who I am is part of you,
And you're not far away.

Rena set the guitar down without a sound. The crash of the waves beat a cadence in the silence. A log crumbled, sending orange sparks into the night air that turned black as they rose. Dani looked around the circle, in awe of the talent, depth, and creativity she was witnessing, and yet every one of the kids sitting around the fire had probably been labeled a throwaway by someone. She wiped her eyes with the back of her hand. *Please, God.* She wasn't even sure what she asked for.

Rena took two steps and froze. Her eyes widened then darted toward Dani.

"Hey!" A male voice broke the silence. "China's here."

Dani's chest locked. Evan's grip tightened. Head low, she turned.

China stumbled toward the group. In spite of the darkness, it was clear she'd been drinking. Two of the girls ran to meet her, and each grabbed an arm. As she got closer to the firelight, Dani caught a glimpse of the crazed look in reddened eyes. China pushed away the girls who were supporting her. From behind her back she produced a gun. "Anyone want to do this for me?"

Gasps rose over the crackle of the fire.

"That's what friends are for, right? No? Fine, I'll do it—"

"Rabia! Grab it!"

A heavyset boy with an eagle tattooed on his arm grabbed China's arm. The gun went off, pointed straight up.

China's legs folded. She sank to the ground. Wild eyes swept the group. She blinked and shook her head in confusion. Her eyes lasered into Dani's. Her breath came in short, loud gasps. "Perfect. You come to watch—" She bent toward the fire, almost losing her balance, and grabbed a burning stick. Holding it out in front of her, she lunged at Dani.

❦

Using Evan's arm for support while holding an ice pack to the back of her head, Dani tried to absorb the instructions the emergency room nurse listed. Stitches closed the gash above her left elbow. Loose gauze covered spots of third degree burns. The back of her head bulged with a lump the size of a kiwi. She nodded at the nurse, but her brain was fuzzy and the tears wouldn't stop.

Evan kept his arm tight around her waist as they walked out into the waiting area. Rena, wearing shorts and a tank top, was curled like a kitten in a plastic chair. She looked up when they got close. Evan handed her a red plastic bag. "The nurse tried to rinse out your shirt."

Dani touched Rena's bare shoulder with the backs of her fingers. Air conditioned air blasted. "You were probably freezing without it."

"I'm fine."

"You should be a nurse," Evan said. "You moved fast."

The past two hours were a blur, and whatever they had given her for the pain was doing strange things to her head. She remembered bits and pieces. China lunging at her with the glowing stick. White hot pain. Rena taking off her shirt and wrapping it around her arm. The next few moments came into focus then faded.

Evan pulled out his cell phone. "I'm taking you to Anna's."

"No. Her mom's visiting."

"Then Vito and Lavinia's."

Dani opened her mouth to protest, but Rena spoke first. "She can stay with me. She can have my bed, and I'll sleep in my dad's room. He doesn't use it, somebody should." Dani shook her head, but Rena continued. "It'll be fun. Nicky's trying a new brunch promo on weekends, so he makes cinnamon rolls and—"

"Not Nicky." She'd just proven once again she was all he'd said, silver platter and all.

Rena laughed. "He'll be working all night and in bed before you wake up."

107

She shook her head again and the room tilted. She leaned against Evan and closed her eyes. "No Nicky." Her voice sounded far away. "But I don't want to wake Vito again."

"Then it's settled."

She walked between them on a floor that bounced and rolled like an inflatable gym. As they eased her into the car, she wondered what it was that was settled.

⚜

April 13, 1925

Tag smoothed back his hair with both hands, opened the car door, and offered his hand. As if he were some kind of gentleman. "You're a natural, doll."

Francie checked her lipstick in her compact mirror and straightened her necklace, "You've been training me for six months."

It seemed so much longer. Impossible that half a year ago she'd been a barefoot farm girl in overalls. She ran her hand along her skirt, smoothing three tiers of gold satin, and got out of the Model T without the aid of his hand.

"Gorgeous gams." Tag lifted the hem of her dress and laughed in a way that not long ago had made her heart flutter. "It's been that long, huh? At Thanksgiving you were still the pudgy kid playin' the part of my little sister. Every time I think of that teller in Rockford... ah, good times. But no more banks for you, no more hooch runs. You help me move up, I return the favor. Look at you, all svelte and acting like a lady, but knowing just when not to. Like I said, you're a natural."

Francie sighed. Not that he'd notice.

"Maybe time for a little anniversary celebration." As he ushered her, hand on her back, toward an unremarkable door on the dimly lit street, he pulled a long, slim box from his pocket. "Get Mr. Carson out of here tonight, and what's in here, and more, is yours." He knocked three times, paused, and gave a fourth sharp rap. The door opened.

They hurried in and the door closed behind them. Soft lamplight illuminated a haze of smoke hovering over small round tables. Women in jewel-toned gowns lounged on overstuffed sofas,

108

laughing with the men they leaned against. A jazz piece Francie hadn't heard before jangled from the piano in the corner. Tag helped her out of her coat and dipped his head toward a thin man leaning on the bar. The man lifted his glass.

"Go do what you do so well, just don't do it too well." Tag laughed and walked toward a group of men in the corner.

Francie applied a coy smile the same way she'd put on lipstick and sidled up to the man. "Mr. Carson. Remember me?"

An hour and a half later, Mr. Carson pulled up at a house two blocks from the one Tag had bought for her. "You're sure you'll be all right?"

"Yes. I just need to lie down." She rubbed her temples and winced. "I'm so sorry to take you away from everything."

"My pleasure to be of service. Will I see you next week?"

"I do hope so, Chester." She gave the kind of smile a woman with a migraine would give and waved as he drove away.

Her job was done for the night. She'd given Tag the time he needed for plans to be made and money to change hands. In exchange for what, she hoped she'd never know. She took off her hat and walked home to the part of her life that wasn't a total lie—the little boy her sister had given a name "as close to yours as I could for a boy."

Suzette met her at the door, high heels in hand. It was all Francie could do to look her in the eye and say good-bye. What her sister had become since she'd gotten pregnant and left home was unspeakable. "*I did what I had to do.*" Francie hated the line. Especially when she used it herself.

Francie kicked off her shoes and went straight for her nephew's room.

"Hi, Aunt Frazzie." Franky sat up in bed. He lowered the ladder on his fire truck, set it on the window sill, and slid under the covers.

Francie grinned at his name for her. Folding a white sailor suit, she sat on the edge of the bed. "Hi, little man." She pushed aside a dark ringlet and smacked a loud kiss on his forehead.

"I'm not little. I'm almost this many." He held up four fingers.

"Only three more months." She picked two books from a basket. "*Winnie-the-Pooh* or *Ring O' Roses*?"

"Tell me about Applejack."

"Again?" She pulled the blanket up to his chin. "Applejack was the tallest, strongest horse for miles around. All the farmers wished they had a fine plow horse like your grandpa's Applejack. His hooves were as big around as a dinner plate. . . ." Dark eyes fluttered as she spoke. In minutes, his soft, deep-sleep breathing filled the tiny room.

Francie turned off the lamp, walked to her room, and pulled out her diary. This wasn't the life she thought she'd be writing about.

Chapter 13

Teeth, long and sharp, sank into her arm. Some animal, a dog or a tiger with a massive head, gouged a huge chunk, shook her, and bit again.

Her own cry woke her. Her left arm throbbed. She opened one eye. A thin square of light from a street lamp outlined a window to her right. Faint music played somewhere beneath her. Katie Melua. "The Closest Thing to Crazy." She breathed a sigh. She was home.

A light blazed on above her.

"What the—"

Dani grabbed the sheet and pulled it up with one arm.

"What the heck are *you* doing here?"

Nicky. Her eyes shot open. "Where—"

"What's with the tattoos? Where's Rena?"

"In your father's room."

Nicky folded his arms and stared. Katie Melua sang about the link between being close to crazy and close to you.

Dani shook her head to clear it. A wave of dizziness stopped her. She closed her eyes again then opened them slowly, hoping the statue-stiff figure in the doorway had slipped back into her nightmare. "I got hurt down at the beach and Rena came to the hospital with me. The stuff they gave me for pain made me a little foggy, so she offered to let me stay here."

He didn't blink.

She turned away and saw the prescription bottle sitting on the nightstand. She reached for it. The bedside lamp swayed before her eyes. Her head hurt, her arm throbbed, and Nicky's silence magnified it all. *Say something. Scream, kick me out, don't just stand there.* She squeezed the childproof cap and willed tears not to fall. "Rena's a good kid. It was nice of her to let me stay."

Nicky snorted and took two strides into the room. Dani pulled back.

"Give it to me."

The bottle shook. The sheet fell off her bandage. Blood soaked through the gauze in a crisscross pattern.

"What happened?" His voice lost some of its edge.

Once again, the change in his tone unnerved her, brought the tears closer than his anger had. She didn't trust herself to answer. Nicky read the label on the bottle then put one white pill in her hand and put the cap back on. Dani pulled the covers back with her good arm. "I need to get some water." She stood. The angles of Nicky's face swam like the bottle painted on the building next door. She sank onto the bed, head down.

"I'll get it."

She held up her hand. "Just give me a minute. I'll be fine." By the time she lifted her head, he was standing in front of her with a glass of water. She swallowed the tablet and stood slowly, determined to take the glass back to the bathroom herself.

"It says you're supposed to take this with food. I'll get you something." He turned toward the door.

"No. Thank you, but I'm fine. I need to get going anyway."

He turned back to her slowly, rolled his eyes and shook his head. "Good idea." Two words, thick with sarcasm. "It's not safe to sleep in a locked car around here, but walking the streets at night is no problem, especially if you're good and drugged up."

If he'd said it in jest she would have had a comeback, but there was not even a hint of amusement in his voice. She narrowed her eyes to block the glare from the overhead light. And his eyes. "Where's my phone? I'll call a friend to pick me up."

"At two in the morning?"

"*Yes*, at two in the morning. Believe it or not, I have friends who will pick me up at two in the morning."

She stood, slower this time, and stepped toward him. He didn't budge. She moved to his right. He blocked the way.

No command in her repertoire would stop the tears. Her breath shuddered. The next thing out of his mouth would be a sarcastic jab about women using tears to get their way.

"Look." Nicky rubbed the dark stubble on his chin, leaving several unguarded inches on his left. She moved. His arm shot out. His hand grasped the doorframe. "You're quick." Ripples deepened above one eyebrow. He sighed. "Come downstairs and get something to eat first."

More of a command than an apology, his words seemed to compound the effects of the pill. She nodded, subdued as if the jagged tiger teeth hovered over her.

⁂

Dani sat on the stool Nicky pointed to and looked around. Crocks of rising dough covered with white towels sat on the back of the black iron stove. Racks of drying pasta as long as Nicky was tall lined the counter. The smell made her stomach growl. Nicky buttered a piece of bread and cut several slices of cheese, then poured a glass of milk and set it in front of her without a word. He nodded at her thanks then turned his back on her, washed his hands and punched his fist into a mound of rising dough.

He wore khakis, a form-fitting white T-shirt, and an apron folded at his waist. Biceps bulged as he worked. He stood at a slight angle, giving her a perfect view of his profile. Did he know how gorgeous he was? He could easily have been a model. All he lacked was a smile.

"This place has so much atmosphere. What does it feel like to stand in the exact place your great-great-grandfather stood, making bread the same way he did?"

Nicky shrugged. He rolled out dough, sliced it into strips, and lined them on baking pans. He brushed the breadsticks with melted butter and sprinkled them with parmesan cheese.

This is going well. "I worked at a pizza place in high school. A

113

chain. The breadstick dough was frozen, and we had to put this thick yellow junk on it—coconut oil and artificial who-knows-what." She took a bite of the bread. "Nothing like this. Nothing. This is incredible."

He looked over his shoulder. "Thank you."

She watched his hands, mesmerized by his speed and skill. "Can I ask you something?"

"You can ask."

"Did Rena say something to color your opinion of me before you met me?"

He turned toward her, wiping his hands on his apron. "No. Did she know you before that night?"

"Not really. I came in for dinner earlier, and I fed her some lines."

Nicky raised one eyebrow, walked to the sink, and washed his hands then dried them on paper towel.

She'd seen glimpses of a smile. Flashes that disappeared like match light. Somewhere deep inside this man, there had to be more. What would it take to make Nicky Fiorini laugh? "When she told you you had delusions of grandeur—that came from me."

His eyes held just the slightest gleam. "Figures."

"So you formed your opinion of me simply on the fact that I fell asleep in a car."

"Yeah."

"So if I had met you before you called the cops on me, you would have had an entirely different attitude?"

"Maybe."

For no reason she could come up with, she felt like laughing. She cocked her head to one side. "So if we started all over and pretended I'd never been here in the middle of the night—the first time—would you be nice to me?"

Without a word, Nicky walked over and picked up the prescription bottle and read the label. "Maybe. When you're done with these."

She giggled. "Can I ask you another question?"

"Why not? You're on a roll."

"When's the last time you really smiled?"

He opened a massive stainless steel refrigerator, took out a tub of butter and a carton of cream. Angled toward her now, he raised hinges on an industrial-sized mixer, raising the beaters out of a bowl. He added cream without measuring then put the carton away. Back at the mixer he paused, finger on the power button then sighed. He walked away from the mixer and pulled out the stool across from her. "How about if I ask the questions for a while?"

Dani pushed her plate aside, folded her hands in front of her, and nodded.

"You were at the memorial at the beach."

"That's not a question."

Nicky bit the corner of his lip. "I'll take that as a yes. So you do have a death wish, or the cost of my ad in the *Times* just went up because they're paying you guys enough money to make risking your life worth it."

"Still not a question."

"Here's one." He fingered a strand of her hair. His fingers brushed her arm just above the bandage. "What's with the weird hair?"

"I was trying to blend in."

"With what? Tomatoes?"

"With the kids. For a story."

His eyes widened. "You were trying to pass yourself off as one of them?"

"What better way to get the inside scoop?" She smashed a crust crumb with her fingertip and let a slow smile spread. "It worked."

"Then how'd you get hurt? They didn't beat you up for being a poser?"

"No." She took a gulp of milk. "China was there. She saw me and flipped out." She left out the part about the gun. "She hit me with a stick, and then she passed out. I'm guessing she's on her way to juvie."

Gripping the bottom of the stool, she waited for a blast like the one he'd ambushed her with the night they'd met.

It didn't come. Smile lines framed sculpted Roman lips. "Gotta learn when to duck."

I thought I had. All her training in bobbing, weaving, and blocking, and she hadn't even had time to strike a defensive pose. "Guess I need some lessons." *If I'm going to keep up this charade.* "So it takes a woman making a fool of herself to get you to smile?"

"That's some of the best motivation I can think of."

Her head felt suddenly heavy. She propped it up with her hand. "You're really a lot nicer than your sister says you are. And you're cuter when you smile. You look scary when you're mad."

"Can I have some of that stuff you're on?" Nicky stood and walked back to the end of the table. He sliced the rest of the dough into strips, put them on pans, and set them on the counter next to the massive stove. He scrubbed the area where he'd been working and where he'd been sitting across from her, then lifted another enormous bowl of dough and carried it to the table. He punched the smooth, rounded dough until it hissed and fell, then dumped it on the table directly across from Dani. "Cinnamon rolls. Want to help?"

"Sure."

"Wash your hands."

She wobbled to the sink. Warm water flowing over her wrists seemed to slow time.

"You okay?"

She blinked. "Yeah. Sure." She cranked the faucet to cold and splashed some on her face.

Cutting the dough down the middle, Nicky pushed half toward her, handed her a rolling pin, and set out containers of butter, sugar, cinnamon, and pecans. Dani pushed the rolling pin out across the dough and winced. Without a word, he rolled it out for her then went back to his own. She didn't thank him in words, just nodded. "Did you always want to do this—run the restaurant?"

"In a way. I always thought when it was my turn to take over I'd transform Bracciano into something spectacular. I wanted to live in Italy for a year, just soaking up the atmosphere and learning techniques to make our food even more authentic. I wanted to keep the flavor of this place, but buy the building next door and turn it into an upscale dining room."

"What stopped you?"

"Life. And a father who can't handle responsibility."

Dani reached for a gob of butter and slathered it across the flattened dough. "What happened to your mother?" Her voice lowered of its own accord. "Is she still living?"

Nicky handed her a paper towel. "More or less. It's a long story."

Sprinkling sugar over the dough, Dani stared into eyes haunted by stories she wanted to hear. If she could stay awake. "I've got all night."

⚜

Nicky sharpened a knife and laid it on the table. "My dad cheated on her. A million times, according to the arguments I heard. One day—I was eleven and Rena was just a baby—my dad came home after being gone for three straight days. My mother handed Rena to him and waved a plane ticket in his face. She never came home."

Dani slid her hand over his. "I'm so sorry."

He didn't breathe until she pulled her hand away. He rolled his cinnamon-covered dough into a cylinder and cut it into one-inch slices then handed the knife to Dani.

"So that left you in the role of parent."

"Yeah. There's a lady who stepped in to help. That was huge, but Rena's not a little girl anymore." He looked toward the back door. "I see how she's messing up, and I get mad. So I yell and she shuts down, and we never get anywhere."

"She's at a scary age. One wrong choice can alter the course of her life. But you can't make decisions for someone else. I know. That's what I tried with China. Maybe someday I'll learn I can't keep taking on other people's problems as my personal project."

"No, you can't, but living with regret is worse than saying too much."

Her tired eyes took on new focus. "I get the feeling you've experienced regret."

"Haven't we all?" For a moment, he considered saying more. But he couldn't lose sight of the fact that she was a reporter. He stood. "You need to get back to bed."

"Only God can fix broken people, you know."

"Convince Rena to let Him, and I'll be forever in your debt."

She stuck out her hand. "Deal."

He shook it and held it. "Just name your price."

117

"I think I already have."

"What's that?"

"Lunch. Today."

⸎

"Look at this." Rena slid her phone across the counter.

Dani wiped cinnamon roll frosting on her napkin and read the text. WDYT ABT LN? CHI CRAZY. CHICK OK? SC. CM.

"Um. . ." Dani bit the corner of her lip. "It would be a lot faster if you translated rather than me guessing. I text, but I'm an English major. My friends know I'll go nuts on them if they do that to me."

"You gotta learn this stuff if you're going to be writing about us." She ran her finger across the screen. "This is from one of the Sisters."

"Sisters?"

"I'll explain that later. One of the girls who was at the beach last night. It says, 'What did you think about last night? Chi's crazy. Chick'—that's you—'okay? Stay cool. Call me.'"

"You got all that out of *that*?"

"Yup. You'll learn. I'll teach you." Rena set the phone down. "Last night didn't scare you off, did it? It was a freaky night. I keep thinking what woulda happened if Rabia hadn't charged at Chi like that. She'd be. . ." Rena shivered. "Anyway, do you still want to do this?"

Dani sucked frosting off the side of her hand. "I'm scared, but not ready to quit. If you think we can still pull this off."

Seven silver earrings, four in one ear, three in the other, jiggled. "I think what happened last night gave you a little street cred, girl."

"Even though I wasn't smart enough to duck?"

"You wait. You're already turning into kind of a hero." Rena picked up her phone and typed a message so fast her fingers blurred. She held it up." ICBW, BUT IMHO, UR IN.

Dani dug her fingers into her hair and faked a scream.

"I could be wrong, but in my humble opinion, you are in."

"I hope you're right." She fingered the bottom edge of her bandage and stared over Rena's shoulder, picturing the man who

118

slept upstairs. The man who was, now and forever, in her debt. Lines were blurring, and she couldn't blame it on the pain medication. Lines between her job and her heart, the law and her passion.

She forced her foggy thoughts back to the moment. "At least I think I hope you're right." She slid her hand in the back pocket of the distressed and now blood-specked jeans she'd borrowed from Rena, and pulled out a digital recorder. "We only have a few minutes."

Rena's spine seemed to stiffen. Her hand rose to her mouth, and she bit down on what was left of the fingernail on her pinky finger. "You're not going to use my name, are you?"

"No."

"And no one in my family will hear this?"

"No."

She got up and closed the door to the stairway, sat back down, and nodded.

Dani turned on the recorder. "Renata Fiorini, do I have your permission to record you?"

Rena swallowed audibly. "Yes."

"What do you see as the biggest problem facing—"Dani's phone dinged. She pointed the screen at Rena and shut off the recorder. "See? This is how old people text."

Evan's message—I'M OUT FRONT. ARE YOU READY?—forced her to gulp the last bit of coffee.

"So what's with you and Razzi? You said you weren't going out with anyone."

Dani laughed. Evan would be thrilled she'd used the nickname even though, after hours in the waiting room, she knew his real one. "We're just friends. We met at church, and I got him a job at the paper. He's an amazing photographer. Always my first choice."

"How old is he?"

"Twenty-two. He's kind of like the little brother I never had."

"Is he single?"

"Yes. He is."

Rena nodded. A slow, contemplative nod. "He's cute. And funny."

"I'll tell him you said that."

"Don't you dare."

"No names, remember?" Dani slid off the stool and picked up

the recorder. "I'll just tell him one of the girls from the bonfire has a crush on him."

"I do not. I'm with Jarod." No love-light lit her eyes. "So what are you guys doing today?"

"He's just giving me a ride home. I have a. . .lunch meeting at noon." She walked around the table and gave Rena a quick hug. "We'll talk."

"No." Rena grabbed the napkin and marker and scrawled T2UL.

Dani laughed, took the pen, and wrote a series of letters. TRKOTULU

"I don't get it."

Dani turned around when she reached the door. "Think about it. You will." She walked along the side of the building to the H1 parked in front.

Sliding into the passenger seat, she grinned at Evan. "I've always wanted a private chauffeur."

"Hope you realize you're buying me lunch for this."

Dani swallowed hard.

Evan pointed to a poster on the front door. "Let's come back here. They have a buffet on weekends."

"I really need some time to relax." It wasn't a lie. She'd relax. At the park. With Nicky. "How 'bout a rain check?"

"Tomorrow then. After church."

"That sounds"—her mouth felt lined with beach sand—"fun."

CHAPTER 14

Dani waved a honeybee away and pulled a sweet-and-sour chicken wing out of the box. Her fourth one. She rested her elbows on the picnic table. "This wasn't what I expected."

Nicky dipped a celery stick in bleu cheese dressing. "Do you eat potatoes for every meal?"

"That's a weird question."

"Gallagher. That's Irish, right?"

She laughed. "So there's more to you than pasta and pizza. I get it." She looked out across an expanse of green grass bordered by a split rail fence. In the opposite direction, birthday balloons swayed in the breeze under the roof of a field stone shelter. Two young girls pushed toddlers on swings. "Do you come here often?"

"A few times a year. When the weather's decent, I pack roller-blades and try out different parks. Pet Springs might be my favorite. I can't do vacations, so I need mini getaways during the week."

"I should do that. Kind of resets your brain." She glanced at him. "There must be some way you can do vacations once in a while. Your father's around some of the time, isn't he? Do you own the restaurant or does he? Can't you—sorry. Questions are my life."

"You're good at it." He shifted so he faced her without turning his head. "You'd think it would work that way. My grandfather owns the business. He's in a nursing home. My dad doesn't have the heart

121

to have him declared mentally incompetent. My dad's a chef, not a businessman."

"So a lot of the responsibility falls to you."

Nicky nodded. "We have good employees, but my dad and I are the managers and he's AWOL half the time. If I left I just might come home to no business at all."

"Does he drink?"

"No. He. . .carouses. It's embarrassing. When I got old enough to know what was going on, in my early teens maybe, he reminded me of some of the kids at school. Living for the moment, you know? I always thought my dad would grow up when I did. He didn't."

"Have you ever thought about striking out on your own?"

A ghost of a smile flickered at the corner of his mouth then disappeared. "Millions of times. But I couldn't stand watching ninety years of family history fade away."

"Why don't you buy it from your grandfather? If your dad isn't interested—"

"It's not that simple. My dad has a brother. They aren't talking to each other, but someday my dad and Uncle Sal will inherit the place together." He tossed a chicken bone onto his plate and wiped his hands on a napkin. "So what did you find across the street? What's this secret meeting all about?"

"It's not secret."

"You just didn't want anyone else to know about it. Or was it just the guy you were with at the funeral who shouldn't know about us. *This*."

"The guy is just a friend, and I don't want too many people hearing about *this*"—she tapped her bag with the toe of her shoe—"until we know more."

"The 'this' is in there?" Nicky nodded at her bag.

"Yes. Can't take it out till I wash my hands."

"They teach you that in school? To give your reader just a nibble so they want more."

"It's called a hook."

"It works." He held her gaze. "I'm hooked." Dani stopped breathing. He pointed at her bandaged arm. "How's that feel?"

Delicious. "The arm? Sore."

"You gonna stop pretending you're a teenager?"

No. "Guess I'll just have to brush up on my street smarts before I do it again." She tore open a towelette pack as she watched his mouth set into a rigid line. *When's the last time you laughed?* She picked up her cup of root beer. Two bees crawled around the inside edge. She dumped the rest of her soda into the grass and tossed their plates into a trashcan. She handed the diary to Nicky. "I found this behind the house across from the restaurant. It was in a basket with China's school notebooks. I thought it was hers, but it's not."

Nicky opened the front cover. "1924. Osseo. That's up by Eau Claire, isn't it?"

Dani nodded.

"It looks interesting, but what's this have to do with me?"

She sat beside him and turned to the page in the middle of the book she'd marked with a sticky note. She pointed to the entry at the bottom of the page dated June 24, 1928. Nicky's eyes widened. His lips moved with the words. *Busy but fun night at Bracciano again.* He turned the page then several more. His finger landed on an entry dated July 30, 1928. "Did you see this?"

Dani's arm pressed against his as she leaned over the book.

"Renata. That's my great-grandmother." His tone held a reverence that seemed completely out of character for Nicky Fiorini. "Look at this. 'Renata helped me find a way to hide the things T left. They are safe. I don't think I will ever see him again, but I'm afraid to believe we are finally free.'" He looked up, eyes dancing with questions. "What does that mean?"

Dani shook her head. "I'm still in 1924, and I hate reading the end of a book first, but I had to show it to you. I thought maybe we should. . ." The heat from Nicky's arm spread through her veins, melting her thoughts.

"Start from the beginning? Together?"

She nodded.

His eyes locked on hers. "I think you're right."

"Is she blind?"

Nicky rested his chin in his hands and stared at Dani next to him on the picnic table bench.

"She's fifteen. She's never been in love before."

"I thought girls were born with antenna to pick up those signals. Guys are supposed to be the obtuse ones." He shifted the church bulletin Dani had laid on the page to keep their eyes from wandering away from 1924. He ran his finger along a line of rounded, girlish script. " 'Theo can have dreams of moving to India, but I'm just a girl. I shouldn't trouble my empty little head over a silly notion like a career. I should only worry about embroidering luncheon cloths for my hope chest. Theo doesn't say such things, of course, but I know he thinks them. Men!' "

"I so agree." Dani looked up at him with laughter in her eyes. "Keep reading. Maybe she catches on."

" 'Sheriff Bakke came today. Mama shook so bad I had to pour coffee. Mama doesn't know that daddy's reputation for not watering down his product makes him popular with more than just the farmers. Mama knows the sheriff's car. She doesn't recognize his horse when it's tied outside the barn!' " He tore his gaze off the page. "This is priceless."

"Any idea what kind of trouble Francie's dad would have been in if the sheriff hadn't been one of his customers?" Dani reached in her bag, pulled out her phone, and typed in a question.

"I'd like to know what would have happened to the *sheriff* if he'd gotten caught."

"This says a thirty- to a hundred-dollar fine and or a night in jail and confiscation of your liquor. I wonder how much money a guy like this could make in a week?"

"It was da big guys what made all da mooo-lah, ya' know." Nicky doffed an invisible cap. "Da Big Fellow, my buddy Al—Capone, ya know? He had it figured out. Get the little people to do all da dirty work and you rake in da dough."

She laughed. "You're related to him, right? That's what Todd meant about you being descended from criminals."

"Best keep that to yourself, doll face." He wiggled his eyebrows at her. "You don't know what you're getting into, messin' wit' us Italians."

Her lips pressed together. Tiny divots formed in her cheeks. "You forget. I've seen the soft side of this one."

"I beg your pardon." He flattened his hand against his chest. "I don't have a soft side."

"Tough guys don't rescue shoes."

The wells in her cheeks deepened. He folded his hands to keep from touching one.

"So true. Tough guys"—He changed his mind and gave in to the temptation. The tip of his finger covered the dimple perfectly—"only rescue dames."

⚜

Her seventh-grade math teacher had a favorite cliché—"Don't check your brains at the door." Why did it come to mind now, and not fifteen minutes before agreeing to a picnic lunch with Rudolph Valentino?

Dani squinted at the diary entries and pretended she was sitting alone. She'd read of people lowering their blood pressure by visualizing tranquil scenes. If the pressure in her head and the choking sensation were any indication, she'd be suffering a massive stroke in a matter of seconds. *I am alone in this peaceful park. There is no gorgeous man next to me. No tanned, muscled arms. No burning hole where he touched my cheek. . .*

The offending fingertip landed on the page. " 'Suzette has a little boy. I still can't believe it. She wants me to come and help her. Mama and Daddy don't know I overheard. They burned her letter and said they'd never let me go to Chicago. But I will. It's not New York, but there are fashion designers there, too.' " Nicky yawned and rubbed a hand across his face. "That gets her a little closer to Kenosha."

"She's a fifteen-year-old farm girl. How's she going to manage in Chicago?"

"Is it bugging you that you can't give her advice?" The glint returned to his eyes.

"Yes. I want to fix her before she does something stupid."

"Save all that repressed fixingness for my sister."

She laughed. "I'll work on that."

Nicky went back to reading. " 'Today began with my hand in Theo Brekken's on the way to school and ended with my hand in a fist on Earl Hagen's nose, blood spurting everywhere.' "

"Go, Francie! What did the guy do?"

125

" 'He told everyone Daddy's a bootlegger. So I punched him. My hand still hurts, but I feel good. Theo walked me home. I tried to tell him I'm going to Chicago.' "

Nicky stroked the stubble on his chin. "Feisty kid. Not too bright, but gutsy." His shoulder tapped into hers. Not by accident.

"Gutsy is good."

"Not always." His expression hardened, and he turned back to the diary. "You want to read for a while?"

She silenced the questions begging to be asked and turned to the next entry. She ran her fingers through damp bangs. The spot of shade they'd found an hour ago was now dappled with sunlight. "Should we keep going or are you getting tired of it?"

"I'm tired but not tired of *it*." He glanced at his watch. "We won't get to the part about Bracciano today, but let's read a couple more." He stretched both arms out straight. Muscle shadows landed on the open pages.

Dani averted her eyes. She focused on the aspen leaves turning lazily over their heads. When the stretch was over, she swallowed hard and went back to reading.

" 'Applejack is sick. Daddy says something's twisted or blocking his intestines. He's tried everything. I've been helping him all day, but we can't get him to stay on his feet anymore. I'm so scared. Mama's downstairs on her knees. I tried praying, but I can't.' " She turned the page. The top lines were blank. She flipped through page after page. "The next entry for 1924 is November 8."

"What happened?"

Keep them wanting more. Mitch's motto flitted through her head. "Maybe we should stop here, with a cliff hanger."

"That's cruel."

But it will give us a reason to get back together. Soon. She closed the book. "You have to get to work."

"You can't look ahead without me. No cheating."

She rested her left hand on the diary and raised her right. "No cheating. I solemnly swear."

♔

"Thanks for the ride." Nicky grabbed the car door handle as he

126

watched a platinum strand drift lazily across pale, freckled skin. Would a quick kiss, just a brush of his lips across that cheek be out of line? Probably. Maybe he'd just squeeze her hand. "Maybe next time I'll pick you up."

"Don't know how you live without being able to hop in your car whenever you want."

"If my Javelin were parked here I'd be hopping into a car without wheels. But I have a bicycle and rollerblades and a delivery truck. What more can a guy ask for?" *Twenty-four hour access to a sleek black car. And a gorgeous blond in the passenger seat.* "It's not a problem if you don't have a life outside of work."

"We have that in common. But we can live vicariously through the adventures of Francine Tillman."

"When do you want—"

"Nicky!"

Heels clacked on the sidewalk. He turned to see Gianna, shopping bags and massive purse looped over both arms, heading toward them. He turned to Dani. "Do you have a minute? I'd like you to meet this lady."

"Sure."

They got out of the car and met Gianna on the sidewalk next to the side door. Her lipstick matched orange pants absurdly tight for a woman her age. Long gold earrings with red stones swung beneath huge hair. She set the bags down and pulled him into a smothering hug. She smelled, as usual, like the cherry-scented deodorizers used in public restrooms. He kissed her cheek.

"Gianna, I'd like you to meet Danielle Gallagher."

Dani held out her hand. "It's Dani. Nice to meet you."

Nicky put his arm across Gianna's shoulders. "This is the amazingly tolerant woman who raised Rena and me after our mom joined the gypsies."

Dani shook her hand. "Nice to meet you, Gianna."

"So who are you, Dani, and how do you know my Nicky?"

"I'm a reporter for the *Times*. I was working on a story one night, and Nicky called the cops on me."

Gianna laughed. "Hope I get to hear the rest of that story someday." She nodded toward the restaurant. "He home?"

"Nah."

Gianna turned to Dani. "Don't judge my Nicky by his crazy relatives. Whatever you've heard about us, it's all true. Not that I'm family by blood, but I've invested enough tears and prayers in this boy to count as DNA, you know? You ever hear of a generational curse?" She didn't wait for Dani to answer. "My boy's breaking it. He might look mean on the outside, but—"

"Gianna." *Stop scaring the girl.* Nicky put his hand on her arm. "What's in the bags?"

"Sheet sale at Target. I got plaid for you and. . ." She pulled a set of sheets from one of her bags. It looked like a used drop cloth. Gray background with splotches of orange, green, and blue. "I know she'd prefer black, but I thought this might appeal to her inner artist."

Nicky picked up the bags. "You know you don't have to—"

"Shh." Gianna touched an orange-nailed finger to his lips. "Don't be a blessing stealer." She winked at Dani. "You two going inside?"

"No."

"Well then I'll leave you alone and get to work. So nice to meet you, Dani." She picked up her bags and shot a finally-you-bring-home-a-girl look over her shoulder.

"Sweet lady." Dani brushed stray hairs off her neck.

"She's a saint." He ran through his next move. Grab both hands in his. Look into her eyes. *I've had a wonderful time, Dani. Let's get together—*

Bicycle brakes squealed. He turned to see Rena and her best friend half a block away. Rena's mouth opened wide then closed. She turned to Trish and said something requiring a lot of hand gestures. Trish took off in the opposite direction. "Dani! Hi!" Rena's smile seemed somehow off-kilter. "How's your arm? And what are you doing here?"

Dani's face reddened. "I was just—"

"Picking up a spinach calzone," Nicky filled in the blank.

"Cool." Rena hoisted her bike onto her shoulder.

Nicky held the door open for her then turned and took just one, not two, of Dani's hands in his. "Thanks for today."

She'd already turned the corner when he realized he didn't know when he'd see her again.

❧

October 2, 1926

Francie pulled her cloche low over her forehead and raised her fur collar to cover most of her face. She scanned both sides of the street for a two-toned Alfa-Romeo. Tag went to visit his mother in Aurora on Sundays, which meant Sunday was her day off. She was free to go anywhere as long as she didn't take Franky. Or get serious about another man.

Turning in the leather seat, she gazed through the square rear window, searching for headlights. "Kiss me quick." She leaned toward the driver's side of the Model A.

"That, my sweet, will require more self-control than this man possesses." A lock of blond hair fell across Albert Hollanddale's temple. His lips touched hers, but he didn't linger. "Next Saturday?"

Francie's throat tightened. Once again the dizzying tightrope feeling swept over her. With each passing week, the game grew harder to play. But if she didn't get out, didn't have some fun, she'd go crazy. She clasped the lapels of his trench coat. Behind the tan fabric, she crossed fingers on each hand. "It's my day to mind Franky."

"You take care of that boy more than his own mother."

If Albert only knew the half of it. "How about a picnic on Sunday?"

"In this weather?"

"We'll bundle up. Together."

He sighed, long and loud. "If I must wait until Sunday. . ."

"Peachy. Be here at three on the dot in knickers and a polo shirt." She opened the door and stepped onto the running board. Bending down, she kissed the tips of her fingers and blew the kiss across the seat. "We'll make believe it's spring." She hopped down and ran onto the porch of the bungalow without a backward glance until the car sped away.

Skin prickling, she looked up the tree-lined street, then searched the opposite way. Nothing out of the ordinary. She turned the handle and stepped inside. From the kitchen radio, Marion Harris crooned "The Man I Love."

She clicked both locks then hung her coat on the tree by the front door, petting the black fox fur as she stuffed her gloves in the pockets. "I'm home," she called, soft enough not to wake Franky.

The rattle of a cup and saucer answered her.

"Good movie, Suze. I was rooting for Jean Hersholt's character, but he didn't win the girl." She set her hat on the side table. "Pola Negri's part was a bit overdone, I thought, but she wore this hat that was ab-so-lute-ly delish. I have to make one just like it." She kicked her shoes off. Swinging them by the heels, she padded in chiffon stockings toward the kitchen. "Did you know 'The Secret Hour' was originally a play called—Tag." Her pulse thundered in her ears. "H—how was your mother?"

Diamond cuff links caught the light as he folded his arms across his chest. Cold green eyes nailed her. "Who is he?"

Francie blinked into character with a vampish flutter of her lashes. "The boy? Don't be silly." She leaned forward, letting her rope of pearls brush his knee. "You're not jealous, are you, Tag?" Straightening, she put one finger on her chin. "Oh my, I believe you are. I think I rather like that."

The eyes didn't change. "Who is he?"

With a move calculated to be alluring, she skimmed her hands along the pale blue crepe flowing over her hips. "His parents own the diner in the South Bank building." No need to mention that Albert's parents owned the bank, too. "We made a Sunday visit to his poor grandmother." Albert's poor grandmother had not seemed to take note of them as they'd snuggled in the car near her headstone at Mount Carmel Cemetery. "Just doing a favor for his mother." But he'd heard the part about the movie. "Thought we'd stop and catch a movie on the way home."

"I give you everything you need." His eyes roved to the opposite end of the kitchen. Suzette stood with her back pressed against the refrigerator, anger glowing in her eyes. "What do I ask in return? You stay true to me. I don't mind a little hanky-panky. I'm a tolerant man. But this—"

"He's just a friend."

Tag stood. Blazing eyes locked on her as he reached for his coat on the back of the chair. "Don't lie to me. I got eyes everywhere you go." He stepped toward her, bent down, and picked up Franky's fire engine.

"Tag." She ran her fingertip down the front of his coat and tried playing dumb. "You see other wom—"

"What I do is none of your business. We have an agreement. *Capisce?*"

"I won't do it again."

He grabbed her chin and jerked her head up. "I know you won't." He lifted her hand and slammed the truck onto her palm. "You've got a lot to lose, doll. A lot to lose."

He turned and strode through the living room, stopping only long enough to lift her coat off the tree and loop it over his arm before walking out the door.

Chapter 15

*"W*hy don't you buy it from your grandfather?"
Nicky opened one eye and glared at the clock. Five after eight—a.m. The middle of his night, but he hadn't slept. Dani's questions invaded his personal space like swarming honeybees. He turned on his side. *"Have you ever thought about striking out on your own?"* He angled a pillow to block the light. *"Why? Does he drink?"* He yanked the sheet free from the foot of the bed.

He'd read somewhere that people who fell asleep in less than five minutes were sleep deprived. It never took him more than a minute. He'd counted clock ticks and rarely made it past thirty. This morning he could have topped ten thousand.

Hiring, firing, inventory, and unpaid bills didn't keep him awake. What gave the girl with hair the color of a sun-licked beach the right to mess with his sleep?

She'd be a lot easier to dismiss if she only looked good. If she didn't also make sense. He got up, yanked the door open, and walked across the hall to the bathroom. He drank a glass of water and splashed his face. Trying to trick his body into starting over. But the questions followed him back to bed.

Footsteps climbed the stairs outside his door. Too heavy to be Rena or Gianna. His father knocked.

"Yeah?"

"Can I come in?"

"Yeah." Nicky sat up and stuffed two pillows behind his back.

"I heard you up." Carlo Fiorini took the rounded-back wood chair from the corner, flipped it around, and straddled it. Thin blue and black lines formed small squares on his short-sleeved white shirt. *Why was it he never wore T-shirts?* Khaki pants sported a sharp crease. It had never occurred to him before that Gianna ironed his dad's clothes.

"What's your take on things, Nick? Anything I need to know?"

Your daughter might be involved in a gang. I might have a girlfriend. I'd like to buy the business. "We need to get the new menu printed and think about hiring a new waitress. Maria's going on maternity leave. Friday night was nuts. Rena wasn't here and we got two ten-tops..." He rattled off facts as if reciting a grocery list. His father would look thoughtful, nod, slap his knee, and leave.

"I'll give it some thought."

"Hey. A journalist friend of mine was asking about our history. I was wondering if we had any old letters or anything."

"You have a friend who's a journalist?" A thick black eyebrow, scattered with gray, peaked. "Sal's got all that stuff."

"Why?"

"Why does Sal do anything? He's the oldest. He can call the shots. He can walk away and start his own place and still call himself a partner. He can bad-mouth our business and tell people it was my son's fault his—"

"*Dad.* So tell me what you know about the early days, about your grandfather. You used to tell stories." Nicky cleared his throat.

His father rested his chin on his arms on the back of the chair. His eyes lost their dullness. "This was a place full of music. My grandfather and his three brothers took turns cooking and singing. They played the *vihuela*, the *guittaron*, the trumpet. They say my grandfather had a voice to make ladies swoon. If my grandmother caught him serenading a particular lady, she'd pull him back to the kitchen by his apron strings. Can you imagine the laughter?"

Yes. I can. Maybe we should try that with you. "We should try live music."

Carlo Fiorini laughed. "No one wants that these days. They want to eat fast and get on with their lives. People don't linger anymore.

My grandmother used to tell of meals when she was growing up in Bracciano. Meals that didn't start until eight o'clock at night and lasted two hours."

"Is that what they tried to recreate when they moved here?"

"No. Americans were too busy, even back then. Even Italian Americans. They had to adapt to a whole new way of life. And remember, they opened during Prohibition. The words my grandfather used to describe the idiocy of an Italian restaurant that couldn't serve *vino*, I would never repeat."

"So they didn't serve drinks?"

"Never a drop of alcohol in this building. My *nonna* would not allow it. Her father was an alcoholic. An angry drunk. She joined the Women's Temperance Union as soon as they moved here. So"—he slapped his knee—"Friday night was good, huh? Things are looking up." He stood. "Go back to sleep. But maybe later we can talk, huh?"

"Friday was nuts, Dad. We got buried. Alonzo and I can't keep this up. We need another cook." *To take your place.*

His father chewed on the inside of his cheek and nodded. "That won't be necessary."

Nicky scrunched the sheet with the hand his father couldn't see. "Why's that?" Stupid to ask when he knew the answer.

"It won't be necessary. I'm going to be staying home more."

Sure, Dad, whatever you say. Now, about that new cook. . .

"Dani!"

The laughing voice floating across the church parking lot stretched Dani's smile. "You *do* exist!" She waved as Anna broke her connection to Jon's arm and ran toward her.

Anna, three inches taller than Dani before the three-inch heels, engulfed her in a citrusy scented hug. Strange that the girl who had it all dabbed her pulse points with Covet.

Sunlight concentrated on a square diamond as Anna pulled away. Dani shielded her eyes. "You just destroyed my retinas."

Anna laughed. "Oh, I've missed you. I'm so sorry I've been hard to get in touch with. Mom and I have been trying to pack as much as we can into—what happened to your arm?"

Dani tugged at her shirtsleeve and covered the gauze peeking out just above her elbow. She lifted her shoulders and let them drop. "It's nothing. I ran into a tree branch while I was covering a story on Friday. So what did you and your mom get done?"

"I took her over to the hall and we figured out where everything's going to be and took pictures of the chapel and—"

Jon cleared his throat.

"Let's save the details for this afternoon over dress patterns." Anna waved as Evan walked toward them. "Where should we go for lunch?"

"Applebee's? Olive Garden?" Dani positioned herself between Anna and Evan. *Anywhere but—*

Evan stepped next to her. "Dani found a cute little Italian place about ten blocks from here I'd like to check out."

"Love Italian. Let's go."

"I. . .um." Dani lagged a yard behind Evan as they headed for the H1. *I wanted to. . .wash my hair. . .do my nails. . .* She slid her hand into her purse in search of the prayer list in the church bulletin. There must be someone in the hospital she needed to visit.

Evan stopped and waited for her. "You okay with this?" He leaned down, forcing her to look at him. "Is it dangerous for us to be in that neighborhood after Friday night? Will anyone recognize us?"

"I don't know." That was the least of her concerns. She hadn't had a chance to tell Anna or Evan about Nicky. Evan might not catch on, but Anna's radar would pick up the heat, and she'd ask questions. So many questions. She glanced at her watch. Nicky would sleep for another hour. Maybe he'd go for a run after that. Maybe he'd run far, far away from Bracciano.

She pictured the dynamics of the gorgeous Italian walking into the dining room like a grid of laser beams. Dani staring at Nicky. Nicky staring back. Evan watching her then Nicky. Anna gaping at Nicky then her. Draw another line between Rena and Evan and what she had was a diagram of a mess.

"It said on the sign they have cinnamon rolls."

"Mm." Butter slid across the soft dough of her mind. Cinnamon drifted like gold through royal fingers. She tried to swallow but couldn't. "Delicious."

✧

"Nicky!"

Rena's voice clawed through layers of exhaustion. Nicky woke feeling exactly like he should after four hours of sleep. "What?"

"The fryer's overheating."

"Is Dad still here?"

"He said to wake you. We're in the weeds."

And he's cooking? What was happening to his nice, predictably dysfunctional family? His father was cooking at noon on a Sunday. "Eighty-six the fried stuff and drain the oil. Give everybody a fifty-cent discount and apologize profusely." In the latest ad, he'd posted testimonials about Bracciano's calamari and fried eggplant. Now they couldn't deliver. "I'll be down in a minute."

A shower would feel good. A run first would be even better. He picked up his jeans from the floor and stumbled into them. If he owned the place he would have replaced the fryer months ago. If his dad had to actually pay for repairs, he would have gotten rid of it. But repairs were free. *Go wake Nicky.*

He took time to brush his teeth. A small act of rebellion. He'd fix the thing but on his terms. Frank Sinatra sang in his head. *I did it my way....*

In the storeroom, he set his toolbox on the wrought-iron table then took down a box of hi-limits, thermopiles, and gas valves. He shouldn't have to keep all of this on hand. By the end of the weekend, he'd show his dad the jump in revenue since he put out the ad. That amount was going toward a new fryer.

Right.

He nodded at the three-legged chair the way he'd acknowledge an old friend. He needed think time. Hand on the light switch, he stared at a patch of wallpaper. Did Nonna Renata decorate this place as a refuge from the busyness or a respite from the man who serenaded customers a little too intently? He called up his one dim memory of his great-grandmother. Bumpy white hands with blue veins that reminded him, at six or seven, of angleworms. "Dominick," she'd whispered, her accent thick, "you have the light of God in your eyes. Never let it go out." One hand had lifted slowly and rested on top of his head as she prayed for him in Italian.

His father had translated the prayer. His mother wrote it down. He still had the paper, framed and tucked away in a drawer. *Heavenly Father, give Your angels charge over Dominick. Keep him safe from harm and the evils of this world. Show him the special gift You have given him. May he walk in Your ways always and may his children and theirs acknowledge You. In the name of Your son, Amen.*

A week later she died, with her hands folded on her Bible. Beneath her hand they'd found a card with the names of her children, their wives, their children, and their children's children. Her prayer list.

Her prayers had not kept her grandchildren's children from harm.

Locking the door he'd entered, Nicky walked through the one that led to the kitchen. His father looked up. "Morning." The man smiled as natural as if being there was what he did every Sunday. "The pilot must be shot."

Not likely. Nicky knelt beside the five-gallon can filling with hot oil. He reset the hi-limit and relit the pilot. It stayed lit. "It's the thermostat." *Again.*

"Got another one?"

"Of course. I keep a box of—"

"Nicky!" Rena popped through the swinging doors along with his name. "There's somebody out here who wants to compliment the baker."

"A regular?" He was in no mood to face the chatty, Sunday-dressed crowd.

"No. She was here once before. Actually, she's been here a few times." She giggled. "She says the cinnamon rolls are fit for a king."

"Do you cater?"

Dani watched Anna's mouth form the words then followed her gaze to Rena's bobbing head.

"What's the occasion?" A silver butterfly bounced amid the rings on Rena's left ear.

"Our rehearsal dinner. We have the venue, but we haven't decided on the menu. Everything here is so yummy."

As they volleyed food words—vermicelli, mostaccioli, parmesan, and penne—over her head, Dani stared at the house across the street and contemplated how and why every aspect of her life seemed entwined, like a ridiculous strand of spaghetti that began and ended at Bracciano.

Movement caught her eye across the street. A man walked out of the downstairs apartment where China had lived. He pushed a For Rent sign into the ground. Without a conscious reason for her action, Dani entered the number on the sign into her phone.

"I'll go see if my dad's free to talk to you." Rena's voice brought her back into the moment. "Not sure Nicky's going to show. He's in the middle of fixing our fryer."

Dani nodded. It had been Rena's suggestion, not hers, to compliment the baker face-to-face.

Rena left and Anna leaned forward. "Who's Nicky?"

Swallow. Speak. "Rena's older brother. He's one of the cooks. I met him while I was doing a story."

Anna flipped flat-ironed platinum bangs. "You are so going to tell me everything this aft—"

"Benvenuto."

A man in his late forties or early fifties stepped up to the table between Anna and Jon. "I'm Carlo Fiorini. So glad you could join us today. My daughter tells me there is going to be a wedding. Which one of you beautiful women is the bride?"

Dark eyes framed by thick black lashes stared out of a face lined with life experience. If Nicky looked like this in twenty-plus years, he'd still be causing women to tumble out of their shoes.

Anna raised her left hand and wiggled her fingers. Even inside, the square rock attracted sunlight.

"Congratulazioni."

"We're looking for a caterer for a rehearsal dinner. About forty people in all."

"Wonderful. My son and I would love to sit down with you and—and here he is."

The room tilted as Dani stared up at damp hair combed straight back from a perfectly chiseled face.

Rena popped up behind him with a pitcher of water. She bent low as she filled Dani's glass. "World's fastest showerer."

The room righted. "N–Nicky, I'd like you to meet my friend Anna Nelson and her fiancé, Jon Weber, and this is Evan Carr, he's a pho. . .tog. . ."

Across the street, the man who'd put up the sign held his hand out to a girl with long black hair.

Dani pushed back her chair and stood. "Excuse me."

"Don't." Nicky's hand clamped on her arm.

She tried to pull away. "I'll be back in a minute."

"Or dead." Eyes locked on hers, he let her go.

CHAPTER 16

One foot off the curb, Dani waited for a line of cars. As the last one neared, China looked up.

Stay there. Dani darted toward the back fender of the passing car and stepped into the street half a breath behind the rear bumper.

The man hammered the top of the sign. China turned her chin to the right and folded her arms across her belly.

Dani slowed her strides, kept her arms down, palms up. Four feet away, she stopped. "Are you okay?"

Tears gathered. No mascara rimmed the reddened eyes. Seconds passed. China turned, gaze landing on Dani's arm. "Are you?"

"I'm fine."

The man walked back toward the house.

"Turned my keys in."

Dani nodded. "I was afraid you'd be in juvie. I'm glad—"

"Miguel wasn't a bad person." Dark tendrils framing China's face quivered. Her breath shuddered. "No one ever loved him until me. He didn't know how to give back. I thought I could show him. I thought I could make him feel whole. But it didn't work. I couldn't—"

"It wasn't your job." Dani took a step toward her.

"It was his mother's job. A mother should love her child no matter what. No matter what people tell her, she should love her baby." She looked up, eyes glazed, her face expressionless.

140

"China, Miguel was—"

"Maybe it *was* my job to make him whole, and I just didn't do it right. Maybe I didn't listen like I should. Maybe if I'd heard things he wasn't saying, picked up on things, I could have made it all right. If I had more time. . ."

"No one can do that for another person. It's not our place to make someone else feel whole." She sucked in a breath. "Only God can do that."

China raised her chin. Tears coursed down pale cheeks. Dull eyes met Dani's. "Then why didn't He?"

Dani opened her mouth, took another step, and stretched out her hand.

"You think you have the answers. You don't." China shook her head then turned and ran.

Strong hands grasped Dani's shoulders.

Evan. *Always there when I—*

"You said what she needed to hear."

Nicky. His breath feathered her cheek. Heart slamming her ribs, she didn't move, just breathed in the fresh-showered smell of him.

"I shouldn't have tried to stop you. You knew what you were doing. This time."

"I wish."

"You did the right thing." He paused. A long, breath-tickling-cheek moment. "But you still don't have any street smarts."

She heard the smile in his voice. "It takes a woman making a fool of herself to make you smile."

His grip tightened. "Not this time. This time it took a woman doing what she believes in."

"Whoooo is he?"

Anna stood in the doorway of her apartment, not bothering to invite Dani in or even to waste breath on common courtesies like "Hello."

"He's just a guy who's giving me some info for a story."

"Right. And Jon's just a guy I hang out with once in a while." Anna stepped back, opening the door wide. "You have approximately ten minutes until my mother gets back to tell me how you met, how many times you've seen him, every word he's said, and what his intentions are."

Dani tumbled inside, kicked her shoes off, and followed Anna onto the balcony overlooking a courtyard. A glass-topped table held wedding books, fabric swatches, a plate of cookies, and a pitcher of lemonade.

"You're the perfect hostess."

"Thank you. I was just sitting here imagining the courtyard with banquet tables, lots of candlelight, floral centerpieces to match my colors, and a buffet of the best Italian food I've ever eaten, cooked by a guy you haven't told me about yet." She filled two glasses, thrust one at Dani, and sat down. "Sit. Spill."

Settling into a white wicker chair, Dani took a long drink. She pulled her phone out of her purse, set it on the arm of the chair, smoothed her blouse, and smiled coyly.

Anna glared. "Talk. Fast."

Dani held the glass to her forehead. Leaving out trespassing in the apartment, she recapped the story, starting with the call from China. When she got to the part about Nicky saving her, and her shoe, from a near nosedive, Anna stopped her.

"That's so Cinderella-ish."

"Yeah. He said that, too."

"He called you Cinderella?"

She moved the glass to her cheek and nodded.

"So what's next? What's going on in your head? When are you going to see him again?"

She'd save explaining the diary for later, when she knew what it was all about. "We didn't make any plans. I needed some facts about the history of the restaurant, and he was going to check with his dad—"

"Who, by the way, is like *wow*. He's old and I'm happily almost married, but the man made my knees weak. What a charmer. 'Which one of you beautiful ladies is the bride?' That whole accent thing. . . Okay, back to Nicky. You like him, of course. But how much?"

Dani slid the glass to the side of her neck. "Can you imagine how many girls are standing in line for a date with a guy who looks like that?"

"Who cares? Just get to the head of the line and stay there."

Closing her eyes, Dani shook her head. "You're a lousy accountability partner."

"I am not. I'm keeping you from talking yourself out of what just might be God's will for your life."

"How about focusing your energies on talking me out of a guy I have absolutely nothing in common with?" Her phone dinged. "I have no idea what he believes. I don't know if he's ever even been out of Kenosha. He works six nights a week." She picked up her phone. "We're from opposite sides of the tracks, completely different backgrounds. Not that *I* care, but can you imagine me telling my parents I'm going out with a guy who makes pasta for a living?" She touched the screen. "And why are we having this conversation, anyway? I have no idea if he's even interes. . .ted." She stared down at the text.

ARE YOU BUSY MONDAY NIGHT? THOUGHT WE COULD READ SOME MORE. AFTER TAPAS AT PAZZO'S.

"Him?" Anna jumped out of her chair and bent over Dani's shoulder. "Yep. You're right. I need to save you from possible heartache. Let's go shopping Monday night and then go get manis and pedis and—"

"Not on your life."

⬥

Her phone rang as she pulled out of Anna's driveway. She answered without looking at it.

"Dani? This is Todd. Metzger? The policeman?"

"Yes." *Uh. . .* "Hi, Todd, how are you?" *And what do you want with me?*

"This is really late notice, but I was wondering if you'd be interested in going to the coffeehouse thing at my church tonight. I'm only playing a few sets, so it's not like I'd leave you stranded all night. It starts at seven. I could pick you up." He laughed. "Guess I should have stopped at 'Would you be interested?' and let you answer."

Would I be interested? I don't know. Is this social? Professional? Are you asking me out on a date or to pick my brain about Miguel's death

143

or to appease Lavinia or warn me about Nicky? The last possibility intrigued her. The guy probably knew Nicky better than anyone. But how do you ask a guy about another guy you're interested in if the guy is asking you out because he's interested in you? "That sounds fun. I'm just on my way home, but I don't have plans for the rest of the evening."

"Great. Oh, and just to put your mind at ease, I promise I won't be asking a single cop question, okay?"

Cross that one off the list. "I appreciate that."

"And I think it might be best not to mention this to Lavinia. She gets a little. . ."

"Intense. I know." Check two. That left actual interest, or a warning.

"I know we're 'practically neighbors,' but where do you live?"

She gave him the address.

"I'll pick you up about quarter after six then. We usually wrap up around nine, and then I thought maybe we could go out for pizza. If that's not too late for you."

"I'm a night owl. That sounds good."

"What do you like on your pizza?"

"Everything but anchovies."

"Great. Me, too. I'll call ahead and let Nicky know to have it ready. Bye."

"Bye." She croaked her closing word and turned off the phone.

Did everything lead back to Bracciano? She closed her eyes, picturing a ridiculously long piece of spaghetti. One never-ending snake of linguine entangling every piece of her life.

♛

Dani sat at a table with three of Todd's friends. Until the music started, they'd sipped iced tea and chatted over popcorn and trail mix. When the lights dimmed and soft guitar chords lured them into worship, all talk stopped. Todd's drumsticks tapped out the opening rhythms of "He Reigns." A keyboard and three guitars joined him.

Dani sang to the beat vibrating in her chest. At the next table, a girl with short bleached hair nodded in time to something other than the music. Something in her spirit. Dani imagined China in this place, arms raised, grateful tears streaming down her face. *Lord, she needs you.*

As always, the song birthed a picture of the earth from outer space. Millions of voices rising in a grateful choir from every continent, praising God in thousands of languages and dialects, all blending in one glorious song of joy. This time, as the chorus filled the room, she imagined China, Rena, Jarod, Scope, Broom. . .maybe Nicky. . .standing mute on the sidelines. Without a song to sing.

Her chest ached.

The song ended. Another one began, more piercing than the first. Matthew West's "My Own Little World." Dani brushed away a tear. Todd caught her eye and nodded. Not to the beat of his drums.

The tightening of her chest, the pressure behind her eyes, was a familiar sensation. When Jesus' disciples healed a lame man, the man went away "walking and leaping and praising God." People saw him and were filled with wonder. Curling the edge of a napkin, Dani let conviction wash over her with the words of the song.

When it ended, Todd set his drumsticks down and pulled the mic close to his mouth. "I don't know about the rest of you, but that song always makes me question what I'm doing to make a difference. In my job I see abuse and addiction, rage and loneliness daily. I've had to harden myself to a lot of it just to be able to do what I have to, but the faces haunt me sometimes, especially the innocent ones, the victims. I could do so much more. What are we—the church, the hands and feet of Jesus—doing to bring light into their darkness?"

He picked up two black-handled brushes and began a soft, hushed cadence. His eyes connected with hers. "Lord, show us the greater purpose so we can start living it out."

Dani nodded and mouthed *Amen.*

♛

"You'd be amazed how many life lessons you can squeeze into a game of horse or one-on-one." Todd eased the car to a stoplight. "A kid who would never answer a direct question if you were sitting face-to-face will open up with a ball in his hands."

"I made an appointment to tour the Boys and Girls Club. Can

I get some insider quotes from you?"

"Sure."

"Does Nicky ever join you?"

Todd clicked his tongue. "This is going to sound rude, but every time I hear or play 'My Own Little World,' I think of Nicky."

"Why? Is he really that self-focused?"

"Yes." One shoulder shrugged. "Maybe self-protective is a better word. We used to get games together with the kids in the neighborhood. They loved Nicky. He was good with them, but something happened four years ago that changed everything."

"What happened?"

"You should ask him. He needs to talk about it. Maybe your reporter skills can draw him out. Someday something's going to crack that wall. Once in a while I can distract him, and the old Nicky comes out—funny as all get-out, and man, what a way with the women. That Italian charm just knocked 'em dead."

She wasn't sure she could handle meeting the old Nicky.

"If we're working on his car or I get him out on my uncle's boat, he forgets for a while. Hey, you don't want to hear about Nicky."

Actually. . .

A boy in sagging jeans sidled through the intersection, holding his pants up with one hand. Todd tipped his head toward him. "That kid right there needs somebody to care enough to spend time with him. He needs a Nicky in his life."

"The old Nicky."

Todd nodded.

"So you really believe the face time makes a difference."

"I'm seeing it. Kids join gangs for a lot of reasons. They're bullied into it, or they want protection, but the bottom line for most of them is a place to belong. If they don't feel wanted at home, they'll find a place where they are. Give them a good place that feels like family and lets them just be kids with the right kind of people watching their backs and they thrive. I mean, it's not that simple. There are so many influences on a kid, but I see it working all the time."

"What can you tell me about the Sevens?"

Todd shook his head slowly and sighed. "They aren't much of a problem yet. Just a neighborhood gang, but we've seen some changes.

A few of the smaller gangs have merged. I picture the whole Midwest like a big sticky web with Chicago right in the middle. Like a black hole. There are a lot of wannabes around here, kids who wear the colors, talk the talk. A lot of them are taggers—they get involved in graffiti wars, but nothing else. Most of them will probably break away and lead decent lives, but the ones who really scare me are the kids who don't fit in anywhere. They're so desperate to belong they'll do whatever they're told. It's like those kids walk around with targets on their backs. Leaders watch for loners and suck them into the system. I see that look of desperation in a kid, even if he's only nine or ten, and I know I'm going to be putting cuffs on him someday."

"That's so sad. But you're doing your part. You've found your greater purpose."

"For now."

"I envy you."

He turned to her and smiled. "I know that kid we just saw. You tell people his story, and you'll break their hearts. You'll move them to move, to do something about the problem. Can't you see God's hand in that?" He turned a corner and Bracciano came into view.

Dani's pulse skipped.

Todd parked behind the restaurant. As they walked along the side of the building, he grabbed her arm. "This way." He nodded toward the side door.

Her stomach doubled over like a slab of just-punched bread dough. "Here?" she squeaked.

"Sure. The rush is over. We can eat in the kitchen."

With Nicky. Her knees stiffened. Did Todd know she had plans with Nicky on Monday? Did Nicky know who Todd was bringing to share his pizza? Were they competing or clueless? *Speaking of clueless.* She pressed her hand to her right eye. *It's not a date, Nicky. Todd and I just came from church. It's not a date, Todd. Nicky and I are just doing research. Over tapas and candlelight.*

October 7, 1926

Franky was asleep. Tag didn't need her. Strange to be home on a Friday night, but then everything about the week since Tag had caught her with Albert had been odd. She was sure he was having the house watched. She'd seen the same car parked three doors down every day. Twice she'd seen a man in a suit get out, lean against the car, and smoke a cigarette. She hadn't bothered to check the back. There was probably someone out there, too.

Strange, also, that it barely fazed her.

Francie tucked her legs beneath her on the pink chenille rug. Leaning against the ruffles of her bed skirt, she dog-eared another page in McCall's. She couldn't decide if she liked the spring green silk chiffon with the tiered petal skirt better than the black net with the handkerchief hemline. Both had beading, which she loved to do. "Black for evening, green for day." She clicked her tongue to add finality to her decision. "When in doubt, choose both."

But where would she wear them? Out with Albert? She laughed to herself. Tag didn't like it when she wore her own creations. Made him feel cheap.

Her mood was quickly becoming as stale as the room. She jumped up and opened the window. A cool breeze rustled the curtains and turned a page in the magazine. It opened to an advertisement that caught her attention.

Wash Away Fat

and Years of Age

with La-Mar Reducing Soap

She brought the magazine closer to her face. " 'Results quick and amazing with nothing internal to take. Reduce any part of body desired. No dieting or exercising. Be as slim as you like. Money back guarantee.'" She bent another page corner.

Why hadn't she been born into her mother's era where rounded actresses like Lillian Russell were the epitome of beauty? Suzette ate like a farm hand and still had the body of a twelve-year-old boy. Life was not fair. And neither was Tag.

She'd pored over the stack of books on her nightstand the way Mama used to read the Bible. She'd combined the grapefruit and melba toast of the Hollywood 18-Day Diet with the slow chewing and daily enemas of Dr. William Howard Hay's Medical Millennium Diet and had lost the weight. Keeping it off was a killer.

In response to her thoughts, her stomach growled. She stood

and took a long drink from the water glass on her vanity. Water cleansed and flushed and could fool your body into thinking it wasn't hungry.

Standing sideways, she appraised the figure in the floor-length dressing gown. "You're one foxy lady, Francie Tillman." She said it in a low voice, imitating Tag's. Her lip curled, and she sank onto her vanity stool. She'd transformed herself into the woman Tag wanted her to be. But inside she was just an eighteen-year-old farm girl, transplanted but not at home in the city.

She opened a drawer and pulled her diary from beneath a stack of hankies. As she wrote the date with a gold-nibbed fountain pen, a gift from Tag, the words on the pen registered in her mind: SHEAFFER PEN CO./LIFETIME PEN.

Lifetime. Like her sentence.

She lifted the pen from the paper. The phone rang. Jumping up to answer before the shrill ring woke Franky, she slid across the polished wood floor to the alcove in the hall. She lifted the candlestick phone. "Hello?"

"Francie?"

"Albert."

"What's going on?" His voice shook. "A man came into the bank asking about you. Are you involved with him?"

Francie took a tight breath and painted on her smile. "You know you're the only boy for me."

"I don't know that. I don't know any such thing."

"I'll bet it was one of those guys we met bowling last week. I told you all about the boys hanging around us girls after you left, remember? It was all perfectly harmless. I bet they're just trying to razz you and have a little fun."

"There was nothing fun about this man. He was over six feet tall and had arms like tree trunks."

So Tag had sent his brother to check him out. "I'm sure it's nothing. I don't know anyone who looks like that." It suddenly dawned on her that her casual response might actually be making her look more suspicious. "Albert?"

"What?"

"I'm sorry you had to go through this. I can't imagine who

149

that man was or what he has to do with me, but that had to be frightening."

"We'll get to the bottom of this." His tone had softened drastically. "I promise. I'll talk to the police."

Her pulse skipped. Somehow she had to stop him from reporting it. "I really can't talk now. Let's decide the right course to take when we're together. I can't wait to be with you. I'll feel so much safer when we're together." She did her best to act the part of a wilting violet. "Let's meet at the park on Sunday."

"I suppose a public place like that is safe."

She laughed. "I don't think anyone's tailing me like they do in detective novels."

"This isn't funny."

"I just think you're overreacting a bit."

"The man. . .as he was leaving. . .I saw a shoulder holster."

Francie closed her eyes. *Stupid move, Tag.*

"Did you hear me, Francie? The man had a *gun*."

CHAPTER 17

A timer buzzed. Nicky strode toward the oven, keeping Todd and Dani in his peripheral vision. His irritation ping-ponged between the guy who was supposed to be his best friend and the girl who'd vowed, "No cheating, I solemnly swear."

Too bad it didn't apply to men.

He smacked the timer button and yanked the handle on the middle door of the pizza oven. Shoving a spatula under the crust, he gave serious thought to catapulting sausage, pepperoni, and mushrooms across the kitchen.

Stay cool, Fiorini. Or at least look it. He slid the pizza onto a pan. Instead of picking it up by the edge, he balanced it on his fingertips. As he ambled across the room, heat from the crust seeped into the aluminum and transferred to his skin. Pain radiated down his arm. As he reached the counter, his reflexes reacted without permission from his brain. Or his pride. His hand dipped. The pan tipped. Dani jumped off her stool, hands out. She caught the pan by the cool edge at the same moment his other hand figured out what was happening. Eyes locked, they lowered it together.

"That was a close one," Todd said.

Dani laughed, high and stilted. Like the shoe he'd slipped from her foot.

"Fast work." She had to know he wasn't talking about the pizza.

"What do you two want to drink?" Had he really put that much emphasis on *two*? He headed for a rack of glasses. He didn't care what they wanted to drink.

His father walked in carrying a mountain of dirty dishes on a round tray. On one hand, steady as a rock. He set the tray down and bowed to Dani. "Danielle, *si*?" The man was second-generation American, born and raised in Wisconsin, yet he could conjure the just-off-the-boat routine at the bat of a female eye.

"Call me Dani. Nice to see you again, Mr. Fiorini." She smiled coyly.

If three made a triangle, what do you call four—when one was as old as dirt?

"I did not have time to talk much on Sunday." The accent deepened. "My son tells me nothing. My daughter says you work for the paper. So you are the journalist friend asking about our history. Si?"

Dani nodded. "I don't have any specific questions yet, but I'm doing some research, and I'd love to sit down with you in a week or two if you'd be willing."

"I would love that." He pulled a basket of calamari out of the fryer.

Nicky filled two glasses with 7UP. Todd's slopped over the side when he set it down.

The swinging doors opened again. Rena walked in, head down. "One chicken parm, two gnocchi, one white, one red." She hung the order on the wheel and turned around. "Hey! Dani, you gotta just move in here, girl."

"Renata! Show a little respect."

"Sure, Pops." She ladled minestrone into three soup cups. "What are you guys up to?"

"Todd invited me to his church tonight. I got to hear him play."

"Poor you. He and Nicky used to—hang on." She reached in her apron pocket and pulled out her phone.

"Not while you're working, Rena."

"Right." She answered the phone and walked toward the back door. Her lips parted. Her face blanched. Nicky made out four words: "I can't" and "Five minutes." Rena turned around, slipping her phone back in her apron. Without looking at anyone, she filled a basket with bread, set it next to the soup cups, picked up the tray, and walked into the dining room.

Todd looked from the swinging door to Nicky. "What was that all about?"

"She's seventeen."

"That explains it then." He took his first bite and mumbled his approval of the pizza, making Nicky wish he'd added the red pepper he'd talked himself out of.

Rena came back in. "Dani?" She shot a glance at Nicky then turned back to Dani. "I've only got a minute, and I wanted to show you something in my room."

Dani wiped her mouth with a napkin, nodded, and slid off the stool. "Okay."

Their footsteps flew up the stairs.

"What was that all about?" Todd took a swig of soda.

"They're female."

"That explains it then."

Nicky smacked two empty lasagna pans onto the counter next to the dishwasher. Dean Martin's voice poured through speakers in the ceiling. His father sang along to "That's Amore" as he ladled marinara into a plastic container. Not an environment conducive to punching your best friend.

"So what's eating you?" Todd garbled over a mouthful of pizza.

"Nothing." Nicky's gaze wandered to the back door.

"*Her*? That's it? You're ticked that I asked her out first?" Todd's laugh echoed off the ceiling.

His father joined in. "All's fair, my boy."

Of all the people unqualified to give a lecture on what was fair in love, his father topped the list. Nicky tossed a serving spoon into the sink and sucked a calming breath. He grinned at Todd. "Why should I be ticked? She's going out with *me* tomorrow."

Todd's eyes jarred wide. Nicky laughed. "All's fair, my boy."

"Go around back to the building next door." Rena stood on a stool and reached for something near the ceiling of her closet. "He'll meet you on the other side. There's a row of bushes. Just give him this and get back here as fast as you can." Rena's icy fingers placed a roll of money in Dani's hand.

Dani closed her fingers around it. "Who's out there? Jarod? You don't want him coming to the door because Todd's here, right?"

"I'll cover for you. I'll say you're trying on some shirts that don't fit me anymore. It'll only take a couple minutes. Here." Rena grabbed a hooded sweatshirt off a chair. "Put this on." She opened a drawer and pulled out a pile of shirts. "I'll leave these on the bottom step. Bring them when you come back in the kitchen."

The hoodie reeked of cigarette smoke. A moment of claustrophobia speeded Dani's already thundering pulse. She yanked it over her head and took the hair band Rena held out to her.

She still hadn't said she'd do it.

Rena lifted the sweatshirt hood over Dani's hair. "Walk down with me so they don't hear your footsteps. I'll keep the door to the kitchen door closed. Be careful when you come back in. Open the door slow so it doesn't squeak."

"Rena. This is crazy. What's going on? I'm not doing anything illegal or im—"

"It's not illegal. I earned this money."

"But why are you—"

"Do this and I'll answer questions. You want a story, so go."

Shutting out the warnings in her head, she followed Rena down the stairs and stepped out into the hot, still night.

The slap of her sandals reverberated off Bracciano's brick wall as she ran into the alley. The roll of bills in her hand grew warm and damp. Fighting the effects of adrenaline with every step, she passed the grassy space between the restaurant and the two-story garage. *Lord, what am I doing?* She didn't wait for an answer she didn't want to hear.

She slowed her steps as she neared the corner. Behind her, something clanged. A trash can lid. Her breath froze in her throat. She stopped, pressed her shoulder to the wall, and inched toward the corner.

"Have nothing to do with the fruitless deeds of darkness, but rather expose them." She'd memorized the verse from Ephesians years ago.

She shouldn't be here.

154

Do this and I'll answer questions. She ordered trembling legs to walk. Sweat trickled down her sides and she shivered.

In the bushes just feet behind her, a twig snapped. A figure stood between her and the street.

Dark eyes blazed in a thin, pale face as the boy neared. "How much?"

"I don't know."

"Count it."

"It's too dark. I can't—"

The boy swore and grabbed her left arm. Pain shrieked from the stitched cut. She bit back a scream. A moan escaped.

"Count it."

Trembling fingers unrolled the bills and held them in a thin finger of light from the street. "Twenty, forty, sixty, eighty, a hundred. . ." Where did Rena get it? What was she paying for? "Two hundred eighty-five."

"Lucky." He grabbed her good arm and pushed her bad one against the bricks. Points of silver light shot before her eyes like falling stars. A police cruiser drove by at a crawl, tires close to the curb. She tried to pull away.

His fingers formed a vice around her arm. "Rena trusts you. That doesn't mean I do. Don't forget that." He shoved her toward the alley. "Go!" His foot landed on the back of her thigh. She stumbled but caught herself. When she reached the alley, she heard the soft groan of metal on metal. Flattened against the back of the building, she looked around the corner.

White shoes, incongruous with the black, glowed in the thin light. Silhouetted against the light from the street, the boy crouched on what appeared to be a thick metal door. Curved hinges connected it to the brick wall. He raised his shirt, pulled out something she couldn't make out in the dim light and tossed it into an opening in the wall. He turned. Locking eyes with her.

Holding her breath she ran into the green space, pressed against the wall, and waited. Footsteps pounded the gravel.

Away from her.

Nicky tossed an empty pizza box at Todd. Rena pushed through the double doors and rattled off an order. Her eyes darted to the door leading to the stairs.

Something wasn't right.

"What's going on, Rena?"

"Huh?"

"What's she doing up there?"

"I had a bunch of shirts for her to try on." She patted her belly. "Your cinnamon rolls are making me fat. Oh yeah, that scampi wanted vermicelli instead of—"

The door opened. Dani came in with a stack of folded shirts balanced in one hand. Her cheeks were flushed. A pale ring surrounded her lips. "Are you sure I can have these? That's really sweet of you."

"Hey, they don't fit me anymore."

Nicky recognized the gray one on the bottom. It wouldn't be too small for Rena if she gained forty pounds. "You're giving her your Twin Shadow shirt?"

"Yeah. I thought they were cool for a while, but I got sick of their stuff."

Nicky scraped the griddle as he eyed Dani. "And you, coincidentally, got sick of Nora Jones, and now you're crazy for metal?"

Dani laughed. "This is my new paint shirt." She tilted her head to one side. "I minored in art in college." Her smile wavered when he didn't return it. She reached for her glass and took a long drink. The side of her right hand appeared bruised. He looked again. Dropping the spatula, he walked toward her. Not bruised. Paint. Mixed with grime. He'd seen the exact same color many times. On his own hand.

She looked up at the clock. "I didn't realize it was so late." Faint smile lines curved around her mouth. "I've got a busy day tomorrow."

"So I hear." Todd dumped room-temperature pizza into the box. "Here. Take this—in case you don't find time for supper in your busy schedule."

Picking up his keys, he led the way to the back door.

👑

"I take it Nicky mentioned I'm having dinner with him tomorrow night."

156

"He did." Todd stared straight ahead, the glow from the dash lending a bluish cast to his features.

"Did he tell you why?" She pressed her hand over the throbbing part of her arm. Her head pounded in unison.

"There's a why? Other than the obvious?"

She looked out her window. She didn't have the strength for this. The last time two males had fought over her she was nine and didn't like either of them. "I wanted some history of the neighborhood for a story I'm working on. Since his family's been here for generations, he seemed a likely place to start."

"And he agreed?"

"Yes. Does that surprise you?"

"If I thought he was doing it just for your story, I'd be surprised beyond belief. He hates reporters."

Now what? Make things worse by saying she wasn't interested in either of them? It had worked in third grade. Her two pursuers became best buddies—a friendship based on the common ground of tormenting Dani Gallagher.

They passed two boys leaning on a utility pole, smoking cigarettes. "Do you know them?"

"Yeah. Two *un*success stories of the Boys and Girls Club." He tapped the steering wheel with an open hand. "I just thought of something."

"What?"

"You need stories of kids like that, right?"

Saliva sat at the base of her tongue with nowhere to go. "Yes."

"So if you can go out for dinner with Nicky tomorrow night and call it work, why don't you go out with me on Friday night and call it work?"

"Uh…"

"You can ride with me on my shift—right here in this neighborhood. You'll get firsthand stories. What do you think?"

"I think…" *It sounds like a conflict of interests. For both of us.* "That sounds interesting."

Chapter 18

AREA YOUTH FIND INNOVATIVE WAYS TO EARN MONEY

In a Monday midmorning fog, Dani scowled at the line, pushed the backspace key, and tried to reword it. Kenosha Teens Create Unique Summer Jobs. She rubbed her forehead and took a sip of room-temperature coffee. The website created by a sixteen-year-old boy and his fourteen-year-old sister was colorful and creative. The two charged a flat rate for setting up and promoting garage sales and had almost more business than they could handle. Dani had spent an hour with them and had more than enough material for an interesting story. But it wasn't the story she wanted to write, and she couldn't keep her mind on it.

She picked up her phone and dialed Rena's number.

A sleepy voice answered.

"Good morning. It's Dani." She forced a smile into her voice. She needed cooperation not defensiveness. "Do you have plans for the next couple of hours? I'd like to take you out for lunch."

The time on the computer changed from 10:23 to 10:24. "Uh. Yeah. Okay. I have to be somewhere by two."

"That'll work. Can I pick you up in half an hour?"

"Sure. I'll be outside. Wait. Are you free the whole time until two?"

"I can be." *For the answers you promised.*

"Let's go shopping first. No offense, the retro thing's cool and all, but you need some girly-girl clothes for my brother." She giggled. "For *you* for my brother."

"Rena. I'm not. . ." Not what? Not interested? "Fine." When girls shop, they talk. "We'll shop."

⚜

Rena sat on the cement step and leaned against the side door. She spent too many afternoons working and never seemed to get her fill of sunshine.

Or maybe it was something else that made her crave light. She was tired of the dark, tired of feeling the need to hide in her secret room with the light off to shut out the world, tired of the person she became after the sun went down. She'd teased Jarod about being a vampire, about sleeping all day and prowling the streets at night. It wasn't funny anymore.

Ever since the moment at the park when Jarod took off his sunglasses, everything was different. He'd looked at her, but he hadn't seen her, and for the first time she realized he never had. One of his favorite lines was, "I look good when I'm with you." It used to make her laugh. Now it made her sick. That was her job, her role in Jarod's life. He was the winner. She was the prize.

A single cloud slid over the sun, stealing the heat from her skin. Blocking the light. She pulled rolled-up paper and a pencil stub out of her pocket. There was a song in the tug-of-war of black and white. The moment reflected her life. People like Gianna brought warmth and light. People like Jarod blocked the sun.

And where am I?
Child of the shadows
Longing for the light.
Dare not think of heaven.
Dare not long for right.
Child of the darkness
Cowering in fright.
Must not wish for—

The door handle clicked above her. She sat up straight and stuffed the pencil and paper back in her pocket as Nicky walked out and sat beside her. His hair stuck out and eyes narrowed in the light. Nicky was a night person but not by choice. "You look bad. What're you doing up so early?"

"Todd's bringing the car over. I'm going up to see *Nonno*."

"You're amazing. You get the world's best grandkid award."

Nicky shrugged. "You need to give him another chance."

"Nuh-uh. Nobody's ever yelled at me like that in my whole life."

"If you sit with him long enough sometimes things get clear for a while, and he knows who you are and he talks about the old days. He'd like to see you."

Rena shivered. "I can't stand that place. Old people smell."

"So will you someday." He nudged his shoulder into hers. "What are you up to today?"

"Shopping."

"With Gianna?"

"No." She turned to watch his face. "With Dani."

She hadn't seen the dimple on his cheek for a long time. He seemed to be trying not to smile, but it wasn't working. He turned and looked up the sidewalk. *Gotcha!* "So what's going on with you two?"

"Nothing." He pretended to act surprised. "She's working on a story about some things that happened around here back in the 1920s."

"And you're an expert on stuff that happened sixty years before you were born."

The smile popped through. "So maybe I like her. What do you think of that?"

She copied his smile as a little blue car pulled up to the curb. "I think it's just fine."

He stood before she did and opened the passenger door for her. She gave him a minute to poke his head in and say hi. They looked good together, and something had changed in Nicky in the past few days. She wouldn't exactly call him happy, but he wasn't blowing up nearly as easily. She got in the car, and Nicky closed the door.

"You ladies have fun."

"We'll try." Dani giggled. *So* not mature.

"See you tonight."

Dani's face turned pink, and she waved with fluttery fingers as they pulled away from the curb.

"You liiiike him. You think he's handsome." She said it in a singsongy voice. "You want to kissssss him."

The pink turned to the color of the stop sign in front of them. Dani put on the brake and put the car in park. In slow motion, she turned her head then her shoulders. Her eyes got squinty. Her lips tightened. "So this is how it's gonna be, huh, punk?"

Laughter spewed out. For a second Rena didn't even realize it was hers. "You got the street thing goin' on, girl. Scared me right outa talkin''bout how much you want my bro." With a smile locked in place for the first time in months, she fastened her seat belt and leaned back. Dani was a sunlight person.

Dani dipped her fork in french dressing then jabbed a piece of lettuce as she tried to figure out how to segue into deeper topics. They'd spent the last hour in the vintage corner of her favorite consignment shop, trying on goofy hats and chunky jewelry. She'd found the perfect dress for tonight—a pale yellow A-line from the sixties. Sleeves just long enough to cover her bandage, with a turtleneck and a bright orange belt around the hips. Rena had tried on a flowered gauze blouse that made her look very feminine. Dani bought it when she wasn't looking and surprised her with it when they got to the car.

The morning had gone so well, she hated to change the mood, but she had to. "What do you want to do with your life now that you're out of high school? Do you plan on staying at the restaurant?"

"What do I *plan* on doing, or what do I want to do?" Rena swirled a french fry in ketchup.

"Both. Let's start with what you want to do."

"I'd like to go away to college. I'm *planning* on going to school right here, if I go at all, but I'd love to get away. See something new, and have the whole experience."

"What would you go to school for?"

"Music. Or English. I love poetry and music and songwriting."

"The song you sang at the memorial service was beautiful. With all the craziness, I don't know if I told you that."

"Thank you. Yeah, that's what I'd like to do. Be a singer-songwriter. I don't have big goals. I don't need to be the next American Idol. I just want to get better at it and get a job where I can sing songs that make people think."

Dani set her fork down and leaned forward. "You're not the kind of girl I'd expect to be mixed up in a gang." There, she'd laid the question on the table.

Dark lashes closed then slowly opened. "I know," she whispered. Dani waited.

"Geography. If I had all the same heredity, but I was born to a rich family in a rich neighborhood, I'd be a whole different person. I'd go to football games and school dances, and maybe I'd be dating the class president or a guy who plays basketball and goes to church instead of. . ." She wrapped her straw wrapper around her finger and stared out the window.

Dani waited then moved on to another question. "Tell me about the Sevens. How do you join?"

Rena shook the hair out of her eyes, looked out the window for a moment then took a drink of her soda.

"You promised to answer questions if I did that one thing for you." *That thing you're going to explain before I take you home.*

"Yeah. I did." Rena pushed her plate aside. "The guys don't have to get rolled in or anything, they—"

"Sorry. Rolled in?"

"Fighting. Some gangs make the guys fight the leaders, or a couple members at a time, to prove themselves. The Sevens don't fight unless we have to. We're more about taking care of each other. Protection, you know? As long as a guy can prove he's got something to offer the family and he doesn't have any bad connections, he's in." Rena traced the path of a drop of water along the side of her glass. "I'm actually one of the Sevens' Sisters. We're the SS."

Dani cringed. "So the girls actually have a separate. . .group?" She wasn't up on the lingo.

"Yeah."

"What do you do?"

"We hang out. Sometimes we run. . .errands."

Did the girl have any idea how much she gave away by what she *didn't* say? "How do the girls get in?"

"There are two—I guess you'd call them levels—with the Sisters. To get in the first level you just have to know somebody." Her gaze fastened on her glass. "To hang with the guys there's an. . .initiation."

"So if I want to take this further I can get in because I know you."

"There's one other prob."

"What's that?"

"Hafta live in da 'hood, girlfriend."

"O. . .kay."

"You could move in with me." She grinned. "And my bro."

"Right. We'll work on that one. So, if you're one of the Sisters, and you want to get out—"

"You can't." She looked away. Another subject closed.

"Tell me about Jarod. What attracted you to him?"

This was the point where a smile should have brightened the tired face. It didn't. "He's confident. I like that in a guy. I see how my dad pushes Nicky's buttons, and it makes me mad that Nicky lets him. Jarod doesn't let his dad control him."

"How old is he?"

"Twenty."

And you're a minor. Dani filed the information away. "What else? How do you feel when you're with him?"

Rena shrugged. The straw wrapper snapped.

"You didn't finish your sentence earlier. You said if you lived somewhere else you might be going out with a guy who played basketball and went to church instead of what?"

Dark bangs slid over one eye. "You know, like we talked about before—Jarod's not the kind of person who wants to let you in."

"How did you meet him?"

Rena stared out the window. "Last year I was walking home after school and a guy grabbed me and pulled me between two buildings." Her voice shook. "All of a sudden, just when the guy was. . .Jarod showed up and pulled him off me." Something close to a smile curved her mouth. "Love at first sight."

"But things are different now?"

"I guess I'm not exactly what he was looking for."

"Does he ever talk about breaking up?"

"No. I'm still. . .useful." She tucked her hair behind her ear. Muscles bulged at her jawline.

Fingers tightening around a clear glass mug, Dani listened to echoes of the advice she'd given to China—words thrown back in her face to blame her for someone's death. *You're worth so much more than this.* "Are you paying him for protection, Rena?"

Face expressionless, Rena stared straight ahead. "Yes."

Afraid she'd break the glass, Dani pulled stiff fingers away from her mug and clasped them in her lap. "Does Jarod sell drugs?"

"I don't know."

Dani leaned in. "There's a door in the side of the garage building."

Rena nodded.

"What is it?"

"Why?" Rena tapped her foot. A telegraphic beat beneath the table.

"Jarod threw something into it." She analyzed every twitch of the girl's face as she waited for a comment.

Rena rolled the edge of her napkin for several seconds then her chin jerked up. "Did you tell Todd?"

"No. What does the door lead to?"

"Nowhere. It says COAL on the door, so I guess it's an old coal chute, but it doesn't lead anywhere. It's just a room."

"Who owns the building?"

"Nobody. It's abandoned."

Then the city owns it. Still trespassing.

"Nicky told me about it. He hid in it once when he was a kid, but he was scared of the dark. I'm not."

"What was Jarod hiding?"

Rena scooted to the edge of the booth. "I'm going to the bathroom."

Dani reined in her sigh, pulled out her phone, and flipped through her contacts for a listing she'd labeled FOR RENT.

This is insane. Mitch's words argued with her common sense—*"I think you were gutsy. I like that about you, Danielle."* And then Nicky entered the conversation in her head. He'd used the same word for Francie, and Dani had replied, *"Gutsy is good."* His reply rang in her head. *"Not always."*

Silencing Nicky, she dialed the number and requested an application then worked on her next few words. They weren't going to be easy.

Rena came back, sat down, and picked up her soda.

"What would happen to you if you broke up with him?"

Storm clouds roiled in dark eyes. Rena looked down at the time on her phone. "I have to get back." She shoved her glass aside. Soda slopped onto the table. "Jarod's waiting."

⟡

March 29, 1927

Opening her desk drawer just enough to see the mirror on her compact, Francie retouched her lipstick. With lips the color of maraschino cherries, she went back to typing invoices.

When Tag had made her apply for the job, she'd assumed she'd only be here a few weeks, but nothing had happened yet. She wasn't complaining. Her evenings were free to watch Franky.

She'd started as a clerk, learned to type at night school, and worked her way up to secretary. Tag had already told her to set her sights higher.

He'd also promised he wouldn't make her steal anything and said she'd be out of the way when something went down. She believed him. Tag had a distorted code of honor when it came to women. *"I may own you, babe, but you'll never end up behind bars."*

After each invoice, she allowed a moment to look around the room and out the window. As the light changed throughout the day, it caught new facets of the pieces on display. Emeralds set in gold, pearls surrounded by silver. Rubies, sapphires, diamonds. She paired each one with an outfit that walked past the window.

Wabash Street was a never-ending source of couture inspiration. The warmer it got, the more color was displayed. The thermometer outside the break room window hovered in the low sixties today, and the stick-thin woman walking past the storefront wore only a fur scarf over a champagne-colored dress that appeared to be silk. The skirt had godet inserts of deep, rich brown.

"Swanky." Doris, the other front desk secretary, chewed on the end of her pen as she stared, starry eyed, at the dress.

"I could make it for you."

"For how much?"

"For nothing." Though he disapproved, Tag kept her well supplied with fabric for her "little hobby." "I think blue looks best on you."

Doris put her hand to her collarbone. "You'd do that?"

"Of course." Francie picked up a pencil and sketched on the pad next to her typewriter. "But I'd make the neckline like this and make a scarf out of the same fabric as the skirt inserts. That is, unless you want mink like she has."

"You slay me," Doris deadpanned. "You got a sugar daddy or something?"

Her phone rang, giving her a reason not to answer. "Good afternoon. Walbrecht Jewelers. This is Francine, may I help you?"

"You do that so, so well." Tag's laugh filtered through the receiver. "You just say what you gotta say to make it look good, okay?"

"Yes, sir, I believe I can do that for you."

"I heard a rumor today." He laughed. "Actually, I started the rumor. Mr. Walbrecht's personal secretary is giving her notice soon. She doesn't know it yet, but she is."

Francie's hand went to her throat. Harriet Jones was the sweetest person. If Tag did anything to that woman— "Yes, sir."

"You're going to take her place. But first you gotta make yourself known a little bit. So here's the deal—the big guy has lunch at Berghoff's every day. I want you to bump into him and ask his advice about something. A pair of earrings for your sister, something like that. And you be real friendly, okay?"

"Yes, sir. I'll make out that order immediately."

"You do that, doll."

CHAPTER 19

Evan crouched beside Dani's desk on Monday afternoon, resting his chin on the corner. Absurdly sad eyes stared up at her.

"Any room in your packed social calendar for an old friend?"

"Hmm." Dani arched one brow. "It depends. Can you compete with Tuscan shrimp bruschetta and a ride in a cruiser?"

"As a matter of fact, I can."

She sat back in her chair and folded her hands on her lap. "You have my full attention."

"I offered to help one of the guys in my study paint his house."

"And you want me to help." She pressed her fingertip to her chin. "How thoughtful, knowing I love to paint and all."

"Yes. I want you to help."

"I was kidding."

"I'm not. Hush up and listen. It's an old house. Brick, layers of paint."

Dani tipped her head toward her shoulder. "If you think you're feeding me clues, it's not working."

"Hang on a minute. I was over there Saturday morning and staring at this huge brick wall. . ."

"A blank canvas."

"You're catching on. So I left there and went back to the beach and found the guys with the goofy names."

167

"Who love to paint."

"Exactly. And I asked them if they knew anyone who'd had experience painting street art."

"You're good."

"Not so good at first. They didn't happen to know anyone."

"Until you said there was money it."

"I might have mentioned a small stipend for helping me with my project."

"You're really good. And they agreed?"

"Once I assured them they wouldn't get arrested, though I'm guessing that concern has never stopped them before. They're going to meet me there on Thursday afternoon, and I thought, if you could possibly rearrange your calendar, you might like to join in."

"Join in—as in paint with them?"

"I thought it might give you a little 'inside' feel."

She'd had enough 'inside feel' to last her a long time. "I'll be there. This'll be good. We know at least one of them will talk. I need to get some emotion out of them; find out why they do it or if they've ever gotten caught, and what the consequences were. If all I have is a how-to on defacing property, it might not be so great for sales."

"We'll make 'em talk." He used his best *gangsta* voice. "A little food, a little dough. They'll talk."

Dough. Her brain drew a short line to Nicky. Her stomach rolled as she glanced at the time on her monitor. In two hours he'd pick her up, and she'd spend the evening trying to ask more questions than she answered.

"What's your story about this week?"

"Young entrepreneurs." She curled her lip. "I interviewed two dog walkers this morning."

"How cool to be you."

"It was fascinating. Really. But what's wrong with me that a story about what motivates someone to paint gang signs on overpasses gets my adrenaline pumping but talking to really nice, enterprising kids is boring?"

"Maybe you're living vicariously through the trouble makers. Deep down you really want to rage against society, but you won't allow yourself to break the rules."

Usually. "You may be onto something."

Evan groaned as he stood. "Well, I'm off to capture the artistic beauty of a bunch of sweaty bicyclers gearing—get it?—*gearing* up for the International Cycling Classic at Library Park. Bet you didn't even know that was coming up."

"Sorry. No. But how cool to be you."

Finger on the elevator button, Evan looked back at her. "That's not always a bad thing."

"What?"

"The rage against society. Jesus was a rule breaker."

As the elevator door closed, she tried to focus on the dog walkers in their matching pink jackets embroidered with "Fuzzy Friends," but the words slipped away like sand through her fingers. She wanted to write about Jarod—the kid whose face had haunted her all night. Gaunt, scared—raging against something. He'd come into this world a blank slate, just like the girls in the shiny pink jackets. At what point in his life could something or someone have intervened and made a difference?

That kid needs a Nicky in his life. The old Nicky—the one who cared enough to make a difference. She wanted to meet that Nicky.

She stared at a picture she'd taken this morning. Not Evan quality, but not bad. All feet—two pairs of pink sneakers in the middle of a jumble of dog paws. The girls had been giggly but articulate. Smart kids. Innocent kids. She'd asked what they did with the money they made. They both had savings accounts. The rest went to clothes and makeup.

At their age, she'd gone to Haiti on a two-week mission trip and come home embarrassed by her home, her clothes, her parents' jobs. The food they ate. The food they threw away.

Two weeks after the trip, the team got together to swap pictures and to support each other in the reentry process. The leaders reiterated the things they'd taught in the airport debriefing before leaving Haiti. *"People won't understand. Don't judge them, teach them. Don't lose what you've learned. Let the images and the memories shape who you become, how you relate to the world, and how you respond to Jesus."* They'd stood in a circle in the church basement and prayed while a slideshow of wide-eyed children with distended bellies played on the cement block wall. All she'd wanted at that moment was to go back. To build schools and dig wells and feed babies. To make a difference.

And then the mothers—in cheery Ocean Pacific blouses covered with palm trees and dolphins and fruit baskets—brought out the food. Haitian recipes, they'd said. Surprise! Corn fritters, fried bananas, pork meatballs, red beans and rice—more food than most of the Haitian kids they'd met would eat in a year.

Dani had made a vow that night.

It was the moment that should have changed her life forever.

♔

Nicky pushed aside an empty square plate. "I remember studying in a psych class in college—"

"You went to college?"

"That shocks you?"

"No. It's just. . .if I had a family business to fall into. . . I mean. . . that makes it sound like it's easy, like falling off a log or something, and I know you had to—"

He pressed his index finger against the blur of lips. Very soft lips. "I remember reading about children who go through some traumatic event, and they get stuck in a certain phase. I think you're stuck, Miss Gallagher."

The mouth opened beneath his finger. He pulled his hand away before it travelled to her cheek. Or hair. Or traced the arc of her eyebrow.

"I'll hold off being insulted until after you explain that."

"Have you ever been around a three-year-old? No matter what you say to him, the answer is 'Why?' That's you. You don't even come up for air long enough to eat."

"I'm sorry. I know I make people nuts."

"Did I say I didn't like it? I just don't want you starving to death before my eyes."

She picked up a stuffed mushroom. Instead of popping the whole thing in her mouth, she took a bite and set it down. "According to my parents, the "Whys' started when I was a year and a half. They bought me a storybook about a kitten named Curiosity."

"Did it die in the end?"

"No. But it had splints and bandages on every appendage."

He pointed at her left arm. "How fitting."

She smiled.

"Voltaire said, 'Judge a man by his questions rather than by his answers.'" He slid his hand over hers. "You ask good questions." Her cheeks colored. He pulled his hand away. "I'll read while you finish eating."

She nodded, wiped her hands on her napkin, and took the diary out of her purse. "I haven't read a word. Really. I was tempted but I didn't."

"I believe you. Really." He opened to the marker and centered the book under the light. She pulled a penlight out of her purse and handed it to him. "Much better." He ran his finger along the date. " 'November 8, 1924. My life has turned upside-down. I gave Daddy the money for Applejack and got a ride with two suppliers headed to Chicago. They stole a truck on the way. They talked about killing me. Maybe I would have been better off, but I have given up freedom because I had no choice.'"

"She got a ride with suppliers? They're gangsters! And what does she mean by—"

"Uh-oh. Here come the questions."

"Fine. Read."

Nicky scanned several pages, looking only at the entries at the top of each page. "She only has six lines each day, you know. It looks like she's trying to do catch-up. Mini flashbacks." He took a sip of water. " 'Daddy always says be careful what you wish for. I wished for money and beautiful clothes. I wished for a rich boyfriend. I have all of that now. I did not wish for someone to control my life, but I have that, too. Mama always says this too shall pass. I used to think that was true, that all bad things were for a season, but this is not a season. This is my life.'"

He turned the page, not bothering to read dates. " 'One thing I know to be true. If you look for good you will find it. My cloud has a bright and beautiful silver lining. His name is Franky. Suzette named him that because it was the closest thing she could get to mine and still be a boy name. He says the cutest things.'"

The next one was only two lines. "'What would mama say if she knew what I had done? How does God view a person who sells her soul to the devil to keep a child alive?'"

A tiny gasp escaped the lips whose softness still lingered on the tip of his finger. Dani pushed her plate aside and leaned closer. "That's all?"

He nodded.

"Keep reading," she whispered.

"'There are things from my childhood I want to remember forever. It helps me pretend that I can have that kind of life again. I need to record those memories before they slip into the darkness. My earliest memory is of my birthday when I was four. It was snowing that day and—'"

Dani sighed. "She's not writing anything about what's going on in her life *now*."

"It's not now. It's then."

"I know." She flicked her finger at the back of his hand. "Should we skip to the good stuff?"

"No. It's frustrating, but suspense is good, right?"

"Right." For the next hour he read stories of Sunday school picnics, a bee sting, and Francie's first ride in an automobile. The name Theo came up regularly—the boy who carried her books, shared his lunch when she forgot hers, and picked daisies for her birthday.

He rubbed his eyes. "That boy is so in love with her." He looked across the table. "And she is so clueless."

"*Is*? He *is* in love with her? She *is* clueless? It's not now, you know, it's *then*."

He laughed and turned the page, realizing in the first few words that Francie was back in real time.

"'February 21, 1925.'" He looked up at Dani. "She skipped right over Christmas."

"And her birthday. Maybe living in the past is easier."

He nodded. "'T asked last night why I still insist on sewing my own clothes—'"

"Who's T? Theo?"

"I doubt it. Theo seemed like such a nice kid, and she mentions him by name in her childhood memories. Seems strange that she'd do that if she's afraid to write his name when she's talking about her present-day stuff." He found the spot where he'd left off. The interruptions were growing on him. " '. . .when he buys me gowns from Paris. I told him I do it because I am impatient. That's true, but it's not the only reason. When everything around me belongs to someone else, I need something to call my own.' " He turned the page. "There's a sketch in the margin."

Dani slid out of her seat. "Can I sit next to you?"

He felt his Adam's apple slide up and wondered for a second if the thing could get stuck. He moved over. Not too far. Her arm touched his as she stared at the penciled drawing of a dress that billowed out at the bottom like thin curtains fluttering on a breeze.

She ran a fingertip along the lines. "It's gorgeous."

"You'd look good in that."

"I love vintage clothes. There used to be a shop downtown on Fifty-Eighth Street with clothes from every decade. I've always wished I had a time machine."

"Be careful what you wish for." He nudged her arm. "What decade would you travel to first?"

"Maybe this one." She tapped the diary page. "I love the styles from the twenties and thirties, and I love the thought of a simpler life. Economically things were bad after the stock market crash, but people pulled together. They helped each other."

He tapped the book, mimicking her gesture. "Some of them just helped themselves."

"As our Francie can attest."

"Every era has its good and bad, I guess." Nicky cleared his throat. Something about the *our* in her statement messed with his voice.

Dani yawned.

"Want to quit for a while?"

"No. I want to cheat."

Nicky feigned shock. "I can't believe you just said that."

"I want to skim for a while. Look for key words and important things. You do realize, don't you, that five years times three-hundred-and-sixty-five is like a bazillion."

"But she skipped a few days." He chucked her under her chin. "I'm all for it. If it were up to me, I would have gone straight to the end."

It was her turn to give a faux gasp. "Okay. You skim while I go to the restroom, but you have to stop if you get to something good, okay?"

"Aye aye."

She got up and the waitress brought coffee. He ran his finger across page after page. Childhood memories, cute things her nephew said, here and there an argument with her sister. He'd reached October of 1927 by the time Dani returned.

"Find anything?"

"Listen to this. " 'I don't think I mentioned that Suze works for T now. Don't know what he paid or did to get her. I hate the time of day when Suze gets ready for work. Watching the makeup go on, watching her transform into something she's not, deep down. I can't sleep at night thinking of her on the street.'"

"Whoa." Dani fingered an emerald ring on her right hand. "Her sister was a prostitute?"

"That's what it sounds like."

"These two are like living right smack in the middle of a. . .sin pit. Okay, take a little nap if you want. I'm going to skim."

Nicky closed his eyes. If he were asleep he wouldn't be responsible for his head dipping down to rest on hers. When it happened he was wide awake, and he figured she knew it, but she didn't move. The rustle of pages lulled him.

"Wake up. I'm in 1928. 'I feel so free at work. For now, it's a neutral country in the middle of a war. Sometimes when I punch the time clock in the morning, I feel like a refugee crossing the border to freedom. Before the doors open, I wander around display cases, pretending I am royalty, walking through my own collection and choosing the gems I'll wear that day.'"

"Gems?"

"The newspaper clipping!" She described an article that had fallen out of the book. "I bet she works for that jewelry store."

"I bet she robbed it and my great-grandmother helped her hide the loot. Our girl's a hard-core criminal, and my father's sainted grandmother is an accomplice."

"But did they set her up, or did she do it herself?"

"They did, for sure. Her job's a cover."

She smiled. "Or she's there to case the joint."

"Or unlock the safe for them." He pointed her back to the book. "Keep skimming. Wake me up when they break in."

He stirred when she fished in her purse for a tissue and blew her nose.

"Are you crying?"

"Listen." She stuffed the tissue back in her purse. " 'If I hadn't been so full of unreachable dreams, I might have simply gotten a job up north and sent the money to Suze. I might, right now, be in India with Theo. Will a man ever again look at me the way he did when he said I was meant to marry a missionary?' "

She wasn't actually crying, but her eyes were glassy. "It's so sad," she whispered. "I really want to skip to the end to find out what happened to her."

"But we won't." *Because we need a reason to keep on seeing each other until the day we no longer need a reason.* He hid a smile. He was starting to think in the roundabout way she talked. "Will we?"

"Maybe you should take it home with you."

Wonderful idea. He moved away, just enough to allow room to angle toward her. "Do you trust me?"

Green eyes lost their glassy sheen. She nodded. "You're not the tough guy you want people to think you are."

He blinked. "Who says I want that?"

"Don't you? Think of how you sounded the first time we met."

"I don't come off to everyone that way. That was justifiable anger. You were. . ." He let the sentence die.

"Dumb. *And* stupid. But even at Vito's you came upstairs with a major attitude."

"That was Rena's fault." He caught the twitch of her eyebrow and smiled. "But it bothered you, huh? You like me better without the 'tude."

Her eyes closed for a fraction of a second. She shook her head in what appeared to be a gesture of resignation. He'd take that. "Yes. I like you better without the 'tude."

Like a middle school kid who'd just heard the cute girl in the front row had a crush on him, he imagined doing handsprings on the way to the car. *She likes me!*

"Read." She looked down at the diary, a deliciously restrained smile gracing her lips.

He cleared his throat again. " 'I had a dream last night that I was trapped in a cage. It was smaller than the one they locked me in, but—' "

"What? Who are these people?"

"You're not a terribly patient person, you know."

"Of course I know. Patient people sit back and wait for life to happen. They don't ask questions, and they don't meet writing deadlines."

"But impatient people go crazy when they have to wait till next time to find out what happens next." He closed the diary.

"You can't stop there!"

He tucked it behind his back, inhaling the scent of her hair as she lunged for it. "Oh, yes I can."

CHAPTER 20

"Who was she?"

Through jaws clenched almost shut, Jarod breathed the question again.

"A friend." Rena lifted her chin and tried to pull away from him. "What did you hide in there?"

She pulled away from Jarod, watching his face in the streetlight as she waited for his answer. It was after nine, but he still wore sunglasses. She'd know if he was lying if she could see his eyes. If he actually said anything.

Leaning against the lamppost, Jarod flicked ash off a cigarette, looked up the street, turned and looked the other way, and snorted. "When I asked you to be my girl, did you think I was askin' you to be my mama? 'Cause I already got one of those." His laugh lifted goose bumps along her arms.

"It's my place. I have books and things in there. If you get caught, I'll look like an accomplice. I have a right to know."

He threw the cigarette at the sidewalk and straightened to a stand. "You have a right"—he pulled his sunglasses off—"to ab-so-lute-ly nothing." He reached for her. She stepped back. His hand clamped around her arm, squeezing until she moaned. The harder she pulled, the tighter he held. "I take that back." He yanked her toward him. "You have the right to love me." His laugh hung in the heavy air. His left hand dug into her hair. His lips smashed against hers.

Ignoring the pain, she tried to turn away.

"Is this how you want it? Don't make no difference to me. I like a good fight." Again, the cold, evil-sounding laugh. "Or maybe you want to introduce me to your friend. Maybe we'll make a deal. You get rid of me, I get your—"

Rena felt the car approaching before she heard it. Music reverberated through the sidewalk. Jarod swore and shoved her away. She fell, her knee skimming the cement. She gasped and he swore again. "Shut up and stay there."

A bright purple car with Illinois plates pulled up to the curb. The music shut off. She didn't recognize the car or the driver, but Trish's boyfriend, Rabia, sat in the passenger seat. His eagle tattoo looked like it was staring at her. Jarod walked over to his open window. "You're early."

Rabia didn't respond. "Got it?"

Jarod nodded and opened his jacket.

"Chick's cool with lettin' me in. We got a history now." Rab's laugh drifted up like the smoke still spiraling from Jarod's cigarette on the ground. "But just in case. . ." He held out his hand.

Jarod pulled out a gun.

Rena gasped.

Rabia pointed to Rena. "She gonna be a problem?"

Jarod handed him the gun. "Nothing I can't handle."

"See to it. Be at. . ."

Rena eased to her feet and stepped out of the circle of light. The lawn behind her sloped up from the sidewalk. She took another step into the shadow, and another.

". . .be the only one home. . .in and out like. . ."

"Later."

Jarod patted the roof of the car. The music rumbled to life.

And Rena ran.

❧

Dani stood on the sidelines at the preshift briefing on Friday night. She recognized streets and businesses and the name of a store that had been robbed several times in the past few months. After the briefing, Todd took her out to his cruiser—to begin a shift in her new neighborhood.

Probably wouldn't be smart to mention the lease she'd signed two hours ago.

"You've never done a ride-along?"

"In school we got to choose a ride in an ambulance or a patrol car. I chose blood and gore over coffee and doughnuts." She ducked the hand swinging her way.

"This is a state-of-the-art doughnut-mobile. It has all LED overhead lights." He gestured toward the top of the car. "The rack has a much lower profile than the old ones." His grin matched the expression Evan had every time he bought a new lens.

Men and their toys. "You've come a long way from Barney Fife's bubble light."

"Are you making fun of me, Miss Gallagher? This is serious stuff."

"I wouldn't dream of making fun of an officer of the law." She touched the glass on a spotlight fastened to the side mirror.

"You wouldn't believe how many people don't have reflective numbers on their houses or mailboxes. They call 911, we get to the neighborhood in time to save the day, and then we can't find the house. Somebody should write an article about that problem." He nodded toward the spotlight. "Also works well for blinding a driver."

"That sounds malicious."

"When I pull someone over, I park so that the middle of the cruiser lines up with the right hand corner of the vehicle on the side of the road. That protects my back."

"And you point the spotlight at the car's mirrors so they can't see you walking up to the car."

"Exactly." Todd opened the driver's side door and pointed out the radar system and mounted laptop then reached in and flicked a red button, turning on the lights he'd been bragging about. Red and blue light splashed the building behind them.

"Déjà vu."

"That had to have been scary to wake up to. But, hey, it's how we met."

Dani inched away. It was also how she'd met the Italian with the attitude.

"Go open the back door on the other side."

She walked around, opened the door, and stared at the stark gray interior. "It's hard." The whole back seat appeared to be one big piece of molded plastic. "No creature comforts."

"We can just hose it down when needed. I'll leave the reasons to your imagination."

"Gross. What are these indentations?"

"Handcuff room. See, we do make a few concessions for comfort. We're not as inhumane as some people think." He swept his hand toward the seat. "Get in."

She thought of the bottle of hand sanitizer in her purse as she slid in. "The seat belt is strange." She fingered the massive buckle.

"You, I wouldn't have a problem reaching around, but I don't want to be that vulnerable with a guy who wants to bite my face off. Literally. The cage"—he tapped the grate between the front and back seats—"is open on this side and Plexiglas on the other in case I have two passengers and the one over there decides he'd like to spit at me."

"My respect for your job is growing by the second."

"Thank you. Another storyline, maybe."

"Maybe."

"Put your hands behind your back."

The words, even though said in a calm tone, gave her a chill. She did as she was told. Todd closed the door.

She wasn't normally claustrophobic, but the cramped space and hard seat combined with a door that didn't open from the inside made her chest tighten. She looked up at the shotgun mounted on the other side of the cage and thought of a wad of money and a boy with fire in his eyes hiding. . .*what?* Mitch's words floated through her head.

Just keep it legal, Miss Gallagher.

Jarod's curses still rang in her ears as Rena ran up Trish's back steps and let herself in. She pulled off her shoes and padded through the kitchen. The clock on the microwave illuminated piles of dirty dishes. The room smelled of rancid oil. In the living room, somebody, probably one of Trish's cousins, slept on the couch. Someone else sprawled, probably drunk, on the floor. Trish stood at her bedroom door, wearing pajama bottoms and a T-shirt and rubbing her face. She closed the door without a sound when Rena walked in.

Trish flopped onto the bed. "Better be good."

"What's Rab doing tonight?"

Pulling her knees to her chest, Trish yawned. It looked fake. She wrapped her arms around her legs. One hand played with the hem of her pajamas like a fidgety little kid. "Taking care of business." She glanced down at her phone.

"What's going on? What do you know?"

"What do *you* know?"

For the first time in their ten years, Rena knew in her gut she couldn't trust her best friend. "I know he's got a gun."

Trish shrugged. "It's just for show."

Right. "So you know what they're doing tonight?"

Uncoiling from her fetal position like a snake getting ready to strike, Trish lifted her shirt, showing the 7 curled around her navel. "You forget what this stands for?" She jumped off the bed. She picked up her dark green sweatshirt, put it on, and zipped it, then pointed at the seven embroidered on the front. "You see this? You know what it means?"

"Quit the drama."

"*You* quit not knowin' who you're loyal to. You don't wear the colors, you hide your tat, you question everything. A couple a months ago Jarod was all that to you, all you could talk about. You woulda done anything for him, like it should be. Now you're talkin' stupid about leaving him. I don't even know you anymore. I don't even know if I want to know you anymore."

Rena's muscles tightened like a piece of steel stretched across her hipbones. For a second, she couldn't make her lungs expand. "Maybe stupid is not ever thinking about leaving. Is this where you want to be ten years from now? Still wearing the colors, your tat stretching over and over with Rab's babies? Bein' a nothing? Hoping you live to see your kids grow up? Hoping *they* live to grow up?" She slid off the bed, almost tripping over something. "I don't want that. I want to be somebody. I don't want to be *owned* by somebody."

As she walked to the door, Trish laughed with the same kind of tone Jarod had used. "You're gonna so regret it if you try leavin'."

"I don't think so. I think you're going to be the one who's sorry." She walked to the door. As she turned, she noticed something she hadn't seen when she walked in. Dresser drawers. Empty and stacked on the floor. The thing she'd almost tripped over was a duffle bag. The steel in her belly quivered. "Where are you going?"

"Vacation. We're leaving early in the morning."

"And you didn't tell me? Who's we?"

"My family. We'll be gone a week or so."

Hand on the doorknob, Rena stared. "You forget. I know *you.* And I know when you're lying." Without saying good-bye, she turned her back on the girl who once shared all her secrets—and wondered if she'd ever see her again.

♔

The claustrophobic feeling didn't leave. Dani had expected the ride to be exhilarating, but as she sat in the narrow space between the passenger door and the laptop mounted between the seats, watching Todd approach a car he'd just pulled over, anxiety kicked in. The Kevlar vest bit into her ribs, and she fought the sensation that she couldn't completely fill her lungs.

China had left the beach in a car like this. Dani had hid from one in the dark with a roll of cash in her hand. The boy who'd hid something in a coal chute should have been picked up in one. Because of her, he'd gotten away.

Dash lights and a soft glow from the computer lit the interior. Red and blue lights strobed the pavement and the gray siding of a warehouse. The spotlight bathed Todd in white light. He knocked on the driver's window. "Open the window, sir." His words piped into the car.

Reaching into her purse, Dani pulled out her recorder and turned it on. With the pen and notebook already in her hand, she wrote her impressions. He took the man's license, asked several questions, and came back to the cruiser. She recorded his gestures

182

and the expressions on his face as he ran a check on the license and plates. And for once she didn't ask questions.

Todd gave the driver a ticket and came back to the cruiser. "I was fully expecting the guy to be intoxicated. Driving without headlights is one of biggest cues you have to DUI." He entered the details in the laptop. "This is the biggest part of my job. Not too glamorous. I hope something story-worthy happens tonight, but you could just end up seeing the boring side."

"Hey, I've spent my week interviewing young entrepreneurs who walk dogs and make stationary out of recycled paper. You've already topped—"

The radio crackled. A woman's voice broke through the static. "Respond to corner of Forty-Eighth Street and Thirty-Seventh Avenue for a possible B and E in progress. Caller says two SPs barged their way into an apartment across the street from caller. One appeared armed. Witness heard screaming. Stand by, getting further info."

Todd spoke into the microphone. "Twenty-two. Three blocks from location. Responding." He pushed the other red button. A siren wailed. The lights were already flashing. He peeled away from the curb.

"Copy twenty-two. One SP still in apartment. Other fled on foot. Be advised at least one person was on premises at time of B and E." Several seconds passed. "SP running is Hispanic male, early twenties, dark sweatshirt, white shoes."

Todd nodded. "Do you have an apartment number yet?"

"Not yet. It's street level. Caller unsure of directions. Says it's the only apartment with all lights on."

"Twenty-two." Another voice broke in. "Fourteen answering Twenty-two. I'm on Thirty-Ninth Ave and Forty-Fifth Street. Responding."

"Copy."

The cruiser slowed at a stop sign then took off again. Todd mashed the brake, stopped the car, and turned to her. "Stay here and stay low. Don't get out of the car."

Dani slid down. "I won't." Her pulse hammered. B and E . . . breaking and entering. If someone had seen her barge into China's apartment. . . The thought took a backseat to the description of the "suspicious person." Male, twenties, dark sweatshirt, white shoes. It fit hundreds of young men in the area. It also fit the boy she'd met in the shadow of the old garage.

The radio chatter increased as the second and then a third cruiser slid in front of the row of apartments. Four officers flew out. Two covered Todd as he approached a door that stood ajar. One officer darted toward a cluster of people in the front yard of the next block of apartments.

"Sargeant Metzger, witnesses say one SP headed north on Thirty-Seventh on foot, and a second just ran behind the building."

"Copy." Todd pulled his gun out, held it straight out, supporting his wrist with his other hand. Two officers stood on either side of him, several feet back. "Kenosha Police. Open up."

Dani held her breath as seconds passed and he repeated the command, waited, then kicked the door open. He walked in, a second officer at his heels. Dani leaned toward the radio speaker, waiting for his voice. A knock on an inside door. "Police. Open the door." Then the banging of a door against a wall.

"Apartment's empty. Whoa—ho." It was the voice of the second officer. "What do we have here?" A long, low whistle followed. "Must be two ounces at least."

"A little home business," Todd replied, the radio breaking up his voice. "Looks like we interrupted some pretty productive young entrepreneurs."

⚜

A one-pound brick of marijuana and two and a half ounces of cocaine lay on a table in the back bedroom. Gloved policemen recorded everything on the table. A scale, scissors, a box of plastic sandwich bags. *A little home business.*

Trying to stay out of the way, Dani wandered into the next room. Children lived here, but it was anything but a home. A crib with a broken spindle took up one corner. The sheet, stained with juice spots and who-knows-what, was so dirty it looked stiff. Two bare twin mattresses lay on the floor. A handful of toys and children's books were almost buried in the dirty clothes and disposable diapers littering the floor. Her heart broke for the children. Her mind raged at the adults.

"That's not always a bad thing."

Todd had said Child Services would be notified. He'd also added, "There's no chance whoever lived here is coming back."

So where were the children? What possible hope did they have for a decent future? Again she wondered when it was too late to intervene in the life of a child. *Lord, what can I do?* She walked down the narrow, dirt-streaked hallway.

The only furniture in the living room was a stained flowered couch with a cushion missing. There was no kitchen table. Counters overflowed with empty chip bags and pizza boxes. The walls were bare. One dirty towel lay on the floor.

Todd walked in and opened the refrigerator. "Breakfast of champions."

A half-empty bottle of orange juice and two cases of beer.

"Those poor. . ." Her voice disappeared as a picture magneted to the refrigerator came into focus. A Hispanic woman, early twenties, her head leaning on the shoulder of a bald man. . .with an eagle tattooed on his arm.

Dani's pulse skipped. "I've seen that guy," she whispered. "I know his name." *Rabia.*

A direct link to the Sevens. And maybe Jarod.

Whose arrest could set Rena free.

⬥

April 29, 1927

Francie poured a second cup of coffee and set it next to the melba toast she'd barely nibbled. She crossed her legs and stared down at the invitation. She'd had it for a week. She now had half an hour to decide if she should join Albert and his mother for lunch.

She hadn't talked to Albert in months. Not since the second time Tag's brother had shown up at the bank with a bulge the shape of a revolver in his breast pocket. The invitation made no sense.

The bathroom door opened. Footsteps shuffled in the hall. With dark circles under her eyes and hair wild as a dust mop, her sister plopped into the chair by the wall, jarring the table.

185

Coffee sloshed onto the oilcloth. Francie leaped out of her chair. "Watch it!"

"Sorry." Suzette yawned and reached for a Lucky. "Aren't you just the cat's meow this morning." She moved her finger in a circular motion.

Francie turned in a slow pirouette. The irregular hem of the rust tunic dress flared as she turned. The print chiffon overlay drifted back into place when she stopped. "I just finished it last night."

"Love the belt." Suzette blew smoke out of the side of her mouth and reached out to touch the brown velvet sash on the dropped waist. "Very chic. Guess it means I'm stuck with Franky."

Francie cringed.

Suzette brought the cigarette to her lips then stopped. "Going out on the town with Timothy?"

"Suze! How'd you find that out?"

"Asked the right person after the right amount of champagne. *You* wouldn't tell me. 'Tag.' Makes him seem kind of weak, doesn't it? Timothy Arthur Gaines. Who goes around being called by their initials?" Her mouth curved into a sneer. "Why don't you go by your initials, Francie Avril Tillman? That would have been perfect a few years ago."

In spite of the way her sister's attitude irritated her, she couldn't help but laugh. "Oh, yeah, and how about you, Suzette Orlene Tillman, you drunken sot!"

Suzette held her head with both hands as she laughed. "I guess mine fits."

Francie took a sip of cold coffee. "What did you do last night after—" She couldn't say "work."

"George and Betsy and I hit a little joint on North Broadway, the Green Mill. Drinking room only." She pointed at the band of fabric across Francie's forehead. "Pretty. You do good work. So where did you say you're going?"

"I didn't. Albert's mother invited me to have lunch at the Palmer House."

"Albert? Thought you dumped him eons ago."

"I did. That's what's so strange. I'm not sure if I'm going."

Her sister's bloodshot eyes widened. She waved her hand, the sign that Suze was slipping into pretend world. "Not sure? Are you crazy? Five years ago, you thought you were living high on the hog if you got a chunk of side pork in your beans for Sunday dinner. Now look at you. All dolled up like Greta Garbo and actually questioning if you should go to the Palmer House. *Go.* Albert's a nice kid. I like him. He could be husband material."

"Never. He's a mama's boy."

"His mama's got enough money to make you forget that little problem in a jiffy. If you don't want him, I'm next in line." Her eyes danced. It was a strange game they played, imagining they led normal lives. Sometimes it lifted them out of reality. Today it just seemed to make it all more depressing. Still, she played along.

Suze traced a vine on the oilcloth with her fingertip. "I can see you pushing a buggy down Michigan Avenue, cooking supper every night, going to church on Sundays. Tell me what your life will be like in five or ten years." She closed her eyes, as if shutting out the present.

Swinging her foot, Francie leaned back and counted the pearl buttons she'd sewn on the satin T-strap on her shoes. "I'll be married. To a man I haven't even met yet. He's tall and dark, with Valentino eyes. He's insanely wealthy, but money hasn't turned him into a snob. He'll treat me like a queen and spoil our three kids. I'll have a governess to push the buggy, a cook to cook, and a maid to serve, and on Sunday mornings we'll have champagne and strawberries in bed."

"Guess that means no church."

Francie laughed. "Definitely no church." She took a drag on her cigarette. "Hear anything about the job yet?"

"No." She'd done what Tag had asked. She'd "bumped into" Mr. Walbrecht and forced out every ounce of charm she possessed. The next week he and his wife had sailed to France. Where she thought she'd be by now. "The Walbrechts are in Europe."

"Ta-ta."

"Yeah. Ta-ta. Can you imagine how much money they have?"

Suzette tapped the letter from Mrs. Hollanddale. Her expression turned serious. "With enough money, we could disappear."

CHAPTER 21

Todd walked her to her car at the police station just after three on Saturday morning. He'd been laughing off and on for the past two hours. "Too weird," he said for the tenth time at least. "How is it you just happen to be riding with me, and you just happen to recognize..." She tuned him out as she searched for Agatha's keys. "I'm telling you, tracking down this kid could unravel something big." He gave her another slap on the back. Gentle, but annoying. "So when do you want to do your next ride-along, partner?"

Her shoulders ached. The back of her neck felt like it was held in the grip of a massive hand. She forced a smile. "I'll let you know after I recover from this one. Thank you so much."

"If not a ride, how about dinner later this week?"

"I'll check my schedule."

"Good enough." He bent toward her.

She offered her cheek. "Good night, Todd."

He followed her home and waited in the cruiser while she trudged up the stairs to her apartment.

She walked in and kicked off her shoes then fixed a cup of chamomile tea and ran a hot bath. As the tub filled, she checked her phone for messages. She'd missed a call from Anna. And a text from Nicky. ON A SCALE OF ONE TO TEN, HOW IMPORTANT IS SLEEP TO YOU?

He'd sent it at 9:45. She glanced at the time and texted back. ZERO IF IT'S WORTH IT. WHAT DID I MISS?

Tapping fingernails on the edge of the tub, she pictured him finishing up for the night, taking bread from the oven, wiping down the table. Would he know when his phone signaled a message that it was from her? Would he smile? She counted the seconds it would take for him to set down a hot pan or a blob of dough, maybe walk to the sink and wash his hands before picking up his phone or pulling it out of his pocket. As she imagined him drying his hands on his apron, he answered. I THOUGHT YOU MIGHT LIKE TO COME AND READ TO ME WHILE I WORK. WHY ARE YOU AWAKE?

She replied that she'd been out working on a story, and she would have loved to read to him.

HOW ABOUT TONIGHT? I'LL HAVE A MIDNIGHT SNACK READY.

"Time with you *is* a midnight snack." She grinned at the phone as she sent a self-controlled SEE YOU THEN.

Nicky tossed his jeans over a chair and flopped onto the bed. Five minutes later, he was still staring at the same spot of light on the wall. And thinking about the same girl.

So Todd's e-mail earlier in the day hadn't been just idle conversation. Sandwiched between the cost for an oil change for the Javelin and "Want to go out on the boat on Sunday?" was a seemingly casual comment: "Got a woman doing a ride-along tonight. Always makes me nervous."

Mighty strange coincidence that Dani was working on a story in the middle of the night.

Let the battle begin, buddy. You may have sirens and flashing lights, but I've got a time machine.

He sat up, turned on the lamp, and grabbed the photo album he'd taken from the shelf in his grandfather's room. A portal—for stepping into a simpler time. With a beautiful blond at his side.

He'd driven to the nursing home on Monday with an agenda, but it hadn't been one of Nonno Luca's better days. He was glad Rena hadn't joined him. Nonno had yelled at him for not bringing the books for him to look over. When he'd explained, as he had often before, that they kept everything on the computer now, his grandfather had thrown a glass of water at him. "My sons I can't trust. But you, I had hopes for." The words stung, even if, like he'd told Rena, Nonno wasn't always responsible for what he said.

He never got to voice the question about Francie Tillman he'd come to ask. But he did get pictures. He'd deliberately not mentioned them to Dani on Monday night. The timing had to be just right.

The first photos in the album were taken in 1924, the year his grandfather was born. One shot, of his great-grandmother holding her newborn, was taken from across the street from the restaurant. Renata Fiorini stood next to a Model T. She wore a dress with a low belt like the one Francie had drawn in her diary. Around her neck was a long string of pearls. It was the kind of scene Dani had described the day they'd stood on the sidewalk and imagined the street the way it had been decades ago.

Most of the girls he knew wouldn't have a clue what life was like in the Roaring Twenties, but this girl wanted a time machine. He couldn't do much better than that. When he got to the last black-and-white image, he yawned.

She might have spent the night cruising with Todd, but tonight she'd be all his, and that pale boy had nothing on him. He came from a long line of men who knew how to romance a lady. *And* he had pictures.

He turned off the lamp. *All's fair, buddy.*

♛

"You gotta have some talent to start with." Scope outlined an *H* in white on the brick wall and handed the spray can to Dani.

Evan looked on through the lens of his Nikon, laughing. "She's got talent."

Scope appeared skeptical. "It's art, you know? Not everyone can do it."

Dani slipped her digital recorder into her shirt pocket and took the can. She stepped back to take in the whole picture. Evan had set the tone by suggesting they create something upbeat and explaining that young children lived in the house. So far, a smiley-faced sun peered out of a swirling, Van Gogh-like navy background covered with stars and indecipherable letters. The boys claimed all of their names were written on the brick canvas, but Dani's imagination didn't stretch that far. Scope had decided it needed a "Happy Day" message—"like the hippies did." She guessed this was a far cry from the masterpieces he once did.

"How did you learn?"

"I watched. I copied. I drew a whole lot of stuff on paper before I ever picked up a can of paint."

"Let's see if I've learned anything from watching you." She outlined an *A*.

"Not bad. Try a couple more."

"Thank you." She stepped back, thought it out, and painted the next three letters. "It's fun."

Evan coughed. "But not cool to do it illegally."

Way to shut them up. "Of course." *But we could get to that part after we get them to talk.* She handed the can back to Scope. "You guys each do specific things. Does everybody know what his job is before you start?" She turned around to include the two who sat like mute, slouchy statues on a picnic table bench.

Back resting against the table, skinny legs stretched out, Broom stared at the wall. His face wore a mask of boredom. Next to him, Zip sat bent over, head down, with his arms folded across his belly. As close to a fetal position as a kid could get with his feet still on the ground. Dani waited for an answer. Finally, Broom nodded at Scope. "He's the boss."

He speaks! He still hadn't cracked a smile or made eye contact, but three words was a start.

Scope nodded. "I've been doing it longer, but they're learning fast. I do most of the designing and outlining and they do fill-in."

The kid was a strange dichotomy of tough guy and compassionate big brother.

"Do you have the whole picture in your head before you start?"

"Sometimes, but other times it comes to me while I'm doing it. The wall talks to me." He finished the lettering and nodded to Zip, who somehow saw the signal even though he appeared oblivious to the world outside his small personal space. He got up, picked out a yellow can, and began filling in the letters.

Evan slung his camera strap over his neck. "I hear there's food in the fridge. Anyone interested?"

Scope nodded. "Sounds good."

As Evan headed for the house, Scope sat at the table and Broom, on some unspoken cue, turned around and faced him. Dani sat next to Scope. "You guys spend most of your time together, huh?" She looked at Broom.

"Yeah." Not surprisingly, it was Scope who answered. "These guys are like my brothers, you know?"

"A lot of kids join gangs to get that sense of belonging, but you three seem to take care of each other."

Scope looked over Broom's head at the wall. Dani followed his gaze, watching Zip shadow Scope's yellow sun with orange.

"Gang bangers say they protect you, but being part of a gang makes you a target. Might as well paint a bull's-eye on your back."

"You know people who are involved?"

"Sure."

As Scope answered, Broom raised his head. Dani watched the muscles in his neck tighten and relax as he swallowed. "Scope got me out."

The Hallelujah chorus burst forth in Dani's head, but she switched the volume off, took a slow breath, and calmly asked. "You were in a gang?"

Scope raised and lowered one shoulder. "Almost. They tried conning him, but I knew their scams. My dad and me and some of my dad's friends stood up for him."

Broom nodded. "The Vamps got a freaky way of recruiting. They beat people up then send one of their guys to beat up their own guy like some superhero."

Icy fingers slithered along Dani's spine. "Good cop, bad cop."

"Yeah." Broom held out his arm and showed off a diagonal scar. "I got jumped after school a couple years ago. While one guy's poundin' on me, another one suddenly shows up and smashes the first guy, then tells me I can't be alone in that part of town, ever, and I need to join his people so they can watch my back. I just moved here. I was one scared kid, so I said I wanted in. Scope lived next to me and somehow he heard about it, and he and his dad went all

192

Batman tough and got me out." A slight smile rippled the skin on one side of his mouth.

The slithering cold on her back and the sick feeling in her gut overrode the sense of victory over getting the boy to talk. She'd heard another version of his story in Rena's voice.

Scope's hand had been clenching and unclenching the whole time Broom talked. "Once somebody gets jumped in they can't get out without getting hurt bad. . .if they're lucky."

Evan appeared with a tray of sandwiches, chips, and a pack of soda. As Scope reached for a sandwich, Dani caught a glimpse of a tattoo on the inside of his right arm. It appeared to have been created in two stages. Bluish-black lines formed a shape she was familiar with. A stylized number. But darker ink formed two bars, one sticking out of the top of the 7, the other at a right angle to it.

Forming a cross.

♔

Nicky spread a damp towel over a bowl of dough as he waited for Dani's head to bob up with another nugget from the diary. He didn't have long to wait.

"Francie wants to know who came up with 'When the cat's away, the mice will play?' Her cat is away for three days and she's playing."

Nicky touched the tops of two cake layers cooling in pans. He wiggled an eyebrow at the girl who sat at the end of his server counter then set a plate on top of one of the layers and turned it over. "You may have to bleep out parts of this."

"Nooo. Our Francie isn't like that."

"Right. She's a nice girl who just happens to hang out with gangsters." His chest tightened. "Speaking of which, what are you learning from my sister?"

Dani's gaze dropped to the bruschetta she'd been nibbling on. "She's opening up."

"Good. What can you tell me?"

"If I want her to keep talking, nothing." Her nose crinkled as she gave what seemed to be an apologetic smile.

He eased the second cake layer onto a plate then washed his

193

hands and took the photo album off a top shelf. He sat down across from her. "Guess I'll have to trust you."

She looked into his eyes with a steadiness that made his throat constrict. "I guess you will."

The air conditioner was worthless tonight, and he hadn't even turned on all of the ovens yet. He handed the album to her. "I can take a break for a few minutes. I wanted to show you this."

She ran her fingers across the worn suede cover and the tooled letters spelling out PHOTOGRAPHS. She sat back and looked at him. Waiting for an explanation. Not asking questions.

"My grandfather is in a nursing home in Milwaukee. I went up there on Monday to ask him about Francie." He pressed his lips together to dampen the Fiorini charm rising to the surface. It scared him to realize how much like his father he could be if he didn't rein it in. But there would always be one significant difference.

Dominick Fiorini, unlike his father, was a one-woman man.

"Go on."

He could almost hear the interrogation wheels grinding under the force of her restraint. He hated to disappoint her. "I didn't get a chance to ask. My grandfather has good days and bad days, and this wasn't a good one."

"Well, we know that Francie was here in 1928. When was your grandfather born? Would he even have been old enough to remember her? And if he did, is there a chance—"

Once again, he stopped the flow of questions with the tip of his finger. It gave him a strange sensation. . .not of power, more of awe that she so readily responded to his touch. What would their relationship look like if he exercised no control on the charisma embedded in his DNA, and she let loose every question that crowded her mind? "If we keep reading we just might find the answers to all our questions."

"I suppose we might. But pictures first."

He walked around the counter and sat beside her. As he opened the album, Dani pressed her hands together as if she were praying.

Black corners fastened the photos to black paper. Captions were written in white ink.

"Aww. What a cutey." Dani pointed to a picture labeled "Luca

Fiorini, August 1926." "I see the family resemblance."

"All Italians look alike."

She laughed and turned the page. She commented on hats and dress styles for two more pages then stopped at an over-exposed picture of two men and a woman sitting on bar stools. Each had a cigarette in one hand and a drink in the other. The caption underneath read "Stardust 1928."

"Either they were drinking root beer, or that place was illegal."

"I asked my grandfather about that one years ago. I don't think I got a straight answer. My great-grandmother was an activist in the temperance union, and family legend says she kept a pretty tight leash on my great-grandfather. I don't think he would have been allowed in a place like that."

"I've read some taverns switched to soda and ice cream to stay open."

Nicky pointed out the row of bottles in front of a massive mirror behind the bar. "This doesn't look like an ice-cream parlor."

"Sure it does. That one's chocolate syrup and that one's butterscotch." She nudged him and turned another page.

Two women held the hands of two young boys, maybe five and seven, dressed in matching sailor suits. There was no caption. It was the picture he'd been waiting to show her.

"Could it be. . . ?"

"I think it could be."

Dani reopened the diary to the place she'd marked with a napkin. Needing some outlet for what felt like a caffeine buzz, she tapped her sandals together under the counter. She had a sudden flashback of watching *Wheel of Fortune* with Grandma Agatha. Sitting on the floor, inching closer and closer to the TV with each added letter until she finally let out a squeal.

Francie's story was practically writing itself in her head. *I'll give you something big and meaty, Mitch.* "Okay, back to the mice playing while the cat's away."

Francie's handwriting seemed to change with her mood. The letters in this entry were less slanted and more open. " 'Last night

Doris and I went dancing. Doc Cooke was at the White City Ballroom. I wore my yellow chiffon and got so many compliments.'" She moved to the next entry. " 'Saw Louis Armstrong at the Sunset Café. So many men. I know I was being watched, so I was a good girl.'" Dani looked over at Nicky. "See? Told you so."

She stared at the sculpted Roman nose and the mouth that at this moment laughed at her feigned defense of Francie. She'd found fault with that face when she first met him. Something that wasn't all together perfect about it. Hard as she tried, she couldn't remember what it was. "Read," he whispered, close enough that the single word wafted garlic-scented heat onto her cheek. People talked about garlic breath as if it was something bad. It wasn't. Not at all.

Back to the book. " '. . .I danced and danced, but never more than twice with anyone. I didn't give out my number, and I ducked every kiss.'"

Nicky inched closer. "So that's the definition of a good girl, huh?"

His eyes smoldered with more passion than one man should be allowed to possess. Her lips parted of their own accord. Her mind played out the leaning in, the lift of her chin, the warmth radiating from his skin even before his—

"Good girls duck every kiss?" He smiled and eased away. Not a teasing smile, it was a look of sweet, shared restraint. "I have dough to punch." His hand rested over hers for a too-brief moment, and then he got up and walked to the sink and scrubbed his hands.

Dani stared at the heather gray shirt conforming to his back. He hadn't given her a chance to answer his question. She breathed a silent sigh and went back to Francie's world. Nicky slammed his fist into a mountain of dough.

"That looks like fun." *And frustration-relieving.*

"Wash up and come here." He fixed her with a gaze like a heat-seeking missile. "I'll save the rest for you."

Was his radar reading what he was doing to her? "Okay." She closed the diary and slid off the stool. *But I'm warning you. . .good girls don't always duck.*

Do good boys?

CHAPTER 22

Heard on the radio of another robbery attempt foiled downtown last night and read in the paper about the police department hiring new men and purchasing more cars.'"

Dani closed the diary and stifled a yawn. "Something's going to happen soon. I've got a bad feeling about this."

Nicky picked up the last double pan of bread and opened the oven door. "Not to spoil the drama, but you do realize that whatever happens happened over eighty years ago."

"Spoiler. Must be a blast to watch a suspense movie with you."

He slid the bread in the oven and set the timer. "I just don't want you losing touch with reality."

"And I think it would be good for you to lose yourself in the story. Think of all the 'what ifs.' She's mentioned three people who were killed. One in a police raid on a gambling operation, three during robbery attempts. They could just be people she's read about in the paper, but something about the way she writes makes it sound like she knows them."

"So we need to look up those names and cross reference them with all robberies, sting operations, and bad guys gunned down in Chicago in da twenties." The *Godfather* voice came easy. He'd grown up surrounded by great-uncles who talked that way without pretending.

"Are you making fun of me?"

"A little." He took the stool across from her. The one next to her looked risky.

"Whatever makes you happy."

Sitting on that stool would make him happy. "Okay, I'll behave. Go on."

"Let's guess. What do you think happens in the end?"

"T is slaughtered in the Valentine's Day Massacre, and Francie lives happily ever after on her parents' farm."

"Could be. I like that, but we have to get her to Kenosha. Maybe she married somebody from here."

"My great-grandmother introduced her to a friend of the family, an Italian lover"—he slid his hand across the counter, picked up hers, and kissed the air millimeters above her fingers—"and she became Francine Napoletani or Pontecorvo." He rested her hand back on the table.

Face flushed, Dani laughed. "Or Fiorini. Maybe she changed her first name, too. Maybe you grew up with her great-grandkids."

"What do you think she turned out like? Did she have a come-to-Jesus moment and join the Temperance Union with my great-G-ma to atone for the sins of her father?"

"She's got a few of her own to atone for. She's apparently hiding stolen goods, so I'd rule out a total life change. And what about Franky? Think he rebelled against his mother's profession and became a priest?"

"Nah. I can see him joining the mob. Boy had bad blood. He got filthy rich and lived in a penthouse with cute little maids in white aprons peeling grapes for him."

"I Googled Francine Tillman and Suzette Tillman and didn't find anything. I didn't stop to think that if her sister never married, little Franky would have the same last name. We need to see if we can find Frank Tillman,"

"Let's do it now. Unless you're too tired?"

She shook her head. Champagne-colored hair glimmered in the overhead lights and slid across her shoulders. "Sleep is a zero, remember?" She picked up her phone. The screen came to life.

"It would be easier on the computer. Follow me."

Not smart, Fiorini. A smaller room, with a door that closed automatically. How many waitresses had his father, grandfather, great-grandfather and countless uncles—three generations of philandering Fiorinis—lured into the storeroom?

He opened the door for her and flipped on the light. "This is the all-purpose room. Storage, office, break room." *Thinking room. Hiding place.*

He'd flirted with his share of waitresses over the years but never considered bringing anyone in here. This was his hideaway, his middle-of-the-night sanctuary. He was safe here, maybe even from his own runaway thoughts about the girl in front of him. This was not a place to desecrate, and not a place to share with just anyone.

Then why her? He could have brought the laptop into the kitchen.

He stepped to the side and watched her face as she touched the ceramic-tipped hooks on a wall-mounted mahogany coat rack, then walked over to the only square foot of wall not covered with shelves or hooks. "Beautiful wallpaper." She bent closer. "It's embossed. Is it original?"

"Yes. No one's ever going to take the shelves down to tear it off, so it'll be here as long as we own the place."

"I love that. So nostalgic. My parents built three new houses while I was growing up. No sense of family history at all."

"At least your parents didn't have to tell you not to chew on the windowsills because you'd end up with brain damage."

Her soft laugh filled the small space as she ran her hand along the scalloped bottom edge of a shelf.

"These were all cupboards once upon a time. My grandfather took the doors off to make it a more efficient—and junky—space."

Dani nodded and looked up at the wooden crucifix hanging by the back door. "That looks really old, too."

"It came from Italy with my great-grandparents." He fastened the chain lock on the door and propped it open. Night air, several degrees cooler than inside, seeped through the narrow space.

Nicky picked up the three-legged chair, carried it to the desk, pushed the padded desk chair to the side for Dani, and turned on the computer.

"Are you Catholic?" Her voice, so small, seemed to have floated down a long hallway. She still stood in front of the crucifix, staring up.

"I was raised in the church."

She turned around, crossed her arms, and rubbed them as if she were cold. "And now?"

Now. He chewed on his bottom lip. He couldn't put it into words even for himself.

Dani crossed the room, her sandals ticking on the wood floor. She sat down and swiveled to face him. As he stared at the screen coming to life, he balanced on three chair legs and tried to formulate an answer.

"Why is that hard to answer?"

Her hushed question slid over him like a caress. For no definable reason, his eyes stung.

She touched his arm, tentatively at first then conformed her hand to his forearm. "Talk to me."

He pressed his teeth into his lip, willing the pain to overtake the emotion. He shook his head. He was not going to fall apart in front of her. The pressure on his arm increased, and then she let go. The spot felt cold. She folded her hands on her lap and bent toward him. "What happened four years ago?"

Anyone could have told her. Vito, Todd, Rena. She could have looked back and found his name in the paper she worked for. But if she knew, why was she asking? Just to make him talk? Because asking questions was what she did? She had a right to know. He'd tell her about it, just not now. Not at this time of night or in this room. Not with the smell of baking bread, the heat of summer, bringing it all back. Too sharp. Too vivid.

His fingers curved in toward his palms. He watched them, as if they belonged to someone else. Someone else's hands covered with blood. Not his. Someone else's fist jutting at a dark, cloudless sky. He shook his head. "Not now."

In his peripheral vision, he saw her nod, but he couldn't see her expression. Was she hurt? Angry?

"Okay," she whispered. She gestured toward the screen. "Let's leave all this for another time." She stood.

He'd pushed her away. She stood less than a foot from him and yet the room already felt empty. *Don't go. Don't be mad.* His stomach clenched. They were the words of an eleven-year-old boy running after his mother. *Please stay.*

But she wouldn't. He stared at the door, seeing her walk out even though she hadn't moved.

At the moment he expected her to say good-bye, she reached toward him. Her hand rested on his cheek. She bent down, lifting his face to hers, and kissed him. Light, soft, too brief. "I'm praying for you, Nicky."

With a half smile that stopped his next breath, she walked out.

✦

Nicky pulled the sheet over his head and closed his eyes. The cloth touched his lips, making it easier to relive the kiss. But when he closed his eyes, it was too easy to imagine he'd just dreamed it.

"Nick? Can I come in?"

"Sure." He pulled the sheet down and turned on the lamp as Rena opened the door. She wore plaid shorts and an oversized black T-shirt with an old-fashioned silver microphone sparkling on the front. It brought to mind the shirt she'd given Dani. He'd never gotten a satisfactory answer about what had happened that night. He glanced at the clock. "It's five o'clock in the morning. You really need to sleep once in a while, kid."

"I was asleep until I heard Dad come home." She sat down on the end of his bed, curling long legs beneath her. "It's Gianna's birthday."

She knew he knew. Something else was going on here. "I made the cake, if that's what you mean."

"I was just thinking. . .she'd love it if we went to church with her."

"Church? You?"

One shoulder lifted. The neck of her shirt dipped. What was that on her shoulder?

"I just thought it would be nice to do it for—"

"What's that?" Ice coursed through his veins as he leaned forward and pointed at her collarbone. The light was bad. It was just a shadow.

Rena's eyes widened. She clenched the top of the shirt. Her expression froze.

201

"Let me see."

She pulled back. "See what? You're being weird."

"Let go of your shirt."

"Why? Quit acting like a perv."

"Rena. Stop it." His voice came out rough and louder than he'd intended. Every second she resisted convinced him he hadn't seen a shadow. *Dear God...* Heat rose from his belly. He gripped the sheet to keep from grabbing the hand that held her shirt.

He expected her to run. She didn't. She stared back. Tears pooled in her eyes. "It's not what you think."

"Then what is it?" Her tears slowed his rage. "Show me."

Her eyes closed as she slowly released her grip and pulled the neck of her shirt to the side. In the hollow triangle above her collarbone, a 7 seemed to vibrate with the pounding of her pulse. Like subscript, a small *S* curled around the base of the seven.

Anger seeped from him. As if the plug had been pulled, and he couldn't retain it. In its place it left deadness. "What's the *S* for?" Once again, he felt like an observer. The flat, emotionless voice wasn't his.

"Sisters. We're not...what you think."

"You said that."

"It's more like a club."

He laughed, hating the sound. "Right. Like the Girl Scouts."

"We're just...it's just a way...to be protected."

His turn to close his eyes, but the picture stayed. His cousin had ignored a promise of safety. "And what do you have to do to earn the protection? Sell enough cookies?"

"What do you mean?"

A thin line of fury, like a white-hot needle, rose through the numbness. "What do you pay for your safety? What do you give in return?" He suddenly realized he had no idea what his sister did with the paycheck he gave her each week. "Money?"

"Do you honestly think I'd do that?"

"Then what? Your body? Do you—"

"Nick? Rena?" Their father didn't wait for an answer before opening the door. "What are you two talking about?"

His cheery tone fanned the heat, bursting it into flames. "We're talking about—"

Rena's fingernails bit through the sheet, stabbing his leg. He stopped and stared at the stark fear in her eyes. Trembling with the pressure of unspoken words, he smiled. His father didn't know him well enough to recognize it for what it was. "We were talking about Gianna's birthday."

"Oh. That's today, isn't it?" He shuffled from one foot to the other. "Do you have plans?"

"Yes."

Silence. Nicky wasn't about to fill it. Rena stared at the floor.

He wouldn't ask for details. He knew he wasn't invited. "I was wondering if maybe we could go out for breakfast today."

Rena shook her head, a barely perceptible motion.

Nicky copied her response. "Sorry. We're going to church with Gianna."

"Oh. Good. She'll like that. You two don't need to be back here for brunch. We'll handle it. In fact, take the rest of the day off, both of you."

Rena raised an eyebrow. "Thanks." She slid her feet to the floor. "I'm going to bed." She raised her face for a kiss on the way out. "Night, Dad."

"Maybe we can talk about what you hear at church when you get back. We should do that more, you know. . .talk about things that matter."

"Yeah. Sure." Rena answered from the hallway.

Great idea, Dad. Or would have been. . .years ago.

⁂

"Fabulous." Gianna smashed the last chocolate crumbs with her fork, slid her plate onto the patio table, and leaned back in the chaise lounge. Eyes crinkling around Sophia Loren-worthy teal-rimmed sunglasses, she waved at Rena, perched on the diving board. "She looks cute in that suit."

Nicky curled his fingers around the ends of the armrests. Try as he might, he couldn't force his body to conform to the lawn chair. "What did you call it?"

"A tankini. Nice to see her in something modest."

He'd agree if he didn't know she'd bought it to cover the skin graffiti. "I guess."

Gianna raised her leg and wiggled her toes. Bright red toe nails sported little white flowers. "Did I tell you my prayer partner took me to the spa yesterday? Hot stone massage, cucumber mint sugar scrub, steaming towels. Must be so sad to be a man."

Nicky laughed. "I pay fourteen bucks for a haircut and three-ninety-eight for deodorant. How sad is that?"

"It's why it's fair that you guys foot the bill for everything." She lifted her glasses and eyed him. "Footing any bills lately?"

"Smooth. And yes."

"Danielle, right? That wasn't just a casual acquaintance."

The woman had radar. The day she'd met Dani was the day he'd decided he wanted to see more of her, in spite of her lack of street smarts. "There might be some potential there."

"Hmm." She lowered the glasses and turned her head back to neutral, but the tight, red-tinted lips fighting a smile said more than all the Italian exclamations of joy she was holding back. "You should have invited her to church this morning. Do you think she would have come?"

The woman should work for the CIA. He gave her the answer she was looking for. "Yes, I think she would have come."

"And what would she have said about Ecclesiastes 4:9?"

Grateful he'd been listening, he laughed. "I think she would agree that two are stronger than one."

Gianna's sunglasses rose as a grin lifted her cheeks. " 'How can one keep warm alone?' Verse eleven." She folded her hands and in minutes was softly snoring.

April 29, 1927

The Palmer House lobby bustled with well-dressed, well-heeled patrons. Francie clutched her handbag against the front of her wrap coat. She still missed the black fox.

Scanning the room, she took in more than just the latest fashions. Tag wouldn't be awake this early on a Sunday morning, and this really wasn't his kind of place anyway. She stared at a man reading the Sunday paper, half hidden by a massive rubber plant. Was he one of Tag's men?

She glanced at her watch. Tag hadn't returned the fox coat, but not long after the Albert incident, he'd given her the Gruen Cartouche bracelet watch with its face encircled by diamonds—"just because."

Needing to set her thoughts on anything but Tag, she stared up at the vaulted ceiling supported by stone columns resembling gold-topped palm trees with fronds branching toward exquisite mythological murals. It still amazed her that she could walk into a place like this and blend in—still couldn't believe she was in this place, sporting a watch worth more than her father made in a year.

"Francie!"

Albert's boyish yell pulled her into the moment. He strode toward her, his hand on his mother's elbow. As they approached Francie darted a look toward the rubber plant. The man was gone. She breathed a sigh. Would the day ever come when she could stop watching over her shoulder, imagining eyes following her everywhere?

Albert embraced her with a brotherly hug. No trace of hurt or anger. What was this all about?

"So glad you could join us, Francine." Mrs. Hollanddale leaned forward, and Francie kissed her cheek. A delicate cloud of Chanel No. 5 hovered around her.

"Thank you for inviting me."

They walked to the dining room where sumptuous smells assaulted Francie's willpower.

Chew slowly. Drink lots of water. She read the menu, see-sawing between indulgence and restraint. Aiguillette of Striped Bass, Potatoes a la Hollandaise, Medallion of Spring Lamb, Asparagus Tips au Gratin, Breast of Chicken a la Rose. Irrationally close to tears, she listened as Mrs. Hollanddale ordered beef tips in sage gravy over toast points, in a voice as rich and buttery as the sauce her name resembled.

With a smile she wanted to feel but couldn't, she ordered lamb chops and steamed asparagus with pearl onions. Albert asked for the Salisbury steak.

A waiter brought salads. Fresh greens drizzled with vinaigrette and topped with raspberries. Francie picked up her salad fork. Albert cleared his throat. "I'd like to say a blessing first."

A blessing? Albert?

"Heavenly Father, Mother and I thank thee for allowing us time to share Your truth with Francie today. Thank you for this food and the many blessings You provide. In the name of Your perfect Son, Jesus, we pray. Amen."

Francie's fingers, laced together as if her hands were one, pulled stiffly apart. For all her practice at pasting smiles, she couldn't conjure one now. She'd come here for two reasons—curiosity and the possibility that Suzette was right. Money meant power. She'd never before considered the far-fetched idea of Albert's family buying their freedom, but she was more than willing to pursue it. What had happened to the Albert she knew?

Mrs. Hollanddale patted her hand. "I know you're wondering why we invited you here."

Not anymore. She nodded.

"Don't let my son's newfound boldness scare you. While it's true, we feel God would have us share something with you, that is not the only reason we invited you. Albert has often spoken of your gift as a seamstress, and I have recently been convicted about the money I spend on my wardrobe. That's when Albert brought you to mind. I am wondering if you would consider coming to work in my employ as a—"

"Excuse me." Francie looked up into the round, florid face of the man who signed her paychecks. He bowed slightly. "Mrs. Hollanddale, Albert, how good to see you. Hello, Francine."

He remembered her name. Francie wiped her palms on the embroidered napkin.

Albert's mother extended her hand. "Mr. Walbrecht. How was your trip?"

"Far too short. Aren't vacations always too short?"

"You have a home in Paris, am I correct?"

"Yes. Couldn't tear my wife away from it. Business demanded my return, but she'll be there for another eight weeks."

"Paris is so lovely this time of year."

"Indeed. I won't take any more of your time. When I saw you,

I just had to stop by and say hello to you. . .and to my soon-to-be personal secretary."

Francie gasped.

"I'm looking forward to a profitable working relationship, Miss Tillman."

CHAPTER 23

Rena stepped out of the shower and wrapped herself in a towel. Her new bathing suit lay in a wet lump in the sink. She combed her hair straight back. The dramatic look used to make her feel like a super model. Now it only emphasized the grayish circles under her eyes.

She hadn't fallen back to sleep after talking to Nicky.

Nicky knew. At least part. It should upset her, but in a strange way, it was a relief.

Things were strained between them. She'd expected questions, but he'd been quiet on the way to church. On the way home from Gianna's he'd handed her the church bulletin. "Read those verses again."

She'd read them out loud. Part of it was inked in her brain. *"Pity anyone who falls and has no one to help them up!"*

When they got home he'd headed to his room and she'd turned into the bathroom. She was just about to shut the door when she heard him say, "I'm here when you need me, Wren."

Tears slid down her cheeks. She swiped them away. She pictured the pathetic scene when Jarod shoved her down and she'd crept backward into the shadows like a frightened cat. With no one to help her up.

No more. Two are stronger than one, the pastor had said.

There were ways of getting out. Like China, she could leave. She thought of the things she knew. That Jarod had had a gun. That he might have stashed drugs. Was it enough to make her a threat? Enough to make him come looking for her if she left? Most likely he wouldn't bother. He'd just move on to someone else who'd make him look good and give him what he wanted.

But if she left, she couldn't come back. Jarod might not come looking for her, but if she dared show her face in the neighborhood... She shuddered.

Maybe she'd try disappearing right under his nose. Just fade away emotionally. Not fight, just play dead. Not respond to anything he said or did. He'd get tired of her. And she'd be free.

Or she could find out what was going on and expose him. Blow the whole thing up in their faces.

The Sevens had a reputation for being wannabes. That was mostly true, until you got to the middle of the circle. The eye of the hurricane, Jarod called it. It was where he wanted to be, he said. She'd always laughed. There might be an eye, but there was no hurricane. They defended their streets and their people. They fought if they had to. They didn't move in on other neighborhoods or take what wasn't theirs.

But things were changing, she could feel it.

"Two are better than one."

She tore off the towel, put on shorts and a tank top, and flew into the hallway. Nicky was walking down the steps, wearing running clothes.

"Nick?"

He turned around.

"You don't have to worry, okay?" She rubbed her tattoo. "I'm getting out."

His eyes closed for a second then opened. Sad eyes. He sighed. "Can you?"

She nodded. "Sure."

"What can I do?"

"Just pray."

She had no idea where that had come from. Or why Nicky didn't look surprised.

"I will."

Walking into her room, she picked up her phone and punched Jarod's number. No answer. She left a message.

"Hey, babe, I'm sorry about last night. I was scared for you. I just didn't know how to process it, you know? Call me and I'll make it all up to you."

⚜

Pink and purple layered the western sky as Dani walked along Third Avenue with Evan on Sunday night. He'd left the H1 at her place, and they'd walked to their singles group meeting. Neither of them had said a word since leaving church a mile ago. They'd spent the entire meeting processing the death of one of their members. Two days ago Lori Mills, a girl Evan knew from high school, died of an intentional overdose.

Dani stopped in front of a two-story redbrick home with a gabled attic window. A black wrought iron fence surrounded the property. Tiny lights bordered a curved stone walk. Two children chased each other on a side lawn as wide as some parks in other neighborhoods.

"Where did Lori grow up?"

Evan stuck his hands in the back pockets of his jeans. "Four blocks from here."

Two-story homes built in the sixties, well-kept yards, nice cars. It all negated Rena's theory. *"Geography. If I had all the same heredity but I was born to a rich family in a rich neighborhood, I'd be a whole different person."*

They walked along the sidewalk that bordered Eichelman Park. *"When the weather's decent, I pack rollerblades and try out different parks."* Did Nicky ever come to this one? Who would he be if he'd grown up in this neighborhood?

She thought of the girls in the pink jackets and sparkly shoes who walked groomed dogs with jeweled collars. Who knew what those girls would turn out to be? Maybe Lori Mills had worn cute shoes and walked spoiled dogs. Geography hadn't made a difference to her. "Do you ever feel like a major hypocrite?"

"All the time. Why?"

"I see kids over by Bracciano. The little ones look scared. The big ones look cocky because they have to be to survive." She pointed to a family with three little girls. The parents folded blankets and picked up toys while the girls twirled until they got dizzy then fell to the ground giggling. "Around here, you see little girls in boutique clothes dancing around without a care in the world. I want to do something about the scared kids, but what does that make me if I live in a place with marble countertops in a neighborhood of massive houses with stained glass windows and wrought-iron fences?"

She was working up the courage to tell him about the phone call she'd made after lunch with Rena.

"You live in a one-bedroom apartment. It's not the Taj. Don't be so hard on yourself."

"But I've been thinking maybe I should downsize, you know?"

"Did all this start in Sunday school this morning?"

"It didn't start there. It got worse there."

" 'If anyone, then, knows the good they ought to do and doesn't do it, it is sin for them.'" He recited the verse scrolling through her brain. "So what good are you not doing that you know you should be doing but aren't doing?"

She popped his arm with a slow-moving fist. "I'm trying to stay morose. Quit interfering."

"Sorry. Okay, so you want to make a difference. Where, specifically?"

"I don't know. If I did—" Her phone beeped. She pulled it out of her pocket. "If I knew what God was calling me to do—" Her words faltered as she read the text from Rena. WANT STORY? MEET ME @ COAL CHUTE 11 2NITE. PARK IN BACK. DISGUISE.

She answered with two letters—OK—and kept talking over the drumming in her ears. "Isn't that the hard part? If God sent texts"—her laugh bordered on a squeak—"we'd know what we were supposed to do."

"I'm guessing by the sudden giddiness that one was from the Italian rather than God."

I wish. No, she didn't. This—whatever Rena was pulling her into—was what she wanted. Still, a message from "the Italian" would be nice. She hadn't second-guessed the kiss until a few hours ago. He had the diary, and he was off tomorrow, but she hadn't heard a word from him. "Nicky? No." *God? Maybe.* Thunder rumbled in the distance, promising a downpour. *Phones, thunder. . .* God could use anything to move a person in the right direction. "We should head to my place."

Evan stared up at the pink-tinged sky. Black clouds hovered low over the lake, far to the east. "Whatever you say." A thread of irritation wove through his answer. So unlike Evan. But then, it was unlike her not to tell him who'd sent the text.

She set a faster pace. "Were you happy with the pictures of the boys painting?"

"Yeah, I was. I mailed my finished project last night."

"You did? And you didn't tell me?"

He shrugged. "You've been pretty distracted lately."

"I guess I have. I'm sorry."

"No apologies. It's not like I sit around with nothing to do. My schedule's overloaded with all those girls clamoring for a little sliver of my time."

She looked up into his elfish face and smiled as an idea sparked. "Did I tell you I know a girl who thinks you're really cute?"

His head jerked back. He blinked four times in rapid succession. "Do I know her?"

"Yes. The text was from her, actually."

"Who—"

"No questions. I'm the question-asker."

"But—"

Nerves tingling about what lay ahead, she walked the rest of the way home a step ahead of Evan with one finger in the air and a "Shh" on her lips. As they walked, she wrote a mental list of everything she'd need.

Skinny jeans, hair color, tattoos, lip stud. . .

CHAPTER 24

Rena fluffed her hair. "Man, it's hot." Her hands needed something to do other than shake.

Yamile, self-proclaimed "Queen of the Sisters," sat on the curb, hands clamped on her waist as she faced Dani. Her thick dark hair concealed the scar on her right cheek.

"Go easy on her." Rena swallowed hard. "I've known Cerise for a long time. I checked stuff. She's okay." She picked a spot on the curb in front of a handicapped parking sign and sat next to Leah, Yamile's shadow, who hadn't said a word yet. Her spiky hair, white-blond over black, wobbled as she nodded with every question Yamile threw at Dani. A few feet away, Venus leaned on a parking meter, bracelets stacked on her wrists, green bandana tied around her forehead. Rena motioned for Dani to sit. "Park it, Cerise."

"Nah. I'm good where I am." Dani folded her arms across a faded green T-shirt.

Rena hid a smile. She'd been sure Dani was going to overplay it and act all gangster, but her attitude was perfect. Even her posture said, "Take me or leave me. I don't care." If she looked too anxious to be accepted, Yamile would have told her to leave. Yamile hated "cling-ons."

Yamile took a step toward Dani. "You were at the memorial. You knew Miguel?"

213

"I know China."

"Where you live?"

Alarm bells went off in Rena's head. She tried to get Dani's attention but couldn't. *You're moving in with me, remember?*

"Across from Bracciano."

What?

"Haven't moved in yet, but I rented Miguel's old place."

You did?

"Freaky." Yamile laughed, deep and throaty. "Place is probably haunted. Where you get your money?"

Dani widened the distance between her feet and stuck out one hip. Way casual. "I got a job. Working for the *Times*."

"La-de-da. Paper girl, huh? Make it sound all that when it ain't."

"It's money."

Rena let out a loud sigh. "Lay off, Yamile. You never asked me all these crazy questions."

"Didn't have to. You had Jarod and Trish vettin' you. This chick's got nobody." She tipped her head toward Leah and started a slow circle around Dani. Rena's gut tightened. Dani didn't have the sense to keep her back to the wall. Where she stood, out in the open, she was a perfect target from any angle. Leah slowly rose to her feet. Rena copied her.

Yamile slunk like a jungle cat. "Know what I'm thinkin', girls?"

Leah fell in step behind her. "I got an idea."

Dani didn't move. To her credit, her fear wasn't showing.

"I'm thinkin' I don't trust this"—she used a word that surprisingly didn't make Dani cringe—"and I'm thinkin' maybe she got to prove herself. Maybe she got to get jumped in."

"Don't be crazy." Rena stepped toward Dani. "We never—"

Yamile lunged at Dani, arms outstretched. In a blur of motion, Dani's right leg shot straight out and up, smacking Yamile's chin with a *thwack*. Yamile slammed against a parked car, shook her head, and pushed off the car, eyes blazing. With a roar, she whipped a knife from her back pocket and charged. Dani stared her down. At the last second, she twirled away in a move that looked like ballet.

Rena leaped back. Her mouth opened.

Leah and Venus closed in. Rena's pulse thundered in her ears.

She could take Leah down if she caught her off guard. Yamile spun around, four-inch blade glinting in the streetlight. Dani turned slowly, her chest heaving, but her face showing no emotion. Without warning, she kicked—a smooth arc—foot slamming Yamile's wrist. The knife flew, clattering on the concrete. Venus bent to grab it, but Dani's knee smashed into her shoulder. Leah backed away, hands up. Yamile held her wrist, spit out a string of dark words, and suddenly broke out laughing. Letting out a whoop, she raised her good hand in the air.

"Proud to call you a Sister, Cerise. You got wicked feet. I trust you to have my back any day."

Dani slapped her hand.

Rena dropped to the curb, wondering if she was the only one who noticed just how bad her knees—and "Cerise's" high-five hand—shook.

⸙

It worked. It actually worked.

Dani sat on the hood of a red Grand Am, repressing a grin. Every synapse quivered, and her legs had all the strength of bread dough. Her face felt cold and clammy, but the adrenaline rush, and Rena's look of pure awe, rivaled any award she'd ever win. The words came together in her head. Change the names and the locations, and the identity of the girl with the wicked feet, and she'd have a story to razzle the socks off her boss. She bent down, under the pretense of rubbing her foot. What she really needed was blood to her head.

"Where'd you learn that?" Yamile still held her wrist, but her eyes held nothing but admiration.

"I took classes."

"You pulled back, didn't you? You coulda broke my face if you wanted."

Dani pressed her hand against the back of her neck. "I could have."

Venus rubbed her shoulder. "Can you teach us?"

"Maybe. There are rules to it. You'd have to promise only to use it for self-defense."

Leah nodded. "Like *Karate Kid*."

215

"It's an honor thing." Dani straightened as her equilibrium returned to normal. "There's a code, you know? You gotta respect the art."

"I get it." Yamile walked over to the curb. As she started to sit down, a siren blasted. Loud and close. Maybe a block away. "Let's get." She took off between two cars, crossed the street, and ran into the alley.

Dani looked at Rena, who nodded. "Follow her."

The siren grew louder then stopped. Dani glanced over her shoulder as she ran. Red and blue lights swam across the garages at the end of the alley. Yamile crossed a second street, Venus and Leah close behind her. Dani heard Rena's labored breathing.

Red and blue light splashed onto the garage next to her. She bent low and followed the two girls in front of her as they darted behind a garage and ran through two back yards and onto a back porch.

"Trish isn't home," Rena gasped.

"So what." Yamile opened the back door and all five ran in. Rena caught the screen before it slammed. They passed through a porch strewn with beer cans. Towers of empty blue beer boxes tottered along the screened-in windows. Rena pulled her into a fluorescent-lit kitchen that smelled of rancid oil and burned food. A woman in her forties or early fifties sat at the table, cigarette in one hand, old-fashioned glass in the other. "What you girls up to?"

"Just havin' fun." Yamile answered.

"Any of you know where Trish went?" Her words ran together. "She left a note. Said she was going out with Rab, but she took clothes." Red-rimmed eyes looked from Yamile to Rena. "She movin' in with that boy?"

Rena's mouth opened, but it was Yamile who answered. "Probably. She'll get sick of him before long and be back."

The woman shrugged. "Cheaper when she's gone."

Yamile laughed. "Can we hang out in her room?"

"Go ahead. Just don't wake Buddy and whoever that is sleeping on the floor."

Lungs burning and legs trembling, Rena sat on the floor, hugging

216

her knees the way Trish had last night. Dani sat next to her. The other three poked around the room, looking in empty drawers. Rena stared at a stack of empty frames on the desk and a vacant spot on the bookshelf that had once held the scrapbook she and Trish started in fifth grade and traded back and forth on their birthdays. They were going to travel together someday. *"See the world and fill the book,"* they'd said.

She thought of the moment the innocence had faded and her life took a wrong turn. A cold, moonless night in February. Walking home from a journalism club meeting at school. Alone.

Alone because Trish hadn't shown up for the meeting and hadn't called.

She stared at a single green bead on the floor under the dresser as a piece from the puzzle of that night chinked into place.

Trish had been in on it. Her best friend had set her up.

Rena shivered. Dani put her hand on her arm. "You okay?"

"Yeah. You were awesome," she whispered.

"Can't believe I pulled it off. I've only kicked dummies and punching bags."

Yamile flopped down on Trish's bed. Leah and Venus crawled around her and sat against the wall. "Rena tell you how we roll?"

"She told me you're all about protecting each other, being a family. I like that."

"Yeah." Yamile looked down at her feet. "We do what we gotta do to take care of our own. If it's fighting, we fight. If it's gettin' money to take care of somebody who gets pregnant or don't have a place to stay, we do it." She turned to Rena. "You hear what went down last night?"

"Heard some chatter before it." She leaned against the wall and concentrated on even breathing. Jarod hadn't returned her call.

"Rab almost got busted. Wasn't your man in on it?"

"Not in the middle of it." She talked about "it" like she knew.

Dani picked up the green bead and tossed it from one hand to the other. "What happened?"

"Rab got in on a payback with some Chi-town guys. Had it all set up with some chick going to let him in to grab some weed and coke from the Roses, but it went bad. Neighbors ratted to the cops and started screamin', so he ran."

Another chill shimmied up Rena's spine. Jarod was in on this. Trish was an accomplice. What would the charges be if they got caught? Dani leaned toward her. "Is Rab the guy with the eagle tattoo?" she asked.

Rena nodded, forcing herself to look calm. She looked at Yamile. "What was the plan if they'd gotten it?"

"Doesn't your man tell you nothin'?"

Pressing her knuckles into the carpet, Rena shrugged with one shoulder. "I knew enough. I was there when Jarod gave Rab the gun."

Yamile smacked her lips, a weird sign that she approved. Only weeks ago Rena had craved that approval.

At the moment, it meant nothing. She waited for an answer.

"They were going to kill the girl and take the stuff."

♔

Dani fought nausea as she stared at the girl who'd just mentioned murder in the same tone anyone else would use to say she was going to brush her teeth.

Yamile lay on a pile of pillows, leaning on her elbow. She could have been any teen at a sleepover, except for the two-inch scar tugging at the tender skin beneath the outside corner of one eye. Yamile stretched and yawned. "I'm starving."

Had this cold, hardened kid ever been a little girl who played with dolls and sang her ABCs? "How'd you get to be the leader, Yamile?"

"Blood."

Dani winced.

Yamile laughed. "Not like that. My brother was one of the original Sevens, so I didn't have to prove nothin' to hang out with them. But they exclude females on lotsa stuff, so when I was like twelve, I decided the women oughta have their own thing, ya know?"

"So you started the Sisters."

"Yeah. We got some wannabes hanging around, but there's maybe fifteen solid. My girls take care of each other." She sat up. "And now we got you." She slid off the bed. "I gotta find some food."

She opened the door. "Hey," she whispered. "You guys see who's sleepin' on the couch? It's Chi."

Bile rose in Dani's throat. Her fingers curled around the green bead. "Chi. . .*na?*"

"Yeah." Yamile closed the door. "She's who we needed the money for. Her aunt kicked her out 'cause she found out she's pregnant."

The clamminess returned. Dani swallowed twice and sucked air through parted lips. She rose slowly on wobbling legs. "I have to get up early. I'm going to run."

Yamile nodded. "We're meeting at your place from now on."

Dani wiped dampness from her upper lip and reached across Yamile to grab the door handle.

"Hey." Venus pointed a black-nailed finger at her. "This is perfect. Chi can live with you."

♔

August 31, 1927

Francie straightened the papers and rose from her desk. *Her* desk in *her* office. *Mama, if you could see me now. This part of my life is good.*

For now.

The swell of pride deflated as she walked into the hall and past the locked closet. The door concealed a row of loaded guns. She quickened her steps. Exactly a week had passed since another failed attempt to murder Al Capone. Three men, all friends of Tag, men she knew, were dead. Tony Russo, Vinnie Spicuzza, Ben Giamonco. All shot.

Tag's time was coming. She could feel it in her gut. Soon.

Outside her boss's door, she took a deep breath then knocked and opened the door.

"In triplicate, Mr. Walbrecht." She raised her voice to be heard over the jackhammers on the third floor. She smiled at the man behind the sprawling mahogany desk and set the file on the corner. As she did, she glanced down at the paper unrolled in front of him. It appeared to be a diagram of a maze, but Francie knew what she was looking at, knew exactly what to look for. Every day for weeks now she'd gotten an inside glimpse of a different phase of the construction just beginning above them.

"Thank you." Her boss leaned back in his chair and put his hands behind his head. "I'm thinking we should have lunch at Municip—*Navy* Pier today. Can't get used to the name change. What are you in the mood for, my dear?"

Tag's coaching resounded in her head, but she ignored it. She was playing this one her way. No pouts, no dew-eyed looks. She knew how to get to a man like this. "You'll laugh."

"Try me."

"Lunch would be wonderful"—she looked for, and found, a square red box on the diagram—"but I'd love some hot roasted peanuts."

A deep, rich laugh echoed off the dark paneling. "That, we can do." He stood and offered his arm. She took it, but discreetly pulled away when they reached the elevator. Mr. Walbrecht never used the back entrance, which meant that every day at half past twelve she tried to ignore the stares from Doris and the woman who sat at the desk she once occupied, as she walked beside one of the richest men in Chicago past glass cases teaming with sparkling diamonds and gleaming with pearls.

She hated that part of her day. Hated the stares and the way she had to act better than Doris when she was anything but.

They walked out into oppressive heat and into a waiting car, the door held open by a man in a black uniform with gold buttons.

Leather seats the color of butter welcomed them. A small fan mounted on the dashboard stirred the air. Francie adjusted her hat and folded her hands on her lap. As they pulled away from the curb, she ducked, looking up at the boarded windows on the third floor. "When will it be open?" she asked, with the air of a child anticipating Christmas.

"Can you keep a secret, my dear?"

Heart beating in time with the puttering motor, she slid her hands behind her back, crossing her fingers like the child she no longer was. "Of course."

"The new vault is being made in Germany as we speak. It should arrive in June and coincide perfectly with the end of the reconstruction. The security company assures me the wiring and alarms will be installed and everything ready by June. So. . ." He hung on the word as if giving a drum roll. "We'll switch over to the new system on my birthday, at the very moment I was born."

Francie smiled. She didn't ask the obvious questions. There were other ways to find that out. Mr. Walbrect's mother belonged to Mrs. Hollanddale's book club.

And Francie made all of her gowns.

CHAPTER 25

Dani stared at the time in the corner of her computer screen, begging it to change. The time, and her brain, were in worse-than-usual Monday morning slo-mo. She'd taken a half hour shower when she got home around one a.m.—shampooing three times, scrubbing off the tattoo and makeup. And guilt.

She'd spent the night connecting dots. Jarod had given a gun to Trish's boyfriend Rabia—the guy whose picture she'd identified for Todd. Rab's intention was to kill the woman who lived in the house—the mother of the baby who slept in the filthy crib? After two hours of wrestling, she'd gotten out of bed, driven to a gas station, and called the police, telling them all she knew. Anonymously.

That left her mind freed up to panic over China. There were moments during the sleepless night when the irony sank in and she'd laughed, in a twisted sort of way. China didn't have a place to live because Dani had told her to leave her boyfriend, and when she did, he killed himself, leaving the apartment empty for the person China blamed for killing him to move in. . .and invite China to live with her.

Even now, hysteria stalked the edges of her remaining sanity.

She couldn't think about it now. She had to focus. After work she'd go home and pray her way through it and decide what to do with what she knew. But right now she had to multitask her way into a mental fog that allowed no room for fear.

Between rewriting the end of her story on a girl who'd earned her college tuition sewing vampire costumes, she made notes on things she wanted to ask the director of the Boys and Girls Club, and instant messaged a seventeen-year-old boy who fashioned yard art out of old wheel covers.

Her e-mail icon popped up.

You kissed *him?*

Anna. Responding to the plea for advice she'd sent what now seemed like years ago.

Yes.

What she'd wanted, twenty-some hours ago when the kiss thing seemed monumental, was assurance—that she hadn't done the wrong thing, that a girl initiating the first kiss wasn't the end of the world. That she just needed to be patient. He'd call.

But maybe he wouldn't. She deleted the last sentence of her story, redid it three times, and sent it to Mitch.

"Great copy."

Mitch leaned on her partition. Sleeves rolled up and tie askew, he looked like a Friday afternoon.

It took her a moment to realize he referred to the garage sale tycoons and not the story she'd just sent. "Thank you."

"The kids' mom sent an e-mail. They've been swamped with calls since yesterday." He lifted his coffee mug in salute. "You're making a difference."

She held back her smile and refrained from explaining that what she'd had in mind was more along the lines of world peace and a cure for cancer. "I hope what they're doing will inspire other kids." *To get real jobs that don't include guns and illegal substances.*

Mitch nodded. "How are you doing on the Swamp story?"

"Still researching. I've established some good contacts. I did a ride-along with a police officer on Friday." *And got rolled into a gang on Sunday.*

"Can't wait to read it. Keep up the good work."

She sucked in her cheeks, poker-facing the end of their exchange. "Thanks. I'll try." *To stay out of jail.*

Warring emotions made her punchy. Recollections of last night sent adrenaline coursing along nerve paths. Thoughts of Nicky spawned a whole different brand of jitters.

Another e-mail appeared in her inbox.

Did he kiss back?

She had far more pressing matters to decipher than the force of lips pressing hers.

He had kissed her back. Hadn't he?

Wouldn't he have called her by now if he had? Was it better if he didn't? She hadn't figured out a way to tell him about her double life, to show him she was doing it partly for Rena. If she was going to live across the street, Nicky had to know and had to swear to protect her cover. For Rena.

She had to figure it out and tell him face-to-face. Besides, they had to finish the diary.

She stared at the black words on her computer. *Did he kiss back?* With all the shades of gray she was dancing in these days, she needed one area of her life where she was totally transparent. At least to one person.

I think so.

She pushed SEND. And then she pushed another button. The little green icon on her phone. Next to Nicky's name.

His recorded voice made her heart fumble the next beat. She took a deep breath. "Hi. It's Dani. Um. . .I have something to talk to you about, and it's time sensitive, and I can't tell you on the phone. And, yeah. . .about that k—what I did. . . I'm sorry. Can we get beyond the awkward and finish the diary? Call me." Only then did she glance at the slow-moving time on her screen. She'd just done the equivalent of someone calling her at four in the morning. "Oh! I'm so sorry. I didn't look at the time. It's not even eleven, and you're probably sound asleep. I hope your phone is off and I didn't wake you. I'm sorry. Guess I said that, didn't I? Okay then. Bye."

Face flaming like a tiki torch, she ended the call. And began the wait.

⚜

Monday. Six p.m. He still hadn't called.

Dani added two things to her list and told herself not to overthink it.

Dishes, silverware, lamp, sheets, towels, futon mattress. Survival gear for a double life. She crossed off each necessity as she shoved it into a box or on top of the pile in Agatha's back seat. She'd already made one trip to her new digs with hair supplies, makeup, books, and a week's worth of jeans and T-shirts. She planned on stopping back at her Third Avenue place to change clothes before and after work every day. It didn't seem smart to keep skirts and heels in her new place. Could blow her cover. She'd found a special at Walgreens on spray-in hair color. Wild red. Three cans for twelve dollars.

Could she get a story in three cans?

After fighting with the futon through the living room and halfway across her kitchen floor, she surrendered. "You win." She'd settle for a pile of blankets. Flopping across the futon, she stared up at the ceiling fan and wondered again why she hadn't asked Evan to help. *Because he'd stop you, dummy.*

Evan didn't know she was moving. Neither did Anna. Technically, she wasn't actually moving, she was visiting—hanging out after work and on weekends. The landlord had agreed to month-to-month and hadn't even asked for references. A working vacation, that's what it was. She could afford the rent on both places for a few months, but her goal was to have the story in by September, to time it with school starting—she'd make a heart-wrenching contrast between the lives of these kids and the dog walkers in their satin jackets.

She dragged the futon back to its frame, pulled three blankets from the linen closet, and took a plate, a bowl, and a cup from the kitchen cupboard. She wasn't planning on entertaining.

"Chi can live with you."

Venus didn't seem like the type to make idle threats.

Neither did Yamile. *"We'll meet at your place from now on."*

She started another list. *Paper plates, plastic cups, toilet paper, pizza, soda. . .* How many Sisters were there again? Having them in her apartment would be the best way to get to know them and still have some control. Maybe. She thought once again of the girls sitting on Trish's bed and imagined slumber parties with pierced and tattooed "chicks" crashed on the floor from one end of the apartment to the other. *Pardon me, Venus, but would you mind snuffing out that joint? Yamile, honey, I thought I said no alcohol. Leah, watch the language. Rena, turn the music down. I'm really not fond of rap. Boys? Who invited boys?*

This was a bad idea.

But it was a necessary idea. The only way she'd get the story angle she wanted. *Ladies and gentlemen, as I write this, I am embedded with the notorious Seven Sisters in an undisclosed Kenosha neighborhood. This is a part of this beautiful harbor city few ever see. The scene before me is not one you'll find on tourist brochures, but this, ladies and gentlemen, is the sad reality for far too many of our youth whose potential will never be realized thanks to*—Her phone buzzed. Nicky?

Vito.

"Hi Vito, how's my angel?"

"The question is, how are you? Did I just see Agatha at the house where that kid shot himself?"

"Ah. . .yes. I was working on a story."

"Funny, looked to me like you were moving in."

"Really?"

"I dropped Lavinia off to get an order at Bracciano and drove around the block, and I see you carrying in a box, and I see a guy taking down the rent sign. I didn't stop 'cause I didn't want Lavinia to know. She'd go nuts. You need money? A place to stay? We got two empty bedrooms. You know—"

"Thank you. That's so sweet. I'm not really moving, I'm just. . .hanging out for a little while to work on a story."

"Bad idea."

I just said that.

"Does Metzger know?"

"No. Vito, I need you to keep this a secret. Especially from Todd. Please? It's just for a couple of weeks. I'll be fine. I'm a kickboxer, you know."

She could swear she heard him spit. "Fat lot of good that'll do against a .45. Just the other night a guy busted into somebody's apartment in Wilson Heights with a gun and—"

"I'll be careful. Besides, I've got Nicky right across the street."

Another spitting sound. "That kid can't even keep his own fam—" He sighed and said something in Italian she probably didn't want translated. "I'll keep it to myself, but you better believe I'm going to be watching you. And you better answer your phone every time I call, you hear? If I so much as hear somebody on that block sneeze too loud, I'm calling you, and then I'm calling the cops. Got it?"

"Got it." She stretched and rubbed a sore spot on her foot. "Vito? Thank you. It's nice to know you got my back."

A snort sounded in her ear and he hung up.

Dani put two dish towels and a pot holder in the drawer between the aqua sink and the white stove then walked through her new vacation home. A pile of folded quilts lay on the floor of the bedroom. On the ridiculously remote chance that China came to live with her, there were more blankets in the closet.

She hadn't thought about curtains. There were blinds on the windows facing the street, but the rest of the windows were bare. She hung bath towels over bent white curtain rods then peered between the slats in the blinds and around the crack running down the center of the living room window at the neon CLOSED sign in the window across the street. Bracciano was dark and silent. Like the man who worked there. What was Nicky doing on his night off? What was he thinking? About her? About her question? She'd said she was praying, and she was. Over and over. *Lord, help him. Help him open his heart enough to let You in.*

Would there be a moment in the middle of whatever he was doing when he'd stop and think about that kiss? Would he smile or swipe his lips with the back of his hand to erase the memory?

She let the gap in the blinds close.

The apartment walls had all been repainted, but she'd set a green and white webbed lawn chair in front of the place where the stain had been. She hadn't sat in it yet. Would it be creepier to look at the spot where Miguel had died or to sit on it?

Scuffed and worn wood floors whined under her feet. A toilet flushed downstairs. Seconds later her landlord laughed. She'd heard the intro music to *M*A*S*H* on one of her trips up the stairs. Working up the courage to sit in her lawn chair, she turned on the floor lamp she'd taken from her "real" living room and pulled out her voice recorder, legal pad, and iPod. She searched for the right song to fit her mood. As Eddie Vedder sang "Longing to Belong," someone knocked on her door.

Her heart skipped a beat then stumbled back to normal rhythm. *I'll be fine. I'm a kickboxer, you know. Besides, I've got Nicky*—who doesn't know I'm here and will kill me himself when he finds out—*"across the street."*

She parted the dotted swiss curtain a fraction of an inch. Rena. She opened the door.

"Hope this is okay, *Cerise*." She walked in with Yamile, Venus, Leah, and three girls Dani thought she'd seen at the bonfire.

"Hey. Sure." In her own apartment, unfamiliar though it was, she found it hard to shift into tough-girl mode.

Yamile pointed at her shoulder. "Thought you had a tat."

Busted. "It was fake. Just figuring if I wanted it or not."

"Do it." It sounded more like a command than an opinion. She pulled aside the strap of her tank top, showing off her 7 with a snake-like *S* coiling around the bottom—at least twice the size of Rena's. "Need this, too."

Dani gulped and nodded. "Sorry I don't have a place to sit. I'm just. . ." Her thought trailed to silence as the girls hauled all of her blankets into the living room.

Venus plopped on a folded blanket and leaned against the wall. "Doesn't it gross you out that somebody shot himself here?"

She opened her mouth to deny it—a lie—when a girl with stringy blond hair streaked with green made a retching sound. "Where was it? Where did he do it?"

Reminding herself she wasn't supposed to know, Dani asked if anyone wanted pizza. Just like a sleepover. *And then we can do each other's nails. Sorry, fresh out of black.*

Like the queen overseeing her minions, Yamile sat in the folding chair with her arms perched on the arm rests. At least a dozen rings adorned each hand. Probably more purposeful than fashionable. Street-girl brass knuckles. "I couldn't live here," she said.

Leah stretched out on the floor and clutched her throat then let out a wicked laugh. "*You* couldn't live here, but you told Chi to move back in. As if she wasn't already psycho."

"Chick's gotta crash somewhere."

Dani wiped her palms on her jeans and edged toward the kitchen. No one had answered her pizza question.

"She'll sleep in a Dumpster before she comes back here. That'd be too weird livin' here with Miguel's kid in her—"

"Pizza sounds good." Rena threw a blanket in the corner. "I'll help." She followed Dani into the kitchen and stood a foot away from her as she opened the freezing compartment. "You look scared. Chi's not coming, you know. You didn't think for a second she'd come back here, did you?"

Dani shrugged and turned on the oven. "Depends on how desperate she is. I'm going to run into her sometime. What'll she do if she sees me?"

"Spaz."

"Thanks for the reassurance." Dani tugged at her faded army-green shirt. "How am I do—"

A short round girl wearing a black tank top that looked like it was sprayed on opened a cupboard door. "Ashtray."

"Sorry." Dani pointed to the smoke alarm straight above the girl. "Landlord won't allow it."

The girl rolled her eyes and tucked her unlit cigarette behind her ear.

"What's your name?" Dani tried matching the irritated tone. It wouldn't pay to be too polite. She grabbed a paring knife, the only knife she'd brought, and cut the plastic off a pizza.

"C.J." The girl scratched her belly. "You do karate, huh?"

"Kickboxing, actually." *What's your specialty?* "How long have you been with the Sisters?"

"Dunno. A long time."

"Why'd you join?"

C.J. shrugged and walked over to the fridge. "Don't wanna get beat up mostly." She opened the refrigerator door and took out a can of Mountain Dew. Sticky spray hit Dani in the arm. "Yamile wants a powwow. We better get out there."

The oven hadn't finished preheating, but Dani slid in two pizzas. The timer knob spun like a top. Both hands of the clock on the back of the stove hung limp and lifeless. She followed the girls and sat on the floor.

Yamile twirled the rings on her index finger. "We gotta tell Cerise wha'sup. She don't know the rules yet."

Leah's hand shot in the air, a move sickeningly close to a gesture once accompanied by "Heil Hitler!" She lowered it, still stiff, to her side. "Don't steal my man."

The others nodded and laughed.

"Oh yeah."

"So true."

"Y's the boss," C.J. added, pointing at Yamile. "Do what she says."

The scar pulling at Yamile's eye lost its tightness as she smiled. "Rule number one."

"Stay loyal."

"Gotta have honor. Be true to your people."

"Respect."

"Take care of your sisters."

Rules ping-ponged across the room. Dani pulled her knees to her chest as a reality hit with the force of a fist. *What they're trying to be is what the church is supposed to be.* Where were the Christ-followers, the hands and feet of Jesus, in this neighborhood? A song she'd sung in Haiti filtered through the four-letter words and raucous laughter. *"Let peace begin with me."*

Yamile wrapped a strand of hair around her finger, let it spring loose, and did it again. "And what happens if you break the rules?"

"Consequences." Like a classroom of first graders, they answered in unison, adding fist-in-hand gestures and pantomimes of cut throats.

Dani nodded. "Got it."

"You better." Yamile leveled a warning glare then dissolved in laughter. "So what's goin' on with everybody?"

What followed was a time of gut-honesty that reminded Dani of the "sharing and caring" times in her singles' group—minus the prayer. And the hope.

"My dad's back in jail."

"My sister's pregnant."

"Me and Jay had a fight again."

"Anybody heard from Rab and Trish?" Leah asked.

Rena shook her head.

Venus stretched and yawned. "We gotta figure the Roses are gonna retaliate, right?"

"Maybe not. Rab didn't get anything."

"Somebody bust into my house with a gun even *thinkin'* about takin' my stuff and I'm gonna—"

"They know they ain't got a chance. We'll—"

The rattle of the kitchen doorknob interrupted Yamile.

"Chi!"

Ice slithered through Dani's veins. She couldn't run or hide, but she could stand on her feet and pray she wouldn't need to use them to defend herself against a pregnant woman.

China wore no makeup. She'd lost weight. Dani watched her eyes. She dropped a grocery bag on the kitchen counter. It made only a rustling sound. Clothes? China looked at Yamile. "This stinks, but I don't have a choice. Who's Cerise?"

Dani flattened her hands against the wall behind her. "I am."

"What the—" China spun from Dani to Yamile. Vile words sliced the air. "What kinda sick joke you pullin'?"

Yamile stood. Her hands flexed. "What you talkin' about?"

"Why do you think I tried taking her out at the bonfire? She's a poser. What'd she tell you?" She turned on Dani. "You're renting this place? And you want me moving in with you?" Tears mingled with a screeching laugh. "You're hoping I'll blow my brains out just like Miguel, aren't you? I didn't give you the Romeo and Juliet story I promised. Did you bring the poison? Or a gun? I'd like pills, if that's okay with you. Tried the gun. Oh yeah, you saw that." Her dark eyes lost their depth. "Her name is Danielle. She's a reporter. She's the one who told me to break up with Miguel. I listened to her, and now he's dead."

Yamile closed in on Dani. Venus and Leah flanked her. Yamile's scar puckered. "That true?"

C.J. rose to her feet. Instead of joining the half circle moving in on Dani, she slid around the corner into the kitchen. The oven door opened and closed.

Yamile glanced at Dani's feet. "That true? You're not Cerise?" She shifted from right to left and back again.

Dani held her gaze. "That's true."

"You doing a story on us?"

"Yes."

Yamile stopped pacing and clenching. Her head tipped to one side. Dani had the sudden realization that her life literally hung in the balance. Seconds passed. And then Yamile smiled. Her right hand relaxed. Dani's silent sigh half-emptied her lungs when a blur to her left ended with a head-rattling slap. A shower of light points distorted her vision. When they vanished, Yamile's face loomed inches from hers.

"Nobody lies to me. You really thought you'd get away with this? You come here and listen in on our plans. . . . You wearing a wire like on TV? Recording all our secrets? And you think you can put it in the paper and nothin's going to happen to you?"

Leah clamped hands on her hips. "Let's show her."

Two of the other girls stood. "Can't mess with the Sisters."

Yamile shoved her against the wall.

"Don't you—" Rena grabbed Yamile's arm.

Yamile shook her off. "Whose side you on, girl? You defending this poser against the rest of us? Sorry mistake. No wonder Jarod don't treat you good. We been feelin' sorry for you, but maybe it's all your problem. You got a loyalty problem, Fiorini? Sergeant Metzger getting to you?" She grabbed a handful of Rena's hair and jerked her toward the floor.

The action shocked Dani out of paralysis. "Let go of her. *Now.* Your problem's with me. And guess what? This is my place. And guess what else? I proved myself, and you let me join the Sisters.

So if you say you believe in loyalty, and you want to be true to your rules, you have to hear me out. There's nothing honorable about beating on somebody when you don't know why she's doing what she's doing."

For once her wordiness had a positive effect. Yamile's jaw dropped, she blinked, and laughed. "Man, you talk good. Okay. Sure." She motioned for the others to sit. "Make it good, *Cerise*."

CHAPTER 26

Dani leaned against the wall, hoping she looked casual. In truth, she needed it for support.

Forearms tightened over her abdomen, China glared at Yamile, walked into the kitchen, picked up her paper bag, and walked to the door.

Dani cleared her throat. "I'm going to tell you the most important thing right up front. I'm a Christian. I believe in Jesus Christ, the Son of God, and the main goal of my life is to surrender to Him and give Him honor."

Venus cocked her head to one side. "He teach you to fight like that?"

Swallow. Think. *Lord, help!* "That's a fair question. I don't claim to make the best decisions, okay? But I use martial arts to defend myself, not to cause harm. Anyway, I met China while I was doing a story a few months ago. She confided some things. If she was telling me the truth, Miguel was controlling her big-time, and it made me mad. I told her she deserved better than that. Any of you disagree? You think some guy should use you and have power over you?"

Heads shook.

"Nuh-uh."

"No way."

Out of the corner of her eye, Dani saw China, still standing by the door, arms still hugging her unborn child.

"I told her she should try to go on to school and maybe find a church to connect with so she could break out of the cycle of poverty and violence and become the kind of person she could feel good about. Any of you think that's a bad thing?"

Leah snickered. "Dreamer. Easy for you to walk into our world and say that. Any of us try getting out, we get knocked down."

C.J. gave a fake smack to the side of Leah's head. Leah crumpled to the floor. "Jus' like that."

"I can see me walkin' into church." C.J. spun the chain encircling her wrist. "All the little church ladies havin' heart attacks."

As they all, including Rena, laughed, Dani eyed her car keys hanging on a hook on a kitchen cupboard and considered walking out. She'd have to get past China first. "But what if the church started acting like the church?"

"What's that supposed to mean?" A girl with stringy black hair and knees drawn to her chest asked the question while picking black nail polish from her fingernails.

"Anybody know anything about Jesus?"

"He was born in a manger."

"He died on a cross."

"He fed a bunch of people with a couple fish."

"Okay. Let's take just that. Jesus is God. He helped create the world. He left all the splendor of heaven to come here as a baby born in a stable to show us He gets us. He knows all the hard stuff we deal with every day."

"Great. And then they killed him." Leah rolled her eyes. "Not such a smart move to come here."

Sweat dampened Dani's sides. If she couldn't make this make sense, they'd devour her. "But it *was* a smart move. Yamile, what would happen if you made a rule and Leah deliberately defied it? What if she broke every rule you made?"

Yamile leveled a finger gun at Leah, aiming right between her eyebrows.

"So God's the same way. Only He's totally perfect."

Yamile pointed to herself with both thumbs. "You sayin' I'm not?"

Dani smiled. "God made this world and made people to fill it and then gave them rules. Since He's perfect, He couldn't put up with anyone breaking His rules. You break 'em, you die." She waited for a chorus of affirmations to quiet. "The problem was that He loved the people He created. They're His kids. So He gave them a way out. He let them kill an animal, a lamb or a goat, in their place so they wouldn't have to die when they broke His rule."

"That's disgusting."

"Gross."

"A sacrifice," Rena added.

"Exactly." She chanced a quick look at China. The girl seemed frozen in place. "And then, because He loved his kids so much, God sent His own Son to Earth to be the very last sacrifice. Jesus was perfect. He never once sinned. When soldiers nailed Him to a wooden cross, He could have gotten away, but that was what He came to earth to do—to die like a slaughtered lamb, a sacrifice, to pay the price for the sins of God's people."

The room was quiet for a moment. Yamile nodded. "So like, if Leah broke all those rules, and I had to off her, but I loved her so I killed my kid instead 'cause somebody had to die for what she did. . . that would be the same, huh?"

"Yeah." *Sort of. Lord, don't let me mess this up.* "The difference is that even though it had to hurt God unbelievably to see His Son suffer, He knew that after Jesus died He'd bring Him back to life, and they'd live in heaven together. And by doing that, He showed us that we can live forever, too. We don't have to sacrifice anything. We need to get to know Jesus and believe how much He loves us. We need to grow to love Him and believe that He gave up His life here on earth to pay the price for everything we do wrong. That's how we have eternal life in heaven after we leave this life."

Again the silence. C.J. crossed her legs in front of her and furrowed her brow. "That's crazy stuff. So what about the church being the church?"

"Somebody mentioned Jesus feeding a bunch of people. The time He was here on earth was spent caring for others. He healed sick people, made blind people see, and told everyone about God. He wants His followers to do the same thing. So that brings me back to what I'd like to do with you guys. Most Christians care about people. Most of us do things like sending money to feed and clothe hungry children in other countries and to support missionaries who go to places like Africa or India to tell people about Jesus. But a lot of us, myself included, are scared to get face-to-face with people with real problems, people who desperately need to hear about Jesus."

"People like us, you mean." Attitude laced Yamile's words. "So you want to put stuff in the paper to show people how bad we got it so all the church ladies can come to the 'hood on Sundays and give us cookies and then go home and feel all good about themselves the rest of the week."

Like uncapping a shaken soda bottle, Yamile's comments started a flow of cynicism.

"God bless you, poor underprivileged Sistuh."

"Jesus love you even though your daddy don't. Just belieeeeve."

"Your mama's a crack head, but don't you worry none, 'cause Jesus loves you."

"Have a cookie, Sistuh."

Dani pressed her hands over her face. This wasn't working. "I'm not talking about cookies. Not charity. I'm talking about people giving you their time—training you for jobs, tutoring, helping you finish high school or get your GED, maybe teaching life skills like cooking and budgeting and"—she pinned her gaze on China— "parenting."

C.J. did another sweep of eyes to ceiling. "I seen those people. They painted my ma's house one time. Whole bunch of squeaky cleans in matching shirts." She jabbed a finger toward her tonsils. "Made the house all pretty outside while my brother's shooting up in the basement. What's the point?"

Venus shook her head. "Maybe the point shoulda been showin' your brother how to paint his own house and get off his lazy—"

"Stop it." The quiet command came from the doorway to the kitchen.

Dani's jaw unhinged. All eyes turned to China.

"We sit around complaining about the way things are, and then somebody comes along who wants to change things, and we put her down. I say we give her a chance."

Yamile swiveled on her throne. "One second you want to kill her, and now you're sayin' give her a chance?"

"Yeah." China glanced at Dani then back at Yamile. In that second, Dani sensed a significant change. "We owe it to the younger ones." She pointed at C.J. "I don't want her thinkin' she's gotta do whatever some guy says just to survive. We owe it to them to give them choices."

Dani finally found the presence of mind to close her mouth.

Venus narrowed eyes thick with mascara. "What do you want from us?"

"Tell me your stories. Your hopes and dreams and hurts. I'll make up names so no one will know who you are. Leave me out of anything that isn't legal, but let me hang out with you for a couple of weeks."

Yamile tapped fingernails on the chair's aluminum arms. Leah leaned forward. "The guys won't like it."

The scarred side of Yamile's face tightened, puckered. A steely gaze swept the room. "Then we don't tell them. Everybody got that?"

Like a roomful of bobble head dolls, they all agreed.

Nerves stretching and thinning like violin strings, Dani waited for the conditions. Yamile rose slowly to her feet. The room hushed. "Two weeks. Fourteen days. You write your story, and I get to read it. If I say change something, you change it." She stepped closer, face within inches of Dani's. "Like Chi said, we'll do it for the younger ones. But you turn on us, you make one wrong move"—she pointed at her scar—"you'll be lucky if you look like this. Got it?"

"Yes."

Yamile brushed past her. "Let's get."

She walked out the door, Leah and Venus at her heels.

C.J. stopped at the door and turned, her face void of expression. "You tell those church ladies if they want to make it outta this neighborhood with all their teeth, they better bring cookies." Laughter sparkled in her eyes.

Relief coursed out of Dani in a rippling laugh. "You give me two weeks, and I'll throw in chocolate chip and oatmeal and peanut butter and snickerdoodles."

"Oreos."

"Yes. Oreos. Lots and lots of Oreos."

C.J. walked out the door and down the steps.

China dropped her paper bag on the floor and stared into the living room.

Dani rested a hand on her back. "You can have the bedroom."

♔

Unanswered questions woke Nicky before ten on Tuesday morning. He'd spent his evening off in the kitchen, gluing down loose vinyl floor tiles, soaking stove burners in degreaser, and replacing a pot handle. He'd even fixed the three-legged chair.

Mind-numbing work that didn't help him figure things out. Or tire him. Even after four hours of baking, his thoughts still raced. At best he'd gotten five hours of restless sleep. Disjointed dreams had haunted his night. A lingering kiss, a crucifix, an angry black seven dripping red.

Face down on the mattress, he pulled a pillow over his head. *Sleep. . . sleep. . .* He tried a hypnotic chant followed by counting backward from a hundred. *Ninety-nine. . .ninety-eight. . .ninety-seven. . .* Rena was in a gang. *"Is that why they leave us alone?" Ninety-two. . .ninety-one. . .* "You don't have to worry. I'm getting out." *Eighty-one. . .eighty. . . seventy-nine. . .* "Can you?" *Seventy-seven. . .seven. . .seven. . .seven. . .*

Crack! The sound zinged through the open windows and reverberated off the kitchen walls. *Wake up.* The nightmare again. He knew he was in it, knew it wasn't real, but he couldn't get out. The sound was so close. Just outside. He dropped the spoon, ran to the back door, but stopped and called 911. *This isn't real. Wake up.*

"Stay inside, sir. Someone's on the way."

Stay inside when he didn't know who was outside? This was his neighborhood. His people. He opened the back door. The smell of the gunshot filled his nostrils. It came from the alley.

"Nicky!" Not a boy's yell. . .a cry. Weak and desperate.

Tony! Where are you? Dear God. . .

Wake up!

Sides heaving, sweat soaking his pillow, he flopped onto his back. *Make it stop.* The nightmare that had been in retreat was back. Thanks to his sister.

He had to do something. Punching walls wasn't producing results. He sat up and grabbed his phone. He needed advice, needed to talk to Todd about Rena. That wasn't going to happen until they made peace.

Todd was no longer competition. Not after that kiss.

Unless she'd only meant it as a token of sympathy. Or unless she'd meant it as a starting point, and then he'd gone and ignored her for two days. She might be spitting tacks by now.

He hadn't had time to figure out the next step. He definitely needed a better grip on his emotions before spending time with her. No more soap opera scenes. He still couldn't believe he'd been on the verge of losing it like that. Every time he thought about it, it was like watching some bad actor on TV. Whoever that mental wreck was, it wasn't Nicky Fiorini. Though the end result was sweet.

He pushed a button on the side of his phone. If Todd didn't have plans until work, maybe they'd take his uncle's boat out and hash over the Rena problem on the lake. Then again, if the Kenosha Police had the answers, he wouldn't have to be asking the questions.

The screen came to life and nagged about his missed calls.

Dani. *Yesterday.*

Tacks. She'd definitely be spitting tacks.

He glanced at the leather-bound book half concealed by his jeans on the chair. She would have been expecting him to call to set up a time to get together on his day off. Would she get it that he'd needed some space after finding out his little sister was in a gang? Would she get it that he'd hoped to have an answer to her question before he saw her again?

He dialed his voice mail. Her voice, stumbling over an apology for "that k—what I did" washed over him—the perfect antidote for the nightmare.

The smell of coffee wafted through the vents. Throwing off the covers, he loped down the stairs and threw open the kitchen door. "Morning, Dad."

"Morning. Things look good around here."

"Thanks. Hey, Alonzo's working tonight, and I was wondering if you're going to be around—"

"You want the night off? Take it."

YESTERDAY'S STARDUST

"Thanks."

"A girl?"

"I hope so."

He took the steps two at a time, pushing her number as he reached his bedroom.

"Hello." Her voice held a cool edge.

"Hi. Hey, I know I didn't call, but. . .I've been thinking about you." The smooth voice could have been his dad's. Not what he was shooting for.

"You have?" She paused. "I'm afraid to ask what."

"So don't ask." Had his great-grandfather laughed in the same way as he coaxed a young flapper into the storeroom? "I got the night off. Do you have plans after work?"

"No."

"Want to have plans?"

"Y-yes."

"You don't sound so sure."

"I'm just. . ." Her sigh echoed in his ear. "Yes. I'd love to. We'll talk. About things. Then."

"Okay. What time are you done?"

"I'm getting a lot done this morning. I could leave early—for a story."

"So that's all I am to you, huh?" He grinned at the wall.

"To be honest, Mr. Fiorini, I'm not quite sure what you are to me. But I'd like to find out."

His lips parted then puckered in a silent whistle. "Well then, you name a time and maybe we can figure it out together."

"How about noon?"

That barely gave him time to shower and pick up the car. But it gave them what? Eight or ten hours together? The thought did strange things to his gut. How would they fill all that time? *Think fast.* "How would you like to go with me to visit my grandfather? Late afternoon is the best time to visit. You can read on the way, and maybe we'll get lucky and it'll be a good day for him. Maybe some female charm will spark his memory."

"Sounds like a wonderful plan. Pick me up at my place."

She gave him directions. He knew the area well. It was a

neighborhood he passed through but had never had reason to stop. "Are you a cold pizza fan?"

"Love it."

"Then I'll bring lunch, and we can eat at Veteran's Park. See you then." *And we'll figure it out together.* He left the words in his head where they belonged. "Bye."

⚜

As Nicky turned onto Sheridan Road, Dani opened to the bookmark in the diary. Nicky gestured toward the page. "I hope the cat goes away again. It was fun to see her enjoying life."

"And it's fun to see you getting into her story like it's all happening now."

"Imagine this playing out on Facebook. Status: owned and controlled by bf."

She laughed. "Think how different her situation would be if we could rewrite her story and add technology. She could meet prince charming on a dating site, and he'd locate her with his GPS."

"And he'd sneak in and steal her away right under T's nose with his night-vision goggles, and if the guy came after them, he'd blast him with an RPG."

"I think you're writing a different book."

"I'm writing a bestseller. Women swoon for the strong, silent good guys who pack antitank weapons."

Your eyes are weapons enough for me. "Men."

"Can't live with us, can't shoot us." He pulled into the right lane. "Before you start reading, maybe we should talk."

Did he hear her gulp? "So you're not the strong *silent* type." At the moment, she wasn't so sure she wanted him to be in touch with his feelings. If he said anything—

"About that kiss. . ."

Her teeth sank into her lip. She let her grimace serve as an answer.

"It was nice. Very nice."

An unplanned sigh rushed from her lungs. She closed her eyes and sank against the seat. "I'm not usually that forward. I've been second-guessing and wondering what you thought of me." She

242

heard the tick of the turn signal. "I just gave in to an impulse, and it seemed the right thing at the time, but then afterward I—"

The car stopped. She opened her eyes. They were parked at a gas station but not at a pump.

Nicky stared at her. He unfastened his seat belt. His gaze caressed every inch of her face, lingering on her eyes then her lips. "It was nice. No second-guessing, okay?" He leaned closer. "I give you permission to always"—his hand conformed to her cheek—"give into"—his lips grazed her mouth—"your impulses." He pressed his lips to hers, and she responded in a way that would leave him no doubt she'd kissed him back.

♛

"Hey." Dani shook her finger at him. "I just saw something important we skimmed over. *You* skimmed over. 'T caught me with A.'"

"I don't remember reading that. So our good girl got caught with another man." Nicky took his eyes off the road long enough to wink. "The infamous triangle. A common theme throughout history."

She opened her mouth to read the next sentence when his meaning hit. Her lips still tingled. Didn't his? One kiss—*keep them wanting more*—and she couldn't have come up with the color of Todd's eyes or even his last name if her life depended on it. "And people throughout history have been seeing triangles where none exist."

"None?"

"None."

The dimple made an appearance. "Then you can keep reading."

"Thank you." She ran her finger under the next line. " 'He took my black fox—' "

"She owned a fox?"

"Fox fur. That was back before PC and PETA."

"Right."

" 'He took my black fox and left with a threat—"You've got a lot to lose, doll." He's right. I have everything to lose, but I can't lose my mind while I'm trying to save my family. There are ways to get around everything, and I will find a way around T to get to A.' "

They passed the Seven Mile Road exit. "The Alphabet Game."

"She plays it well." She scanned up, going back a year, then turned the page. "Someday I want to read this all over again." Nicky had skimmed much faster than she'd realized. They'd missed whole chunks. "Listen to this. 'When I was in the cage, T told the man I was useful and convinced him to let me live. I thought, at that moment, that I was in love with T. He saved my life. It took me a long time to admit my life wouldn't have been in danger if it weren't for him and his kind.'"

Dani rubbed one arm to fend off a shiver. Francie's story was eerily familiar. Stockholm Syndrome. Jarod held Rena captive but made her feel safe. Apparently even loved at one time.

Nicky shook his head. "Sounds like every gang kid I've ever known."

"That's just what I was thinking. Nothing new under the sun." She continued reading. "'T drove me to Suzette's apartment. He reminded me of what would happen if I tried to get away from him, and I cried. Just when I thought he was going to hit me, he kissed me. A grown-up kiss that made me not care that I would belong to him forever.'"

"What a"—Nicky gave a short, throaty groan—"sociopath, psychopath. Take your pick."

"And she's so naive, gullible, needy. Take your pick."

"I think we're in need of a subject change, but the one I want to talk about isn't much lighter." His shoulders rose with a deep inhale. "Did you know my sister's in a gang?"

Dani smoothed the seam on the sleeve of her blouse. "Yes." Her pulse rate kicked up a notch. Now that she was face-to-face, telling him what she'd done didn't seem like such a great idea. "She wants out."

"So she says. Do you believe her?"

"To be honest, I think she's torn. I'm not sure she's ready to do what it takes, to turn her back on Jarod and the girls she thinks are her friends."

"She needs to get out of here." Nicky's right hand formed a fist. "I wish we could afford to send her away to school."

"There have to be answers. If every church in the city had an outreach to kids in their own neighborhoods, think of what that could do. You get parents to volunteer, open up a church basement after school, pair kids with people who care, and in the process they're learning about Jesus. It would be radical."

The muscles in Nicky's jaw bulged. His fingers whitened.

"What are you thinking?"

"Nothing." His voice negated his answer. "Let's get back to Francie."

"Okay. I'll go back to where we left off before."

" 'Franky loves to play school. I'm going to invite the Bullis children next door to play with us. I worry about them. Mr. Bullis is not a nice man, and Mrs. Bullis is too harsh with her children. She reminds me of Mama. That makes me scared her children will rebel like Suzette. My sister didn't love the man she ran away with. He was just her ticket out.' "

The next day was a continuation. " 'I read books and played games with the children today. Maybe I can play a small part in keeping them from turning bad. They just need to be children, and they need someone to love them. I can do that.' "

Goose bumps skittered along the backs of Dani's arms. "Nothing new under the sun. She's doing her version of what I was just talking about." She looked at Nicky. His eyes narrowed as if they were driving into the sun. They weren't. Something she'd said had changed his mood. "What—" She cut off the questions she'd already asked. With all of her training, she couldn't make a man talk if he didn't want to. Not this one, anyway. She closed the diary, keeping her finger in it to hold their place. She wasn't good at silence, but sometimes it was necessary.

She leaned back and watched the Milwaukee skyline unfold. The Bradley clock tower, the twin smokestacks as they neared the National Avenue exit. Nicky turned onto 794. Suspended ribbons of freeway overlapped like strands of cooked spaghetti. She hid a smile under her hand. Her life was spaghetti. And the silent man beside her was the sauce.

Nicky didn't talk until they pulled into the parking lot at Veteran's Park. "I'll bring the pizza if you get the iced tea."

The class she'd taken on tone of voice and body language didn't prepare her for Nicky Fiorini. This guy had some kind of stealth mechanism that let him fly under her radar. Analyzing the set of his jaw, the tightened muscle bands in his upper back as he opened the car door, she had to dismiss the analogy. She tracked him just fine. She just couldn't decode him.

They found a tree where he could sit in the small circle of shade, and she could have her back in the sun. He'd even remembered a blanket. He spread it out. She sat down, legs crossed beneath her. He tossed the pizza box onto the blanket and sat down across from her—mirroring her pose, knees touching hers. A reflexive swallow closed her throat.

His hands rested on his legs, fingertips less than an inch from her knees. His eyes closed.

She waited. And prayed.

"My cousin died." He opened his eyes, sought hers. "That's what happened four years ago. Tony was twenty-one. We grew up together. He was full of life. And Jesus." He blinked and gazed beyond her, toward the lake.

Dani touched his arm. "I'm so sorry."

"Tony was crazy about Jesus. Those were his words. Crazy about Jesus. It was contagious." He reached up and fingered a lock of her hair. "You remind me so much of him with your passion to fix things and start something." He swiped his hand across his face. "One summer Tony and a friend of his started a Bible school at Bracciano. They invited the neighborhood kids. They put on plays and taught them songs. Because of what they were doing, Todd and I started getting some of the older kids together for basketball."

"He told me about that."

"I'd never felt so alive, so free of anger. The kids loved it, and we got to talk to them about what was important." He rubbed his hands on his thighs. "My aunt and uncle thought Tony was taking his religion too far. It caused a lot of tension, so he moved in with us. There were people who didn't like what he and his friend were doing. Tried roughing them up a couple of times."

"The Sevens?"

He shook his head. "The Vamps. Tony's answer was to tell them about Jesus."

"And that just made them more angry."

Nicky nodded. "One night Tony and a girl went to a concert at some mega church near Chicago. She drove, and they said they'd be home late." The brown in his eyes seemed to darken. His fingers arched like claws on his thighs.

"I was in the back room taking a break around one in the morning. I had the door propped open, and I saw their headlights drive into the parking lot. It crossed my mind to yell at them not to stay out there, but I didn't. I just went back to work, and about five minutes later I heard a shot. I called 911. I heard another shot and a scream while I was talking to them. The dispatcher told me to stay inside, like she knew what I was going to do. I ran out. I could smell the gunshot, but I didn't know where to look. And then I heard him. . .crying my name. . . ." He swiped at his eyes. "They were in the girl's car behind the restaurant. The windshield was shattered. The girl was unconscious. Tony's eyes were open, but"—he took a ragged breath—"he'd been shot in the head." He raised a finger and pointed to a spot above his right brow. "I opened the door, and he fell into my arms. I didn't want to move him. I crouched there holding him. 'Pray,' he said, 'Pray with me.' So I did. I begged God to save him. I thanked Him for what he was doing through Tony. I bargained. I praised Him. I said the Lord's Prayer and the twenty-third Psalm. I. . ." His voice caught on a sob.

Dani wrapped her arms around him, and as he pressed his face into her shoulder, she prayed.

⚜

October 16, 1927

Going to Moody Church with Albert and his mother was her good-bye gift to them. She hadn't told them she was moving, and she wouldn't. A little longer, and maybe she would have confided in Mr. and Mrs. Hollenddale. She'd come close several times, while pinning a dress for Albert's mother. She'd convinced herself so many times, standing in a foyer that rivaled the Palmer House, that she could be happy as Albert's wife. But there were too many things that could go wrong.

She'd done the same with Mr. Walbrecht—come so close to asking him to take her to Paris. He would have done it, but would he have taken Franky and Suzette? That was the catch in every plan she'd come up with in almost four years. She'd never have, or want, the luxury of thinking only of herself.

Folding gloved hands on a borrowed Bible, she turned her attention to the stout man with a white goatee waving a Bible over his head.

"I remember R. A. Torrey, standing on this very spot, speaking of a painting he'd seen in an art gallery in Munich, Germany. Close your eyes and picture it—trees bending in a fierce wind, roiling black clouds overhead. Horses, cattle, and a small group of men, women, and children running from the storm, terror etched on their faces as they searched for a hiding place."

The man pointed at the crowd. "Are we so very different from these people?" Fierce brown eyes seemed directed at her. "Every one of us needs a hiding place."

Francie turned away. She focused on a hat in the front row. Black velvet, gathered at the side in a wide gold buckle. *I could make that.*

". . .from fear. If you do not yet know the grace and the mercy of an all-forgiving God, you know that haunting sense of fear that never leaves. Dr. Torrey put it so well—we need a hiding place from the torment of an accusing conscience."

Francie slipped her fingers beneath the jeweled clasp of her coat. She longed to slip out of the constricting wool. It was warm in here. Too warm.

"Not long ago a man about my age, thin, bald, unhealthy in appearance, came to me and confessed a grievous sin." The man stroked his goatee. "His employer had caught him in the act of dipping his hand into the till. In a panic, to cover his sin, he committed a far more grievous one. He killed the man."

Gasps echoed off the domed ceiling.

"The guilt, the burden of his conscience, was eating him alive." The preacher stepped to the edge of the platform. "This is the part I want you to hear, dear ones. The man is my age, in his sixties. He had committed the crime that robbed him of sleep and health. . .when he was *nineteen*."

A sharp, silent inhale brought Francie's hand to her mouth. Perspiration dampened her upper lip. *He knows. He knows what I've done. And what I'm about to do.*

Heat rose to her cheeks. She thought of the diagrams on Mr. Walbrecht's desk. The ones she'd so carefully described to Tag. The details she'd coaxed from him. The facts his mother had too willingly shared as Francie measured her for another gown. A sob shook her shoulders. Mrs. Hollanddale slipped a handkerchief into her hand.

"I pray you have not experienced anything like this man, but this I know, if you have not given the burdens of your past to Jesus Christ, there is something. Something that you carry. Something that is chasing you like a gale force wind."

Francie closed her eyes. She wanted to cover her ears. Her head felt light. Her fingers tingled.

"But there is hope. There is freedom. There is a hiding place. I handed this book to that man with the conscience so heavy he could carry it no more. I walked him through the truths about Jesus and asked if he believed what was in it. 'Yes, sir,' he said, 'I believe it all.' And do you, I asked, believe that Jesus Christ is the only Son of God and that He gave His life as a payment for your sins? 'Yes,' he said, 'I believe.'"

The preacher paused, walked from one end of the platform to the other. "I told him then to read these words from the book of Isaiah—'And the Lord has laid on him the iniquity of us all.' And then I said, 'Friend, where is your sin?'" He stopped pacing and pointed. Again, Francie felt the finger aimed directly at her.

" 'It is on Jesus Christ!' he cried. 'My sin is on Jesus, and I am free.' Dear ones, Jesus Christ is the only answer to a heavy conscience. He is your refuge in the storm. Who will come to this hiding place tonight?" His gaze swept the crowd. "Will you?"

CHAPTER 27

Nicky steadied his breathing and pulled away, breaking the circle of her arms. Tears dampened her lashes. His fingers submerged in her hair. "When I saw you. . .that night in the car. . .with your head leaning against the window. . ."

Dani inhaled, sharp and raspy.

"I didn't get close enough to really see. I just went nuts. The whole thing with Tony played back. It was so real. I couldn't look. I called Todd and told him some kid had stolen Vito's car, and somebody'd knocked him off outside the restaurant. Finding out you were just sleeping made me feel stupid, but seeing you were a girl made me crazier than ever. I'm sorry I went off on you like that."

She skimmed his face with a soft hand. "Your reaction makes sense. And you were right. It's not a safe place."

"I look at Rena, and I think of Tony."

"And she doesn't see it as protectiveness."

He gave a soft laugh. "Everything my cousin was doing was good. All for God, and he's dead. What chance does Rena have if she's playing with the devil? I found her lip-locked with that guy she calls her boyfriend, and I got so mad it made me scared of what I was capable of."

"Does your father try to control her at all?"

"Not like he should. He's too scared to clamp down, afraid he'll lose her." He wiped his face on his sleeve. "I haven't told him the latest. Maybe finding out how deep she's in would be a wake-up call."

"Where is God in all of this?"

He knew what she meant. It wasn't rhetorical and *she* didn't need an answer. She wanted to know where his head was—if he viewed God as sovereign, in control of the good and the bad, including Tony's death. Nicky raised his right shoulder. "We really need to lighten things."

At the outside corner of one eye, a tiny muscle jumped—the only indication his failure to engage had affected her.

"Is that why you hate reporters? Did they swarm after your cousin was killed?"

"Swarm. Yeah. Like bees on a hive. For two weeks I didn't leave the restaurant. Didn't even go into the dining room. You guys are masters at disguise."

Dani seemed to cringe at his choice of words.

"A waitress would tell me someone wanted to compliment the chef, so I'd walk out to a nicely dressed, hand-holding couple and *bam!* they'd turn into piranhas. 'What did you think when you saw your cousin shot in the head? How do you feel about the person who did it? What will you say to him if he's apprehended?'"

"And was—" She looked away. He could practically see the pressure building in her head, but she let it drop. "Let's eat pizza and think up questions to ask your grandfather."

"You and your questions." He slid his fingers deeper into her hair and leaned toward her lips. "I might be changing my opinion on reporters. At least one of them."

⁂

An hour later, as Nicky drove out of the park, the feel of another kiss still lingered on her lips. She was supposed to be reading, but for a moment she wanted to stay in the make-believe bubble where happily-ever-afters were the law of the land—where a guy like Nicky could care for a girl like her—even after he found out her new address. With a sigh, she went back to reading.

"'I lie awake at night and think of ways to escape with Franky.

251

I imagine him at home on the farm, flying into the creek from my old rope swing or sledding on the hill. I see him sitting in church next to his grandma. Mama would spoil him so. All this is simply dreaming. Mama and Daddy have not answered my letters. I think they have disowned us all.' "

Dani tapped a fist to her sternum. "How can parents be like that?"

"Good question. I have no answer. Is there anything happy in this girl's life?"

"Here. 'I had brunch with Mrs. Hollenddale at the Palmer House again. I won—' "

"Did you know the brownie was invented at the Palmer House?"

"No. I didn't know that vital little tidbit."

"They put an apricot glaze on it."

"That sounds awful." She wrinkled her nose at him and turned back to the diary.

" 'I wonder what people would say if they knew that the girl with the stylish bob and classy new hat eating off china plates under chandeliers dripping with crystals had been milking cows just a few years ago.' "

"The Palmer is the oldest continually running hotel in history."

"Is this boring you, Mr. Trivia?"

"A little. Skip to the good stuff. When do they hold up the jewelry store?"

"*Men.* Okay. Give me a minute." She turned several pages. " 'T took me dancing last night. It was nice. Just the two of us with no agenda.' "

"She is one messed up girl."

"No more confused than some present-day teens I know."

"Yeah." His cheeks bowed with a heavy sigh. "I still keep wondering if that book dropped into your hands right now because there's an answer in it for Rena."

She looked at him out of the corner of her eye.

"What? You think I don't believe things happen for a reason? God is in control, okay? Is that what you've been waiting to hear me say? I maybe believe that more than you do. God is God, and He can do whatever He wants to do." He rapped the steering wheel with the

252

heel of his hand. "And there's not a thing we can do about it."

As Nicky turned left, Dani took one last look at sunlight dancing on the lake. "I believe from personal experience that God answers our prayers, and there's certainly evidence in the Bible to support that, but what if He didn't?"

"What do you mean?"

"What if He planned every detail eons before we were born?"

"I don't know what you're getting at."

"Think of what you know to be true about the character of God. What's the first thing you learned about Him when you were a kid?"

"God is love." His sing-songy tone broadcast his irritation.

"If that's true, then why do we need input?"

His lips parted. He glanced at her then back at the road. She waited for a comment or a nod, but Nicky stared straight ahead in silence.

She turned the page, skimmed through two weeks of dreams and fashion sketches and cute things Franky said before a two-line entry grabbed her. She looked at Nicky. " 'March 23, 1927. I'm finally getting a clue about why I'm working here. T wants me to cozy up to Mr. W so I can get a promotion. I can't do that. He's a nice man with a nice wife, and he's three times my age. But I have my ways to get what T wants.' "

"The plot finally thickens."

Dani groaned. "This poor girl. What does T want her to get from the old man? Money? Jewels?"

"The combination to the safe is more like it. Or her own key."

"Promise me we're going to finish this today. If we don't, I'm skipping to the end."

Nicky wagged a finger in front of her face. "Rules is rules. I promise we'll finish tonight. Nonno starts to get cranky after just a few minutes, so we won't be there long. I don't have to start baking until midnight. You can follow me back, and we can read right into tomorrow."

"Sleep is a zero."

"Exactly."

"Where are we going anyway?"

"Dessert."

By the time they parked at a coffee shop on East Brady, Francie had been promoted to "Mr. W's" personal secretary.

✧

The waitress brought their pie and coffee, and Dani opened to July 1927. " 'Had lunch with Doris today. She told me people are calling me Little Orphan Annie. She asked if the rumors were true. I laughed. It was easy to laugh because the rumors aren't true. Mr. W is not like that, and I feel so bad I'm tarnishing his reputation. What are people saying to his wife?' "

Nicky snickered. "Forgive me for saying anything bad about our Francie, but she's probably going to rob the guy blind, and yet what bothers her is tarnishing his reputation."

"He's got a gob of money. Only one rep."

Nicky rolled his eyes. "Read."

" 'I've decided that every day I have to write at least one happy thing. Happy thing for today: Franky said, "When I grow up I'm going to be a pirate and only have one eye and one leg and hunt for buried treasure.' "

"That's all very cute, but could we skip the happy thoughts?"

"Curmudgeon. One more. 'My happy thought for today is the emerald on my right hand. T buys me jewelry but never rings. This morning there was a little box with a big gold bow on my desk. The card read, "To my Right Hand Girl." Mr. W was so pleased when I danced around the office with it. He has a nice smile.' "

Nicky cleared his throat with a machine gun sound. "I'm sorry. I know you want to think the best of her, but she's pathetic. First she falls for the gangster who's blackmailing her, then it's the old married boss."

"She's not falling for her boss. All she said is he's got a nice smile."

"That's how it all starts."

"She is not going to fall for this guy."

"If she isn't ga-ga over Daddy Warbucks by the last page, I'll cook a seven course meal just for you."

"Deal."

"Not so fast. What do I get if I'm right?"

254

"A big head. Okay, you don't want me cooking for you. I'll write a glowing piece about Bracciano. New customers will flock to you."

"I like that. Maybe you'd better let me read for a while."

"And let you rewrite...re*read* history? Nev*uh*." She scanned the next few pages then picked one. " 'I dreamed I was walking over the hills back home holding Theo's hand. Earl Hagen caught up with us in a Model T and leaned out the window yelling, "You are nothing, Francine Tillman. Your father is a bootlegger, and you are nothing." I dropped Theo's hand and ran. Theo called after me. He told me to stop. I wanted him to catch up with me, but he never did.' "

You are nothing. Francie's dream resurrected a dialogue Dani had overheard between her parents the year after her mission trip to Haiti. She'd stuck to her vow that year. By riding her bicycle, taking her lunch to school, and buying her school wardrobe at garage sales, she'd been able to donate most of her clothes and entertainment allowance to charity. She was ready to step through the door if God opened it for her. And then the letter from the mission board came in the mail.

"Dani needs this, Deborah. It's what she's called to do."

"Quit the melodrama, Gary. What she needs is a normal life. She needs to go off to school and meet boys and be a normal eighteen-year-old girl."

"But she's not normal. Thank God she's not normal. She cares about people. She wants to make a difference in the world. She wants to be involved with something vital. A mission, a purpose, something bigger than herself."

Her mother's laugh ricocheted in her head. *"So you'd give her your blessing to skip college and go straight to being a nobody in a filthy hut in some God-forsaken country exposed to every disease known to man?"*

"If it's what she's called to do, yes." Chair legs scraped the floor. The door handle turned. *"But* my *daughter* will *never be a nobody."*

"Dani? You still with me? Yoo-hoo. Are you walking the hills with Theo?"

Nicky's words bounced on the edge of long-buried memory. She blinked as if coming out of anesthesia. "Sorry."

"You okay?"

"Yes." She pushed her untouched pecan pie toward him. "No." Arms planted on the table as if to stabilize herself, she told him about Haiti and the conversation between her parents.

Nicky's forearms paralleled hers. Tan, muscled arms created a fortress. The slightest smile gentled the planes of his face. "All those years I was longing for a mother to help direct my future, and here you were wishing yours would keep her opinions to herself." His hands conformed to her elbows. "It's not too late to follow those dreams."

She raised an eyebrow. "Says the man who wants to open his own restaurant."

"Touché. What a couple of losers. We were meant to meet so we could be miserable and unfulfilled together."

"You're probably right." She hid a smile behind splayed fingers and lingered on a mournful sigh. As she played along, the cloud of bitter memories evaporated into the steam from her coffee, leaving a rain-washed feeling. "I'll feel sorry for you if you feel sorry for me."

His hand rose to her cheek. His fingertip trailed along her jawline then glided up to trace her lips. "Poor baby." She closed her eyes. His butterfly-light caress slid along the other side of her face. "Poor, pretty baby. I could just sit here feeling sorry for you for the rest of my life." His fingertip skimmed down to her chin, Slowly, gently, he lifted. "But I'd rather do this."

Warm lips. A hint of caramel, a touch of cinnamon. A kiss more delectable than apple pie. Eyes still closed, she sighed as he pulled away. "Mmm."

A soft laugh tickled her cheek. "I suppose, while we're wallowing in unfulfilled dreams, it wouldn't hurt to pray."

Her eyes shot open.

"I do know how, you know."

"I. . ."

"Shh." His finger returned to her lips. "Close your eyes."

She obeyed.

"Lord God, You know the cry of Dani's heart is to make a difference for You, and You know the dreams I've tried to ignore. Right now, we bring our dreams and lay them at Your feet, trusting You will put in us the desires of Your heart."

He fell silent. Dani opened her eyes and whispered "Amen" through her tears.

CHAPTER 28

Nicky turned the page with one hand. His other arm was occupied with holding Dani close to his chest. The waitress set a second pot of coffee on the table. He'd switched to decaf three cups ago. He rested his cheek against Dani's hair and skimmed through several weeks of happy thoughts and dress designs. He stopped when a familiar name jumped off the page. "Here we go."

Dani looked down at the spot he pointed to and sat up straight. "Finally."

" 'I'm moving. I say the words, but it feels like someone else is talking. I will live in an upstairs apartment across the street from Bracciano, the restaurant where I will work.' " He looked up. "So she lived—"

"In m—where China and Miguel lived." Dani rubbed her arms. "China must have found her diary somewhere in the house."

Shaking his head, he bent over the book. " 'T took me up to meet the people who own the restaurant. I like Renata, the wife. She is just a little older than me and has the sweetest little boy, but her husband scares me. He is nice and funny, but he looks at me like I'm wearing a FOR SALE sign.' "

Nicky smacked his lips. "Way to welcome the new girl, Great Grampa Santo. I'm so proud of my heritage."

"You inherited all the good parts. The flirt without the sleaze."

He laughed—something that was beginning to feel natural. "I try. I've made it a life goal to never look at a girl like she's wearing a FOR SALE sign."

Dani answered with a soft laugh.

" 'I don't know how long I'm going to be there. I don't know if this is a cover or if T is hiding me there to keep me safe. I want to take Suze and Franky. I didn't bother to ask. T would never allow it. His threats to Franky form my prison walls. No one needs to watch me. I might as well be chained in a medieval stone tower.' "

Nicky rolled his eyes. "Quite the little drama queen, isn't she?"

"She has every right to be. Read." She nudged the book closer to Nicky.

" 'I gave my notice to Mr. W. It was all I could do to look him in the eye. I said I was moving back to Wisconsin to be near my parents. When I close my eyes I still see the pain in his. I have decided I cannot let this horrible thing happen. I have to find a way to stop it.' "

Nicky skimmed over to the entry for Sunday of the following week.

" 'The preacher spoke as if only to me. I—' "

"Preacher?" Light danced in her eyes. "Our Francie went to church?"

Nicky laughed and continued to read. " 'I fell to my knees. I couldn't stop crying for all the horrible things I've done. He laid his hand on my head and helped me to pray. I will never forget his words. "God has set you free. You are safe in His arms. He is your hiding place.' "

Dani's hand slid over her mouth. Her eyes brimmed with tears. "Don't you feel like. . .we're living this kind of parallel life? She comes to Jesus just as—"

"I start finding my way back." He looked back at the page. Here again, it seemed Francie had too many words for the six lines allotted, and her thoughts spilled over into Monday. " 'When the service ended I felt like nothing could ever take that peace away from me. But as we walked out, someone called my name. I turned and there was *Theo*.' "

Dani gasped and leaned over the book.

" 'My Theo.' " The words of the next two sentences were water-spotted and blurred. Three words were legible—" 'kissed my cheek.' "

"She was crying when she wrote this," Dani whispered then

sighed. "Finally, Theo to the rescue. This is too much to process all at one time."

Nicky continued. " 'He had to catch the train back to Minneapolis. He asked for my address. That's when my peace shattered. I told him I was moving, and he gave me his card. He made me promise to write. I gave him my word, but I will break it.' "

Dani pulled out of his arm and turned sideways with her leg bent. Her knee touched his thigh. "This is exhausting."

"Let's go back to skimming."

"But it's all important. What if we'd skimmed right over Theo?"

"Then you wouldn't be exhausted." He glanced at his watch. "We should leave in ten minutes." He edged the diary closer to her. "Hit the highlights."

"There's another time gap." She flipped pages. Eight...nine weeks." She rested the diary on his arm. Midafternoon light shimmered on her spun-gold hair.

" '...is why they believe you must never reenter or take anything from that place.' "

Nicky came back into the moment. Dani rubbed her arms. "Creepy." He had no idea what he'd missed. He tried to focus on the pale blue teardrop hanging from her earlobe, but the dip on the top edge of her mouth drew his eyes, and he got lost in outlining her lips, tracing the pattern in his head.

" '...made her a few dresses, and I'm teaching her to sew. She is encouraging me to open my own shop or at least let their customers know I design gowns. She believes in Jesus and talks to Him like He's right here. We pray and study the Bible together. I read to her and try to explain the words she doesn't know. Renata is the friend I have wanted all my life.' " She flipped a page.

" 'Renata has known T since he was younger than me. She says he used to be a good kid, but the business made him hard. She says "the business" with the same look on her face Mama used to. She hates what her husband does, but she says God commands wives to submit to their husbands and be a helpmate.' "

"What business?"

Dani looked up. "I'm guessing your great-granddaddy was selling booze."

"Or maybe just fooling around with the ladies."

"*Just?*"

"Sorry. Don't mean to make light of the family curse. No For Sale signs."

The corners of her mouth drew up, giving him a whole new shape to memorize.

" 'I miss Franky so much, but Luca is here when my arms feel empty. I have not seen T, but Renata says he calls Santo. I love the customers and the music. For the first time since I left the farm, I'm actually happy.' "

" 'Santo took us to see Hoagy Carmichael. Santo knows him personally! Rumor has it he wrote a few bars of "Star Dust" right here. It may not be true, but I choose to believe it. It was so surreal to hear him live.' "

Dani turned several pages. " 'I'm so ecstatic sometimes I think I'll split wide open! I am starting my own business! It will be private—not a storefront—just for regular customers. Santo has ordered the room behind the shop to be totally renovated to suit my needs. He is not the fiend I once thought he was.' "

Her elbow bumped his ribs. "Resist it, girl," she whispered. Her hair tumbled across her cheeks as she spoke to the book as if were a walkie-talkie connecting her to the past. "Don't fall under the Fiorini spe–ell." She sputtered the end of the sentence as he nuzzled her ear. She barred him from further nibbling with a hand against his chest.

"*She* should resist. *You* shouldn't."

She scooted away from him. "Where's the 'shop'?"

"I don't know."

Dani smacked the table with her palm. "Your storeroom. That would explain the wallpaper and the roses on the light fixtures."

"I can just picture her stitching away between the olive oil and the anchovies."

With an exasperated sigh, she shoved him out of the booth.

"*Bella ragazza.*"

Luca Fiorini's large hand engulfed Dani's and pulled her toward him. A feathery kiss brushed her right cheek and then her left.

Nicky set two chairs in front of his grandfather's wheelchair. "He says you are a beautiful girl."

"Thank you. *Grazie*. Did I say that right?"

Thin lines fanned from dark eyes that sparkled like his grandson's when he smiled. Could Nicky see the resemblance? Did he get the sense he was gazing into some future mirror when he looked at his grandfather? "Irish." Thick white hair fell across Luca's forehead as he shook his head. "My father will not approve."

Dani glanced at Nicky, who shrugged and smiled.

"Danielle writes for the *Kenosha Times*, Nonno. She's a reporter."

"I don't like reporters." His finger ticked back and forth like a metronome.

Nicky nudged her arm and mouthed, "Ask him."

"Mr. Fiorini." Dani pulled the diary out of its plastic bag. "I found an old diary across the street from Bracciano. It was written back in the 1920s by a young woman named Francine Tillman. Do you remember her?"

Weak eyes stared at her. "Fran...cine. No." Gaunt shoulders rose and fell as he sighed. His eyes fluttered closed.

"Nonno." Nicky patted a thin hand networked by raised blue veins. "Francine knew your mother. She mentions Bracciano and says that Renata helped her hide something important. It sounds like Francie Tillman worked at the restaurant. You would have been just a little boy then."

"Francie?" Heavy-lidded eyes opened again. "I know..." His thick white brows converged. "No." He stared at the wall behind Dani.

Dani turned to look at the spot that drew his attention. A framed picture of Bracciano hung on the wall. She recognized the people standing in front—Santo and Renata Fiorini with little Luca between them. She got up and walked to the picture. "You would have been about this age when Francie met your mother. I bet Francie played with you. She—"

"I don't know her!" White fingers curled under.

A CNA they'd spoken to on the way in poked her head in the door. "Everything okay, Luca?"

"I don't know her!" His voice rose even louder. "I don't..."

"It's okay, Nonno." Nicky continued to pat his hand. "We just had to ask. You didn't know her. That's okay."

Luca's chin dipped to his chest.

The CNA turned off the overhead light. A pale glow from the tube light above the head of Luca's bed softened the room. "Mood lighting," she whispered. She turned to Nicky. "This hasn't been a peaceful day. Maybe next time." She offered a sad smile. "I think I said that last time you were here, didn't I?"

Nicky nodded. He stood and put the chairs back against the wall.

"He'll remember you were here. He talks about you all the time. 'My Nicky,' he calls you. 'My Nicky has a dream. Can't trust my sons with it.' I hear that all the time."

"What's 'it'?"

"I never asked. The restaurant? He talks about Bracciano so much I feel like I've been there. He says your tortellini is better than his mother's."

Nicky covered a look of little-boy pride by bending to kiss his grandfather on the top of his head. "I'll see you soon, Nonno. *Ti amo*."

The aide said good-bye, and Nicky put his hand on Dani's back. "Sorry."

"It was worth the drive just to see you with him." She leaned on his shoulder. "You have a tender heart."

He pulled her close. "That will be our little secret, okay?"

"Okay." She kissed his cheek, stepped over to Luca, and crouched beside the wheelchair. A soft snore ruffled through his parted lips. She slid her hand over his. "It was a pleasure to meet you, Mr. Fiorini. You can be very proud of your grandson. Your Nicky is a fine man."

She waited for a sign that her words had pierced his sleep, but none came. She stood and looked around Luca's small world. Pale blue walls, bedspread to match. A bedside table and a small dresser. A bookshelf lined with family pictures and a few books. On the wall, a crucifix hung next to a shadow box displaying medals, including a Silver Star and a picture of a tall, broad-shoulder Luca in a World War II Army uniform. "Where did he serve?"

"Italy."

"My great-grandfather, Charles Gallagher, fought in Italy in 1918. The Battle of Vittorio Veneto. I have a picture of him with his chest full of medals."

"Then my family is indebted to your family for sacrificing for our homeland."

She smiled. "So your nonno went back to his roots to fight."

"At one point he was only twenty miles from the little town of Bracciano, where his parents grew up. He went AWOL for two days so he could meet his mother's parents for the first—and only—time."

Dani rubbed the goose bumps popping up on her arms. She pointed to the Silver Star. "How did he get this?"

"Actually, he got that for going AWOL. My great-uncle fought with the Italian Resistance—against Mussolini. He met up with my grandfather in Bracciano and gave Nonno intel that helped the Allied forces blow up a dozen brand-new German tanks."

Dani turned back to the man whose posture had once been military straight. Luca's limp hands rested on a navy-blue lap blanket. "I'd love to hear that story from him."

"I come up here twice a month. If we hit the right time, you could fill a book with—"

"Franky."

They swiveled in unison. Luca looked up, eyes clear and bright. "It's not Francie. It's Franky."

The goose bumps returned. Dani knelt in front of him. "You knew Franky?"

"Of course. He hated peas. Used to hide them in the cuff of his pants. Every week the old woman who did our laundry would come to the back door jabbering. '*Piselli nell'acqua!*' she'd yell. Peas in the water!"

Nicky laughed. "I can only guess how much fun two little boys had with that."

"We played in the tunnel, hunting for bad guys. He moved." Luca looked up at Nicky, eyes glazed. "Did they want to hurt him, too, Papa? He wrote to me. Franky Becker. . ."

Nicky shook his head and dropped his chin to his chest. Dani felt the weight of disappointment as if a hand pressed against her chest. Was it a bizarre coincidence, or a delusion? Had he known a different boy name Franky? What could they believe from someone who thought his grandson was his father?

263

Luca's gaze clouded. "Brecker. No. What was it? And why—"

Nicky suddenly looked up. "*Brekken?*" His finger jabbed at her purse. "Diary," he whispered. "Theo. Was it Franky *Brekken*, Nonno?"

The white head gave the slightest nod. "Franky Brekken. He sent me a postcard."

The soft snore began even before he closed his eyes.

⁂

As they walked across the parking lot, Dani looked up at him with wonder in her eyes. "How did you remember Theo's last name?"

He could get used to that look. "We get our mozzarella from a farmer in Stoughton named Ed Brekken. It's an unusual name, so it stuck in my head when you read it."

They reached the Javelin. He opened Dani's door and helped her in as she focused on her phone.

"Where do we start?"

"Let's use a process of elimination. Look up Frank Brekken Kenosha then Chicago, maybe Osseo."

Dani's thumbs beat a frenzied rhythm as she searched. "There's one on Facebook. Nope. He's our age. Another one in Minnesota. . . high school kid. . .wait. *Pastor* Frank Brekken? He's a missionary. . .with Overseas Outreach." A tiny gasp. She turned to him and grinned. "A missionary to *India*."

Nicky drummed the steering wheel. "How old is he?"

She tapped the keys again. It sounded like raindrops. "He has a blog."

"That can't be our Frank. No ninety-year-old guy has a blog."

"This one does." Her squeal filled the car. "Look."

He leaned over her shoulder, inhaling a dizzying mix of spice and flowers, and looked at the picture she pointed to. An elderly man stood between a dark-skinned man in a white shirt and tie and a woman in a blue sari. Dani clicked on a tab labeled "Bio."

" 'When I was a young boy, my adoptive parents were the overseers of an orphanage in New Delhi. I grew up speaking English and Hindi. We moved back to the States when I was seventeen. After college I wanted to start a church. God had other plans, of course. My story mirrored my parents'—my wife and I honeymooned in

264

Bombay.'" She clicked the "Contact" button. "He lives in Maryland. I'm calling him now."

As she dialed, his fingers wandered to the back of her neck. She'd put her hair up in a ponytail. It was ninety-three degrees, and he couldn't blame her, but he wanted to rip out the band that held it high off her neck. Then again. . .he bent and kissed the spot where a fine gold chain fastened.

She pushed him away. "I can't concentrate."

"Ignore me. You just do your thing, and I'll do mine." But the moment she said "Hello," he pulled his hand away.

"Mr.—Pastor Brekken, my name is Danielle Gallagher. I live in Kenosha, Wisconsin. I found a diary that I believe belonged to your aunt, and I'm wondering if you have a min—"

"You found it?" The man's voice carried even before Dani put him on speaker phone. "You found Francie's book? Lois! There's a woman on the phone who says she found Frazzie's diary!" A soft shout sounded in the background. "I'm sorry. That's my wife. You have to understand. . .my aunt died ten years ago, and on her deathbed she told me her diary held the key to my future." Frank laughed. "Imagine hearing that when you're eighty years old!"

⟨⟩

February 19, 1928

Francie stepped out of the beige crepe dress, threw it over the chair in the corner of her bedroom, and slid a simple cotton floral over her head. She went through this metamorphosis several times a week. A change of clothes brought on a change of personality. The seamstress kicked out of her high heels, put on comfortable shoes, and changed her vocabulary from pleats and darts and gussets to lasagna, rigatoni, and cannelloni.

She loved every minute of both worlds.

A spritz of perfume, a touch of rouge, and she was ready. Slipping into her coat, she ran down the stairs.

Fresh snow covered the tracks she'd made just minutes earlier. She lifted her face and stood statue-still as flakes dotted her eyelashes. Seductively delicious smells—onions, garlic, thyme, and oregano, drifted across the street, hovered on the still night air. This little corner of the world, this triangle hemming her life, was her slice of almost heaven.

A car passed, honking as it sprayed wet snow in her path. As she sloshed across the street, stepping high to keep the snow out of her shoes, a giggle pulled her gaze to the snow-filled space next to the restaurant. Luca lay on his back, arms and legs flailing. Snow angels. The vision made her laugh. And then her chest tightened. Her arms ached with an emptiness only one little boy could fill. *If only. . .* She lifted a prayer and walked around the corner to the side door.

Rich aromas welcomed her. Renata looked up from her cheese grater and smiled. "Does Mrs. Cardella like the gown?"

"She loves it. She wants the same pattern in blue."

"Wonderful. You will be famous someday."

Someday. The word had once held so much promise. She nodded at her friend. As she walked into the back room, she marveled at the fact that Paris no longer lured her and New York had lost its fascination. She didn't want to be famous. She wanted nothing more than a future for a little boy. *Someday.*

She took a dust mop out of the closet and slipped it around the polished floor then used a white cloth to dust the light fixtures. When the room looked presentable, she opened the back door and swept snow from the back step. The simple action brought her back to a winter storm that now seemed a lifetime ago. She was fifteen, shovel in hand, doing what she could for "the business." Though she now lived in a different world, some things had not changed all that much.

She walked back in, closed the door, and came face-to-face with Santo.

"*Grazie.*" He took the broom from her and set it back in the closet. "These little extras do not go unnoticed." He reached toward her elbow.

She stepped away. "It's my pleasure."

"My wife, she does not understand how important these details are."

Putting yet more distance between them, Francie laughed. "She understands. She *disapproves.*"

A large hand splayed on the top of the iron table in the center of the room. "Hard times are coming, Francine. I am doing what I have to do for my family."

She shook her head. "I invented that line, Santo."

He sidled closer. "You and I, we have something in common."

"Yes we do." She held up her hand, palm out. "We both work for the same people, and we both want what is best for our families, *don't* we?"

He smiled. "You are a strong but beautiful woman."

"And you are a stupid man." She returned the smile. "You will get nowhere with me."

"But it is the trying that I enjoy."

"Then you'd best decide if you want your wife or your boss to shoot you."

With a laugh and a wave, he opened the door and walked into the kitchen.

Francie picked a piece of lint off a flocked rose on the wallpaper and looked up at Renata's crucifix next to the door. The beauty and craftsmanship of the intricate carving transfixed her. She and Renata had sat here in this room, just days earlier, reading the book of Isaiah. " 'He was despised and rejected by mankind, a man of suffering, and familiar with pain.'" She said the verse out loud. It made her want, once again, to drop to her knees. Her pain was nothing compared to what He had suffered. "Thank You," she whispered.

She lifted her apron from its hook and slipped it over her head. The door opened before she touched the handle. Santo motioned for her. "Telephone call for you."

Her heart missed a beat. Her sister was the only one who had ever called her, and Suzette would not telephone unless something was wrong.

The black receiver dangled from its cord. She picked it up and turned her back on the bustle in the kitchen. She stared at the wooden box with the silver dial, at the black numbers beneath the finger holes, and took a deep breath. "Hello?"

"Hello, doll."

"Tag?"

"How's it going up there? I've been missing you."

The warmth of the room became suffocating. "Everything's fine."

"Good. Listen, I've decided you need a reward for good behavior. I'm sending your sister and the kid up there. For good."

CHAPTER 29

Dani slipped her phone into her purse and turned to Nicky. "We just talked to little Franky."

"Yes we did. What a character, huh? 'Don't tell me a thing. I love surprises.'" Nicky's impersonation was uncanny.

"He's a real live person."

Nicky laughed. She loved the sound of it. Tipping her head to one side, she let her eyes trace the curve of his smile.

"What?"

"When we first met, I remember thinking how ridiculously handsome you'd look if you'd only smile." She fit her fingertip into the divot on his cheek. "I was right."

His hand closed over hers. "I finally have a reason to smile."

"Isn't that a song? Or does the song say a reason to live?"

"Well, I've got that, too, now."

She laughed. "Are Italian men just born with that, or did your father and grandfather give you lessons?"

"It's in the genes, bella ragazza." He kissed her hand. One knuckle at a time.

She stopped him at her wrist. Another second of that and she'd need a defibrillator. "We have reading to do," she squeaked. "Hands on the wheel now. You drive. I read. You do your thing, and I'll do mine."

With a smile that promised his compliance would be temporary, he released her hand and backed the Javelin out of the parking space.

Dani found their place in the diary but didn't start reading. "What have we read so far that would be the key to Franky's future?"

"It's what's coming up that's the key. My great-grandmother helped her hide *things*. It has to be her take from the robbery."

"That can't be it. She hasn't worked at the jewelry store for months. I'm thinking it's some kind of a life lesson, or maybe she just wanted him to hear her story so he could understand what led her to do things she didn't want to do."

Her phone vibrated. She pulled it out and glanced at a text from Rena.

CALL ME. NOW. EMERGENCY

Pulse hammering in her ears, she leaned her elbow on the armrest, striking a casual pose as she scanned the sign for the next exit. "Would you mind stopping at the next gas station? All that coffee..."

"Sure." Nicky put on the turn signal. "I might as well get gas."

She nodded and tried to keep her foot from tapping like a preschooler who really did need to use the bathroom. When he stopped, she walked in and darted to the restroom, dialing Rena's number.

A sob answered. Familiar but not Rena. "Danielle, you gotta come here. Now."

China. A loud thud echoed near the phone.

"Where are you?"

"Dani!" This time it was Rena. Her voice was muffled and hollow as if they had a bad connection. "We went against one of the Sisters, and now they're after us."

"Where are you?"

"The coal chute. You gotta come here. *Please.*" Her words convulsed into another sob.

"I'm calling the police."

"*No!* We were right there and somebody took a picture so—"

"You were where? What happened?"

"Leah tried to rob this lady who had a baby, and Chi and I stopped it. I grabbed the gun from her and this kid took a picture of

269

me holding it so now—"

"Rena, calm down. If you're innocent, the truth will come out. I'm with Nicky. We're about fifteen min—"

"No! Don't tell him. Please don't tell him. The Sisters know what you can do. They won't fight you."

Fat lot of good that'll do against a .45. Not a good time for Vito's wisdom to surface.

"Just. . .you. Come. . .alone."

Her short gasps made Dani feel like she couldn't breathe. "I'm on my way." The stall door slammed behind her.

Nicky was still outside, leaning on the front of the car. She yanked her door open.

His brow furrowed. "You're pale as a ghost. Are you sick?"

"No. It's China. I just talked to her. She's finally ready to talk. She's a mess. We have to hurry."

Nicky hopped in and they spun out of the gas station. As he sped back onto the interstate he glanced at her. "Is she suicidal?"

"Maybe."

"Then you need to call a hotline or the police or something. You're not trained for this."

"She asked for me. I'm not going to let her down."

Nicky's exhale gave his reaction. "Where am I taking you?"

Her mouth felt like chalk. "She'll be waiting outside the restaurant."

"You can talk to her in the storeroom. I'll stay out of your way, but I need to know you're safe."

I need to know. The warmth of his words softened the edges of her fear. "Thank you." She'd figure out how to get around his offer when they got there. She stuck her phone in her back pocket and tried to make words link together in a prayer.

"What will you tell her?"

"I don't know."

They sat in silence for the next few miles. Dani thought of the girls huddled in a coal chute and turned the air conditioning vents away from her.

"My cousin and I talked a kid out of killing himself. His mom had just been sentenced to ten years in prison. Tony caught Rafe with a bottle of vodka and a pile of downers."

She tore her gaze away from the clock. "What did you say to him?"

Nicky stopped at two stoplights before answering. "I told him God had a job for him that no one else could do. We had a neighborhood basketball team, and Rafe was the worst player I've ever seen in my life." His lips curved into the beginnings of a smile. "So I told him that."

Dani chewed the corner of her fingernail as she stared at him. "The kid's ready to off himself and you tell him he's the worst player you've ever seen?"

"Yeah. I told him if he killed himself then this little short guy, Luis, would be the worst player, and Luis couldn't handle it. I said he was the one showing Luis that the game wasn't about winning, it was about being together like a family and supporting each other and having fun."

Feeling as if she were in two places at once, she glanced from Nicky to the speedometer needle. *Faster.* "What did he say?"

"He laughed. And then he cried like a baby and handed over the bottles." His shoulders straightened.

Dani's foot wiggled to a nervous beat. "Wow." Glowing blue numbers morphed. One minute closer. She tried to concentrate on Nicky and what he'd just said. In the wake of her apathetic response, his smile lines disappeared, taking the dimple with them. *Focus.* "That's amazing."

"Could have gone the other way just as easily."

She turned sideways. At this angle she couldn't see the clock. "I don't believe that. God knew just what that kid needed at the moment—a laugh and a dose of reality." She touched his arm. "That boy needed a Nicky in his life."

⚜

The lantern dimmed. Rena hit the base with the heel of her hand. She was out of batteries.

"Don't let it go out." China rocked on the camp stool Rena had salvaged from someone's trash years ago. Her eyes were riveted to the iron door. "You're sure we can get out of here?" It was the third time she'd asked.

271

"I'm sure. I've been hiding here since I was twelve."

"It's creepy." China pointed at the brown streaks. "Is that. . . blood?"

"Just paint." *Maybe.* Rena picked up her phone and checked the time again. Her palms were wet. Sweat ran down her sides even though the room was cool. China's rocking was starting to freak her out. She lifted the lantern over her head, trying to make the room seem bigger.

The far wall was metal, the sides were made of stone blocks. The space was just big enough to stand in. Or stretch out in. Two people could fit on the mattress that now leaned against the wall. Rena wished she didn't know that.

"They're going to kill us." China let out a chilling moan. Her chest heaved. "I can't breathe." She jumped up. Her right hand pressed against her belly. "I have to get out of here."

"Sit down. We're safe. No one knows about this place." It wasn't true. Trish knew, but she was gone. Jarod knew, but she was gambling on him not being around, on the Sisters wanting to handle this on their own. The guys didn't want anything to do with Sister drama. She pulled China's arm. "Tell me about the baby. Do you feel it move yet?"

Dark hair brushed China's shoulders as she shook her head. She sat back down. "My uncle kept telling me to get an abortion. I thought we were going to Walmart one day, and we ended up at a clinic. That's why I couldn't stay there." She laughed, a horror movie kind of sound that gave Rena chills. "Now we're both going to die."

"Stop it! Dani will be here any minute."

"She can't fight a gun. What if they're waiting outside? I don't care about me. I don't want my baby to die. I never saw a dead person until Miguel." The light flickered and she gasped. Her hand clutched the front of her shirt. "What was it like when your cousin died? Did you see him? Miguel's eyes were closed, but I heard that sometimes—"

"Shut up! If you don't—" Her phone dinged. "That's Dani." Her folding chair creaked as she reached for it. Her inhale froze in her throat. The text was from Jarod. I NO WHERE U R.

"It's not her, is it? I can tell by the look on your face. Let me see."

"She's almost here." Rena tightened her grip on her phone and put it behind her back. "Tell me about the baby. What are you going to name it? If it's a boy will you name it after his daddy?"

"I'm scared if I do he'd turn out like—" The lantern dimmed, blazed bright, and went out.

China screamed.

"It's okay. We've got light from my phone. Here—"

China lunged for the door. The latch clicked. The door slammed open, echoing like a gunshot as it hit the ground.

⚜

Dani jumped out of the car as Nicky put it into park. "I'll go get her." She made herself walk toward the corner. Nicky would try to follow. She stopped and turned back to him. "Will you make us a pizza? Hawaiian? Kids talk when there's food."

He nodded, but she couldn't take a chance. She whipped around the corner and ran in front of the restaurant and through the grassy area back to the parking lot. Her heart slammed her ribcage, and she couldn't make her lungs expand enough. The night she'd met Jarod replayed in her head. She plastered her body against the brick and gripped her phone.

A scream, muffled at first, then loud and hysterical, met her ears. She crept to the corner, straining to see through the shadows. Rena held China against the wall, hand clamped over her mouth. Dani ran toward them.

"She freaked." Sweat glistened on Rena's neck. "She won't shut up."

Grabbing China's arm, Dani put her face just inches from her ear. "You have to be quiet to protect the baby. This is Miguel's legacy, you have to—"

With a violent shake, China wrenched her face from Rena's hand. "They're going to—"

"Let her go."

Rena gasped and whirled.

Jarod stood in a halo of light from the streetlamp, sweatshirt hood pulled over his forehead like the Grim Reaper. His hands were in his pockets. A taller, bulkier boy moved in behind him on one side.

273

In the dim light, Rena's wide eyes suddenly narrowed. "This isn't your battle Jarod. The Sisters take care of their—"

Yamile stepped into the larger boy's shadow. "You disowned the Sisters. How dare you—"

Footsteps pounded the gravel behind Dani. *Nicky?* She turned to see three boys, two in hooded sweatshirts, one in a white shirt that glowed against the other two.

"What you waitin' for?" the one in the white shirt yelled.

Jarod pulled his hand from his pocket. It held a gun and it pointed at Rena then slowly turned on China. "I didn't even have to pull the trigger to kill Miguel."

"What are you—"

"Just had to talk, tell him the truth. Bet I can do the same with you."

More footsteps. Too many to count. Leah and Venus burst between the boys who blocked one end of the space between buildings. Another boy, blond, early twenties, strode in behind her.

Dani slipped out of her shoes. Without looking at her phone, she pressed three buttons, and prayed she got it right.

Jarod stepped sideways and began to circle. "Nobody's ever going to want you now with that kid. If I were you I'd just take this gun and—"

"Are you crazy?" Venus took a step toward him. "She's pregnant." Leah shoved her back.

Dani's pulse thundered. She caught Rena's glance at her bare feet and gave a slight nod. Rena grabbed China's arm and jerked her toward the wall, opening a path between Dani and Jarod.

The gun cocked.

Dani leaped. Her foot swung, smacking the inside of his wrist with a crack. The gun dropped. A white package fell from Jarod's shirt. He swore and charged at her, face contorted with rage. Strong hands grabbed Dani from behind. Shouts erupted around her. Jarod grabbed her face, fingers biting into her skin. A roar, almost inhuman, exploded from behind him. Jarod dropped to his knees.

Nicky's hand clutched his neck.

Sirens blared in the distance. Angry shouts pierced the air.

A thud sounded in Dani's ears just before the earth tilted and she slammed the ground.

CHAPTER 30

I wasn't arrested! I'm the one who called the police."

"I don't care." Mitch tapped the end of his pencil on his desk. "This is the second time the cops have—"

Dani paced from the window to the corner of Mitch's desk and back to the window. "The first time doesn't count. I fell asleep in a car."

"I'm sorry. You're good, your passion comes across in your work, but this time it took you over the edge. I didn't make the decision, Dani. I'm just following orders."

"But the story. . . I'm getting into their heads. I get what makes them do what they do. People need to hear it." She put her hand on the window and stared down at men in ties and women in business suits, scurrying along a street that led to stately old homes on one end and dilapidated empty buildings on the other. Laid out in nice, neat grids, her city was a patchwork quilt. Blocks of brilliant color interspersed with worn and tattered squares. She wanted to move the people in the beautiful blocks to care about the ones in the faded patches.

"It's not your job." A rueful laugh bubbled from her gut. *Now it's official.* But it never had been. That had been her problem from the start—trying to fix and change and save what only God could do.

What do I do now, Lord? What's next?

Mitch rose from his chair and walked around the end of his desk. Arms overlapping at his waist, he stood beside her. "Remember what I said about separating journalism and social work? As good a writer as you are, I'm not so sure you shouldn't go back to school for something else. Or maybe join the Peace Corps. Use up all this zeal, and a few years from now, with enough life under your belt, come back and I'll find a place for you here."

Not trusting her voice, Dani nodded, gave her ex-boss a quick hug, and walked out of Mitch Anderson's office for the last time.

Evan sat on her desk, drinking her cold coffee. The sight of him brought the tears she'd held at bay. He took one look at her and opened his arms.

"If I hadn't tried to save China, if I'd minded my own business or called the cops or. . ." Sobs swallowed her words. She pressed her face into his shoulder.

When her tears stopped, she pulled away and mopped her face with her hands. "It's your fault for encouraging me to rage against society." She managed a smile. "Jesus was a rule breaker, too, remember?"

He laughed. "For all the right reasons. Not sure Jesus would have joined a gang just to get a good story."

"I didn't do it just to get a story. I did it to understand. I wanted to get to know those girls and show them there's a better way. You can't say Jesus didn't do that. He joined the human gang for that exact reason."

"Wow." Evan brushed a tear from her chin. "That is so very twisted but so true." He squeezed her shoulder. "There are far worse crimes than doing the wrong thing for the right reason. You just have to find a way to save the world without landing in jail."

"That's what Mitch said. Right before he fired me."

"I'm so sorry."

"Thank you." She opened her bottom drawer, pulled out a stack of files, and slammed them on her desk. "I need boxes."

"I'll go get you some." He disappeared, and she continued to dump the contents of her career onto her desk. Five minutes later he returned with boxes. And Vito.

Dani held up her hand. "I know. You warned me."

"Yes, I did." Vito picked up a stack of papers and set them in a cardboard box. "I'll take this down to Agatha." Keys jingling, he walked to the elevator then stopped and turned. "Now you can move out of that apartment, and I can quit worrying."

She shrugged. "Now it's the only apartment I can afford."

"You move in with us."

Flicking a tear away, she blew him a kiss. "You're my angel, Vito."

Dani tossed the envelope from her final paycheck onto the kitchen table. It lodged between a bowl crusted with two-day-old Shredded Wheat and a cup of long-cold chai tea. Her canvas bag sat on the floor by the door, where she'd dropped it after walking out of the *Times* building with her career in a cardboard box. At least a week ago, maybe more.

Still in the baggy Twin Shadow shirt and worn-thin shorts she'd slept in two nights ago, she padded barefoot across the marble tiles and onto the champagne-colored carpet of her living room. As she stood in front of the window, a red-winged blackbird ducked its tail feathers into the birdbath then hopped in. A series of frenetic shakes and flaps shot water like a spasmodic sprinkler. Midday sunlight reflected off flying droplets. For the first time in a week, walking outside sounded slightly more appealing than sleeping. If she had what it took to put on real clothes, she might actually give in to the lure of sunshine. But she didn't have what it took to think, much less get dressed. There were decisions to be made and she was vaguely aware that she had to make them.

Any day now she'd wake up at a time that could actually be called morning. She'd feel rested and ready to begin this new phase of life. She'd pick up a newspaper—one without her byline—and look for a job. And a cheaper place to live. Or she'd pack her shriveled pride and move back to her old room so her mother could have a fresh start at running her life.

"You move in with us."

Maybe, Vito. Maybe.

Strange to be needing an apartment when she already had two. One in a neighborhood she couldn't afford. The other in a neighborhood she couldn't show her face in. The thought brought to mind the face of the Roman statue.

The last word she'd heard out of his mouth—as an EMT bent on one knee and Nicky loosened her arms from around his neck—was "stupid." After leaving three rambling messages explaining why she'd done what she'd done, she'd given up on calling Nicky.

She'd given up on Nicky. Period.

But she had no idea what to do with the ache in her chest that threatened to double her over every time she thought of him. Did he think of her at all? Did he miss her, or had his anger blocked all the good times from his memory? Had he mailed the diary? Dani rested a fist on the windowsill. She'd expected him to call about that. Even if he couldn't say a civil word about anything else, he should have had the decency to let her read the rest of it.

Rena had called twice and left tear-filled apologies on her voice mail. She had no idea who had told her she'd lost her job. Dani had answered with a text. IT'S NOT YOUR FAULT. TELL CHINA SHE CAN STAY IN THE APARTMENT FOR NOW.

For now. Until the day she'd wake up with the energy to tell China she had to find another place.

As she headed for the bedroom, her phone bleeped. A text message, or the last dying gasp of an uncharged phone? She slogged across the carpet and found the phone buried under two charge card bills.

COMING OVER. BRINGING ANNA AND FOOD. GET DRESSED. Evan. How did he know she wasn't dressed? Salt streaks tightened on her cheeks as she remembered how to smile. With a sigh that rearranged the mound of soggy Kleenex on the table, she trudged to the shower.

꒰꒱

Sweat stung his eyes. It was too hot to run. Nicky's new mantra slowed with the change in the pace of rubber slapping concrete. *Idiot. Idiot. Idiot.*

He'd ignored all her calls. Hadn't even listened to her messages after the first one. *Sorry. . .sorry. . .good intentions. . .blah. . .blah. . . blah. . .*

What he chastened himself for with every step was not the pride that refused to call her back, but the temporary insanity that had allowed him to fall for her in the first place. She was a loose cannon, an accident waiting to happen, and a dozen other clichés that described people a guy should avoid like the plague.

But those eyes. And the blush of sun on ivory skin. And the curves that made him act like his father. He swiped his forearm across his eyes and convinced himself it was only sweat. She'd only been in his life for a matter of weeks. People said it took three weeks to form a habit. This was one he needed to break, and cold turkey was the best way to do it.

He walked the last block home. Taking the steps two at a time, he almost tripped on Gianna, spot cleaning the carpet at the top of the stairs.

"Sit." She patted the top step. "Doesn't matter if you sweat on the rug today." She sat back and leaned against the wall. "Talk."

He sat, leaned against the opposite wall, and closed his eyes as the words roiled inside and foamed to the surface. "Is it too much to ask to meet a girl who is who she appears to be?"

"She lied to you?"

Had she? "Lies of omission."

"Were her motives pure?"

"No. She was after a story."

A damp salt-and-pepper curl rolled onto Gianna's forehead as she bent to look him in the eyes. "And protecting Rena."

Nicky slapped the floor. "*I'm* supposed to protect Rena." His lips didn't come together after blurting his sister's name. Heat rose up the back of his already hot neck.

"So. There you have it."

"What do you mean?"

Gianna smiled, squeezed his shoulder, and picked up her rag. "Think about it."

"You want to help?" Dani punched the couch pillow under her head and rolled on her side to stare at her intervention committee. "Come with me to talk to China tomorrow. Help me pack up my stuff."

Anna crossed tanned and waxed legs. "I have to go to a shower in Illinois with my future mom-in-law. Should you go back there? Is it safe?"

"No. That's why I wanted you guys with me."

"Says the lady with killer feet." Evan squinted with one eye. "Or is it your heart you want us to protect? Worried about running into Spaghetti Man?"

The name, combined with the deadpan face, snapped the last, tight little shred of Dani's sanity, and she laughed until fresh, healing tears, coursed onto her shirt. She stood, pulled Evan then Anna to their feet, and enveloped them both in a hug. "Thank you." She grabbed a snippet of the Nicky dialogue that had become the soundtrack to a string of meaningless days. "I finally have a reason to smile."

"*Isn't that a song?*" she'd answered. "*Or does the song say a reason to live?*"

Find that. A tiny voice whispered in a foggy crevice of her tired brain. *Find your reason to live.*

Her phone rang. Mopping her face, she pulled away from her reasons to smile and picked it up. Was this her answer? *My reason? My Nicky?*

An unfamiliar number displayed on the screen. "Hello?"

"Hello." An elderly woman's voice. "Is this the woman who called Frank Brekken last week?"

"Yes it is. This is Danielle Gallagher."

"This is Lois Brekken, Frank's wife. I hope you don't mind me calling. Is this a good time?"

"Yes." She looked up at Evan. "How can I help you, Lois?"

"I overheard Frank's side of your conversation. Have you mailed the diary yet?"

"No." She thought of the leather book on the floor of Nicky's car. "I've had some things get in the way, and I haven't finished reading it." *And maybe I never will.*

"I understand. That's how life is, isn't it? The reason I'm calling is Frank's birthday is in two weeks. Our boys will be here, and I was hoping Frank could share the diary with them. I don't want to rush you, but—"

"It's no problem. I'll make sure it gets sent right away."

"Thank you. You see"—Lois's voice drew to a whisper—"Frank has cancer. He may not have as much time as he thinks."

Dani wiped fresh tears as she punched the number she'd sworn she'd never dial again. Once again the recording stabbed her heart, and once again she spoke to a machine.

⚜

July 27, 1928

Bracciano's side door slammed. Sweat rolling down reddened cheeks, Franky ran into the back room. "Can I hide under the table, Frazzie? I'm a bad guy, and Luca won't ever find me there."

Francie ruffled his hair and laughed. "Not now." She pulled another linen napkin from a wicker basket and picked up the iron. "Get Luca and you two can help me fold."

The side door slammed again. Footsteps pattered through the kitchen. Luca's dark curls clung to his temples. He swiped the dampness from his forehead. "You're not hided."

Franky's nose wrinkled. "Frazzy wants us to fold napkins. That's girl work."

"It is?" Francie matched corners on the cloth she'd just pressed. "And what is boy work?"

"Catching bad guys."

"And putting them in the slammer."

Francie nodded. "You're right. I'll do the girl work, and you two keep us safe from bad guys."

"And put 'em in the *slammer*." Luca's chubby fingers made the motion of locking a door.

Franky put his hand on Luca's back. "Come on. You be the robber this time."

They ran out the door, leaving Francie alone with her thoughts and the crucifix. And the calendar on the wall.

Today was Mr. Walbrecht's birthday.

She propped the back door open wider and finished the ironing. Renata was alone in the kitchen. Francie picked up a slice of fresh bread and took a bite. "Your husband has his faults, but no mere man has ever made bread this *delizioso*. I think I'll go work on your

281

dress for your anniversary."

Renata's cheeks pinked. "Do you think I'm a silly woman to be still in love with him?"

"No. I think you are a hopeful woman with dreams of a better future."

"Time, and God, will tell." Renata mopped perspiration from her face with a towel then washed her hands.

Francie peered into a steaming kettle. "It smells fishy. What is it?"

"*Risotto ai frutti di mare*. Rice and fish and vegetables." Renata stirred the concoction. Carrots, tomatoes, and parsley swirled around chunks of fish, wafting hints of saffron and fennel. "My mother added clams and mussels. I was homesick today. This reminds me of Bracciano."

Francie nodded. "Do you know what I want when I'm homesick? It will make you gag."

Her friend tipped her head to one side. "What is it?"

"It's called *grut*."

"Groot?"

"Kind of like that. Theo said I never pronounced it right because I'm not Norwegian. It's made of milk and flour."

"And. . .?"

"And nothing. If we were lucky, we had butter on it. On Christmas we got cinnamon and sugar to sprinkle on top."

"Poor families make do. We had this"—she held out a spoonful of rice and fish—"because my brothers fished and my mother grew vegetables."

"Why did you leave?"

Renata leaned the spoon against the pot. "My husband's family is very superstitious. They believe the spirits of the dead will return." She stared into space, as if crossing the ocean in her mind. "They believe you should never enter or take anything from a place where there has been a murder."

Francie shivered. "There was a murder?"

"Santo's father. He owed money he could not pay." She stirred the soup again. "They took his life because they could not get his money. In front of his wife and his children. My mother-in-law said her husband's spirit would return with other angry spirits and never let them live in peace. She turned her back on her home, and that is when we decided to come here and start a new life." She picked up a bowl and ladled soup into it. "We do what we have to do, don't we? Here, take some to your sister."

Francie's hand spread across her throat as she drew in a tight breath. She stared at the bowl held out to her. "You are so good to her."

"She is a child of God."

"How could she have allowed this? She has a child. How could she have done this to Franky? And to *me*?"

Renata offered a sympathetic smile that only seemed to fuel the fire in her. "You have lost the sister you once knew. It is your loss that makes you angry."

"It's her choices that make me angry. I sacrificed everything for her, and look what I get in return."

"You sacrificed for that little boy. And you would do it all over again even if you'd known what your sister had become." One eyebrow tilted. "Look what our Savior gets in return for His sacrifice."

There were times she didn't appreciate her friend's wisdom. "I can't feel mercy the way you do. I don't know how."

"You don't have to feel it. Just do what God is calling you to do."

Francie felt her throat constrict. Renata's challenge pulled her away from the subject of Suzette. Today was Mr. Walbrecht's birthday. She looked up at the clock. She had three hours to decide if she was going to do what God was calling her to do. She took the bowl of soup and carried it across the street. With no feeling of mercy, she spoon-fed her sister then spent the rest of Monday afternoon in her shop, letting the drone of her sewing machine drown out the voice of her conscience.

"Just do what God is calling you to do." Just before six, she left the shop and walked back to Bracciano in the dark, fingertips trailing the cold wall as she descended. A strange peace had enveloped her from the moment she'd decided to do the right thing.

It was time to catch bad guys. And put them in the slammer.

CHAPTER 31

Nicky tossed his damp towel on the bed and threw on shorts and a T-shirt. He tensed at a knock on his bedroom door. Gianna's comment still simmered, and he wasn't in the mood for more psychoanalysis.

"You in there?" Todd turned the handle and opened the door before Nicky had time to answer. He wore a uniform that looked freshly pressed, which hopefully meant he was on his way to work.

Nicky gestured to the chair and sat on the bed.

"Man, you look awful." Todd rubbed his chin. "But the ladies love the scruffy look."

"Are you here for a reason?"

"Yep. I'm here to surrender. You can have her."

"As if you were ever in the running." He shoved his hair out of his eyes. "But you win by default. She's all yours now."

Todd reached in his pocket. "Well *she's* all yours." He held the Javelin keys out to Nicky. "I'm waiving the last payment for all the good times. You can still keep her at my place."

Nicky's mouth opened. "You don't have to—"

"I know." He stood. "Gotta get to work. Just remember this gesture of kindness when I steal your ex."

"You can't *steal* an ex." The damp towel hit Todd in the middle of the back as he walked out.

Nicky stood in the hallway. A single guitar chord drifted through Rena's door. He pushed it open the rest of the way. She sat on her bed, head bent over her guitar, hair forming a shaggy fringe around her face. She looked up. Tears streaked her face.

They hadn't talked much in the past two weeks—other than the night he'd forced her to tell him everything Dani hadn't. He'd been too preoccupied licking his own wounds to deal with hers. Maybe it was time. She'd spent a night in jail, and her boyfriend was still there. As grateful as Nicky was for that fact, Rena had to be hurting. He stuck his head in. "How's it going?"

"Life? It's not."

Uninvited, he walked in and cleared a place on her loveseat. "I don't think I've actually told you how proud I am that you stepped in and stopped that robbery. Mad as all get out that you took that chance but proud of you."

Rena wiped her face on the corner of her sheet. "Thank you."

"Do you miss him?"

"Jarod? No. I'm glad he's gone. He was way more of a jerk than I realized." She tipped her head to one side. "It was a God thing, don't you think, that he happened to have all that crack on him when the cops came?"

Nicky nodded. "I guess it was." He stared at a dark green sweatshirt wadded in a corner. "What happens now—with the Sevens?"

She shrugged. "I don't know. They might retaliate. They won't be protecting me. . .or the restaurant." Vacant eyes knifed him. "Yeah, I lied about that."

"Protecting you, and us, is my job."

A sneer curled her lip. "Should be Dad's job."

He leaned forward, folding his hands. "What're you crying about, Wren?"

She swiped her cheek. "Dani got fired. Because of me. She told us not to involve her in anything illegal, and then I had to go and—"

"You talked to her?"

Rena shook her head. "She wouldn't answer my calls, so I called the paper and they said she didn't work there anymore."

"Maybe she quit." *Maybe she moved.*

"I called her friend Evan. He said she got fired. And she hadn't left her apartment since she got fired. He was worried about her."

His chest muscles tightened. "She's smart. She'll find another job."

A pale ring blanched around Rena's mouth. "You think she's that messed up over a job? Duh. You are so dense. It's *you*. I checked your phone. She's called you like a million times. Did you call her back even once?"

Nicky shot off the loveseat. "I don't need to listen to her trying to justify what she did. She didn't trust me enough to tell me the truth when it mattered. I don't give a rip now."

He stomped toward the door.

"Do you know why we don't have two parents?"

He stopped, smacked the door frame with both hands, but didn't turn around.

"Gianna told me. Dad wasn't like he is now until after Mom left. Mom didn't leave 'cause Dad kept having affairs. It was *one*. Just one night. He made one mistake and came to Mom on his knees, begging her to forgive him, but she wouldn't listen. She froze him out, shut him down. Just like you're doing to Dani."

Nicky's right hand balled into a fist. Without a conscious thought, he thrust toward the wall. Patching plaster crumbled onto bare feet. His knuckles throbbed. Biting back a string of words he never used anymore, he stomped into his room and slammed the door.

He had to get out of here. Away from women who thought they understood him. But first he had to delete the one he'd thought he understood. He dialed his voice mail.

"Nicky, it's Dani. Can we get together? I need to explain—" He pushed 7.

"Your call has been deleted."

"Nicky, I know you're mad. I don't—"

"Your call has been deleted."

"Hi. . .it's Dani. You're probably ignoring all my—"

"Your call has been deleted."

"I just got a call from Frank's wife."

Nicky's finger hovered over the button, but he decided to listen.

"Frank has cancer. He's dying." Her voice dipped. *"She asked. . .if*

we could send the diary right away. His birthday is in two weeks, and she wanted to give it to him then. Her address is. . ."

Nicky saved the call and threw his phone on the bed. His hand shook. Not from the news that a man he'd never met was dying, but from the raw, rasping pain in Dani's voice. He sank onto the bed.

"She froze him out, shut him down." Rena's words scraped his nerves. He was eleven years old again, in this same room. His mother thought he was asleep. She'd walked in, smelling like the patch of lilies of the valley that grew behind the restaurant. "I'm going on a little trip, Nicky. You be good for Daddy and take care of your sister."

He hadn't moved. He didn't know why. Maybe he knew it would do no good to tell her to stay. Maybe even then he knew she wasn't coming back. Only when he heard Rena's cries over his parents fighting at the bottom of the stairs did he get up.

"Nita. Stay," his father had begged. "It won't happen again, I promise. I'll make it up to you. I can't take care of two kids and run a business at the same time. Think of the children."

"No." His mother had waved her plane ticket in his face and handed Rena to him. "*You* think of the children. For once, I'm thinking of myself."

The screen door slammed. Nicky ran down the stairs and out on the street, screaming and running after the taxi as it turned the corner and disappeared.

"Shut him down. . ."

Did his mother know—did she care?—that she'd also shut down her son?

⚜

He'd put the diary in the top drawer of the desk in the storeroom, thinking someday, in the middle of the night, he'd finish it. Sometime when it didn't hurt so much to think of reading it alone.

Now he walked through the kitchen as the lunch rush was winding down, nodded to the servers and cooks bustling around the room. He had one foot through the open doorway of the storeroom when his father walked into the kitchen with a tray in one hand. Nicky waved. He still hadn't figured out why the man was hanging around so much. It was too much to believe he'd actually changed, was actually making good on a threadbare promise.

He headed to the desk in the corner. The crucifix caught his eye. *"Are you Catholic?"* she'd asked.

"I was raised in the church."

Her eyes had searched his soul. *"And now?"*

He hadn't answered. Not until that prayer had sprung from some sealed, forgotten place inside of him. Thinking about it now, he wondered if he'd dreamed that prayer. Was that really him? As he'd listened to her talk about her mother squelching her dreams, something had started to crack inside him, something that made him want to reach out, take her broken dreams in his hand, and mend them. In that same instant he'd known it wasn't his job. As he traced the curve of her face, he'd replayed the conversation they'd had in the car.

"Think of what you know to be true about the character of God. What's the first thing you learned about Him when you were a kid?"

"God is love." He'd spat it back to her in a voice steeped in cynicism.

"If that's true, then why do we need input?"

In that moment, in the replaying of her words, he'd suddenly seen the love of God for the first time in four years. Prayer was the only possible response.

And now?

If God was love, who was Nicky Fiorini to question what He was doing?

Opening the drawer, he pulled out the diary and dragged a chair over to the table in the center of the room. Shoving aside a two-gallon jar of pepperoncinis and a box of napkins, he sat down and opened the diary to the place Dani had marked with her church bulletin. Before he could start reading, Rena walked in, hair still unbrushed, eyes still smudged.

"I'm sorry. I shouldn't have said that stuff." She sat on a stack of boxes. "I just feel so bad. It's my fault Dani lost her job and—"

"It is not your fault. She chose to join your...group." He couldn't bring himself to call it what it was. "She chose to come when you called her."

"To protect me."

Again, the tightness in his chest. *"It's my job to protect you. It was my job to protect Tony."*

"Only God can do that."

Dani's words. He'd heard her express it twice. Once to China, when she'd met her across the street. "It's not our place to make someone else feel whole," she'd said. "Only God can do that." And then again when he'd asked her to fix Rena. She'd answered, "Only God can fix broken people."

But she'd been willing to let God use her to get to Rena. She'd chosen to come when Rena called her, in spite of the risk.

And that, not the fact that she'd joined the gang or that she hadn't told him what she was doing, was what really bugged him. Because he'd been too wrapped up in himself to take the time to find out what his sister was up to and to put himself in a position to protect her.

"Only God can do that."

"Only God."

"What's that?" Rena leaned over the table.

"A diary." Nicky suddenly felt too tired for the anger. He got up and grabbed the mended chair, motioning for Rena to take his. "Dani found it behind the house across the street."

"Oh yeah. Chi told me about it a long time ago."

"You knew about this?"

Rena shrugged. "Chi found it in the attic with a bunch of ancient fashion magazines. She said the girl's daddy was a bootlegger. That's all I heard. Chi's not much of a reader."

He told her about Francie and gave her a quick summary of all they'd read so far.

"That's crazy. Can I read it?"

"I need to finish it now and mail it today. The man, Francie's nephew, has cancer. We need to get it to him before. . ."

"Can I read it with you?"

He didn't have the energy for a confrontation. He positioned the book between them.

July 29, 1928

T is hurt. Bad. His brother was shot, too. Cops interrupted

289

*them, but T called it a successful mission. Thanks to me, he said.
If he knew the cops showed because of me, I'd be dead. He left
something with me. Said he's coming back for it. And me.
I don't know when. I'm so scared.*

"T's the bad guy?"

Nicky nodded.

"What was the mission?"

"Dani found a newspaper clipping about a jewelry store holdup."
He'd never seen the clipping. Nicky flipped through the pages, on
the off chance Dani had stuck it back where she'd found it. It wasn't
there. "I didn't see it, but I remember the numbers. Forty thousand
dollars worth of diamonds and jewelry were stolen."

"Wow. Think what they'd be worth now. And this guy gave
them to Francie? When she worked here?" Her eyes sparkled.

"Don't get too caught up in the drama, kid. It happened over
eighty years ago. I don't think Francie left a pile of jewelry in a
kitchen cupboard for us." He started reading again.

*Renata helped me find a way to hide the things T left. They
are safe. I don't think I will ever see him again, but I'm afraid
to believe we are finally free.*

Only scattered entries filled the next six weeks. Most were about
Francie's seamstress business. On September 14, 1928, Francie had
written:

*Life would be perfect if not for the problem sleeping in the
same room with me. Today I'm doing a second fitting on Mrs.
A. Tomorrow Renata and I are going to a Women's Society
Meeting at the First Congregational Church. I called Mama
yesterday. She actually talked*

That was all. Nicky turned blank pages, hoping for something
more. Rena shrugged. "Well, you know the kid survived." She pulled
the book toward her and stared at Francie's picture in the back.
"She's kinda pretty. How old was she when this was taken?"

"She was fifteen when she started writing in here and"—he glanced at the last date—"nineteen when she wrote this."

"I wonder"—her fingernail slipped under the edge of the picture—"if she wrote on the back."

"Don't do—"

The photo popped away from the back cover.

"She did write something. 'Behind the storm there—'"

"Look."

In a slight recess in the center of the white rectangle the picture had once covered sat a brass key.

CHAPTER 32

A *literal* key?"

Nicky's phone, set on speaker, sat in the middle of the table. Frank Brekken's voice boomed out of it. "Any idea what it's for?"

"No idea. It's a skeleton key, hollow on one end, about two inches long. It doesn't seem large enough to be a door key. Do you have anything that belonged to her—a suitcase or jewelry box or anything? Because we have good reason to believe that at one time your aunt was hiding something. Possibly a substantial amount of stolen jewelry."

Silence. Had he caused the guy to have a stroke? "Mr. Brekken? Are you okay?"

"Yes." He coughed. "I just can't imagine how. . .but that could be the reason Luca's dad. . . But don't tell me anything now. That settles it. We're flying to Wisconsin, Lois. Next week."

A woman's gasp filtered through the phone followed by insistent words not clear enough to make out. "We'll talk when I'm off the phone, sweetie." Frank laughed. "She'll come around. Women always do if you treat 'em right."

"That hasn't been my experience, but I'm glad it works for you."

"Guess we'll have to have a man-to-man when we meet face-to-face."

Again, the woman protested in the background.

"I'll look forward to that, sir."

"Good. Better give me the address. Seems impossible all this time has passed. I remember watching your great-grandfather make ravioli like it was yesterday. Can't remember what I had for lunch yesterday, but, boy, do I remember that ravioli with Renata's tomato sauce."

"I'll make some special for you while you're here. Still the same recipe."

"Makes a grown man misty-eyed. A meal at Bracciano will do me more good than all those drugs they want to stick in me."

"My grandfather is convinced the only medications a person needs are garlic, oregano, and olive oil."

"*Sage* advice." The deep laugh filled the storeroom. He didn't sound like a man who knew he was dying.

"Why don't you just give me a call when you know when you'll be coming in, and I'll pick you up at the airport."

Rena's elbow connected with his ribs. "*We'll* pick him up," she whispered. "You are not going to meet them without Dani. If you don't call her I..."

Over the whir of his sister's warnings, he said good-bye to Franky Brekken.

♔

Dani got out of the H1 and stood next to Evan, staring at the door to the upstairs apartment. Her gaze wandered to the restaurant across the street.

Evan put his hand on her shoulder. "Maybe he's—I mean *she's*— not home."

"I called. She's home." *Is he?* What was he doing with his free hours before work?

Her phone buzzed. Todd Metzger. She didn't have to think too hard to figure out what he wanted. And she just might—for none of the right reasons—say yes. But she'd deal with him later—after she'd packed up her street kid clothes and fake tattoos and moved back to her upscale apartment and her verge-of-poverty reality.

"Did you tell China you were coming to evict her and her unborn child?"

293

"What would I do without you to give me strength when I'm weak?" She reached for the door handle. "No. I didn't tell her."

At the top of the stairs, she almost knocked. Evan reminded her it was her apartment. "Hey, China. We're here."

They found her sitting on the floor with a sketchbook on her lap. The walls were lined with at least a dozen drawings.

"Hey."

For an instant, Dani was almost sure the girl smiled. She walked over to one of the pictures. A sketch of Bracciano as seen through the cracked front window. "You did this?"

"Yeah. Not much else to do around here. Hope it's okay I hung 'em up. It's just tape."

"It's fine. They're amazing."

China looked down at her pencil. A moment later, her head bobbed up. "I've been looking for a job."

To Evan it may have sounded like mere conversation, but Dani knew it to be a declaration of hope. This was a girl who wanted a future. Dani grinned and nodded.

Evan walked up to a drawing of a fire hydrant. Its shadow flowed over the curb and onto a crumpled beer can in the gutter. "You've got talent, China. Real talent."

"Thanks. Can't feed a baby with pretty pictures, though."

"Tell me about it. Wish I could feed myself on pretty pictures." One finger tapped his chin. "Do you know a guy named Scope?"

"Heard of him. He got rolled out of the Sevens a few years ago, right?"

"I guess. He's an artist, too. We should get you two together for an—"

Footsteps clamored up the stairs. Venus burst through the door. "Hey Cerise, or whoever you are. Welcome back to the 'hood."

"I..." Shock evaporated Dani's words. "Thanks." It wasn't the time to mention she wasn't really back. She introduced Venus to Evan.

Even nodded. "What's up, Venus?"

"Nothin'. Too hot to do anything."

"Boredom seems to be a common theme around here."

Venus sank to the floor a few feet from China. "Wait. Almost forgot. I made something for you." She fingered a dozen or more beaded bracelets, slid off one made of solid white beads and handed it to Dani. "White is for new beginnings and for when you want to get rid of prejudice and preconceived notions. I read that in a magazine. I had preconceived notions about people like you. When you fought for Rena and Chi, I knew I was wrong."

"Thank you. I'm speechless. I just assumed the Sisters—"

"Hate you?" Venus laughed. "Most of them do. But I see your true colors, you know."

Still stunned, Dani circled the room, looking at pictures on the wall as others flashed in her head. Leah wrote poetry. Rena wrote songs. Scope painted. China sketched. Venus made jewelry. Evan took pictures. She was a journalist. An out-of-work journalist. She glanced at Evan. Was this a God moment or the meanderings of a tired mind?

The spark in his eyes said he was feeling it, too. "I'm thinking we need to have an art show."

Dani shook her head. "I'm thinking bigger."

"How bigger?"

"I don't know. Teen center or nonprofit. . .something."

"Or *for*-profit something. Magazine?"

"Store?"

"Both?"

Heads turning in unison, China and Venus silently followed the verbal ping-pong.

Dani nodded toward them. "What do *they* want?"

"Let's ask them." Evan dropped to the floor and sat tailor-fashion in front of the girls. "There are places you can go to play basketball and study and things like that, but what if—"

"We started something to provide jobs." Dani sat next Evan. "Jobs that use your talents."

Evan nodded. "Like a place to sell bracelets or a magazine or art gallery."

China's eyes lit. Her posture straightened. "What about people who do other kinds of art—like music?"

Adrenaline floodgates opened. Dani's arms tingled. Her toes wiggled to a silent beat. "An all-kid performing and visual arts center."

Evan put his hand on her shoulder and squeezed. "Maybe a little over the top."

Venus's lips opened and closed, making a soft *pop—pop—pop*. "But you gotta dream big. Remember what you said about doing something to stop the cycle? I got a little sister that's gonna end up jus' like me or worse if somebody don't do something. You guys gotta dream big for her."

Odd advice from a girl whose highest aspiration seemed to be stringing glass beads.

"You're right." Evan tapped his chin. "How involved would you two want to be? If we set up a meeting at our church, would you talk and tell them what life is really like here?"

China seemed to shrink. "I guess."

"We'll do it." Venus held up a hand and got a weak slap from China. "I ain't afraid of talkin' to nobody."

"Well, okay then." Evan copied the high five, holding his hand up for Dani to slap. "Looks like you got yourself a job, Cerise."

"Can't feed myself on dreams."

Nicky's prayer surfaced on her words. *Lord God, You know the cry of Dani's heart is to make a difference for You, and You know the dreams I've tried to ignore. Right now, we bring our dreams and lay them at Your feet. . . ."*

Evan stood. "Let's get you packed up. Ladies, we'll be in touch. I've got a meeting tonight, so I need to get your boss home."

"But. . ." China's dark-rimmed eyes took on the look of a six-year-old.

Dani chewed on her bottom lip. *Lord, you know the cry of my heart.* "Um. . .yeah. . .about that. . ."

Evan's eyes widened. "You're *not.*"

"I am."

His eyes narrowed. "You are not."

"Oh, but I am."

China looked from Evan to Dani. "You are *what?*"

"I am home."

♔

Nicky took the car keys from Gianna. She kissed his cheek. "Be

296

kind. To my car and the girl. 'Love covers a multitude of sins.'"

He snorted.

"'A person's wisdom yields patience; it is to one's glory to overlook an offense.'" She squeezed his arm. "Proverbs 19:11."

He managed a close facsimile of a smile and walked out the back door. Laughter and the clang of a metal ladder drew his attention to the house across the street. The guy who owned the house stood on a stepladder scraping the porch railing. Another whacked at an overgrown bush with a machete.

About time. The place, like too many others, had been a disaster for years.

He started the SUV. The radio blasted. A male singer wondering if there was a greater purpose outside his own little world. Nicky cranked the knob. Amy Winehouse sang "Will You Still Love Me Tomorrow."

The singer's tomorrows had ended in alcohol poisoning.

He smacked the button to silence.

As he neared the Kemper Center, his pulse went into overdrive. His palms slicked on the steering wheel as he cranked it toward the curb. The battle inside made it feel like the power steering had gone out. He stared at the redbrick house with the white-spindled stairway leading to the apartment above the garage.

Why was it he'd only been here once? Was she embarrassed by her posh neighborhood? Afraid he'd feel unworthy if he saw her in her own surroundings?

He glanced at the clock. Frank and Lois's plane was landing in three hours. It would take him a little over an hour to drive there, but then he'd still have to find a parking place and get to the baggage claim to meet them. Why had he waited till the last minute?

Pride.

As he shut the car off, he tried to come up with a first line. "Get in the car, we're picking up Frank" probably wouldn't cut it. Whatever came out of his mouth, she'd be expecting it to include an "I'm sorry."

He hadn't changed his mind on that. He wouldn't pretend he was sorry for being angry about her deception. He couldn't pretend he was fine with her renting an apartment in his neighborhood and getting rolled into a gang without telling him. Dumb. And Stupid. And he'd added a dozen more words in the past two weeks.

But maybe she'd be the one to say it first, and then they could move on from there. She'd learned her lesson, figured out the hard way that all his warnings were for a reason. He wouldn't have to worry about her doing the same kind of stupid thing, but what would she try next? Where would she go where he couldn't protect her?

He slammed the car door and stepped onto the curb. Other than traffic, the street was quiet. No babies crying, no husbands swearing at wives. Unnerving quiet. He wiped his hands on his jeans and walked up the driveway.

"She hadn't left her apartment since she was fired."

He pictured her curled in the corner of her couch, hair in tangles, eyes red. *"You think she's that messed up over a job? Duh. You are so dense. It's you."*

Pride. The rusty voice of his conscience spoke into the quiet. She wasn't the only one messed up because he'd been too stubborn to listen to her apologies. Or give his own.

Dani. I'm sorry. He took the steps two at a time and leaped onto the landing.

The smell of bleach and carpet cleaner wafted through the wide open door.

The apartment was empty.

Nicky sank onto the top step.

He could find her. He had contacts. They were catering her best friend's wedding. That wasn't the reason for the hopelessness that washed over him.

She'd moved because of him. Because he hadn't been protecting Rena the way he should have. Because he hadn't followed her when she'd run off to meet China. Because he'd been too late and not in the right spot at the right time.

Again.

"It's not your job."

Tears stung. *Lord, I just want to hold her. I just want to tell her I don't care what she didn't tell me. I just want to say I'm sorry for being such a—*

A car door opened and closed. He looked up. Dani walked toward him, hair floating around her shoulders in a warm breeze. *Thank You.* He took the stairs two at a time and met her at the bottom. He opened his arms and she slid into them. He buried his face in her hair. "I'm sorry. I should have answered your calls. I'm so sorry. It was just my stubborn—"

"Shh. My turn." She pressed her fingertip to his lips. "I'm sorry I wasn't totally honest. I should have told you about—"

"Shh. My turn." His lips grazed hers. "I forgive you. Do you—"

"Yes." The word blended with her kiss.

His fingers slid into her hair. He cradled the back of her head, drinking in the scent of sun-warmed skin. When his breathing quickened, he forced himself to pull away. Forehead leaning on hers, he kissed the tip of her nose. "I heard you lost your job. I'm so sorry."

She smiled up at him. "Don't be. I have a new job that's better than anything I could ever have dreamed."

He eased back, let his fingers trail through the gold ends of her hair. "What kind of job?"

Her smile widened. "You're looking at the executive director of Street Level."

"What's that?"

"It isn't much yet, but it will be a nonprofit organization that helps teens turn their talents and dreams into careers."

"Wow. That's perfect for you. Where did you find something like that?"

"I didn't find it. I created it."

"Really?" His voice flattened. "Is it operating out of your church?"

Her smile dimmed. "No." She folded her arms. "It will operate out of my apartment. My other apartment."

Respirations that had just begun to slow suddenly quickened. His pulse reverberated through his whole body.

"I know what you're thinking. I know you think I don't have street smarts and it's dangerous, and you're right, it is. But I'm not doing it alone. I'll be working with a whole team of volunteers and professionals who want to help residents reclaim and restore their neighborhoods." The skin on her arms blanched beneath her fingertips. "You're right, it's not safe. But Jesus doesn't always call us to safe things. Sometimes he calls us to risk our comfort and our convenience and even our. . ."

Her voice faded behind him as he strode to the car.

⚜

September 24, 1928

Run!

The voice screamed in Francie's head, but her legs wouldn't move. Her stomach lurched at the sight on the sidewalk below, but she couldn't close her eyes, couldn't turn away. Santo. Still. *Deathly* still. A pool of blood spreading across the sidewalk. Renata on her knees. Screaming. *"Mio marito! Lei ha ucciso mio marito!"* She sobbed and shook her fist in the air. *"Mio Dio!"*

Run. But where? To her friend or away from here?

"Frazzie? What happened?" Franky stood in the bedroom doorway, rubbing his eyes. "Who's yelling?"

She forced numb muscles to make a smile. "That was"—Black spots dotted her vision. She lowered her head—"a long nap, sunshine."

"Why are you crying?" His sleep-roughened voice sounded small, like it used to. Not like going-on-seven.

Francie swiped at her eyes and tried not to think of the little boy across the street.

She should be there for Luca. But she couldn't let Franky see. *God, what should I do?* "Cookies and milk?"

He nodded. "Snickerdoodles?"

A man lay bleeding, possibly dead, on the sidewalk across the street, and she was fixing cookies and milk.

It was a nightmare. She would wake up and iron her dress and walk across the street and there would be no blood on the sidewalk.

A warm hand slid into hers, and they walked to the kitchen. She opened the Frigidaire and took out a bottle of milk. The glass shook in her hand. Franky crawled up on his stool and took the "hat" off the cookie jar shaped like a bear.

Footsteps pounded on the stairs. She grabbed Franky by the shoulders. "Let's play hide-and-go-seek, okay? Take your cookie and hide in the bathtub."

"But then you'll know where to find me."

300

"I hear footsteps. Someone's coming. You can hide from whoever's coming. I won't tell. Promise."

Cookie in hand, Franky ran to the bathroom on tiptoes. Francie slumped against the counter as someone knocked on the door.

"Francie." A sob swallowed Perlita's next words.

Francie swung the door open. The young waitress fell into her arms. "Santo. He was behind the bar. I was setting tables. Only three customers. And then two men came in. Why did no one check them for guns?" She clung to Francie. "They shot Mr. Jones. In the head. And then Santo. Here"—she touched a spot below her collar bone. "It was so loud. They left. No one tried to stop them. I tried to help Santo, but he took the gun from under the bar and ran down the stairs. I followed. He went down to the coal room. I thought he was going to hide, but I heard him open the outside door. He was after the men, but he fell and"—Perlita bent over, clutching her stomach—"so much blood. Renata said you have to leave. All of you. She said they were after what you have, but you musn't go after it. They will kill you, too." A siren wailed. "Hurry, Francie." She flew out the door and down the steps.

Run! Still waiting to wake from the nightmare, she commanded her legs to run, but they moved as if she stood in waist-deep snow. Her pulse beat an SOS in her ears. "Franky! You can come out now." She walked past the bathroom. Too slow. "We're going on a little trip. You and Mommy and me. Put your pajamas and toothbrush and a clean shirt and pants and socks and underwear in your pillow case." Her mouth formed a list. Her brain shouted *Hurry!*

She bent over Suzette. "Get up. Santo's been shot. We have to leave. *Now.*" She grabbed her purse, checked for her billfold. And the slip of paper with the phone number she'd carried for almost a year. "Get up!"

"Too tired. You go."

"No." She pulled the covers off. "Do you hear what I'm saying? Tag's men shot Santo. They'll kill us." She lifted her sister by her shoulders.

"You go. Take Franky."

The woman curled in the twisted mass of sweat-soaked covers was no longer her sister. The opium had leached away everything recognizable.

"If I take Franky, you'll never see him again. Get up!" She screamed it this time and then, still praying none of this was real, she slapped Suzette across the mouth. "Wake up!"

"No. You go."

There was no more time. She let go of the thin shoulders and let her sister drop onto her pillow. "Ready, Franky? Let's go." She scooped up the boy and his pillow and ran down the steps. She'd run until she couldn't. And then she'd find a phone and call the only person who could help. If he hadn't left the country yet.

She was four blocks away when she remembered the diary.

Someday, for Franky's sake, she'd go back for what wasn't rightfully hers.

CHAPTER 33

Dani turned up the music and smiled at the childlike face of the pregnant girl dozing on the couch.

She walked past the place where there had once been bloodstains on the wall and looked away, out the front window at Bracciano. Morning light glinted on the windows. Half a day after he'd turned his back on her, his footsteps still tapped in her mind. The constant ache in her chest had metastasized to an all-over pain she knew she'd have to learn to live with.

Would his reaction have been different if he'd taken the time to hear that she was only using this place as an office—that she and China had moved in with Vito and Lavinia? She turned away from the window. He hadn't cared enough to hear her out.

The music pouring out of her computer lifted her out of her pain and into her purpose. She opened an e-mail from the man at her church who'd started helping her landlord paint the outside of the house.

Dani, Thank you for the opportunity to—

A knock at the door. She slipped out of her shoes and picked up her phone. Standing to the side of the door, she looked through a tear in the flimsy curtain. Rena.

She flung the door wide.

"There's someone you have to meet."

"Who?"

"Just come with me."

"Not to the restaurant."

"They're just outside." Rena turned and flew down the steps.

Dani slipped her shoes on and followed.

An elderly couple stood on the sidewalk.

She knew, without an introduction, who they were.

⚜

Lois's arm rested on Dani's as they crossed the street toward Bracciano. Dani helped her up the curb. Lois thanked her and looked at Rena. "Before we go in, we'd like to have a little talk with Dani. Rena, will you tell your brother we'll only be just a minute?"

"Sure."

Rena walked away, and Dani looked from one soft, lined face to the other. Faded eyes radiated kindness. Lois touched her hand. "Since you're a person who likes stories, I'd like to tell you part of ours."

"I'd love that."

"This part goes back over sixty years. My dashing young man got down on one knee, asked me if I would make him the happiest man in the whole world, brought me to tears and a promise that I would follow him to the ends of the earth, and then decided to mention God had told him to move back to India to live in squalor and poverty. . .with his new bride."

Frank laughed, placed a thin hand against his chest, and fingered a wooden cross hanging from a leather thong. "I was young and impulsive."

"And thoughtless and insensitive." Lois smiled sweetly up at him. "I was furious. I felt betrayed. Angry, hurt, scared. . .I moped and I stomped and I threw things."

"Including the engagement ring."

"Yes." Lois dabbed dampness from the corner of her eye. "After days of that, I was finally too worn out to fight. And that's when I heard that still, small voice whispering 'Trust Me. I'll never lead you to a place where I am not.'"

Tears stung Dani's eyes. A beautiful story, but it was Nicky who needed to hear it.

"We were married three months later." Lois took her husband's hand. "We have smuggled Bibles, preached the Word in places where it was forbidden, and been held at knifepoint because of it. But God has never led us to a place where He was not."

Dani blinked hard and nodded.

Frank touched her arm. "The point of telling you this is that we had a nice long time to visit with Nicky on the way back from the airport yesterday."

Lois nodded. "Frank has a way of drawing people out. Your Nicky has a good heart."

My Nicky.

"And Lois has a way of helping people see God's hand in every situation." Frank nodded toward Bracciano. "If you're willing to wait for God to—"

"Dani."

She looked over Lois's shoulder. Nicky stood, arms at his side, a black T-shirt stretching across his chest.

Frank and Lois walked into the restaurant. Nicky didn't move toward her. His gaze fastened on the sidewalk.

She waited.

A deep breath shuddered through him. "I'm scared. I don't want to lose you." He looked up. A single tear etched a track down his left cheek.

She stepped toward him, but he held up one hand. "I don't have their kind of faith, and I don't know if I can handle worrying about losing someone else. But I know I have to try to trust God to keep you safe because you don't have any street smarts, but clearly that's not going to stop you from doing dumb things. So if you're willing to put up with me hovering around and being overprotective and getting cranky when you take stupid chan—"

She ran the last few steps and stopped his words with a kiss.

Frank stood in the doorway of the storeroom. The diary lay open on the old iron table, but Frank didn't go in. Instead, he walked into the dining room.

"This is so familiar, yet so different." He pointed to the far wall. "There used to be a bar there with a huge mirror lined with bottles of every color alcohol you could imagine. I remember Santo shining those bottles." He walked farther into the room. I don't think there were windows back then. It was always dark. I remember the music and the smoke—so thick you could barely breathe."

Nicky looked at his father.

Carlo shook his head. "There's never been a bar here," he whispered. "And there have always been windows." He gave a look that echoed what Dani was thinking. Poor Frank suffered from mental lapses like Nicky's grandfather.

Nicky pointed toward the doorway. "I'll show you the diary."

Frank walked in the storeroom. He reached out for the book but didn't pick it up. He stepped back. His lips parted and a smile crossed his face. "The tunnel."

The poor man. Lois put a hand on his arm. "Frank?"

Frank grinned at Nicky. "Do you still use it?"

"The. . .table? Yes. All the time."

"The tunnel. Is it still safe?"

Awkward looks shot around the room. Confusion masked Frank's face. "You don't know about the tunnel?" He rubbed his forehead as if that would clear his brain.

Carlo stepped toward Frank and put his hand on Lois's back. "Nicky made cinnamon rolls. Why don't we all go sit down and—"

Frank handed the diary to Lois, grabbed onto one end of the table, bent his knees, and yanked. His wife latched onto his arm. "Frank, what's going on? What are you—"

Nicky gasped. Rena moved in closer. The table, still attached to floorboards, rose up several inches, boards and all.

"Lift the sides," Frank ordered the men.

Nicky grabbed one side. His father took the other. They lifted. The table swung up and back. Thick curved bars rose out of a hole in the floor. The table made a *thunk* as it came to a stop, resting on one end on the floor.

In the gaping hole, dust-covered wood stairs led down into blackness.

Nicky rubbed his thumb across the back of Dani's hand as they descended. Ahead of them, Frank arced a flashlight at messages and dates etched and painted on the pale yellow brick.

J&R 1926

BUD AND LANA - JUST MARRIED!

RALPH E. APRIL 9 '28

DROP YOUR WEAPONS, BOYS.

TELL NOT A SOUL WHAT YOU FIND HERE.

"My initials are here somewhere. Santo let Luca and I use his knife but warned us to never tell Renata." He stopped and shined the light straight overhead. "So many secrets back then."

Nicky ran his hand along the cool bricks. Beside him, Dani counted the steps. There were only eight. Frank bent over when he reached the bottom. Nicky copied his posture. There was just enough room for Dani to stand up straight.

He'd expected to meet a wall at the bottom, expected it to open into a basement they never knew existed. But Frank walked straight ahead. Which meant. . . "We're between the buildings." They had to be directly under the empty lot between the restaurant and the vacant garage. His pulse tripped.

The flashlight beam ricocheted off something ahead. "More stairs," Dani whispered.

Shoes clogged against wood as they picked their way up another flight of stairs. They reached a landing and turned. There was a door to their left, but Frank walked up yet more steps. When he reached the top, he burst out laughing. "And here I thought I was losing my mind."

The room before them was pitch black, but every spot the flashlight beam illuminated sent chills down Nicky's spine. Though dirty and in shambles, the room was a scene straight out of one of his fantasies.

A massive, carved frame surrounded an enormous mirror. In front of it stood a curved bar made of rich, dark wood. Teak or mahogany. A player piano sat in one corner. The center of the room was filled with square tables, some overturned, some still covered in tablecloths, now moth-eaten and coated with a layer of dust.

Dani gripped his arm. "Look." She reached out for Frank. "Shine your light on the mirror again."

The mirror was cracked right down the middle and what could only be bullet holes pocked one side. Scrolled letters etched in an intact pane of frosted glass above the mirror spelled out STARDUST.

"Why did they leave it like this? All these years..." Nicky rubbed a hand over his eyes. Had Dani found her time machine? Had they all stepped back in time with her?

Dani released his arm and shined her light on a spot on the floor. A stain. "Someone died here." She looked up and locked eyes with him. "Renata told Francie the Fiorini family was superstitious and wouldn't enter or take anything from a place where someone was murdered."

Frank's hand slid over his mouth then fell to his side. "My aunt would never talk about what happened here. I've often wondered if it was just a dream." He looked down at Carlo. "Your grandfather. Was he killed by a gunshot?"

An odd look passed over his father's face. "He died when I was about ten. But he had a scar." He pointed to a spot just below his right collarbone. "He told me and my cousins it was how a gangster made him believe in God."

Frank nodded. "That was the night we left. Mama was sick. Aunt Francie begged her to get out of bed, but she couldn't." His voice drifted as if he were miles away. "I never saw my mother again."

Lois put her hand on his back. The sound of her hand rubbing his shirt echoed in the silence. Nicky closed his eyes, sharing the hurt this man felt even after all these years.

"We took a train to Chicago. When we got off, a man I'd never seen before ran up and hugged us both. He kept saying, 'Finally, finally.' I was terrified. My aunt was sobbing. The guy kissed her and she kissed him back."

Dani gasped. "Theo?"

Frank nodded. "He scooped me up in his arms and said, 'How'd you like to ride an elephant?' That's all it took to win me over. A few months later we were on a boat to India."

If her imagination was spinning, Dani could only guess what was twirling around in the head of the man whose arm was around her and whose fingers tapped a nameless tune on her forearm. Nicky's mouth hadn't closed once since they'd walked into the room. While Dani snapped pictures with her phone, he'd gone from table to table, looking as if he were carrying on imaginary conversations with imaginary patrons.

Frank headed toward the stairs and she tugged at Nicky's sleeve. "Follow the light, Nicky."

He snapped out of his stupor and grinned. "I'm buying this building. You all know that, right? I don't care who owns it or how much it costs or—"

"Nicky." Frank turned and looked from Nicky to his father. "Carlo? Don't *you* own this building?"

"N–no." Carlo scratched his head.

"I understand your family's superstitions, but if they'd sold it, someone would have done something with it, don't you think?"

Furrows deepened on Carlo's forehead. He locked eyes with Nicky. "Nonno still owns the restaurant. Property tax bills go to him. I've never seen one—I just write the check and mail it to his lawyer." His eyebrows rose, exactly like his son's. "We shovel the sidewalk for our customers, we mow the lot. We always have. I've never questioned it."

The tapping on Dani's arm turned frenetic. Nicky's whole body shook as his head bobbed. "This could be ours. This. . .could. . . be. . .ours." This time, he pulled her toward the stairs. "What's on the main floor?"

Six pairs of feet clamored like an elephant herd back to the landing. Frank turned a clear glass handle on a yellow-painted door. It swung open. The room was long but narrow. A rectangular table took up one side. A treadle sewing machine sat next to the table. On the other end of the room stood three dressmaker's forms. Two were empty; a sheet shrouded the third. Dani lifted it by the corners. Beneath it hung a knee-length gown. Once white. Maybe never worn.

Dani grabbed the fingers that pummeled her arm. "Francie's shop." She pulled the sheet away. Satin with a sheer overlay. Yellowed, but possibly salvageable.

Frank crossed the room to another door and opened it. "Whoa. . ."

Through the door, Dani saw tools littering the floor. A mechanic's shop. She followed Carlo and could only nod as his "Suh-weeet" bounced off the concrete floor and was echoed by his son.

An old black car, dust caked, but appearing to be in mint condition filled half the room. She knew enough about cars to recognize it as a Model T. She left the men to drool and went back into Francie's shop. Rena followed her. As her phone lit up lavender wallpaper, shelves still stocked with fabric, a rocking chair in the corner, she could almost see Francie stitching on the hem of the satin dress. Her light scanned the ceiling, then down along the far wall. They walked toward a dust-coated picture. Dark storm clouds, trees bent by wind, people scurrying. "Creepy."

Rena gasped. "Lois! Lois, bring the diary in here!"

Footsteps scrambled behind them. Rena pointed to the picture, grabbed the diary, and opened to the back. Francie's picture was loose, tucked in the back cover. She turned it over. "On the back it says, 'Behind the storm there is always a safe hiding place.' She looked from Dani to Nicky to her father and then to Frank. "Storm. . .*safe*."

Frank stepped forward. "Where's the key?"

Dani looked from him to Nicky. "What key?"

"It was behind Francie's picture in the back of the diary." Nicky reached into his pocket.

Frank walked over to the picture. His hands shook as he lifted the picture. . .and touched the tarnished brass handle of a wall safe.

Nicky handed a skeleton key to Frank. It slid into a slot below the handle. The handle cranked, the door opened.

Frank pulled out a box about six inches long and opened the hinged lid.

Rings. Two ruby, one pearl, an emerald, and two encrusted with sapphires. And scattered along the bottom of the box. . .diamonds.

꧁

Rena lagged behind when everyone else went back to the restaurant. With only the light from her phone, she walked behind the stairway at the end of the tunnel. If her hunch was right...

There. Another tunnel. Narrower than the one that connected the two buildings, it led exactly where she knew it would. A metal door, painted gray. On the peeling paint, she made out a dark brown handprint.

Her great-grandfather's blood?

"It was how a gangster made him believe in God."

She looked at the rusted door handle. What if Jarod had found a way to open it? She shivered. All of this history, and so much more, could have been gone.

Maybe the door only opened from one side. Maybe it was only an exit.

A way out.

She positioned her palm over the handprint. A gunshot had put an end to what her great-grandfather had been doing in this building. He'd come to God because of his blood. She pictured the crucifix Nonna Renata, the woman she was named for, had brought from her hometown in Italy so many years ago.

Because of His blood...

She traced the outline of the handprint with her fingertip. As she did, the letters Dani had scribbled on a napkin scrolled through her mind. TRKOTULU. The real King of the Universe loves you.

She turned and followed the passageway back to the stairs.

꧁

The cinnamon rolls were half gone by the time Nicky and Dani finished telling about T and about Francie's job at the jewelry store. Dani looked up from Nicky's laptop. "Walbrecht's Jewelers is no longer in business. If the jewelry store was covered by insurance, the insurance company would probably have a legitimate claim, but if they no longer exist, it looks like it'll probably be a case of finders-keepers."

Nicky raised his coffee cup. "To your future, Frank."

Frank laughed. "I don't need it where I'm going, and I'm certainly not going to keep stolen property, but our mission board could probably find a use for some of it."

Dani lifted her cup. "Francie raised you well."

"She did. I'm still trying to process everything you've told me. I remember so little about living here and nothing from Chicago. I still can't believe she was involved with organized crime. She was such a godly woman."

"She and Theo ran an orphanage?"

He nodded. "And much more. She met Amy Carmichael and was inspired to teach young women to sew. By learning a trade, they could stay off the streets. That mission is still going."

Nicky smiled at the goose bumps dotting Dani's skin and put his arm around her. "Your aunt was a very brave woman. It's a good thing her husband stood out of her way and didn't interfere with what God was calling her to do."

♔

"You two—stand over by the wall."

Evan's breath crystallized in the chilly April air as he barked orders.

Dani laced her gloved hand with Nicky's and dragged him toward the freshly painted wall between the two garage doors. She waved at Zip and Broom. "You guys get in on this, too. Have to give our artists some PR." The boys ambled over. Though they tried to hide it, pride oozed from every pore.

Dani smiled for the camera and pointed at the swirling design surrounding their logo. She'd watched Scope paint it. He'd outlined and filled in a five-foot-high 7 then stopped, pointed one finger to the sky, and added the two extensions that formed a cross like the one on his arm. Next to the cross, block letters proclaimed STREET LEVEL.

Evan snapped two pictures then turned as Rena walked up to him with a steaming cup. He let the camera hang on its strap, took the cup, and brushed Rena's cheek with the back of his other hand.

"When did that start?" Dani whispered.

Nicky shook his head. "I have no idea."

"Hey! A little help here." China waddled across the street carrying a massive vase of flowers in front of a belly that couldn't get much bigger. She was a week past her due date. Rena grabbed the flowers, and Evan helped the mother-to-be up the curb. "Happy grand opening." She leaned awkwardly toward Dani and kissed her cheek.

"Daisies. Thank you."

"Thank *you*." She patted her belly and looked at Nicky. "Did Dani tell you I'm naming the baby after her?"

Nicky shook his head. "No." His voice was low and rough. "Danielle is the perfect name."

China rolled her eyes. "Not Danielle. *Cerise.*"

"Uh. . ." Nicky's eyebrows rose and he laughed.

She'd never get tired of that sound.

An unfamiliar car pulled up and the back door slowly opened. She and Nicky gasped in unison. Frank, a good twenty pounds thinner than when they'd met him in the summer, stepped out. Lois walked around the back of the car. Dani hugged Lois, dampening the collar of the woman's coat with her tears. "We had no idea."

"We couldn't miss this," Frank answered, his voice as strong as ever.

Nicky wrapped his arms around the man. "None of this"—his voice cracked—"could have happened without you two."

Frank laughed. "Lois is wearing the only ring she wants, and what would I do with the money where I'm going?"

"I don't mean just the money. You'll never know how much our talks have meant. I've learned so much from you."

"And you'll never know how knowing you has kept my mind on things above rather than the failings of this temporal body." He gripped Nicky's arm. "Now give us the grand tour."

"Venus!" Nicky called to the girl handing out their brochures at the door. The girl who had proven she wasn't afraid to talk to anyone. "Come here and do your thing."

Bracelets jangling, she sidled over and gave Lois the pamphlet that Dani had sacrificed three nights of sleep perfecting. "Welcome. The mission of Street Level is to provide a Christ-proclaiming environment for teens in our community, to discover and develop their talents, and to make the products and services they create available to—"

"Frank!" Carlo strode toward them from Bracciano. He held up one finger. "I'll be back in a moment."

As Venus picked up where she'd left off, Dani watched as, behind Frank's back, Carlo returned. He was not alone.

"Franky." The soft, emotion-filled voice belonged to Luca.

Frank turned, stared, and broke into tears. His thin frame bent over the wheelchair, and the two old friends embraced.

Her vision blurring, Dani could hardly see the woman who stepped up and hugged her from behind. Lavinia kissed her on the cheek. "I told you I had a feeling the night you came to dinner. So I was a little off."

Dani laughed through her tears. Lavinia reached out and pinched Nicky's cheeks then nodded toward the building. "You two did it."

"God did it. All of it." He winked at Dani then shook Vito's hand. "Welcome to our grand opening."

"When do we get to come for dinner?" Vito pointed to the second story.

Nicky gave a comical bow. "The Stardust Room will be open for your dining pleasure in six weeks. Our grand opening will be May 18. Would you like to reserve a table now?"

"You bet." Lavinia pinched his cheeks and followed Vito through the open garage door just as Todd walked out.

He grabbed Nicky and gave him a bear hug.

Nicky pulled away, looking like he'd just swallowed a lemon. "What's *that* for?"

"I just spent the last half hour talking to Scope. Did you know that kid wants to be a missionary?"

Nicky nodded.

"He gives you the credit for helping him figure out how God has gifted him." Todd looked at Dani. "The kid just needed a Nicky in his life."

"I know the feeling." She leaned against Nicky's chest and sighed as his arms wrapped around her. "So did I."

"Not everybody agrees." Nicky nodded toward a cluster of

kids across the street. Cigarette smoke drifted over their heads. Occasional four-letter words cut the air. Yamile, Leah, and C.J. were just a few of the faces Dani recognized.

Todd, Street Level's community liaison, waved to the group. "We're watching them. Consider them potential clients."

Come on over, C.J., I bought Oreos just for you. Someday, maybe.

Todd clapped Nicky on the back. "Gotta go back to schmoozing the money people."

He walked away, and Nicky leaned close to Dani's ear. "Come with me." He took her hand and led her through the garage door. The space once occupied by the Model T, now on display at the public museum, was filled with aisles displaying artwork. Across the room, Rena picked up her guitar, adjusted her mic, and began to sing. Dani's throat tightened as they walked through the workroom everyone referred to as "Francie's Room." On the wall next to the storm picture were framed pages of the *Kenosha Times*—freelanced stories of kids at risk and the tale of a young girl's diary—with Dani's byline. Nicky led her up the now-lit stairway.

So many unanswered questions still lingered in the old building. Pondering why Francie had never returned for the diamonds had become a favorite date-night activity.

The upstairs was empty. Sawdust and two-by-fours littered the floor. Still, it took her breath away. Like Nicky, she heard the tinkle of glasses and the soft strains of a Frank Sinatra song every time she walked in.

Nicky cleared his throat and took her hands in his. "That dress, the one Francie made. . ."

"Right there." She pointed to a corner. "It's cleaned and ready. It'll look perfect right there."

"Yeah. It will. But I was wondering. With a little work. . .would it fit you?"

Dani swallowed so hard it was audible. "Yes."

"Good." He let go of her hands and framed her face with his. His lips skimmed hers. "Because I've seen the way you stare at it, and I keep thinking how amazing it would look on you, and I was also thinking that maybe the first reception I book at the Stardust. . .should be ours."

BECKY MELBY has been married to Bill, her high school sweetheart, for forty years. They have four married sons and eleven grandchildren. Becky has co-authored nine books for Heartsong Presents and is working on her third novella for Barbour Publishing. *Yesterday's Stardust* is the second of three stories in The Lost Sanctuary series. Becky's favorite pastimes are spoiling grandkids and taking trips with Bill in their RV or on their Honda Gold Wing. To find out more about Becky or her books, or to let her know your thoughts on *Yesterday's Stardust*, visit www.beckymelby.com.

Discussion Questions for *Yesterday's Stardust*

1. Dani could have responded to China's phone call in many ways other than trying to jump in and rescue. She could have called the police or a suicide hotline or taken someone with her when she went to China's apartment. Some people shut down in a crisis. How do you think you would have reacted?

2. While Dani jumps in feet first to save China, Nicky has the opposite reaction. What advice would you give people like Nicky, who don't want to get involved because past hurts have built a wall around their hearts? If you are self-protective because you've been wounded in the past, what's a baby step you can take toward breaking down those walls and learning to trust others—and the Lord?

3. As a young boy, Nicky vowed to become a different man than his father, yet he sees tendencies toward his father's weaknesses in himself. Are there destructive cycles in your family? How are you trying to be part of breaking the cycle?

4. When Dani's boss says, "You'll go far in this business *if* you can separate journalism from social work," Evan reminds her, "We work for God first." What situations have you faced where you knew you had to listen to God rather than man?

5. Dani rationalizes going incognito for the sake of a story by saying, "It wasn't a lie, it was research." Would you struggle with an ethical dilemma if disguising your identity were part of your job description? In what ways do you hide your "real self" at home, work, or church?

6. Did Francie's story frustrate you at points? Did you find yourself thinking, "There must be some way she can break free?" In her shoes, what would you have done?

7. We only see glimpses of Evan's life story—hints of an abusive father and a lifestyle he has left behind by the grace of God. Evan is a stable, encouraging counterpart to Dani's impulsiveness. How has God used the pain and scars in someone else's life to teach or strengthen you? How has he used your wounds to comfort others?

8. Francie grew up attending Sunday school and hearing her mother read the Bible, yet the truth of God's forgiveness as a free gift didn't "click" until she was at a desperate point in her life. When did you reach that point? If you haven't yet, do you long, like Francie, to drop to your knees and hear the words "God has set you free. You are safe in His arms"? (No matter what you've done or what's been done to you, it's never too late.)

9. We can assume Frank ended up with a substantial sum of money from selling the rings and diamonds. With a "You can't take it with you" attitude, he chose to give it all away. If you were gifted with a million dollars and told you had to give it all away, who would you bless?

10. The Bible portrays several mentoring relationships—Jesus and his disciples, Paul and Timothy—and encourages us to teach those who are younger and to share each other's joys and burdens. Do you know of someone who "Needs a Nicky in his life?" Could you be that person?

11. The cry of Dani's heart is, "I want to make a difference." What causes or ministries are you passionate about? Is there an area of service God might be calling you to? What would allow you to take part in an organization championing your cause—or

help to start one? Money? Faith? More time on your knees? (Challenge: Brainstorm ministry ideas with your family, friends, or study group. Discuss a plan for making a difference in your community or in the world. Share your thoughts with other readers at www.beckymelby.com.)

12. It's fun to dream of the future—even for fictional characters! What do you think the future holds for Nicky and Dani, Evan and Rena, and the kids Street Level hopes to reach?